IMMORTAL LOVERS

Annalee Blysse
Jennifer Colgan
Marie Morin

Erotic Paranormal Romance

New Concepts Georgia

Immortal Lovers is an original publication of NCP. This work has never before appeared in book form. This work is a novel. Any similarity to actual persons or events is purely coincidental.

New Concepts Publishing, Inc.
5202 Humphreys Rd.
Lake Park, GA 31636

ISBN 1-58608-743-6

NCP books are available at special quantity discounts for bulk purchases for sales promotions, premiums, fund raising, or educational use. For details, write, email, or phone New Concepts Publishing, Inc., 5202 Humphreys Rd., Lake Park, GA 31636; Ph. 229-257-0367, Fax 229-219-1097; orders@newconceptspublishing.com.

First NCP Trade Paperback Printing: April 2006

TABLE OF CONTENTS

NEVER A SUNSET

Annalee Blysse

Chapter One

The haze of twilight lit the clouds. The rain had just stopped, so the air was heavy with moisture. Victrina took a deep breath as she stepped out of her apartment, thinking how much she'd miss this place when she left.

The truth was, Victrina loved all seasons in Boston simply because they existed. The city was wrapped up in a long, drawn out spring that made an impression. A far cry from Barrow, Alaska. On the northern tundra, spring passed in the blink of an eye and summer dragged on for months on end. Where she'd grown up, the environment wasn't conducive to going for a walk any time of year. Boston was almost always perfect.

Noting the quiet streets, she smiled as she started walking. Then again, most Bostonians hadn't grown up on the North Slope. What was perfect to her was considered a miserable day down here.

New York City wouldn't be that different. Hopefully. In less than one month, she'd be moving. She'd already accepted a job offer on Wall Street and she was in for years of hard work. But she wanted to prove that a girl from the village could make good. More than that, she wanted to prove to her father that her scholarship to Harvard had been well deserved and not just money thrown at an Eskimo so they could make their quotas. She wanted to earn insane amounts of money and show him what she was really made of.

If asked, she told people why she wanted to live so differently from her life back home. A town that small couldn't keep her happy. There was no way she was ever going to settle down and become a broodmare for a man who didn't respect her, who didn't think she was good enough, who didn't feel her goals and accomplishments amounted to anything. What she kept private was the violence that had been part of her childhood home. She didn't want anyone to pity her.

She heard boots clicking on the cement behind her, heard distinct splashes through puddles that she'd avoided. Victrina turned, her eyes met with a tall man dressed all in black.

He nodded slightly, "Victrina Mechnikoff?"

Confused that he knew her name, Victrina confronted him, "What do you want?"

He grinned at her. His long hair was as dark as hers, and it shone beneath the streetlights. "You," he said, his voice low and husky and very seductive.

His black shirt hugged his chest, outlining sculpted muscles and sharply delineated abs. His jeans were fresh-from-the-rack black, and molded to his incredible legs and cock.

Electric blue eyes captured her senses, digging into her soul. Any anger she felt was replaced by a desire that consumed her body and mind. Her mouth watered and moisture pooled between her thighs. Her senses rang with excitement over the unknown. His clothes. His hair. The whole effect was very sexual, yet very dark. Foreboding.

And you can have me. But fear made her hesitate.

He waved his hand at a coffee shop on a nearby corner. "Can I buy you an espresso?"

Victrina was immediately relieved. Her body might be crying out for him to take her to the nearest hotel and make good on the sensual promise in his eyes, in his voice. She might want him to make love to her all night. But, the offer of an espresso was much easier to deal with.

She took him up on his offer and was soon seated across from him, sipping hot mocha, thinking ... *who are you?*

"Michael Levine," he said, staring deeply into her, as if he could see right through her.

"Pleased to meet you," she replied.

She couldn't understand the hold he had over her senses. She was as progressive as the next woman, but she'd never fantasized about jumping into the sack with a complete stranger. And she was having a difficult time keeping her mind off anything but sex around this man.

"I know," he said, angling his head slightly, licking his lower lip.

Victrina couldn't take her eyes off his face. His response was honest more than arrogant. She wouldn't have been surprised if he knew exactly what she'd been thinking. Her whole body vibrated with the sensuality of the moment. Michael's facial features were strong, yet as photogenically perfect as James Dean. *You are the most handsome man I've ever seen.*

"How do you know who I am?" she asked. "We haven't met before."

"I keep my eyes open. You have a promising career ahead of you." He waited for a moment, and when she didn't respond he continued, "I am looking for someone with your ... abilities. I'm here to offer you a position working for me."

Strange. The way he said "abilities" made it seem as if he alluded to something other than the fact that she was one of the top students in her class. Yet he had slightly toned down his flirting. Employers had been recruiting around the campus, so it was conceivable that he was really going to offer a position working for a company. A damn shame. She was still thinking of positions in the Kama Sutra.

"Work for you? Doing what?"

"I need a personal assistant."

Victrina thought for a moment. "In what capacity?"

"In every capacity. I won't sugarcoat the fact that I can be very demanding. I'd even expect you to check the mail, get the morning paper up off the lawn after it's rained. It irritates me when my paper is too moist to read."

Victrina almost laughed at him. Her goal in life was not to be a glorified errand girl. In fact that was why she'd gone to college to get her MBA. The last thing she wanted to do was end up spending her days at a man's beck and call. "I have already accepted employment, Mr. Levine. Your offer is too late."

"Call me Michael, please," he insisted. "And don't worry too much. I have a house full of servants that would do the most tedious errands. You'd supervise them, after all. Though I would have to warn you ahead of time that my butler hates waking up and getting the paper. He's like me ... a night owl."

That was strange--he'd addressed her concerns, without her having voiced them. But then again. That was a no-brainer. He'd probably assumed that a woman with an MBA wouldn't want to fetch his morning paper.

"I want to give a clear picture of what I'd expect of you as my personal assistant. However, I think the part of the job you'll be interested in is that I want you to be my financial advisor."

Victrina was suddenly intrigued. "What kind of business are you in?"

"Several, actually. They are outlined in the contract. If I were not available, you would have authority in my stead. However, I've got very loyal employees who've been working for me for quite some time. They don't need much by way of supervision. The main focus of your position will be investing the venture capital from my holdings in ways that will ensure my wealth works for me far into the future."

After Michael finished describing what he expected, he gave her time to read the contract he had drafted beforehand. She would be given free rein over designated accounts. Her salary would be very lucrative, and the most enticing section indicated that she would receive a healthy bonus based on her level of success with his assets. The better he did, the better she did.

Additionally, there would be no living expenses for the next five years. As his personal assistant it was expected that she'd live in the personnel quarters provided on his property outside New Orleans. As attracted as she was to Michael Levine, getting to know him better wouldn't be a problem. She was unattached, willing and wanting to experience life, and unwilling to be tied down. Come to think of it, getting to know him personally interested her as much as the job offer.

Her name was already typed on the document. All it needed was her signature. Victrina looked up at him, surprised. She couldn't blame him for taking for granted she'd sign on. The opportunity was more than she'd hoped for, considering she wanted to be a multimillionaire before she turned thirty.

"Before you sign, remember that I require absolute loyalty and discretion on all matters, business and personal." The tone of his voice carried a hint of warning. "There will be no getting out of this contract once you agree. Even if the Inquisition was reinstated and I was sentenced to death for being Satan's spawn, I'd continue to demand your loyalty."

Victrina chuckled.

"I'm not joking. I am--"

"I get it. You're demanding. And that won't be a problem." She could deal with a boss who expected a lot from her, and so long as he was honest, she could be loyal. And discretion she was used to.

It was one reason she hadn't responded to his flirtatious opening lines.

He gazed at her, an ominous look in his eyes. "I hope that remains the case. My business pursuits are entirely legal, but I require a 'blood oath.'"

"Blood oath?" she asked, thinking back on a mobster movie she'd sat through in a darkened movie theater. She set the contract down and shook her head. Having an employer that sounded insane gave her second thoughts. "Are you implying if I left my employment, you would have me killed?"

Locked in a harsh stare, images flashed through her mind. She saw a portly man in old-fashioned clothing of the European aristocracy. He spoke in French to a beautiful woman with long, flowing, burgundy hair. Despite her rudimentary comprehension of the language, Victrina got the gist of the conversation. The man shared the location of his "master," and was excited at the prospect of the financial reward promised for revealing his secrets.

The reward turned out to be his death. The woman latched onto his neck, draining him of blood. The woman was a vampire. A shadowy man arrived, and the woman told him that the Frenchman's master had murdered the man in her arms.

She couldn't understand the hold Michael had over her thoughts either. Victrina knew she wasn't remembering a movie she'd seen. Ridiculous as it sounded, it was almost as if Michael had shared the images with her. But, of course, that was impossible.

"I have taken very few lives over the years," he told her.

Very few lives? What is he, a homicidal maniac? Or is he just insane? She frowned suspiciously at the nonchalant look on Michael Levine's face.

"I protect the people who work for me. Leaving that protection is more dangerous than I am." He smiled then. "Ah, you think I am insane? No?"

"No, not at all."

He laughed loudly. "Never lie to me."

"Well ... this wasn't exactly a subject of discussion when the Fortune 500 companies came to campus. Let's just say, I find your statements odd."

"And the opportunity isn't the same as what other companies have offered you. It's your choice. Until you sign. Think about it for a few days. Hire a private investigator to look into my business holdings. Have them look for skeletons in my closet," Michael said, winking at her. "Which you won't find because I'm not a homicidal maniac. I will reimburse you, either way. But I'm confident you'll accept the position."

Yeah, he looked confident all right.

Way too confident.

"Oh, and by the way," he said, "I'm a vampire. That is a secret I insist you keep, even if you don't accept the position."

Victrina couldn't help herself. She laughed.

* * * *

As he walked her home, Michael tried to ignore the physical reaction of his body. He was pleased that Victrina continued to respond in kind--he'd hoped for that, but not so soon. She smelled so sweet, so tempting. Her dark brown eyes shone when she laughed at his small talk. He loved the way her sable hair curled around her soft features and the curve of her lips as she smiled. He knew that if he asked her, she would accept him in her bed tonight. He wanted to do just that, but it was too soon.

Her allure was no surprise. He'd been watching her for nearly a year, and seen her once in person. But more than desiring her, he admired her drive, and knew without a doubt she would be someone he could trust. Well, not right away. That wouldn't happen until she realized he wasn't joking about what he was.

When they reached the townhouse she'd rented, he said it again. "I am a vampire, Victrina. In the flesh, and ... blood."

She shook her head, the scent of her fear surrounding them. "Is that something you can prove? I'd say that was a big skeleton in your closet."

"I spend most of my time trying to pretend I'm human," Michael said, chuckling softly. "And that proof will have to wait until we know each other better."

"Why?"

"The act of feeding is sensual." That was an understatement. He couldn't even think of feeding from her without getting hard.

"I see," she said, and by the way her eyes swept over his body, he knew that she could. She focused on his face again. "You have sex with the women you supposedly feed from?"

"I'd rather not talk about that."

"Talk wouldn't convince me anyway," she said, grinning.

Oh, boy. If she wasn't careful, she was going to get a full demonstration.

Then, she frowned. "Actually, this is something we should talk about. I hope you don't mind my being forward, but you were flirting with me earlier and well ... I need to know what you expect of me along those lines."

"What lines?"

"Sex."

"What about sex?"

She planted her closed fists on her hips and stared up at him. "Is that part of what you expect from your personal assistant? Will sex be something you demand?"

Michael winked at her. "Definitely not."

"Oh," she said softly, sounding disappointed.

He reached over, caressing the line of her jaw. "At least the first time. After that I'd be very demanding."

Her eyes opened wide. He ran his finger along her neck, feeling the rapid beat of her heart. She was so beautiful. God, he wanted to taste her. All of her.

Victrina began to shiver. "I'm not looking for a relationship. I don't ever want to marry."

"I'm not looking for a wife."

"Good."

"I'm a vampire, you're human."

She sighed. "That remains to be seen."

Leaning forward, his lips met the soft flesh beneath her jaw. He licked her skin, tasting her excitement at his touch. He scraped the tips of his teeth along her neck, opening his mouth and biting, softly. When the first drop of her blood landed on his tongue, he was lost. He pulled her against him, grinding his erection against her belly. *Feel that?*

"Yes," she sighed. "Oh, yes. So you like to bite. That doesn't prove anything."

She turned, unlocked her door and nodded toward the dark opening.

Once inside, the door closed against the world, he pulled her against him again. A low, keening sound from deep within her throat drove him past the point of no return. He began to undress her. Her fingers began working at the buttons on his shirt.

"Wait a second," she said. "How did you speak to me? When you were biting me?"

Not enough proof for you?

"But, how?"

Vampires have heightened psychic abilities.

She laughed. "This is going to be strange night, isn't it?"

"One can always hope."

Time passed in a blur after she led him to her bedroom. She kissed him with a fervor that pleased him more than he had thought it would. It was just him that she reacted to, she wasn't under any compulsion. It felt good that the seduction was real and not feigned.

As she tentatively explored his teeth with the tip of her tongue, her hands ran down his back, cupping his backside as he pressed his cock against her hot, moist flesh. "Please Michael, now. Do you have a condom?"

"I can't impregnate you, and vampires don't carry disease."

"A condom would be nice, anyway."

He sent her images of his life as a vampire through the years. Each image revealed the truth of his nature.

"Okay, okay. I believe you."

"You do?" he asked harshly.

She shrugged. "I don't understand, but I believe you."

He stroked into her, sinking to the hilt in her tight channel. So perfect. She was so hot the warmth poured through his body. "You understand this?"

She moved beneath him, her inner muscles undulating around him, caressing him. He began to thrust into her, keeping the pace slow and steady. Victrina urged him through her sighs and actions into faster, steadier, deeper thrusts until she seemed as frantic as he felt. It was as if she could sense him too. Maybe she could. He had suspected that she was a latent psychic, and it looked like he was right.

Finally, he latched onto her neck again. *Can I taste you now?*

"Yes, yes," she said, her voice cutting into a scream as he sank into her neck. He stopped. But she held him close. "Don't stop!"

Her release hit the moment he began to drink. The sweet, sexy taste of her brought him along with her. Immediately his cock tightened as he came. He was shocked at the way she made him lose control. He continued to pull from her, drinking her blood, her body shaking below his.

"I can't believe it. It can't be real."

She caressed his back when he finally pulled back, then her hands went to her neck, feeling the small wound made by his fangs. Her fingers slid through the blood, and a look of fear shot through her eyes. She snatched her hand in front of her face. "I'm bleeding."

"Let me kiss your wound. It will heal faster that way."

"Heal? Wound?" She scooted back, her body shaking, looking so frightened that it tore at his heart. "Oh my God. You hurt me."

"I hurt you?" he asked. "You should have told me!"

"I didn't think you'd make me bleed."

The terror in her voice was more than he could stand. "Victrina, what's wrong?"

"Please, just leave." When he didn't move, she screamed the demand again.

Feeling a little guilty, he reached out, grasping her head between his hands. "Relax, Victrina. Both your body and your mind," he said, willing her to comply. Her body fell into him arms, limp.

He eased her onto the bed, licking her neck until she was clean. "Did I hurt you?"

"No," she moaned, her eyes fluttering, but staying closed.

"Then, why are you scared?"

"He did that. He made her bleed."

"Who?"

She shook her head, tears flowing down her cheeks.

Reaching out and drying her cheeks, Michael knew it was wrong to push her. He wouldn't force her secrets from her. "Go to sleep, Victrina. And when you wake up, everything that happened tonight will be a dream. Until you are ready to accept me, I'll be a man for you. Not a vampire. When you can accept that, you'll remember the truth."

He kissed her eyelids as she fell asleep, then he left.

* * * *

Victrina woke just before sunrise. Her body had that sore feeling that came after a hard night of sex, when the sex came after a long period of abstinence. Curiously, the air was heavy with the smell of her arousal, and ... his? Her bed held the faint scent of his cologne, of his body, just as if he'd been there.

She ran her fingertips across her throat, recalling the vampire kiss in her dream. She felt a tender spot, right below her jaw. Jumping out of her rumpled bed, Victrina stood before the mirror. That was one hell of a hickey. Leaning closer to the mirror, she shook her head in disbelief. It looked like she'd been bitten.

That is impossible, Trina. Don't be an idiot. She jumped into a scalding hot shower, trying to wash away the strange memories.

I'll be a man for you. Not a vampire.

Yeah, right!

Victrina got online. There was more than enough information at her fingertips to suggest that Michael Levine wasn't a wanted criminal. She called his office. The woman who answered had phone numbers ready and waiting for her. It didn't take her long before she found neighbors who were willing to talk.

Victrina hung up after talking with the first woman, thinking that if Michael Levine had purchased his home in the mid-'50's, he definitely had a good plastic surgeon. She pictured his smooth face and lean body, moving over her as he had in the dream from last night. Her body heated at the images and sensations rolling through her mind. There was no way that man was born before WWII. No way in hell!

She tried to corroborate his age with the next woman she called. That woman thought he should settle down and get married--to herself. That conversation didn't last long. The woman hung up on Victrina in a huff.

Apparently Michael Levine flirted with plenty of women. Competition in his personal life shouldn't affect a business arrangement. She was good at separating her personal life from her professional. Victrina was attracted to him, but she wasn't looking for a relationship. Of course, it wasn't like she had a personal life. She'd focused on school for so long.

The achy feeling between her thighs made her think harder about her dream. Sex was the only explanation for why she felt so tender. She squirmed in her chair, wondering why a dream would result in the tender flesh at her core, or her ability to drum up such realistic sensory images.

You're losing it, Trina. Focus!

She called another of Michael's neighbors. The man who answered said that strange things were afoot at Levine's mansion. Then, his wife grabbed the phone and explained to Victrina that he was the neighborhood drunk.

"Mr. Levine is a drunk?"

"Not Michael, my husband. And cheap to boot. Michael Levine is kind and generous, albeit, a bit eccentric. Michael is wonderful."

Yes, she decided, Michael flirted with plenty of women.

A few more calls and Victrina was sure that Michael was someone that she could work for. Unique in many ways. She left a message on his cell phone explaining that she would send the signed contract. She started making arrangements to move to New Orleans.

Chapter Two

Two Weeks Later

Victrina arrived at Michael Levine's mansion outside New Orleans in the daytime. A housekeeper showed her the quarters that were assigned to her, and explained that Michael wasn't available, but had requested her presence at a private dinner at eight. Unpacking didn't take long, so she had plenty of time to bathe and dress for dinner. She chose her most feminine dress and heels to give the impression that she'd be open to more than a meal. A little excited, her mind on the incredible dream she'd had, Victrina left her rooms an hour early, hoping for a tour of the mansion.

She halted upon entering the living room. Michael was kissing a woman's neck. The woman appeared drugged, and she was moaning in pleasure. Victrina watched the woman's fingers twine through his long, straight hair. A peculiar sensation gripped Victrina's loins when Michael's palm covered the woman's breast, his fingers tearing her red velvet bodice.

The woman in his arms was tall, lithe, blonde, and oh so beautiful. Next to her, Victrina felt short, dumpy and plain. Her stomach was tight with realization that the sexual promise she'd seen in his eyes was never going to happen. When she'd accepted the position, she'd known that he was something of a philanderer. But there was only so much a woman could accept in a potential lover. Another woman in the house when he'd invited her to dinner wasn't one of those things. Especially a woman who looked like that.

Embarrassed that she was even watching, Victrina tried to slip from the room unnoticed.

Don't run away. It was his voice, distinct in her mind.

She turned toward him, confused.

He lifted his face, his blue eyes snapping. He had the decency to look shocked. A trickle of blood eased down his jaw. The woman's neck was marred by a single smear of bright red. He leaned over her, licking the remnants of his feast off her pale skin.

Victrina's heart stopped beating. The moment of silence dragged on before she felt her blood jolt forward through her veins in a rush.

My dear Victrina, you weren't supposed to see me feeding.

In the blink of an eye the woman in his arms was seated, slumped over against a leather sofa's arm. She was smiling, still wrapped in the haze of sexual fulfillment. Victrina watched the blonde wrap her fingers around her breasts. Just like her own dream, this woman had been brought to orgasm with just a kiss.

But then, this wasn't a dream. This was real life. He hadn't actually been kissing the woman. He'd been doing something much darker. He had bit her. The blood on his lips proved that.

Suddenly, Michael was behind her. His breath on her neck felt hot. The smell of blood permeated the room. Even stone-cold sober, she had a difficult time believing what her senses picked up. Victrina hadn't actually seen him move the distance that had separated them, it was as if he could move like the wind. She wanted to run for the phone and dial 911. But she'd never be able to overpower him.

Her skin shivered as Michael's hands landed on her hips. A soothing calm spread over her mind as her body warmed. She was ready to experience what that woman had. She craved what she'd felt in her dream. Her body molded against his chest and she absentmindedly turned her head and bared her neck to him.

Jealousy interrupted her thoughts. The woman was still in the room. She wanted Michael to send his lover home, now, before it was too late.

What's wrong with you? He wants her. That is obvious. You need to leave and call the police before he kills her. Before he kills you.

I'm not going to kill you and I will not allow you to run away. As he spoke in her mind, his lips gently approached her jugular. She felt her heart pulsing against his flesh as his tongue darted out and he tasted her. Her body was filled with desire, but her mind revolted at the thought of blood on his lips. For a moment her mind returned to her childhood home. She was ten. Her mother crawled along the floor, trailing blood. There had been so much blood. She'd been so afraid her mother would die, but her father's threats had paralyzed her.

Victrina cringed at the memories. Would Michael try to kill her too? Would he bite her? Would her blood mingle with that woman's?

Despite her fear, her body thrummed with need. How on earth could she yearn for sex with a man capable of such depraved behavior?

The woman will not be harmed. I was only feeding from her.

"You bit her neck like some freaking vampire. You drank her blood. And you expect me to believe she will not be harmed?" *Or that I won't be?*

An empty feeling took over as his hands left her hips. He'd been exerting some kind of control over her? But how? That was impossible.

Victrina could smell his anger over her revulsion filling the room. "Five years," he said evenly. "If you attempt to leave before that time, I will protect myself regardless."

"Protect yourself?" she asked, her voice shaking. He was threatening her. He'd warned her before, and now she knew it was true. If she left, her life would be in danger. "What could I do to harm you?"

"The memories that I shared with you in Boston were not from a movie. Vampire slayers are not fictional characters. If I am to survive, I need to stay alert. And as my personal assistant, it is your goal in life to protect me. That is, if you want to survive yourself."

Oh, God. You've got to be kidding? He actually thinks that he is a vampire, and he's threatening me. "That wasn't a dream I had the night we met. You really did--"

"No." He turned her toward him, his razor-sharp fangs, long and slender against his lower lips. "That was a dream."

Victrina pointed at the woman. "Did you feed from me?"

"You've had demonstration enough for tonight Victrina. Go back to your room and consider how you are mine for the next five years. After that, so long as you refrain from revealing my existence to another living or undead soul, you will be free."

She spent that night thinking about the night in Boston. It couldn't have been a dream. He'd made love to her. He'd fed from her. And now he was more than likely with another woman. But, why? And why in front of her?

Well, that she could answer. She'd shown up an hour before he'd expected her.

She couldn't help but be upset. Her body ached to experience what his lover must be feeling. Just the thought of that woman in the mansion grated on Victrina's nerves, feeding the jealousy building up within her heart.

She imagined, in excruciating detail, everything that was going on behind closed doors. She could almost feel his touch, yet she told herself that his hands were on another woman's flesh. His hold over her was even more powerful than the dream she'd had that night they'd first met, but it didn't matter. He wasn't here with her. He was with another woman.

Finally, Victrina slid her hands into her panties. She outlined a circle around her clit. She was so hot, so soft, so sensitive, and so needy for release. The fingers stroking her moist heat weren't her own. It was as if someone else controlled the rhythm and pattern. She imagined his soft lips against her labia, kissing her in the most intimate way possible.

She thrust two fingers into her vagina, focusing the dreamlike sensations. She yearned for the hard feel of Michael's cock pumping into her body. She wanted what she felt to be real instead of imagined.

As she reached her peak, hot tears welled up in Victrina's eyes. She blinked them back. How dare he tease her, taunt her, and then give the gift of his desire to another woman?

Victrina knew that she was slightly insane to crave the touch of a man who could make love to another woman while she was alone in bed, needing him so badly. But her need for his touch wouldn't go away, and she knew her desire would only grow if she stayed here. Having no choice, she would stay until her contract was over. But before she left, she'd take him as a lover and treat him just as callously. Somehow, someday, she would make him pay for his actions.

* * * *

Victrina was in the living room curved over a book when he woke the next evening, her slender legs pulled up beneath her fascinating bottom. Her soft sable hair shrouded her face. Yet Michael read in her countenance how upset she was. He'd seen that kind of jealousy before, knew how her feelings would fester until she turned on him. "I will not take you as a lover, Victrina."

"What makes you think I care?" Victrina flashed him a look of annoyance, then averted her warm brown eyes. She got up and flounced toward the door, her shapely ass and firm breasts jiggling slightly.

Oh, she cared all right. And he did too.

Michael had no idea how he'd manage to keep that promise. She was all he'd thought about for the last two weeks. His eyes fell on the curve of her spine, narrow waist, then her wide hips and firmly muscled legs. His cock hardened as he recalled the feel of those legs wrapped around his hips, her heels digging into his ass as he drove into her.

He'd planned to seduce her again, eventually. That night in Boston hadn't been enough. Yet, he'd managed to screw everything up. He couldn't tell her he wasn't interested in another woman, that he'd only been feeding so he wouldn't scare her. He'd been full of blood lust and hadn't even noticed Victrina until it was too late. Damn, he knew how incriminating his actions looked. He'd been celibate since he'd met her so his body had screamed for release, and it was true he'd stepped over the line. He regretted that, but it wasn't something he could explain to Victrina. Her reaction last night proved that she wouldn't believe him.

"A jealous heart does not harbor loyalty," he whispered. "I need you at my side, working for me, not against me."

"I'm not jealous," she insisted. "What makes you think I'm jealous?"

"I had extrasensory abilities before I turned." He moved forward and caressed her cheek. "Just like you, Victrina. And now that I am a vampire, those abilities are much stronger."

"Right. I'm working for a vampire. And I'm psychic. Whatever you say."

"I can read the thoughts that you project. And if I allow you to, you can read mine. How else would I know you pleasured yourself last night, thinking of my touch?"

Michael sensed her initial shock, then denial. She thought he'd made love to the woman he'd fed on the evening before. He wanted to explain, but Victrina wouldn't believe him. Not now. She was too angry. That left him with only one alternative. He had to gain her trust without sex getting in the way. He had to find a way that they could both trust each other.

"It is why I chose you, Victrina. When you learn to use your abilities, it will be a great asset. We will get past last night. I need a loyal personal assistant much more than I need a lover. I want us to become friends."

He knew that she wasn't willing to believe him. His presence brought out her empathic abilities, and what she felt around him frightened her.

Watching her, amused, he wrote a few words on a pad of paper on his desk, then folded it in half. His gaze locked on her. She was reading him perfectly, not that it took extrasensory perception for her to figure out his painful erection was for her. “What did I just write?”

“I want to fuck you, but I can’t,” Victrina answered immediately.

He held up the note. The words on the slip of paper were almost exactly what she’d just said.

“I want to make love to you, but I won’t,” she threw back at him.

“No,” he said softly. “I won’t. And the sooner we agree on that, the better we’ll get along. Between you and me, sex will definitely get in the way. I can’t afford the luxury of allowing you to fall in love and--”

“Me? I might desire you, but you’re sadly mistaken if you think I’m some lovesick fool. I will not fall in love with you, Mr. Levine. Remaining strictly professional is a good idea.” Her nostrils flared slightly. “And it’s your loss, not mine.”

It was going to be a problem, definitely. He wanted her again, right now, naked and writhing on his couch. He was hungry to sink his fangs into her warm flesh and taste her blood again. He wanted to bury his face in her sex, suck her until she cried out his name. Sharing the images in his mind with Victrina, he grinned as her body reacted. The heady perfume of her arousal clouded his senses. Michael laughed as her cheeks flushed.

“You think that’s funny? Well, go to hell!” Victrina stormed out of the room.

I’ve seen a lot of vampires who deserved that. Angry as you are today, I am still confident you don’t really believe that about me. These feelings will pass and we will become friends.

“And stop talking in my head!” she screamed from the hallway.

That would be like telling a human to stop breathing.

“Just leave me alone.”

How would he manage to do that? He didn’t have a clue.

Chapter Three

He didn’t leave her alone, of course. She had the duties of her job, and he often made her eat dinner with him. But he didn’t recant his oath regarding sex.

It was just as well. Relationships were difficult enough without throwing something into the mix like vampirism. She believed that about him. She had no choice because it seemed as if he held her life in his hands. Even that first night, it was almost as if he apologized for what he was. Not in so many words. But she sensed the regret.

Weeks blurred into months because, as Michael had promised, there was no sex. Which meant most days Victrina was frustrated with him. At least as the days passed she didn't want him to go to hell anymore. Despite being a bloodsucking vampire, he was kind, generous, funny, and vastly intelligent. Those qualities became obvious as she settled into her position. After all, she was the one who took care of his generous, but anonymous, donations in the community. One night she'd even seen him stop a man from beating a prostitute. Michael had compelled the brute to turn himself into the police.

On the surface, they had become the friends he'd promised. He told her of his life--centuries longer than her own--until she came to respect and understand him. But Victrina couldn't deal with her ever-growing feelings. Thankfully, she had learned enough about her own psychic abilities to mask just how much she had come to love him. She had to hide those feelings. What she felt for Michael was an impossible love. She yearned to give her whole heart, yet knew what she desired wouldn't be returned. How could a woman befriend a man she lived with and constantly desired when she received no relief? The answer was. She couldn't.

So, how was it that she had? Why had she fallen in love?

Victrina didn't think that Michael realized the depth of her emotions. She'd become so adept at hiding her emotions from him that she intrigued him. She was a mystery to be solved. His inability to fully understand her only made her more desirable. Yet she found no comfort in that because he was still adamant that despite their physical desire, they couldn't become lovers. Victrina wasn't sure she'd ever change his mind, and that made her morose when she thought about it. Which was all the time. Her sexual desire had only grown over time.

How she could want him so much didn't make sense to her. It was apparent that Michael continued his nightly feeding habits. Though he hadn't admitted her dream in Boston was real, it was easy to assume that he was making love to the women he fed from. There was nothing she could do about that. But, at least he wasn't bringing the women home.

Okay, so that didn't make things that much easier on her. She did regret that he wouldn't take that step with her. But she could honestly say that the anger-driven jealousy was gone. Victrina didn't want to be owned herself. She'd made it her mission in life to fight entrapment. So she recognized that she had acted too possessively considering Michael didn't want to be possessed. She'd figured out that part of his message at least.

Victrina smiled. Maybe when they traveled to Paris, things would change between them. Paris was the perfect place to prove that she only wanted him, and that she'd given up on her little sexual vendetta.

* * * *

Several days after they arrived in Paris, Victrina stood in line under the blazing sun, a smile pasted on her lips as she completed one of her assigned errands. She wasn't jealous, she wasn't. She could deal with the little things. She had to. After all, as Michael's personal assistant, it was her responsibility to arrange his entertainment. It wasn't his job to entertain her. So she had no right to be upset that he was bringing an "old friend" to a concert.

Unfortunately, her pep talk wasn't working. Victrina hadn't bothered asking. She knew the old friend was a woman. So much for romance in Paris.

The evening of the concert, she walked into his hotel room, unannounced. She'd intended to gather some paperwork she'd left behind in his briefcase to keep herself occupied while Michael was out getting laid. Instead, she found him in the arms of his "old friend."

The woman was the loveliest redhead Victrina had ever seen. Her hair was the color of warm burgundy. Her skin was as pale and smooth as alabaster. Her ruby lips were attached to Michael's neck.

Michael's eyes met hers and Victrina fled.

He followed her, but she slammed the door to her room in his face.

If you don't open this damn door, I'm going to break it down!

He'd probably do that too. Not wanting to cause a scene, she obeyed.

He closed the door and leaned against it.

Victrina's eyes fell to two small wounds on his neck, dripping blood. "I shouldn't have assumed your room was vacant. I should have knocked."

"I didn't intend to repeat that first night. It isn't sex that I had in mind, you assume too much. That first night, I needed her blood. In this case, the vampire I'm with needs mine. You have to believe me." His blue eyes begged her to understand.

"I don't think I am mistaken in believing that she wants sex," Victrina said, turning away from his open stare. "It's okay. Really. I'm not trying to control you. I agree with you. We'll get along much better without becoming lovers. That will only mess everything up. So, go to her." *She's your kind, and she wants you.*

Michael draped his arms over her shoulders. She rested her cheek against his cool chest. He hadn't fed yet. He was a marble statue beneath her skin, cool and cold.

"If I came to you, I wouldn't be able to stop again after one night," he said quietly. "I'd drain you, exhaust you, scare you again."

Victrina wound her arms around his waist, sinking against his hard body. She wanted him to hold her, forever. She wanted him enough that becoming a vampire sounded like the perfect solution. If she was like him, maybe he'd want her too. "You are one of the gentlest men I know."

"You don't mean that," he whispered softly. "I fascinate you, yet you are still frightened. The idea that I live on blood sickens you. I assume it reminds you of something in your past."

"No," she insisted.

"I told you before not to lie to me. I know that you view how I live as violent. It sickens you to see blood."

How could she explain that she had no fear of him without revealing the truth? Even though Michael had threatened her with his "blood oath," she didn't see him as anything like her father. "I did, but not now. Give me a little credit. It's been months. I know you wouldn't hurt me."

"Do you?"

"Yes. And I'm not lying. You do fascinate me. I wonder what it would be like to exist for centuries. I wonder how much more I could learn. I could help people. Like you do. And I would be strong enough to take care of myself."

"No. I will never make you into a vampire. I will never do that to anyone. Never again."

That was one part of his life that he refused to share. He wouldn't tell her how he'd become a vampire, and had said before that he'd never pass vampirism to another. At the time, she hadn't considered wanting that for herself.

"At first, you scared me," she admitted. "But not now Michael. I know that you don't hurt the women who give you nourishment. You bring your lovers pleasure."

"How do you know that?" he asked, caressing her cheek. "You still believe that I have other lovers, and you're wrong."

"I know they want you. Each woman you are with feels joy with you. As if she falls in love. I see that in their eyes."

He closed his eyes for a moment. "You hide so much from me. You are the only one who can. But you don't really trust me. Not if you think I want another."

Victrina sighed, running her fingertips along his eyelids. "Look at me."

He opened his eyes. He needed to know that she was telling the truth. That she truly believed he was good and just and worthy of love. "I still want you, Michael Levine. I know I pretend I don't. But I do. More than ever."

"You will enjoy your time with me much more if you don't hate me," he said, pulling back slightly and capturing her chin with one hand. "Having a personal assistant hell-bent on destroying me is not something I want to happen again. I would never want to hurt you."

"I think I could manage not to hate you. I don't yet."

He laughed lightly. "You are human, sweet Victrina. You are ruled by a human heart. The seven deadly sins are inherent in your nature. You would eventually want to lay claim to my life, and when you find it is impossible, you most certainly will grow to hate me."

"You're wrong," she said, looking into his harsh blue eyes.

"Am I?"

Perhaps she had to share the truth. "I know that you will live forever, and I will live for a few more decades. I know that what I feel for you is impossible, yet I continue to love you. Even though you don't love me."

His lips descended on hers, his kiss stealing the air from her lungs until she was gasping. *Oh, but I do. More than I should. I yearn to make love to you. To taste your sweet essence on my tongue. To taste your blood. You're the woman I need. The only woman. How could I take another as a substitute? I haven't. I can't.*

The words he shared turned up the heat and made her burn for him even more than she'd imagined possible. "I shouldn't have acted the way I did. Yes, I was jealous. I got over that, but not over you. You're the only man I want."

"Vampire," he whispered, dragging his fangs across her throat. She shivered at the feel of them, knowing she was helpless to stop him from drinking from her. "I have not been a man for hundreds of years."

"I don't care." Victrina angled her neck against his lips, offering herself without fear, just nervousness. "I want you as a vampire. I want to feel the passion you give during those moments you feed from me. I want to feel your desire as you soak up my heat, my soul. I know feeding is sensual to you."

He laughed. "Vampires are that obvious, are they?"

"In that way, you are just like a man."

Michael lifted her, one arm resting behind her knees, the other against her shoulders, and carried her to the bed. He laid her against the pillows, then stood back, watching, his eyes devouring her. Even with a set of frumpy old sweats on, Victrina felt sexy and desirable.

"Not yet," he said.

"What?" she asked weakly. *Don't you dare tease me any more. If you don't want me, leave right now.*

A wicked grin spread across his features. "Oh, I want you all right. You're all I've thought about since our first night."

Her pulse quickened at the thought. "I knew that night in Boston wasn't a dream."

He leaned over her body, his hands hooking beneath her waistband. She watched his face as he pulled her clothing from her body. Once she was bared to his gaze, he spread her legs until she felt cool air along her moist flesh.

"You are so beautiful, my Victrina. So lovely and so sweet. I had to taste you then, as I have to taste you now." As he spoke, he lowered his head, moving closer until his breath teased at her sex. When his lips slid across her clit, sucking at her, she gripped the sheets tightly between her fingers and arched her hips against him.

Michael's hands held her hips steady as he explored her sex, his tongue darting against her, teasing her, taunting her. Victrina growled as she twisted from side to side.

Don't be frightened of me tonight. I will not hurt you, my Victrina. All I want to do is bring you pleasure.

I need you too much. You were frightened when I fed from you, so I left you with the belief that you'd dreamed the whole evening.

Really? He'd been protecting her the whole time? "Damn it! Why didn't you tell me?" she insisted, pushing back and sitting up against the headboard. "I could just smack you."

His nostril's flared and he leaned back, unfastening his trousers, allowing his turgid cock to stand free. "Later. I've wanted you too long and too hard"--her eyes fell to his cock, her mouth watering with the need to kiss the head, taste him--"to wait until you punish me for something I can't change."

"That's the whole point," she said, trying to ignore the intense desire to lower her lips and wrap her tongue around his hard flesh. She distracted herself by tearing off her sweatshirt. "I wasn't afraid of you--"

"Yes, you were."

"No, I wasn't! Can't you see? You've guessed it before. It's my own past that frightened me. Not you."

He grabbed her hips and slid her down the bed, spreading her legs wide. "You only remember what I allowed you to remember."

"Which is why I'm upset. We didn't have to wait this long to make love again. If you weren't being so damn stubborn, you could have--"

"Shhh," he said, rubbing his cock against her slit. He was so hard against her, and so incredibly large. Her only memories were the stuff of dreams, yet he felt so right, so perfect. "Trina, you are the most stubborn woman I've ever met. Why are you trying to argue with me right now?"

Before she could respond, he angled into her, pulling her hips up until she was fully impaled. The shock of being stretched so tightly left her wordless. She didn't know why she was arguing, not when she finally had him in her arms. Victrina rubbed her aching nipples against his chest.

Together they set a pace, their lips locked, their tongues matching the pace of his thrusts and her acceptance. To Victrina it seemed as if he was a perfect fit. He filled her, yet left her needing and wanting much more.

He flipped them over so he was below her, leaning her backward until their lips parted. She straddled his thighs as he urged her backward until her hands rested on the mattress behind her. She gasped when his fingers surrounded her clit, massaging her from every angle at once. "Oh, Michael that feels so good!"

"Touch yourself," he urged, pumping into her again. "I want to watch you come."

She ran her hands along her stomach and into the flesh at the apex of her thighs, pressing her clit between two fingers and rubbing herself as he lifted her hips slightly and thrust into her again. She clamped her muscles against him, increasing the friction. She arched her back until her clit was tight against her pelvis.

When her orgasm flooded them both, Victrina screamed her pleasure. He pulled her against his chest, sinking his long canine teeth into her neck. He didn't hesitate. She knew that he couldn't. This is what he'd meant by "lose control." But there was no shock or fear. There couldn't be. His pleasure flooded through her. Her body felt as if it were on fire, as the sensations engulfed her mind. It was him. The heat was his, taken from her and intensified. Michael was joining with her both mentally and physically. They were joined at the sex, by blood, and through their souls.

Her orgasm lasted until he finished feeding, or longer maybe. She wasn't sure. Her mind buzzed with the aftereffects of their lovemaking. Victrina could hardly recall the exact moment his come filled her and his internal voice cried out her name. But she remembered the intense feeling of joy that it had brought her, and for that moment, the world was gone and it was just the two of them.

* * * *

Victrina sat at a small coffee shop beneath the awning, watching the tourists enjoy Paris. She was so anxious for nightfall, all she could do was sip her coffee and relive the night before.

"I won't allow you to interfere again," a woman's husky, thickly accented voice broke her concentration. "The next time you get in my way, I will see you dead."

Victrina met the gaze of the vampire she'd seen with Michael the night before. The woman's eyes were consumed with rage and jealousy. But how could she be here? It was broad daylight.

"I didn't see him running after you," she said, without thinking. "Perhaps you should let go." Victrina immediately regretted her harsh statement. This woman would be dangerous. The death threat was mostly likely real.

"There is no 'letting go,' in our world," the woman said. "Nothing can erase the bond Michael and I have. He made me. I am his, forever."

Victrina sat up straight. "He made you? He said he'd never do that--"

"Did he now?" The woman raised one slim brow. "Of course he would tell you that. He and I may ignore certain vows, but neither of us can escape our marriage. He will never change you, he has me."

"Married?" Victrina asked, her voice scratchy.

"Marianne Levine," she replied. "But enough polite conversation. You will leave, today, if you value your life."

Victrina was in a state of shock. Michael was married? And he hadn't told her. "I'm under contract. I can't leave--"

"I know. You give him five years, then, if you keep his secrets, he'll allow you to live afterward. Typical. A lie, but typical. You will be a liability. He will never allow you to live."

"That's a lie...." Or was it? He'd threatened her. And when it came right down to it, he'd vowed they'd remain friends and business associates. Yet, he'd taken her as a lover. Could he really be trusted?

Marianne laughed. "You know I'm telling the truth. I can read it in your eyes."

The images that Michael shared resurfaced in her mind. This was the woman, the vampire who'd killed his former assistant. They'd known each other for centuries. It didn't matter whether or not she trusted Michael, he had showed her that this vampire would be more than willing to kill her. "He wouldn't harm me. But you would."

"Damn right. You would much rather have me on your side than against you. But you're sadly mistaken if you think Michael is someone that you can trust. You're human. You're nothing but a good fuck and a meal." The woman waved her hand at the sun. "Besides, who should you fear more? Him? Or me? He can't walk during daylight hours."

Victrina didn't know how the vampire before her could reveal herself when the sun was high in the sky, but she recognized how vulnerable that made her. "How can you, and not him?"

Marianne gazed at the sun. "That doesn't matter. All that matters is if you don't leave, tonight's sunset will be your last. I'd say you have four hours to catch a plane and disappear. If you're lucky, you'll be able to avoid Michael. At least for a little while.

You should not underestimate him as an enemy. I'm just much worse."

The realization hit her with a rush of panic. This woman would kill her, and Michael couldn't do anything about it. He'd told her once that he protected those who worked for him. But he couldn't protect her during the daytime. That she knew.

But if she ran, she would test Michael's requirement of a "blood oath." Would he follow through with his threat? Would he protect himself at all costs? Even if that meant killing her? If she ran, he would be forced to come after her.

But there was one place she would be safe. She'd have to go home.

Chapter Four

Victrina squinted into the sun, low on the horizon, as the edges of the European continent disappeared and the vastness of the Atlantic Ocean began to slip beneath the airplane's pale wing. The sunset glinted off the deep blue waters, yet she felt safe. Traveling over five hundred miles an hour brought some comfort. But not enough. The darkness would soon engulf her, and until she escaped the night, she wouldn't be safe.

What a strange turn of events her life had taken. Was this her due for taking the road less traveled, for wanting something new and exciting? As if nursing a broken heart wasn't bad enough, now she was running for her life.

* * * *

Michael threw an end table across the hotel room. It shattered against the wall, leaving a gaping hole. Of course she'd head for the sun. Anyone fleeing a vampire this time of year would do well to head north of the Arctic Circle. Damn ironic that she'd been the first human fleeing his wrath who'd ever come up with that option. But then, Victrina would. Half-Inupiaq, she'd been born in the Land of the Midnight Sun.

Did she think the sun above the horizon would keep her safe? She was so naive....

Where would she go when winter arrived and her homeland fell under complete darkness? He frowned. She had no idea just how dark her world could become.

Her betrayal ate at him. Somehow her actions were related to Marianne, though the bitch denied it. It didn't matter anyway. This complication was his own fault. What in the hell was he thinking when he'd taken her as a lover?

* * * *

Victrina squinted at the sun, high on the horizon, as her jet landed in Barrow, Alaska. The sun would become her refuge, burning brightly from millions of miles away, keeping her safe. As she deplaned, she told herself she had at least a month of freedom. Funny, this place had always felt like a prison before. Facing the dreaded moment, she caught a cab and arrived unannounced at her parent's house.

"Victrina? Is that you?" her mother asked. "I thought you were in France. What are you doing home?"

"I took a much needed vacation."

Her father's face screwed up in disbelief. He thought she'd failed, just like he always believed she would. "You lost it, didn't you? You lost your damn job, and came crawling home for help."

Without answering the accusations, she turned and left, renting a small cabin on the edge of town from her cousin Brad.

She hadn't come crawling home. She'd crawled away from home, hiding from a past she'd had no control over. Even her mother had faced her father's imperfections and decided to accept him. Yet she never had. The funny thing was, the man she ran from now was the man who'd reminded her there was nothing wrong with trusting.

Victrina mentally kicked herself. Trust. She was one to talk. She'd run from Michael without giving him a chance to explain himself. Her actions would force Michael's hand.

It was too late for turning back now. Much too late for that.

* * * *

Two days later Brad showed up after his shift was over at the airlines and pounded on her door. "What kind of shit are you in?"

"Nothing," she insisted, but Brad wouldn't believe that. "Why? What happened?"

"A man showed up this morning, asking about you. Nobody he's talked to can remember meeting him."

This wasn't good at all. "How come you remember him?"

"You know me. I've always been more aware of the supernatural than I'd like to be." He planted his hands on his hips. "But he isn't like anyone I've ever met. He's Russian I think, and he reminds me of Dracula. But he'd make the Count look like a pansy. So who the hell is he?"

Victrina started shaking. "What made you think of vampires?"

Brad slanted her a curious look. "On account of what I saw this afternoon when the second jet for the day showed up. The prettiest woman I've ever seen gets off the plane. The Russian met her and told her to leave you alone. When she refused, your *bodyguard* sent her packing. But not without a fight. She was one kick-ass bitch, fangs and all."

Marianne. Had to be. "Bitch is the operative word. And he's not my bodyguard. I have no idea who he is." *A bounty hunter is more like it.*

"Something strange is going on, and I want to know what it is. You can start with how those two managed avoid federal charges. They broke at least five FAA regulations. The airport is in shambles, and no one can remember they were even there."

Someone pounded on the door. Her eyes darted to Brad. "Don't open it."

"If it's him, he could shred this house into toothpicks." Brad opened the door.

A dark-haired man walked in, exuding power that eclipsed her. His mind swept her own, stealing from her everything he wanted to know. His name was Simeon. She knew without asking that he was ancient.

When he spoke, he used Russian, forcing the meaning into her own thoughts. "You will not leave this place until the next sunset."

"Are you going to kill me?" His power had given her a crash course in Russian. When she spoke Russian fluently, Brad's mouth dropped open in shock.

Simeon grinned at her. Brad was right. Simeon made Dracula look like a wimp. "I'm annoyed enough at the prospect of spending a month away from my home. If you make me chase after you, I won't be pleasant company."

"Then why are you here?"

The sun will set again. She can't run forever. She heard the words in her mind, as if Michael was in the room. Yet he'd spoken those words to Simeon. Fascinating, the idea that the vampire had a photographic memory that spanned centuries.

"I won't go anywhere." How could she? It wouldn't do her any good. She hadn't been successful at running for two days.

"Good. I think Michael would prefer it if I left your lovely neck alone." His nostrils flared and his lips parted to reveal his fangs. "Tempting. But I can smell him on you. That might not matter if you resist me. I've always been a fool over a woman who fights."

His words confirmed she was in danger. But at least she had time to think things through. "Can you answer a question for me?"

He squinted at her. "I might."

"How can you and Marianne walk in sunlight?"

"Not that question."

"But--"

He held up his hand. "Vampirism is a virus that changes the body. It reacts differently in each victim. As a man I was born north of the Arctic Circle. My first summer I tried to burrow beneath the ground but my hunger was too great. I had to come out to feed. The virus mutated and I lived. Just luck, really."

Simeon left after listing his demands again, and Victrina slumped to the floor, feeling drained.

"They are vampires, aren't they?" Brad asked.

She looked at him apologetically. Simeon had forced the Russian language on her mind, so he probably didn't want Brad to know. "No."

"Bullshit."

"Brad, I don't want to put you in danger."

* * * *

Victrina sat on the tundra, picking salmon berries under the midnight sun. A few mosquitoes buzzed around her hands, the miserable little vampires trying their hardest to deplete her of blood, one tiny drop at a time. She swatted them away.

A group of arctic terns dive-bombed the lake next to her. Each summer they flew the length of the globe to mate in the northern hemisphere. It was laughable. It really was. She'd worked so hard to escape the life her mother had found. And now, if she wanted to survive, Victrina would have to migrate here every summer. But not to find her mate. She needed to come here to escape from him. The only man she'd ever wanted ended up being more dangerous than her own father.

After her bounty hunter/bodyguard Simeon protected her from Marianne Levine, she'd wanted to believe that his presence in Barrow was motivated by benevolence. Yet weeks had passed and she'd never heard from Michael. He'd never once called to ask her to return, and his only message had been a veiled threat. *The sun will set again. You can't run forever.*

Victrina sighed loudly, slapping another mosquito as it drilled her knuckle. She was probably alive because Michael wanted to deal with her himself. It probably hadn't helped matters that she'd taken part of her bonus. He obviously viewed that as theft. Okay, so it was theft. She'd broken that contract in more ways than one.

One thing was certain. Michael was out there. Somewhere. He was following the night, coming with the darkness that was quickly approaching the northern tundra. That meant it was time for her to leave. Tonight was the first night the sun would finally set. In a few short weeks, it would be dark enough for Michael's arrival.

She'd made plans by e-mailing an old college roommate whose family owned an air taxi business. She'd arranged for a pilot to arrive at a designated time, so she could board the chartered plane and disappear. The timing had to be precise. Simeon wasn't watching her that closely, but a plane arriving this time of night would send him running. She had no desire to face him should this plan fail.

Victrina jumped on her 4-wheeler and tightened her backpack around her shoulders. It contained everything she dared take with her. A toothbrush, a tube of toothpaste, and the $27,534 she had left from her contract-breaking crime spree.

Chapter Five

Michael watched the lights of the Vegas Strip from his hotel room. He could sense her. She was here somewhere. By tomorrow night, he'd find her. He was sure of it.

Barrow had been a smart choice for a place to hide, but Las Vegas wasn't. Not for hiding from a night walker. He didn't have to sleep in the daytime, and the casinos kept their interiors hidden from the light of day.

But it was fortuitous that she'd chosen this city for her first stop. Marianne was here as well. Only she wasn't hiding. The meddling bitch was gloating. To him that confirmed that Marianne had gotten to Victrina and frightened her. Of course, Marianne continued to deny it. But his ex-wife's true nature had reared its ugly head as soon as he'd turned her into a vampire. Lying was the least of her vices. She was definitely looking for Victrina. That meant he had to find her first. Which he would. Simeon was still helping. Seemed the vampire wanted to see what became of his spunky quarry. Victrina amused the elder vampire a little too much. Yet Simeon wasn't a danger to her.

* * * *

That hair-tingling feeling that she was being followed alerted Victrina that she wasn't safe. She turned, searching the crowd. Ah, Marianne Levine. The vamp was dressed every bit as scantily as any cocktail waitress in the casino, and looked better than all of them. Hard to imagine the woman was hundreds of years old and a hag if ever there was one. Victrina stopped and waited for the vampire seductress to arrive at her side.

"I did as you asked," Victrina said, unafraid. "I think it very rude that you are following me. As if I don't have enough to worry about with your husband looking for me."

"Me, rude?" Marianne laughed. "But you're right about one thing. I'm the least of your worries today. Michael is here."

Victrina had her car packed and headed down the highway within ten minutes. An hour and a half north of Las Vegas, a black sedan sped into view, pulling into the other lane to pass her. She didn't think much of it until the driver slammed into her car, pushing her off the road.

The impact hurt like hell. Her mind was foggy as two men dragged her out of the car and into the desert, forcing her to walk despite the pain. Blood dripped into her eyes. At least ten cars and trucks pass them on the highway. She couldn't believe no one stopped. The farther they walked into the desert, the less it mattered anyway. Her only hope was that one of the witnesses would change their mind and call the authorities in time.

The question was, in time for what? "What are you planning on doing to me?"

Neither man answered. There was something strange about them. But Victrina didn't pick up that they were immortals. Nor did they seem to have extrasensory perception. "You two aren't by any chance vampire slayers?"

Again, neither man answered.

"Did that bitch turn me over to you to use as bait?" she asked. They pulled her up and over a slight rise. Beyond that stood a range of mountains. "I don't get it. If you are vampire slayers, why chase after him? He's nothing at all like his wife."

"Just shut up," one said, backhanding her.

The blow wasn't enough to knock her unconscious. She wished it had as they tore off her clothing. Next thing she knew, she was alone. Spread-eagled. Naked. In the sand.

She struggled against bindings at her wrists and ankles. She was staked out underneath the blazing sun. Her captors were nowhere to be seen. They'd picked an area with enough sagebrush that she wouldn't be seen, so if she couldn't get loose, she was in trouble.

Minutes dragged by as her body heated. It didn't take long before her flesh started to crawl. It was so hot and dry, her perspiration evaporated immediately. The sun was so bright that it hurt her eyes. Her skin looked pale blue. Even closing her eyes didn't protect her vision.

The sun's slow arc proved that hours passed, but pain clouded her mind. A buzzard circled overhead. At first she thought it was a mirage, but she wasn't imagining the bird. She'd lost so much blood that she must smell like a tasty snack.

Terror hit when Victrina realized there was no escaping. She'd been tied up all day. No one had come. She was suffering heatstroke and nearly blind from the sun. Her skin was blistered from a massive sunburn.

I should have flown. If she'd flown, this would have never happened.

All the time she'd spent north of the Arctic Circle, worrying Michael would find her, and it was more than likely the men who stalked him would kill her. She would have rather faced Michael. At least he would have murdered her humanely. He would have drained her of blood, and she would have felt no pain. Only pleasure.

* * * *

"Water...." Victrina croaked weakly, wincing as Michael freed her wrists and ankles.

"Shh," he whispered, gathering her in his arms, trying to touch only the skin that hadn't been burned by the sun. He tried to send soothing thoughts to help mask the pain, but it wasn't enough. She knew that she was going to die. And she was terrified.

Disgust with Marianne curled around his gut as he pushed Victrina's bangs off her tortured, swollen skin. Dried, tasteless blood marred her forehead. Centuries had passed, and he'd never been able to take that final step to rid himself of Marianne. He'd clung to the hope that Marianne's humanity would resurface. Yet as he stared at a weak and dying Victrina something inside snapped. Marianne would pay for this.

Michael leaned forward and bit into the swollen flesh of Victrina's neck. Her mind screamed; her body groaned. *Don't kill me.*

The words repeated in her mind, accompanied by images of vultures circling overhead. She'd spent the past hours terrorized at the thought of being eaten alive.

He didn't have any choice. Like the birds she'd seen, a vampire could smell death. She didn't have long to live. Her mind knew it as well as he did.

The irony hit him as he drained her of blood. She wanted to live. Yet there was nothing he could do for her. He couldn't save her life. But he could save *her*.

Dying is the easy part, he told her as he sat up and sliced open his own wrist. *The change will hurt worse than anything you've imagined.*

"But--"

He covered her mouth with his wrist, rubbing the flow of blood along her lips. She fought him, but her body was too weak. She turned her head, trying to escape his touch, refusing to drink from him.

Michael was angry with himself for his mistakes, angrier that Marianne had capitalized on them. But he wasn't angry with Victrina. He sent her those feelings. "I shouldn't have threatened you. I never intended to kill you. But I can't change what happened, and now, death is all I can give you. If you don't drink, I'll lose you. And I don't want to lose you...."

But you're married.

Relief flooded through his system. That was what was on her mind? "So that is what she told you?"

"Yes--"

"Drink!" he insisted, placing his wrist over her lips again. "I don't have time to explain. If you don't drink now, I'll never have that chance."

It seemed like eternity before he felt the first gentle pull of her lips against his wrist, felt his blood flowing into her body. He sent her images to help warn her of the changes that would start in her body as vampirism infected her. He shared also what had happened to Marianne. *The virus didn't only alter her body; it altered her mind. She became who she is today because I changed her.*

What if the same thing happens to me?

He didn't know the answer. That was why he hadn't changed another human in all the centuries since he'd failed with Marianne. But the unknown was something he was willing to face. The prospect of facing one more moment of darkness without Victrina's ability to light up his existence was unthinkable. The last few months had been irritatingly long. He didn't want to continue. Not without her.

"You have extrasensory abilities, like me. Your mind is strong. You have to fight the insanity. It's our only chance." And he'd help her. He wouldn't leave her. "I'll be here with you. Focus on me."

"We can't stay out here," she said quietly.

That was certain. Marianne was nearby. And his ex-wife had company. Michael sent the thought to Marianne, *Was the trap for Victrina? Or me?*

That little bitch told me, 'I didn't see him running after you, perhaps you should let go.' Me, let go? She doesn't know me very well.

You should run. If you want to continue to exist. The next time I see you, Marianne, I will destroy you.

Marianne laughed as two explosions broke the silence of the night. *Oh, Michael. You just fed her. You're weak. You're miles from shelter. A few hours from now dawn will light up this miserable desert. And as you just heard, you have no transportation. You will be destroyed. Unless you ask for my help that is. Give up your fascination for that woman and--*

"No. That will never happen."

"What's wrong?" Victrina asked. "What was that sound?"

"Nothing," he said. "Rest."

Michael gathered Victrina in his arms and moved further into the desert, toward the distant moonlit range of mountains. It had been more years than he could remember since he'd been forced to find shelter in the wild, but it could be done. And he had no choice. Marianne was right. He was in no condition to fight off skilled vampire slayers and protect Victrina.

Despite her anger, Marianne would keep them from finding him. But Victrina wasn't safe. Now that she was turning, she would be added to their list. He couldn't allow Victrina to be destroyed, so he had to run.

Michael traveled for hours, finally finding a wash where the dirt was firm. He set Victrina down and dug them out a shelter, burying them both inside as dawn hit the eastern skies.

He knew the slayers wouldn't be a problem. Even if they found a way to track him, he'd trekked up and over a mountain on a trail they would not be able to climb. They wouldn't show up today.

That left Marianne to worry about. She wasn't a strong psychic, but shielding his presence from her, and helping Victrina through the change would take all his concentration. Fighting sleep in the daytime was not one of his strengths. Normally, he was the kind of guy whose eyes were shut the moment his head hit a pillow. Well, unless a beautiful woman was sharing that pillow. He could normally stay awake for sex.

Victrina chuckled softly. *Make love to me.*

"I can't."

"Yes, you can...."

He kissed her neck. "Besides the fact that your body is in pain, if you haven't noticed, we're spending the day underneath a pile of dirt. But I'll make it up to you, if you promise to concentrate on surviving the change."

Tell me about Marianne. Tell me about your life, the part you avoided before.

"I met Marianne and fell instantly in love. We were married for less than a month when Simeon changed me. Once Marianne realized what I'd become, she fought the idea of becoming a monster, too. But I loved her so much. I was so young, and so naive. I thought that love could last forever.

"After I changed her, all that was left of her was the hatred and the lust. In a way, that makes her the monster she told me I'd become. Yet she still desires me. As you'll find out, sex with another vampire is ... good."

You've been having sex with her all these years?

"That's a loaded question."

Fair, but I saw you feed her.

"Yeah. And I from her. She's one of the only vampires I trust."

"You trust her?"

"It's complicated."

"I just bet." Victrina was upset. "At least you're divorced. She told me you were still married."

Michael remained silent.

"Please tell me that you're divorced."

"We couldn't go to the church and ask for a divorce. I didn't want her burnt at the stake. She was my wife, after all."

Victrina shook her head. "I'm sorry if I feel no sympathy toward her. She turned me over to those men. If you hadn't found me, I would have died."

Michael nuzzled against her neck. "You are dead, love."

She frowned. "And in love with a married man. Sorry, but that sucks."

He held her tighter. "As I recall marriage vows included words to the effect of 'until death do you part.' For all intents and purposes, we aren't married anymore. We are both dead."

Victrina sighed softly. "It's not enough. Marianne still considers you married. And you did kill her with the intent of spending eternity with her."

"There is no way around it. You just have to trust that it is you I love, not her. I haven't loved her for hundreds of years."

Victrina stiffened in his arms. "I can feel the change starting."

"It will get much worse."

"What if it doesn't work for me? Would you destroy me, if I go insane?"

"She's still unharmed." Michael groaned. "After all these years, I've never considered hurting her until I saw what she did to you. Now I want to rip her throat out. Though I can't see myself chasing her down and destroying her. I'm not a slayer."

"Is she with those vampire slayers now? Why aren't they after her? I asked, but they weren't so talkative."

"Marianne is a day walker. So they are fooled. Were fooled. I lifted the compulsion she gave them. She won't be safe from them." Michael hoped they would stalk Marianne rather than him. That would ensure Victrina's safety. "Now stop talking and get some rest. The change will take all of your energy. But don't worry, within a few days you'll feel good as new."

"A few days?" she whined.

"The worst will be over within a few days, but you'll be punchy for another week." As the virus spread through her, Victrina hovered on the edge of an abyss. Her injuries from the day before had weakened her, and watching her pain only increased his feelings of helplessness. He told her he loved her and didn't want to lose her, but he wasn't sure that would be enough.

Simeon arrived with a helicopter at sunset, a big grin on his face. "You turned her, didn't you?"

"Help her," Michael insisted. "She's so weak."

"You'd have her bond with me?"

"Yes, if it will save her."

Simeon shook his head. "She's got enough fire to not fear me. She'll be fine."

Chapter Six

Victrina stretched, instinctively hiding from the familiar chill outside her downy comforter. But her body didn't gain any warmth by snuggling up beneath it. Her actions were unnecessary. She got out of bed, wandered toward the window. The cool air brushed against her naked flesh, but the air didn't cause goose bumps.

It had been months, and she couldn't get used to the strange sensations her new body fed her mind. She pulled back the curtains. Frost covered the corners, several inches deep. She placed her palm against the thin ice that covered the window. Without any significant body heat, it took awhile to melt it.

"I'm room temperature," she said, moving over to the bed and nudging Michael awake. "But I don't really feel cold. I should be cold. It's freezing in here. This is too weird."

"Okay, I was wrong. You'll be punchy for a long time," Michael said, his voice full of sleep. "Come back to bed. It's after midnight. In a town this small, we need to fake human hours."

Despite the intense desire to follow his suggestion, Victrina left the bedroom and opened the arctic entry. She put on a coat, not because she felt like she needed it, but because from the sounds on the street outside it was 12:43 in the afternoon. Though it was dark outside, it was daytime. She found it amusing that after hundreds of years in the temperate zones, Michael couldn't get used to the lack of sunlight. Being here in Barrow was difficult for him.

You find that amusing? he asked her.

There were definite drawbacks to being with a vampire. There wasn't anything she could hide.

She stepped out on the porch, testing her theory. *Go back to sleep. I'll be back in a few minutes.*

Even in the bitter cold, she wasn't getting goose bumps. She was however, getting colder. But it didn't feel bad. After fifteen or twenty minutes, she started to feel a little lethargic. Maybe vampires were like reptiles. Maybe she'd end up going into some kind of hibernation if she stayed outside long enough. She wondered what would happen if she froze solid.

Her first cousin Brad pulled up on his rattletrap old snowgo. The smell of burning oil assaulted her nose. He lit a cigarette and offered her one. She waved her hand, turning him down. Her sense of smell and taste were so acute that she couldn't handle being around someone smoking three blocks away. "If you're going to keep standing out here without smoking, at least put some snow pants on."

"How cold is it?" she asked, licking her finger. The moisture froze quickly.

"Thirty-five below with a wind chill." Brad coughed as he blew a cloud of smoke into the air. "Everyone in town is talking how you've been standing out on the porch for the past twenty minutes in nothing but a coat. And now that I can see it's true, I'm thinking they're right. You must be fighting with your fiancé. Want me to slap some sense into him?"

"He'd tear *you* into toothpicks."

Brad smiled. "If you don't get your bony butt inside before you freeze to death, I'll slap some sense into you. I'm all geared up for a wedding tomorrow. I don't want to go to your funeral."

She waved him off, laughing lightly, and returned to Michael's side. He was sound asleep.

She shook him until he awakened. Michael was definitely having difficulty adjusting to Barrow's lack of sunlight. But by this time tomorrow, he needed to be awake and ready to marry her at this time of day. "See," she said, holding out her arms. "Not a damn goose bump. You were worried I couldn't stand the thought of drinking blood, and what I miss is feeling normal."

"Would you just come back to bed?" Michael asked, his voice heavy with the inability to think straight. The twinkle in his eyes let her know that he wasn't planning on falling back asleep. Mmm ... now that she could handle. There were definite advantages to being with a vampire. Michael was right. The sex was great.

"Everyone is talking about whether or not we'll get married tomorrow," she said, snuggling next to him.

He shivered. He actually shivered. "Damn, you're cold. Your body must be forty degrees."

"Maybe there is something wrong with me. You can feel cold, but it doesn't bother me. What if I'm like Marianne?"

"You aren't," he assured her. "That I'm sure of."

She sighed as his warm hands started moving across her breasts, teasing her taut nipples against his palms. Still, now that Marianne was a subject of conversation, she forced herself to lie perfectly still. "I can't believe you invited her to our wedding."

"What better way to set in her mind that she needs to move on?"

That was probably true. But that didn't mean she had to like that Michael was right. "You falsified a marriage license, then the annulment. That should have sent her the message."

Michael tweaked one nipple while he caressed her clit. The feelings were too intense to ignore. Victrina was irritated with Michael for trying to distract her. "Would you stop that? It isn't fair."

He leaned over her and grasped her second nipple between his teeth, biting softly. Victrina's sex clenched tightly, as she reached out and grasped his cock. She rubbed the tip of him. His body shivered beneath her touch.

She still owes you a big apology. But she does have her good moments and, after all, if it wasn't for her actions, I wouldn't have changed you. I thought we should invite her so we can thank her personally.

You're much too forgiving. She wound her fingers into his hair, pulling him up toward her lips as she wrapped her legs around his waist, opening to him as his hard member slid into her moist and ready and very needy flesh.

Michael shivered when his cock was fully sheathed within her. *Why on earth did you stand outside so long? Go take a bath and warm up first.*

Victrina laughed as she clenched her inner muscles. "I might not *feel* hot and ready for you, but believe me, I am."

He lifted one brow as she arched her hips against him. He lifted his hips and shafted slowly into her again, then again. The sound of his cock sliding into her was all that she could hear over the rush of blood through both of their bodies. She could feel his heart beating, feel his pleasure as he moved within her.

That was another advantage in having sex with a vampire. There was nothing to hide. *Touch me, Michael. I want to feel you everywhere at once.*

He reached between them, twirling his finger around her clit until she moaned. Even if she hadn't begged for his touch, he always knew exactly what she wanted, yet every time seemed new and exciting.

"I could always join you," he said softly, his cock taking her slowly, sliding into her at a maddeningly slow pace that helped build the tension between them.

"You are joining me," she said. "I love how I can feel your body too. Feel your blood. Sense what you feel when you sink into me. I love knowing how much you want me."

"I meant in the bath," he whispered against her ear, licking the side of her neck.

"Later," she commanded.

He smiled at her, angling his neck. "Then drink. That'll even out our temperatures."

Victrina poked his side. "Didn't anyone warn you that us Eskimo girls like to snuggle up to get warm on cold winter nights?"

Repeatedly. I thought I explained that was the ability that I was seeking out when I found you at Harvard?

If you're implying you wanted me for sex and not my mind, it's a lucky thing you're so damn good-looking yourself. The sharp pang of her fangs extending hit her, and she closed her lips over Michael's neck. She bit him softly, reveling in the love she felt as his blood flowed down her throat. As he warmed her both physically and mentally, she concentrated on what he was feeling. Everything was that clear when they were joined like this.

All she could feel was his blood and his cock moving faster, deeper, pushing past her clit harder with each stroke, bringing her closer to her peak. Michael held her tighter, his nails digging into her as he strained to bury himself farther. Neither could get enough.

Victrina clenched down on his cock, milking him, pushing her hips against him, grasping his hips and pressing him tighter against her. They were joined so closely, she was surprised that he got his hand between then and stroked her clit. He sent her over the edge immediately, and he followed. His seed shot into her, his mind lost with hers as she stopped sucking his blood and wrapped her arms around his neck.

"But nobody warned me that I'd never be able to get enough of you," he said. "I could lie here all day. I never want to leave your body."

She hadn't realized that she'd been clenching him so tightly. She'd been focusing on Michael and his response more than her own. Her muscles were fluttering still, everywhere. Her whole body was shaking in the aftermath. "Me too. I'm so glad you decided to chase me down."

"And I will again if I have to. There'll never be a sunset between us, love."

"Never a sunset," she muttered dreamily.

"Never. So don't think for a moment that you'll ever get away from me by running back here."

He was referring to the fact that Victrina had already threatened to spend next summer in Barrow. She was like Marianne in that respect. She hadn't grown into her vampire body with a fierce allergy to the sun. She could spend hours outside, without being burned.

But her threat hadn't worked. Michael had invited his ex-wife to their wedding anyway.

"I'm here for more than five years. I'm yours forever." Then she laughed. "For better or worse. You listen to those vows tomorrow. I told the minister to take out the part about until death do us part."

"And I told him to add until the end of time. Do you, soon-to-be Victrina Levine, promise to allow me to love and cherish you forever?"

Her lips moved over his neck. She ran her tongue along his jaw line.

What a strange turn of events her life had taken. Maybe running away wasn't so bad. If she hadn't wanted to escape Barrow, she would have never met him in the first place. If she hadn't run back, she wouldn't realize how much he loved her. "I do, Michael. Forever."

The End

FRESH BLOOD

Jennifer Colgan

Chapter One

The sultry beat coming from the interior of *After Dark* competed with the staccato of Erica Talbot's heart as she approached the side door of the nightclub. The white stucco wall, along which the line of hopefuls waited, vibrated from the new age acid rock playing within. The bone-deep pulse made the other young women in the line loose-limbed and excited. They swayed to the beat even though whatever melody the song might have had was inaudible in the alley behind the club.

Erica wanted to act just like the others. She tried to adopt the distant, dreamy expression so many of them wore but she just didn't have it in her. She'd long ago resigned herself to having no rhythm, no sexy sway and no desire to hide the sharp intelligence that shone from her hazel eyes.

Tonight she'd traded her usual style, conservative pinstriped slacks and tailored button-down blouse, for a short leather skirt and a low-cut satin T that did little to hide the black push-up bra she wore underneath. Glitter-dusted stockings and ankle-breaking black stilettos completed her outfit and her golden blonde hair swirled in a wild updo that left her neck suggestively bare. She'd accented her lips with a shade of red that should have been illegal, and applied an extra layer of mascara to her already long lashes.

At least she looked like she fit in. Only her stiff posture gave her away. Anyone looking long enough would have figured out that she had nothing but disdain for the whole affair. This was not her world and it never would be.

It disgusted her that Elena might be found in a place like this. Might be--if she wasn't at one of the dozen other bars like *After Dark* that had sprung up over the past few years when the vampire population in Illinois began a disconcerting upswing. This was just the type of place in which her sister would feel right at home.

"You. You. *Not* you." The muscle-bound bouncer who held court at the metal fire door gestured one of the waiting girls out of line with a tilt of his bald head. The redhead in a black sheath dress, cloggy heels and black lipstick couldn't have been more than sixteen. The layers of kohl that ringed her eyes did nothing to hide the lack of wrinkles, or the hardened edge of lost innocence in her expression.

The vicious curse she hurled at the man--in a voice that spoke of a two-pack a day habit--shattered any illusion of gothic sophistication. She flipped him the bird and sauntered off, mumbling threats under her breath.

The last two women he'd let in lingered at the door watching the girl retreat with smug satisfaction. They thought they were better than her. Luckier. If only they knew.

Erica was next in line, and the bouncer eyed her as though he were appraising a cut of beef. She smiled and lowered her thick lashes in what she hoped was a demure, come-hither look. "Do you smoke?" he asked.

The question surprised her. She wondered if he meant tobacco, or if the question was some type of code she didn't understand. "No."

He looked her over again and then grasped her wrists with his enormous hands. Her first instinct was to jerk away from his grip, but she held her disgust in check. She had to get inside the club, even if only for a few minutes. When he turned her hands palm up revealing the unblemished undersides of her forearms, relief eased the adrenaline rush to her head. "No needle marks," he said. "Do you snort?"

"No!"

He looked at her face, and she held his bloodshot gaze for a tense moment. "You're in," he said finally, then turned to the others. "That's all for tonight."

A wave of recriminations traveled through the dozen or so women left in the alley. "Come back tomorrow." He sounded apologetic just for an instant. But when the women didn't immediately scatter, he cursed at them in a gravelly voice that made the skin on the back of Erica's neck tighten in fear.

He pushed her inside and shut the fire door with a clang that rocked the gritty plaster walls. At the end of the narrow hallway where the chosen ones waited, two other men stood shoulder to shoulder, blocking most of the view into the club. Behind them, blue lights pulsed in time to the music that seemed to have grown ten times louder. While the fifteen women jockeyed for position in the hallway, the bouncer and his two friends did a head count and started on the body searches.

Erica fought to disengage her gag reflex when the men squatted behind each of the women and ran their hands up under each girl's skirt from ankle to thigh. The others didn't seem to mind the frisking, but the thought of some stranger shoving his fingers between her thighs made Erica lightheaded. She bit her lip and sidled through the line, letting other women go ahead of her and shuffling around until she stood with the ones that had already undergone the search.

When the two door guards parted and motioned the girls into the club, Erica's dignity remained blessedly intact. She kept her head down as she passed the men and in seconds lost herself in the river of bodies that filled the dance floor.

Now she had her work cut out for her. In the pulsating light, the scene before her looked like an old-time nickel-movie, everyone jerking around in stop motion. In each flash of neon blue, Erica scanned the faces around her hoping to catch a glimpse of her sister.

The last time she'd seen Elena, her twin had short black hair, and blue contact lenses hid the natural hazel green of her eyes. To a stranger, the Talbot sisters wouldn't have appeared related at all. It still amazed Erica sometimes to think they'd come from the same womb. Even if she were in disguise, Erica would know her sister by the way she moved, her voice, the intensity of her gaze which even contact lenses couldn't hide. If Elena were here, Erica would find her.

She decided to make one complete circuit of the place, checking the bar, the restroom and even the waitresses who carried trays of drinks and plates of food. *Who could eat in a place like this*? The noise alone made Erica sick to her stomach. Maybe you had to be drunk to enjoy it. She figured a person certainly had to be drunk to want to party with vampires.

The only good thing about *After Dark* was the lack of smoke. The lighting was nauseating but the atmosphere inside was crystal clear. She wondered why. Certainly vampires had no fear of lung cancer. Maybe it was the flare of a match that made them nervous. Either way, Erica was grateful that she didn't have to squint through the acrid haze that polluted most of the human clubs.

Pale faces and half-clad bodies swam by in rapid succession until the details of their features began to blur. Erica finally reached the bar and clung to the leather pad that cushioned its edge. On either side of her, patrons leaned in comfort while they sipped drinks and attempted to talk over the pounding music.

Elena's wasn't among the faces that turned to appraise her, so Erica did her best to avoid eye contact until the barmaid slapped a red cocktail napkin down in front of her.

"What can I get you?" The woman was six feet of blonde, Nordic perfection. The only thing marring her appearance was the brilliant white tip of an elongated incisor that peeked out beneath her upper lip. Erica swallowed. Female vampires were known to be vicious, carnal creatures, much less likely to maintain a semblance of their human existence than their male counterparts. Erica formed her answer carefully.

"I'll have a martini."

"Dry?"

"Sure."

The bartender whirled away, her sleeveless sequined T-shirt glittering.

Erica clutched the edge of the bar tighter and stared at her featureless reflection in the polished laminate of the bar top.

I'm out of my mind, she thought. This had to be the last time she came to Elena's rescue. She'd peeled Elena off of too many filthy bar-stools, and sat in the police station too many times, waiting for her sister to come teetering out of a holding cell reeking of smoke and sex.

The fact that this time was different just added to the hopelessness of the situation. This time the static-broken message on Erica's answering machine had sounded truly desperate, not just momentarily needy. "I've been hanging out at ... you know ... the vampire bar. Come get me, Ricki. I need you to help me figure out a way out of this one...."

Erica had listened to the message at least two dozen times and still couldn't make out the name of the bar, so she'd started with the letter A.

By the time the bartender returned with her drink, she'd decided it was time to move on to the next letter, which meant a place called *Danger--Danger* on the far side of town. As far as Erica was concerned, it might as well have been called *Stupid--Stupid.*

That's how she felt.

At least she was reasonably sure no one would recognize her. She didn't know any vampires personally ... at least she hoped she didn't.

* * * *

"What do I owe you?" she asked.

The vampiress laughed. "You don't have to buy your own drinks, babe."

"I--"

"I'll keep a tab for you and when someone picks you up, he'll pay the bill. Sorry, he or *she*--we don't discriminate here."

"No one's going to pick me up. In fact, I'm leaving. I've got ... to be somewhere else." Erica rummaged in her tiny purse and pulled out a rumpled ten-dollar bill. She flattened it out with her hand and pushed it across the shiny surface of the bar.

Before she let go of the bill, a hairy-knuckled hand closed over her arm. "You!"

Erica jerked her hand away this time and the force of the movement sent the top-heavy martini glass skittering down the bar showering patrons with vodka and vermouth.

"What's the problem, Frank?" The barmaid grabbed the glass before it rolled off the bar and swiped at the clear puddle with a rag. She looked mildly annoyed at the intrusion but not as angry as 'Frank.'

"*This* one didn't get searched." The bouncer from the alley yanked Erica around to face him. While those nearby watched in detached amusement, he shoved Erica backward against the bar and spread her legs with one of his massive thighs. With her back arched and her breasts practically even with his nose, there was little she could do but submit. She held her breath against the overpowering aroma of cheap cologne and turned her head. She paled when his meaty hand slithered down her side and he yanked up the hem of her skirt and rummaged underneath.

"I should throw you right out," he said. His face was so close to hers that she was able to make out the gold plated initial F inscribed on his front tooth. At least his breath smelled of a recently chewed Altoid.

Erica looked away again when one of his fingers dipped under the garter that held her stockings in place. "What are you looking for?" She didn't want to sound breathless and terrified, but that's how the words came out.

"Stakes. Bitches always hide 'em up their skirts."

The crowd at the bar backed up a little at that. When Frank finally brought his hand up, empty, they shuffled back to their places.

"You're clean," he said with a leer. Erica felt anything but clean. Her flesh tingled unpleasantly where he'd explored. "Who's buyin' for you?"

"What?"

"You don't have a buyer yet?"

"She said she's leavin', Frank. Why don't you just escort the lady to the door?" The bartender gave Erica a snide look as she tucked the ten--spot into her apron.

Frank obliged by yanking Erica toward him. "Let's go."

"I'm buying for her."

The voice sent a chill down Erica's spine. Deep and sexy with a hint of British accent, it was a voice that could melt a woman or freeze her. Frank let her go instantly as if contact with her skin suddenly burned him.

Erica looked up at her dubious savior and did her best not to react. She'd never thought of a man as beautiful, but she couldn't think of another word to describe him. His hair was midnight black, and his eyes were the bottomless blue of a tropical ocean. His white shirt was open to the second button, and a dark tie hung askew as though he'd just loosened it. A gold pinky ring gleamed on his right hand as he held it out to her.

Frank and the barmaid exchanged a glance before they both went back to their duties leaving Erica on her own. The man's scrutiny left her feeling naked and much too warm and she found herself wishing she'd brought a stake just so Frank would have a reason to throw her out.

"I was just leaving." What a cliché. True, but nevertheless. She might as well have told him she had to go home and wash her hair. He studied her for a moment and his eyes darkened, not with anger, but with something else that made Erica just as uncomfortable. When he spoke, his words left no room for argument.

"The management here doesn't like drop-ins. If a human comes in, it's understood what they're here for. If you want to leave without someone feeding on you, you'll come with me."

Chapter Two

Erica stared at the man before her. He didn't look much like a vampire. His skin wasn't all that pale. His blue eyes practically sparked with inner fire and she didn't see any fangs. She glanced back at the barmaid, but found no ally there. With her spilled drink paid for, the blonde Amazon had no further use for her.

"I ..."

He didn't wait for her to finish her sentence. He reached forward and grabbed her wrist. A second later, he was dragging her after him through the undulating crush on the dance floor.

He pulled her toward the club's front door, the exit reserved for vampires. Humans came and went only by way of the alley. If she hadn't been anxious to leave anyway, she might not have waited until he yanked her down the two shallow front steps and into the empty street to protest.

When they hit the rain-damp macadam, he whirled her around to face him, his long fingers cold as iron around her arm.

She twisted in his grasp but he only tightened his grip.

"What were you doing in there?" His question seemed personal, delivered in a tone of reproachful concern, as if he actually cared.

"I was just looking around." She pulled ineffectually at her trapped wrist and briefly considered using a groin shot to make him let her go. Of course, in her hooker heels, she probably couldn't have outrun her own grandmother.

"Looking for what?"

"Nothing! I was ... just curious. You're hurting me."

"I don't believe you." He looked down his aquiline nose at her with the obvious intent to intimidate. Erica held his gaze, but angled her body away from him in an attempt to keep herself just outside the range of those hypnotic eyes.

"Who are you, anyway? The owner? What does it matter why I came in? I paid for my drink and I left. No harm done, and I won't be coming back."

"No. You won't. I don't want to see you back here. This isn't the place for you."

Erica raised an eyebrow. "*Who* are you again--my knight protector?"

His molten gaze traveled to her wrist and he let her go so abruptly that she stumbled backward a step. "I just don't want to see an innocent drawn into that world. Anybody can see you don't belong in there."

Innocent? Is that what he thought she was? Ha. What she wouldn't give to be innocent again. She tossed her head in a gesture of defiance, gave him a practiced smirk and turned away. "What I do is none of your business."

"Actually, it is."

When she turned back to give him another piece of her mind, a dull silver glint caught her eye. He held out a leather wallet with a round badge and a laminated ID tucked under thin black bands.

A cop? Her mind boomeranged around that one. Since when did cops cover vampire territory? As far as Erica knew, what went on in places like *After Dark* didn't interest human law enforcement. Or maybe they were just afraid to get involved.

Intrigued, despite her desire to get on with her search and rescue mission, she reached out and tilted the badge so she could read the words by the reflection of the halogen lamppost in the club's blacked-out front window. "Maxwell Hart. Vampire investigator?" The thought struck her funny but she caught herself before laughing. "What exactly *is* that?"

"We work for the vampire king. One of our functions is to keep the vampire and human worlds as separate as possible. Feeders are welcome at the clubs, but not drop–ins. Our world isn't a tourist attraction."

Erica gave him a long, appraising look. He *sounded* like a cop. "I couldn't agree with you more, Mr. Hart."

"Then what were you doing in the club when you clearly had no intention of becoming a feeder?"

Knight protector. Wouldn't it be nice? Erica cocked her head and pursed her lips. If she'd known vampire investigators existed, she might have called one before she went trolling the bars for Elena.

"I'm looking for my sister." It killed her to admit it. She hated for anyone to know about her problems with Elena because in her twin's shortcomings, Erica saw her own weaknesses.

"Is your sister a feeder?" Hart asked. He shifted his weight and reached into his pants pocket. Erica rolled her eyes when he pulled out a notebook, the kind with the matching pen attached in an elastic loop.

"I don't need your services, Mr. Hart. I can find her myself."

"She's a feeder?" He wasn't going to give up.

"No ... I don't know. I certainly hope not. She asked me to meet her at a bar, but I couldn't make out the name. I came here because it's closest to her apartment." Her last known address, anyway. Elena didn't stay in one place for long, but she never ranged far enough from Erica to be truly independent, either.

"What's your name?"

"Elena. Her name is Elena Talbot ... but--"

"*Your* name."

Erica looked up. His eyes drew her in. If he were human, he'd have been her type. The crisp shirt, the loose tie, broad shoulders--she fantasized about men like this. The repressed executive type turned her on--proper and polite on the surface, a wild man underneath. That was another thing she kept to herself.

"*My* name?"

He nodded and a faint smile played around his lips. She couldn't help but feel like he had her right where he wanted her.

"It's not important, Mr. Hart. My sister's not here. I've obviously got the wrong place so I'm just going to go home and call her tomorrow."

"If your sister's not a feeder, why would she come to a vampire bar?"

"I have no idea."

One of his dark eyebrows rose. "Do you think she might be a vampire killer?"

Erica frowned. "My sister is a lot of things, but she's not a killer."

"No, of course not. I'm sure she wouldn't hurt a fly. But vampires--we're a little different. We're dead already, so we don't really matter." The bitter edge to his words surprised her.

"She's *not* a vampire killer."

"There's good money in it."

"What makes you think she needs money?"

He shrugged. "Some people do it just because they *like* it."

"Mr. Hart--" Erica turned away but he touched her arm and the contact singed her. How could a vampire's touch be so hot? She looked at the spot where his fingers rested gently on her arm.

"I'm sorry ... Ms?"

"Talbot. Erica."

"Ms. Talbot. I'm just doing my job. There have been a lot of vampire murders recently and when someone comes into a club, like you did tonight, just to scope the place out, you have to understand, it looks suspicious."

"My sister is not involved in anything like that, Mr. Hart. I know that much. She's easily ... led. She may have decided to become a feeder, in which case, I'd like to stop her. No offense, but I don't want to see her become a vampire."

"We don't normally turn our feeders, Ms. Talbot. It's not economical."

"Well, that's good to know."

"We don't force our feeders either, as a rule. So if she's hanging out at a bar, it's probably her choice."

"Then why did she ask for my help?" *Maybe because she always asks for my help?* "She wants me to find her, Mr. Hart, and I intend to do that."

He seemed to approve of that. He folded the notebook and the wallet and returned them to his pocket. Erica followed the movement then looked away quickly, ashamed by her interest in points below his belt buckle.

"Why don't you let me help you, Ms. Talbot? If your sister is in one of the bars or the clubs or a vampire compound, you won't be able to go strolling in for a look around. I could do it for you."

"For a reasonable price, I assume?"

He laughed and she liked the sound, as well as the smile that accompanied it. "No. I'm a public servant, ma'am. I'm on the government payroll."

"The government hires vampire investigators now?" That was a shocker considering the extreme right wing conservative administration these days. She'd have expected vampire *killers* on the payroll, not vampire cops.

"The vampire government," Hart corrected. "Contrary to what you might think, part of our job is protecting humans."

She didn't believe that. But still, the prospect of having a little help seemed, to borrow his word, economical.

"All right, Mr. Hart. I'd appreciate your help. The next place on my list is called *Danger--Danger*, unless you know a club that's closer."

Hart's smile faded. "I'm not taking you with me, Ms. Talbot. Like I told you, a human can't just go into these places unless you're a feeder. That's what these bars are for. It's not like in the old movies where we stalk some virginal society girl and fly into her window on bat wings in the middle of the night. We invite our feeders to come to us. If you give me a description of your sister, and preferably something of hers, like a piece of clothing, something that would have her scent on it, I'll do a thorough investigation."

"Her scent?" Erica pictured Hart leading a yapping pack of bloodhounds. His sardonic look erased the image instantly and she blushed.

"Our senses are much more acute than a human's. Even if I didn't know what she looked like, I could find her by her scent."

"Ah ... well, either way, Mr. Hart, I want to go with you. Elena needs me. She'll be afraid if she thinks a vampire is stalking her. She needs to know I'm coming to help her."

Hart shook his head. "Not a good idea."

"I'll go with or without you. If I have to break into the clubs myself."

"You'll get hurt. Frank was lenient on you tonight. I've seen girls limp out of *After Dark* after pulling what you pulled tonight. I've seen some crawl out." He leaned close and Erica's heart jumped when his breath warmed the skin of her neck. "Some had to be carried out."

Erica swallowed. "Then I'll just have to rely on my knight protector to keep me safe, won't I?"

Chapter Three

Max slid into the driver's seat of his car and tapped the steering wheel in an attempt to keep focused while the woman slithered into the passenger seat in her skin-tight skirt.

The whole set-up was wrong. So wrong. He had to be out of his mind to agree to take her with him anywhere. She had no idea what she was getting into and he had an unpleasant hollow in his gut that told him he didn't either.

He'd handled missing person cases before. Young girls left home all the time hoping to mix it up with vampires. That's why the clubs had rules. No one underage. No one on drugs or drunk when they arrived. Of course, what they got into afterward was up to them.

He liked his job, and he didn't mind that part of it was to keep humans from doing things they didn't really want to do. What bothered him most was the way they looked at him. Even this woman--Erica. She thought he was just a vampire. A monster. He saw it in her eyes. And there, with the keen intelligence and that sweet vulnerability you just didn't see in a woman once she'd been turned, was the fear. What he hated most was that it still got to him, even after one hundred and seventeen years.

Her scent was already familiar to him. She hadn't doused herself in the artificial pheromones humans used to disguise their natural scent. She looked like a feeder, underdressed and over made-up, but she smelled like ... a librarian. She had a faint aroma of books and ink and female musk enhanced by the sharp flavor of a natural soap. Just like all the others, she had no idea that it wasn't the sexy outfit that drew a buyer at the bar, it was the right scent.

Of course, the shimmering stockings on those mile-long legs, the push-up bra that gave her an artfully rounded cleavage and the wisps of golden hair that tickled the naked skin of her neck, would certainly have drawn any male vampire's attention and probably a few females, too. But it was her scent that had brought Max across the surging tide of dancers to find her at the bar.

If she'd been a feeder, he'd have bought her.

Maybe the hollow in his gut was hunger rather than self-doubt. He'd figure out which later on.

"I'm not going to take you to *Danger--Danger*. You're not ready for that. We'll start out at *Club Dead.* It's a little more upscale, not as loud. If your sister's there, we should be able to locate her pretty quickly."

"Fine. I want to hit as many places as we can tonight," she said as she clicked her seatbelt in place. He watched her out of the corner of his eyes as he guided the car out of the parking lot. A block later they were back in human territory and surrounded by late night traffic.

"You have to prepare for some of these places. I'll take you to the lighter ones, where I usually make my rounds on the weekends. Some of the places, even *I* need a reason to go into. I can't just show up and flash my badge."

"Why not?" Her curiosity amused him, and annoyed him at the same time. "If you're investigating--"

"Even human cops need warrants. They can't just barge in anywhere. Some of these clubs are private estates, and what goes on there usually isn't subject to investigation. They have their own security staff and sometimes they work with us. Sometimes they don't."

"So some vampires don't have to follow the rules?"

"It's the same with humans sometimes, isn't it? We have our

own way of dealing with the troublemakers. Don't become a troublemaker." He punctuated his subtle warning with a half-grin.

She nodded but he saw the wheels turning. She wasn't going to be deterred. That made her dangerous to herself and to him.

"You have to trust me on this. I know what I'm talking about. If you want to help your sister, and if she really is in some kind of trouble, you've got to be careful how you go about things. Even in a regular bar, you're not going to just waltz in, grab her by the hand and waltz back out. If someone owns her ..."

Max winced as soon as he said it. He gripped the steering wheel tighter during the outburst that followed.

"No one *owns* my sister! She's not some slave to a vampire. I know that!"

"No. You don't." He shot her a cautious look. With her chin up and her vibrant lower lip caught in her teeth, she looked tough and sexy.

"I don't think you know anything about vampire society, and if your sister is in trouble and she got into something that she wants out of, she probably didn't know anything either."

She sighed angrily. "Then why don't you explain it to me?"

She probably didn't really want to know. "A lot of times, feeders relinquish control to their vampires. Some want to be turned so they do whatever they're asked to in exchange for a chance at immortality." The words left a sour taste. It wasn't a subject he liked to talk about~~it~~. He wasn't proud of some of the promises he'd made when the gnawing hunger robbed him of his reasoning ability. He'd learned his lesson well--never go too long without feeding--never ~~to~~ try to act human for so long that he forgot what he was.

"You think she's selling her soul?" Her pretty voice became a croak. The smell of fear momentarily overpowered her enticing scent.

"I hope we can get to her before that happens. But I want to warn you, you're going to see things you won't like and if you want to get inside, you've got to pretend it doesn't bother you. Are you willing to do that? If not, I will take you home right now, and I'll conduct the investigation by myself ... which is how I'd prefer to do it anyway."

"No."

He tapped the break pedal. Was she really smart enough to back off now while she still could?

"No?"

"No. I'm going to find Elena. I'll do what I have to. I can't let her turn herself into a vampire."

Max laughed but there was no humor in it. "It takes two to make a vampire."

"Whatever. Look, it's not something I like to talk about, but Elena drinks too much. She does drugs sometimes. She likes men who mistreat her. In my opinion, all those things can be cured--with the right kind of help. But there's no cure for 'vampire' ... right?"

He smirked. He'd looked for one, in the beginning, when he thought he'd go mad from the craving for blood. "None that I know of. Except for death. *That* cures the condition pretty quickly."

"Then I've got to stop her. Even if it's what she thinks she wants."

"All right. Then you have to do exactly as I say when we're inside. Do you understand?"

She nodded and he just knew she didn't understand. Not completely. They were going to hit a rocky road. It was just a matter of time.

* * * *

Erica shivered as she got out of Max's car. She already didn't like the way things were going, but she didn't see a choice, but to go along with him. The things he'd told her to expect inside *Club Dead* made her skin crawl just a little. The last thing Erica had the stomach for was anything deviant. Elena had told her stories about aberrant human behavior that still kept her awake some nights. She couldn't imagine what a glimpse of vampire life would do to her, but she couldn't back out now.

She waited while Max came around the car. He took her hand and pulled her toward the side of the building, which, from the outside, looked very similar to *After Dark*. The place was nondescript with darkened windows and no glowing marquis like human clubs boasted. She didn't hear any music coming from within this time, which surprised her. She expected the place to be loud and obnoxious just like *After Dark*.

"Don't we get to go in the front this time?" she asked as he herded her around the corner of the building. Another car pulled into the parking lot just then and Hart shielded her from view, stopping in front of her.

She looked up into his face and stifled a scream. His fangs were showing.

"What the--"

"I promise it won't hurt."

He pulled her to him in a swift movement that caught her off balance. She stumbled forward, putting her hands up against his chest to brace herself. She struggled against his iron grip as his arms came around her and trapped her against him. Fear stole her breath and the bloodcurdling scream she planned came out as an impotent squeak.

Her knees buckled when the needle sharp points of his incisors pierced her neck.

But it didn't hurt.

When he set her back on her feet, she wobbled a little and he steadied her. "I'm sorry about that."

"What did you--" She swiped her hand over the spot, still oddly warm from the pressure of his lips. Bright red blood covered her fingers.

"I marked you as mine."

The words sent a wanton pulse to the suddenly wet spot between her legs. Those were the sexiest words she'd ever heard.

She slapped him.

"You can't just go around biting people!" The sudden adrenaline rush cleared her head a little and she realized how absurd she sounded.

Max rubbed the left side of his jaw and grinned. The humor in his eyes didn't completely mask the dangerous hint of lust Erica saw there. How could what just happened have turned them both on?

"I don't go around biting people. I marked you. I didn't drink any. I just broke the skin so it looks like I've been feeding from you."

Erica stared at her bloody fingertips for a second before Max handed her a folded handkerchief from his back pocket. She wiped her hands and dabbed at the still tingling spot on her neck. "You could have warned me."

"You'd have said no and we'd be out here arguing about it until daybreak."

True. If he'd asked permission to bite her, she would have refused. Biting was ... unsanitary at best. The fact that she liked it--no. She didn't like it. That was ridiculous. She'd been scared out of her mind, limp with terror, unable to scream. She didn't like that feeling at all. Absolutely not. She mentally reserved the right to slap him again later just for good measure. For now, she had to find Elena.

"Anything else I should know before we go in?" She straightened her skirt and fluffed her hair in a vain attempt to recapture some of her dignity. She'd never gone limp in a man's arms before--ever. Frankly, it was embarrassing.

"One thing ..." His wicked smile did something to the muscles just below her navel. "You taste great."

Chapter Four

Max waited until the occupants of the other car entered the club before he led Erica around to the front of the building. He stopped with his hand on the curving handle of the front door and gave her a hard look. "Last chance to back out."

"Open the door."

Her response didn't surprise him. What did, however, was that he found her tough act endearing. She definitely had courage. Maybe on someone else he would have called it unbridled stupidity, but on her it worked. The quiet desperation in her eyes touched a long neglected chord in him and he decided, despite his better judgment, that she just might be smart enough to play it cool.

He opened the door and they entered the sultry atmosphere of *Club Dead.*

Inside, Melinda, the Friday-night hostess, sat on a four-foot high stool next to the inner door. Her skinny legs, sheathed in black stockings, twined around each other and she balanced a narrow leather guest book in her lap. The vampiress smiled at him, showing off her newly sharpened fangs.

"Max! You look great, as always. Who's this? Someone new?" There was just a hint of ferocity in the look she gave Erica. That had nothing to do with Max. Melinda barely tolerated human women. She preferred to feed from males.

"This is--"

"Ricki," Erica blurted the pseudonym, drawing a frown from Melinda. "Hi."

Max yanked her arm, hard. "That's enough talk." He smiled apologetically at Melinda. "She's very new."

The hostess nodded but there was disapproval in her expression.

"Table for two?"

"Yes."

"Go on in." Melinda touched a button on the wall behind her. The inner doors opened and she ushered them deeper into the club.

Max felt Erica stiffen as he pulled her inside the darkened interior where black lights illuminated the carefully painted décor. It looked like a neon garden. Here and there spotlights shone on couples and triples engaged in everything from quiet conversation to blatantly sexual feeding frenzies.

He tugged again and Erica stumbled after him. "Keep walking," he said in his most severe tone.

"I think you--" He cut off her protest with a fang-bearing sneer then splayed his fingers over the bite mark on her neck where he applied just enough pressure to cause discomfort.

"Remember what we discussed. In here, you do everything I say, when I say it. If you have a problem with the way I treat you, we'll discuss it when the evening is over."

He saw her swallow another sharp remark. To her credit, she broke eye contact first, dropping her gaze in nearly perfect subservience.

"Let's get to our table. I'm thirsty." He pulled her gently this time and she kept up with his pace as he made his way through the club to the very back where the B-list patrons got to sit. Once there, he guided her to a chair and then pulled his own as close to hers as possible. Under the table, he put one hand on her exposed knee and squeezed then slid his thumb up beneath the taut strap of her garter.

"Those shoes are too high for you. The next time we go out, wear something more comfortable. I don't want you stumbling all over the place."

She nodded and he squeezed her thigh in approval.

With his index finger he traced a line down her jaw and into the collar of her blouse. He gently pushed the material aside, exposing one thin strap of her bra, which he nudged off the curve of her shoulder. "That's better. Now, I'm going to tell you, in detail everything I'm going to do to you tonight, do you understand?"

Again she nodded and again he squeezed.

"First I'm going to order you a drink. Then I'm going to teach you everything you need to know about being a feeder ... one delicious drop at a time."

* * * *

Erica fought to steady her breathing as Max caressed her thigh beneath the table. The thud of her own wild pulse drowned out much of what he was saying, which was a good thing, because her cognitive skills had bottomed out the moment they walked inside.

The humid atmosphere had surprised her at first. She hadn't expected a tropical feel to the place and if that had been the only shock, she would have been fine.

When her eyes adjusted to the black light she saw the neon splotches of color that dripped from the walls, puddled on the floor and ran in rivulets across the tables and chairs. The décor didn't shock her as much as the patrons, though.

The first couple that had come into view as they entered the club seemed perfectly normal. Seated at a small table, their half-finished meal before them, the man pulled the woman to him in a romantic embrace. Her eyes widened when he bit into her neck and Erica imagined she heard the rush of blood as he suckled. The woman moaned in carnal pleasure and her eyes lit on Erica's for a brief moment. Her short dark hair and thin white shoulders looked achingly familiar causing Erica's heart to pump an overdose of adrenaline into her system. By the time her brain registered that the woman was not Elena, her head was pounding in time to her heartbeat and her legs had begun to tremble.

At the next table they passed, a woman sat on her knees at the feet of a sedate looking man in an Armani suit. Another woman sat on his lap, leaning back against his chest as he drank from her and caressed her breasts through the nearly transparent fabric of her blouse. Erica stared at the thin, glittering chain that connected the woman on the floor to the woman on the man's lap by leather cuffs on their wrists.

She might have left then, but she realized she needed to sit down more than she needed to flee.

With her hands on the cool surface of the table, she concentrated on maintaining control. She'd never felt like this before and she wondered if the sensations were akin to a drug-induced high. Twinges of electrical current raced up and down her spine with detours to the sensitive flesh beneath Max's thumb. With her pulse racing and the humid air dampening her skin, she felt close to having a heart attack.

When a waitress finally brought the drink Max had ordered for her, she reached for the glass and gulped. Only after she'd drained it halfway did she realize there was little, if any, alcohol in it. She set the glass down with trembling fingers.

"Are you all right?" His voice seemed normal when he whispered in her ear. Before, when he'd been giving her orders he sounded commanding in a way that should have made her angry and insulted. The fact that it made her tremor with forbidden desires frightened her and made her feel slightly shameful.

"I'm fine. I don't see Elena."

"This isn't the whole club. What we're going to have to do is wait a little while, then on our way out take a walk through the grotto in the back."

"There's something farther back than this lousy table?" She felt suddenly brave, giddy in fact. She wondered what exactly was in the drink.

He laughed. "There's another room around the corner there." He pointed to a spot where slashes of orange neon paint converged in a caricature of a couple in a fevered embrace.

Erica felt a jolt of anticipation at what might be back there and the still-coherent part of her brain reigned in the aberrant impulse. All she wanted was to find Elena and get out of here, get away from Max Hart and go back to her normal human life. At least, that *should* have been all she wanted.

She concentrated on keeping her hands steady as she lifted her glass for another sip. "Drink it slowly," Max said.

"What ... what's in it?"

"Just scotch and soda."

There had to be something other than alcohol. Only a drug could explain the way she felt. Her eyes drifted back to the threesome, just barely visible in the dimness. The woman on the floor began unbuttoning her blouse and while Erica stared, she rose and switched places with the other. When the man bit into her flesh, Erica looked away.

"Why do they do that in public?" she asked under her breath. She bit her lip as the waitress sauntered by with a tray of drinks and prayed no one but Max heard her question. His response was to inch his fingers a little higher up her thigh.

"Careful. Keep your voice down." He dipped his finger in the cool amber liquid in her glass and brought it to Erica's lips. "Lick."

She hesitated only a second. Some unknown force made her desperate to obey him, and she captured the shimmering drop on the tip of her tongue.

"You'll think this is amusing, but it's a privacy issue. Many vampires lead human lives. They maintain homes in town, hold down jobs. A very small percentage even have families...."

"How--" Erica's question died on her lips when Max dug his fingertips into her leg.

"Shhh. I'll answer all your questions. As I was saying, they have friends and family who may not know they're vampires. It's a difficult existence. They come here to feed without fear of being seen by someone who doesn't know what they really are. They can be free here. Not everyone comes to the bars. Some find feeders other ways and are able to feed privately. I'd say most of us envy them."

Erica lifted her glass but her mind was on the position of Max's hand. She wondered if he felt the moisture on her inner thigh. She wanted to move and relieve the sudden pressure between her legs, but that would only draw his fingers higher.

"And yes, some vampires have families. No, we can't procreate. But some were turned *after* they had spouses and children. There aren't many. It's a terrible burden, to know you won't die--a natural death anyway--and your children will grow old while you remain young."

Erica nodded. The pang of sympathy she felt concerned her. Why would the plight of a vampire affect her? How could she have spent more than a minute thinking of something other than Elena?

"You need to relax," Max said, dipping his head close to her neck again. "Your muscles are like bowstrings. Take a breath."

She tried to comply but a nervous giggle threatened. "What's in the drink?"

"Nothing really."

"Come on."

"What would you like me to tell you? That I drugged you so that you'll be compliant later? So you'll lie still while I undress you and explore your body until I find the perfect spot to sink my teeth into?"

Erica looked up at the swirls of neon pink on the ceiling. Her nerve endings were on fire. She should have gotten up and walked out--run out. But all she could think of was how much she wanted him to do just as he described.

Oh God. This can't be happening. I'm not hot for a vampire. I'm not.

"Finish your drink. It's time to take a walk."

This time Erica had no luck keeping her hands from trembling. The drink sloshed a little and a drop landed on the table. Max glanced up sharply as the remaining ice cubes clinked together like old bones. “Take it easy.”

He touched his finger to the glistening drop on the table then touched the spot just above her exposed collarbone. The cold jolted her, shot an arrow of fire to her core. Involuntarily she arched her back when he brought his head down and licked the spot where he’d just dabbed her skin. The small sound she made in the back of her throat surprised them both.

“Right there. That’s a good spot. I can drink from there and you can hide it under your clothes during the day, but you’ll know it’s there. Every time you see the mark, you’ll remember I was there.”

“What are you trying to--”

“Let’s go, now.” Again he cut her off. He withdrew his hand from her leg slowly, trailing each finger from her aching flesh one at a time leaving her breathless.

He left a folded bill on the table and pulled her to her feet. “Can you walk?”

“Of course,” she said with confidence she didn’t feel. In the time they’d been sitting, she’d forgotten how to walk, how to talk, how to do anything other than exactly what he told her to do. Her body rebelled with a dizzy rush and she swayed.

He caught her around the waist and righted her, tucking her against his side in a possessive embrace. “You’re doing fine. But you’ll need to learn some discipline. I’m looking forward to teaching you all you need to know.”

Chapter Five

Club Dead’s grotto was no place for Erica. Not in the state she was in at the moment, anyway. Max felt her shaking as he walked her slowly through the narrow corridor that led to the club’s infamous back room. If he could have left her out front, he would have, but the way she smelled right now, no vamp in the place would be able to resist her.

The act he’d put on for the benefit of *Club Dead’s* staff and patrons had been a good one. From the delicious scent of arousal on her skin, Max could tell it certainly worked on Erica. That surprised him. At some point she'd transformed from a frightened, naturally defiant ice princess, into the kind of submissive feeder for which the average vampire would pay double the going rate. The way she'd taken his instructions, and the way she'd licked her lips when she watched the couples at the other tables made him hungry and hard.

It wouldn't be easy to shake it off and keep his needs in check until he got her home--and left her there. He'd not only need to feed tonight, he'd need to sate his sexual desires, too. If he hadn't been working, he'd have insisted they forget the grotto and go back to his apartment. Max was fortunate in that most of his neighbors thought he was human and it didn't matter to him if they saw him bring women home. They would assume just what he wanted them too, that he was a bachelor with a lot of dates. The fact that he rarely brought the same woman home twice, was none of their concern.

As he guided Erica down the hallway and into the grotto where a low, insistent beat and the sound of gurgling fountains competed with moans and gasps of pleasure, he reviewed a list of feeders he could call on to provide more than just a fix for his hunger. He refused to acknowledge the fact that none of them would satisfy him completely. He didn't just want blood and sex. He wanted Erica, and that was bad news.

"What are they--" He cut off her query by squeezing her shoulder. When would she learn not to talk so much?

"They're all feeding. There are lots of ways to feed. We'll try them all, eventually." The darker voice he adopted in the clubs reminded him of the early days when he roamed the streets of London doing as he pleased. Such a long time ago, after he'd gotten over the shock of being turned. He didn't miss those times. The loneliness had nearly destroyed him.

Things were better here in the States where vampire infrastructure had taken root so quickly over the last half century. Of course, in Europe, his kind commanded more respect from humans, but garnered more fear as well. There, he was still considered a monster. Here, he was ... something else--a member of a shadow society. A curiosity. Most people who knew vampires existed preferred to pretend they didn't. Whether that was better or worse than being feared, he hadn't decided.

The back room of *Club Dead* had been set up to resemble a city park, with artificial trees and bushes, benches and rocks, dimly lit lamp posts and bubbling fountains, some of which oozed cool carbon dioxide mist across the floor. As they moved through the setting, he gently turned Erica so that she could see each scene as it took place.

He hoped she didn't identify her sister in one of the alcoves. If Elena Talbot was here, lying naked in the arms of a vampire lover, Max wasn't sure how he'd get her out without getting both he and Erica ripped to shreds. They'd have to stake out the door, no pun intended, and wait until Elena left.

Times like this, Max was grateful his heart didn't beat anymore. The adrenaline pumping through his system would have choked him. As it was, he smelled the sharp scents of excitement, fear and desire all around him, but most strongly from Erica. It rolled off her in waves that teased his heightened senses unmercifully. Why hadn't he listened to his inner voice when it shouted at him that this was a bad idea? Was it because he'd been attracted to Erica immediately? Was it because he didn't want to send her back to her safe human world where she belonged if there was the slightest chance he might entice her to spend some time in his?

When she stopped mid-step he tensed. "What is it?" he whispered next to her ear.

She didn't respond. In the alcove before them, a female vampire stood naked and chained to the faux lamppost, her thin arms stretched high above her head. A human male knelt at her feet working to fasten leather cuffs at her ankles. She writhed under the ministrations of a second human male who flogged her thighs with a leather strap.

Max tried to pull Erica along but she stood frozen, her lips parted and her pulse racing.

When the vampiress noticed her audience she bared her fangs and smiled. With a tilt of her head she extended an invitation to join in.

Erica shuddered against Max and he tightened his grip on her waist. He shook his head slowly and showed his fangs, which seemed to satisfy the female. She shrugged her disappointment and turned her attention back to her own pleasure.

Max and Erica moved on to the next alcove where two male vampires fed from a human female. She lay spread-eagled on a flat rock, her eyes wide and her mouth slack. One vampire drank from her neck as he caressed her breasts through the thin fabric of her silk blouse. The other drank from her inner thigh, one hand hidden in the folds of her short, black skirt. The woman moaned and bucked against his hand.

"Do you see Elena?" Max rasped as he pulled Erica forward toward the exit. If he didn't get her out of here soon, they'd end up in one of the empty alcoves.

"No ..."

"Good. It's time to go."

* * * *

The cool night air shocked Erica's senses after the sultry heat of the club. She drew in a deep cleansing breath and broke from Max's grasp as the back door clicked shut behind them.

She didn't dare look at him right now. After what she'd seen inside, and the way it made her feel, she couldn't face him just yet.

With her arms wrapped around her stomach, she doubled over and stared at the pockmarked surface of the parking lot between her feet. A few more breaths and she'd regain control, settle the raging river in her blood and start to feel like herself again. She hoped.

"I told you." His voice reached her from a few feet away. When she peered up at him she saw only his back. A fresh wave of shame washed over her when she realized he couldn't look at her either.

"I'll be all right. Give me a minute."

"It's time I took you home."

She shook her head. "It's only 4:00 a.m. I want to go to another club."

"Sunrise is at 5:03 today. The bars are closing now."

She shook her head, hiding a faint smile as she pulled her hair down from the tight band that held it off her neck. "Of course you know exactly what time sunrise is."

"Did you bring a car to *After Dark*?" he asked, ignoring her comment. She wondered if it offended him to be reminded of the limitations of his kind.

"I walked from the bus stop on Dwight Avenue. I was concerned someone might trace my plates if they saw my car in the lot."

Now Max turned and met her gaze. For a brief moment she thought she saw admiration in his eyes.

"Who are *you* hiding from?"

"I ... have a conservative life." Perhaps that was an overstatement. 'Life' was too strong a word to describe what Erica had. By day, a stoic, proper insurance claims adjuster, filling out complicated forms in triplicate. By night, more often than not,

Elena's keeper. There was nothing in between. She hadn't had time for friends in months, didn't have the energy to make up lies about Elena anymore. She kept her coworkers and neighbors at a polite distance to isolate herself--though she wasn't quite sure from what.

"By vampire standards, so do I." Max smirked again.

"You seemed pretty comfortable in there." She regretted that her statement sounded like an accusation. He didn't seem to notice, though.

"I swing by now and then to keep an eye on things, but that's not where I feed. It's just part of my job."

"They all have jobs, too, don't they? Like regular ... like humans?"

He nodded. "Most of them. The nights can be long and boring. We've all got to do something. Come on. Let me take you home."

Erica straightened and followed Max toward his car. Though her stomach had calmed, a slight tremor played at the back of her jaw and the giddiness hadn't dissipated completely. When she slid into the cool leather passenger seat, she sank back and let the kinks in her spine work themselves out.

"Why?" she asked as he started the engine and backed out of the parking space. She noticed other cars queuing up to leave the club as well.

"Why what?" He glanced at her, and then deliberately looked away as he guided the car through the white painted posts that stood guard at the lot entrance.

"Why everything? Why are they like that? What was in that drink? Why do humans allow themselves ... ?"

"It's a complex symbiotic relationship." Max smirked as he spoke. The line was obviously well rehearsed. "It took centuries for us to come to terms with our true need for humans. Most of us don't think of you as enemies anymore and fortunately for us, there are more and more of you who don't think of us as enemies, either. But on the other side of the coin, years ago no one became a vampire by choice. Turning someone was the closest thing to procreation we could do. And there was the idea that if vampires outnumbered humans, the world might be a safer place for us."

Erica closed her eyes, torn between wanting to absorb what Max told her and understand it, and wanting to drown it all out and forget everything. She had so many more questions but she was afraid of the answers.

"Where do you live?" His question diverted her thoughts from the dark places where she didn't want to dwell.

"On Rochester Drive in the apartments at 101." She answered him easily and regretted it. She should have given him Elena's address and caught a cab from there, but if she had to walk another block in her heels, she'd have collapsed. Her legs ached and she indulged in the fantasy of asking Max to massage them for her when they reached her apartment.

Replaying flashes of the evening in her mind, Erica found herself alternately aroused and disgusted, enticed and ashamed. Whatever spell she'd been under in the bar, she could not have been completely in control.

"The drink ..."

"There was nothing in it. Honest."

She still didn't believe him. Out of the corner of her eye she regarded his handsome profile. A muscle at the back of his jaw twitched. He's hiding something, she decided.

"Right here," she said a while later when her building came into view. "You can pull up over there."

Max stopped the car and turned to her. The look he gave her made her heart pump a little faster.

"Erica," he said her name slowly, his voice low and smooth. "I don't want to put you through any more of this. Let me look for your sister. I'll keep you informed of what I find."

Disappointment surged through her and she glanced away. Why had she been hoping he was about to kiss her?

He reached into his shirt pocket and pulled out his business card. A phone and fax number were embossed below his name in small black letters.

"Call me with any information you have, and like I said, if you can give me something of your sister's that I can trace ..."

Erica bit her lower lip and nodded. "I will. I'll go to her apartment tomorrow and get something. But, I'm not giving up, Mr. Hart. I'm going to keep looking for her myself. I can't just sit around and wait."

"Erica ..."

"No. The things I saw tonight." *The things I did.* "I can't bear to think of Elena involved in that."

"It still may be her choice."

"No. I don't believe that. I'm not saying there aren't people who ..." *Like it? Find it arousing?* She refused to think about how aroused she was at the moment. "It's just not Elena." Who was she trying to fool? She wrenched the door handle and stomped one foot onto the curb.

When he grabbed her wrist, she pulled back halfheartedly but he didn't relinquish his grasp. His gaze was hard, like it had been inside *Club Dead* when he admonished her, when he commanded her. It killed her that her body responded to the authority in his voice.

"If you insist on looking for her yourself, then I'll take you. You have to understand that there are places you just can't go alone. In order to keep their secrets, there are vampires that *will* hurt you. You need someone to protect you."

"I thought we'd been through this already, Mr. Hart. If you want to do that, that's fine. I'll go along with your investigation--only as long as I'm part of it. If Elena thinks that you're a cop or that I've hired you to find her, she'll make herself harder to reach. She'll withdraw and I won't ever be able to help her."

"How far are you willing to go to find her?"

Erica met his gaze and held it as she disengaged her wrist from his grasp. "All the way."

"I don't think you know what that means."

"Then show me."

Chapter Six

Max's growing hunger surged at Erica's invitation. What he wouldn't give to truly show her everything he sensed she wanted to know about his world. Right now, with her eyes flashing, and the scent of defiance mixing with the aroma of her own arousal, she was everything he wanted--and nothing he dared take.

Her conflicting reactions at the club had told him much more than she ever would have. Truly drawing her into his world, maybe even into his life, would destroy everything about her that made her so irresistible.

He wrenched his gaze away from her and tightened his grip on the steering wheel.

"I'll do what I can." He choked out the words. "Tomorrow I'll put out some feelers and let some of my contacts know that I'm looking for someone. I'll see if I can get reservations at some of the other more private clubs and I'll pick you up." What was he saying? Pick her up? Take her with him? He should have pushed her out of the car and driven away as fast as he could. The playacting tonight was just that. It wasn't real. Her arousal--his own--were just illusions. Her fear and her naiveté made her seem, just for a moment, like she was giving herself over to something she wanted but was afraid to admit to herself. He would have given anything to see that happen, to watch her discover that part of herself she so obviously denied. He was kidding himself. When she'd obeyed his command to lick a drop of her drink from his fingertip, he'd caught the most alluring glimpse of something wanton in her eyes.

Then it was gone.

The challenge she'd just issued to him, was no more than a schoolyard taunt. She thought she could handle it, but she had no idea.

"I'll come a little early," he continued, pushing his doubts to the side. "And we'll go over a few more rules. You did well tonight, but tomorrow we'll be in places where vampires don't take new feeders. You're going to have to act like you're used to this world."

She nodded. Something tightened in his groin at the thought that she might be eager to learn more.

"Wear something ... different." He resisted the urge to touch the fabric of her blouse. "Elegant. Preferably black. No jewelry, no perfume."

"Lower heels?" The hint of amusement in her tone disarmed him. If he hadn't been fighting so hard to hold it together, he'd have taken her right then.

"Yes. And ... I'll have to bite you again. Just a little." Would a little be enough? Could he stop again at the smallest taste? Her flavor lingered on his tongue still and the memory threatened to drive him mad. He'd have to make sure he fed well tonight.

"As long as it won't hurt."

"It won't hurt," he assured her as she climbed out of the car. *At least it won't hurt you.*

* * * *

Erica left her clothes in a pile on the bathroom floor and stepped into the steaming spray of the shower. Hot needles of water dug into her flesh from the massaging showerhead and the glorious sensation made her sigh.

The tension that had built in her muscles since the moment she'd laid eyes on Maxwell Hart finally loosened and drained away. In its place a weakness washed over her that frightened her.

She leaned against the cool tiles and gulped the humid air. What had she gotten herself into?

* * * *

Her scent lingered in the car. Max opened the windows and picked up speed to keep the cool air in his face. He had half an hour until daybreak and he had to feed soon or he'd end up back at Erica's apartment. He couldn't go back to *After Dark*. At this hour, Kyra was his only option.

A quick detour to the highway brought him to her development. At 4:45 he knocked on her door.

He sighed heavily and sidled through the door when she appeared. "I need you." He hated taking advantage of her like this, but her seductive smile told him she didn't mind.

Once inside he leaned against the door and took in her familiar scent. The place looked the same as always: clothes and Chinese takeout containers littered every available surface. Under the layer of flotsam, her new furniture looked worn and outdated. A red jar candle flickered on the mantle where a picture lay face down. Max detected the aroma of cinnamon overlaying the lingering essence of moo goo gai pan.

With a sigh, he followed her to the bedroom of the bungalow, his eyes on the faint remnants of the mark he'd left on her neck a week ago. She shrugged off her robe as she walked, leaving the flowered silk on the floor next to the bed.

"Where've you been tonight, Max? You look so tired." He normally found the sensual purr of her voice soothing but tonight he wished for silence. Kyra wasn't the submissive type and if he ordered her to be quiet while he took what he wanted, she'd kick him out. He used to like her independent streak.

"I'm working a new case." He bit the words out as he folded her slim body into his arms. He used to like the feel of her against him too, but tonight she felt fleshless. She made comforting sounds as he sank his incisors into her skin. The warmth of her eased the cold hollow inside him somewhat, and as he drank, he waited for the bloodlust to take him. He needed that release too, but oddly, aside from lessening his hunger, he felt nothing. The hard-on he'd been battling since the moment he'd tasted Erica began to subside as he took his fill.

When he finished, Kyra threw herself back on the bed, ready for what usually came next. She held her arms out to him and smiled. "Come on ... let Kyra make it all better."

He glanced at the bedroom window where a black shade hung

ready to block out the morning light. He could stay. She'd welcome a captive vampire for the day, but if he left right now he might make it back to his place before the clouds parted and the damning daylight took over.

"I wish I had the time." He hated lying. Kyra had always been good to him. Always available when he wanted her. She'd even given up smoking after he told her how the nicotine left a bad aftertaste that most vamps didn't care for. He fished a fifty out of his wallet and handed it to her.

She pouted. "Oh come on, Max! You're going to leave me like this? What's up with you?"

Apparently nothing, at the moment, he thought wryly. That had never happened before. He often fantasized about other women when he was with Kyra but the fantasies had always helped make it hotter, harder. Tonight, Kyra's willing body seemed like a pale shadow. The taste of her blood wasn't quite as sweet as he remembered. He wanted Erica. Maybe if he pictured her, conjured her scent with his mind he could...

"I'm tired. I've got to go. Next time, babe. I'll make it up to you."

Chapter Seven

Erica woke just before seven after barely an hour of sleep.

Frustrated and jittery, she finally flung herself from the sweat-damp sheets and went into the kitchen to brew some tea. She sipped slowly, staring out her kitchen window at the building's rear parking lot. She thought of Max, his dark gaze and the way her body responded to his voice and his touch. She'd never imagined giving up control to someone else, but the thought of him subtly guiding her movements, or openly commanding her, made her knees weak. How could she find it arousing to submit to him? Why did she crave more?

She finished her tea and shook the unsettling thoughts from her mind. It was a fluke, she decided. Everyone talked about getting caught up in the moment--people did things all the time that they couldn't explain to themselves by the light of day. She'd get over it, and move on. As soon as she found Elena.

* * * *

At 6:00 p.m., Erica stood before her open closet and drew out a black dress with trembling fingers. Half a dozen times she'd picked up the phone to call Max and cancel and each time she'd taken a deep breath and steeled herself to do this.

When the doorbell rang, she smoothed her skirt and her hair, and pressed her hand tightly to her stomach to quell the butterflies. This is business, she told herself. *Just business.*

* * * *

This is just business, Max told himself. He'd had less trouble believing that all day while he worked from his apartment. He'd spoken to his contacts and his colleagues and circulated the details he had about Elena Talbot's disappearance. Since keeping a reluctant human from becoming a feeder was within his job description, he felt less like he was using Erica for his own perverse pleasure. The search for Elena Talbot was an official case now, so he didn't have to feel guilty about spending the evening with Erica, even if he enjoyed it.

When he rang Erica's doorbell, his professional resolve wavered. It fled entirely when she opened the door.

Just as he'd requested, she wore black. The dress was strapless and the neckline dipped just a bit between her breasts.

Her neck was bare and now she wore her hair in a loose chignon with a few thin corkscrew curls dangling here and there, just begging to be touched.

Demure black stockings and sharp-toed pumps with old-fashioned pedestal heels completed the look. Her makeup was understated and she smelled like almond soap and indecision.

It occurred to him that if he made this difficult for her, he might still be able to talk her out of it.

"Can I come in?"

"Do you have to be invited?" She cocked her head, baring the pulse-point in her neck to his view.

He swallowed. "No more than anyone else."

She stepped aside and he walked into the apartment where her scent and her taste surrounded him. The overstuffed bookshelves explained the librarian vibe he'd gotten. A stack of hardcovers sat on a low coffee table next to a sofa that begged for curling up and settling in with the latest bestseller.

He smiled. "This is nice. It's a comfortable place."

"Thank you." She seemed unsure of herself now. Despite the outfit and her determined stance, he wondered if she really had the confidence to pull it off. "Can I get you a drink?"

"I don't want anything right now, thanks. We should get started. I made reservations at 7:30 for *Gregori's*. It's a private club that was owned by the prior vampire king. Since he left the country it's under new management, but they kept the name."

"The vampire king owned a club? Didn't he have ... kingly duties?"

"His last duty here was to choose a new king." Max thought of Gregori Nachevik's chosen successor. Jake Beaumont's appointment as the leader of vampire society in this area, had shaken the vampire world pretty badly. Things were still settling, like the aftermath of an earthquake, loose dirt filling in the cracks.

"So how does vampire royalty work? If there aren't any ... bloodlines?"

"It's sort of like a bloodline. The former king chose a successor that he turned himself and the rules are stricter now than they used to be. We need permission from the king to turn someone." Max wished the rules had been in place a century ago, but things were different then.

"What about a queen?"

"There's no queen ... right now. Female vampires usually aren't interested in politics."

"Tell me about the club-... What's it like there?" She surprised him by taking a seat on the sofa. He watched her legs as she crossed them demurely at the ankle. Whatever had stopped working for him last night with Kyra kicked back into gear as his gaze traveled up her taut calf muscles. He forgot vampire politics and concentrated on answering her next question.

"It's elegant. The food is excellent, so I'm told."

"I don't know if it's Elena's type of place. I would have expected to find her somewhere more like *After Dark*."

"*Gregori's* is for vampires who have regular feeders that they like to show off. If she's gotten into a 'contract' with someone, she might not be able to get out of it that easily and that may be why she called for help. Some vampires pay their regular feeders good money for exclusivity, and they help them maintain a certain lifestyle."

Erica nodded. "I'm sorry I couldn't get you something that belongs to her. There's an eviction notice on her apartment and the landlord wouldn't let me in unless I paid two months back rent. I can't get the money until Monday morning so ..."

Max sighed. With Elena's scent, his job would have been so much easier. "Maybe we'll get lucky and we'll find her tonight. I know I don't need to ask but, you haven't heard any more from her, have you?"

She shook her head and the glimmer of vulnerability in her eyes clutched at him. He turned away from her and covered his own uncertainty by placing his suit jacket on a nearby chair.

When he turned back, he was in charge again, ready to teach her what she needed to know.

* * * *

"Let's go over the rules, and the consequences for breaking them," Max said as he turned. His voice sent an unexpected shiver through Erica's body and her nipples peaked beneath the satiny fabric of her dress. Oh, God, if she felt like this now, what would happen if he touched her?

She held her breath while he unbuttoned his shirt cuffs and pushed his sleeves up. He dropped a pair of gold cuff links on the coffee table and gave her a dark look. When he loosened his tie, she arched involuntarily toward him.

"Rule number one: I'm in control at all times. Inside the club you literally belong to me. You have no purpose other than to do as you are told."

She nodded, afraid to speak, afraid that she would sound too eager to obey his commands.

"Rule two: Don't speak unless I give you permission. If someone asks you a question--they probably won't--but if they do, you look at me before answering. If I don't respond, you say nothing.

"Rule three: You never leave my side. Rule four: If you see your sister, don't react to her. Let me know, quietly, and I'll decide what to do from there. There's a chance that even if she's there, we will not be able to get to her tonight. Do you understand?"

"Yes." Erica's response came out as a breathless whisper. "Are those all the rules?"

"The major ones. Get used to doing everything I tell you. You can start now by standing up."

She complied, her eyes on him. When he moved to stand in front of her, her stomach tightened and the tingle between her thighs intensified.

He brought up one hand and traced the healing bite marks on her neck with the tip of his finger. His feather-light touch made something deep within her begin to pulse.

"This healed too quickly. It wasn't deep enough." He ran his finger over her collarbone and across the mounded flesh above the curving neckline of her dress. "There are lots of places I could leave a mark. What would be best? Maybe the other side of your neck?" He smirked and she swallowed hard. His scent was intoxicating, like a warm summer breeze with a hint of spice. She tilted her head back when he placed both hands on her hips and guided her body toward his.

"How about here?" He lowered his head and kissed the spot just below her left ear and she made a sound that could only have been one of surrender.

* * * *

Max hovered over the sweet spot on Erica's neck, lost in the fatal scent of her. Another taste would be his downfall. He wanted her even though he wasn't hungry. Kyra had sated his desire for blood. What he wanted now, he hadn't taken last night.

He told himself the scent of arousal would make Erica seem more authentic. Feeders, as a rule, enjoyed the sexual nature of the vampire symbiosis as well. It raised their internal pressure and heightened their output. Sexual excitement had the added benefit of releasing hormones into the blood that made it sweeter. With that in mind, it was practically a necessity to get her a little hot before he brought her to the club. The anticipation would show on her face in the flush of her cheeks and the swell of her breasts against her dress. He needed her in the same state she'd been in last night, needed her fighting for control so he could offer it to her.

"Turn around." He loved that she didn't question his command.

He pulled her against him, positioning her hips so she could feel his erection. He held her tight around the waist and lowered his teeth to just above her flickering pulse and bent her forward slightly.

The delicious sensation of her pushing against him brought on the bloodlust. He bit down slowly, just enough to let the blood well into a swollen drop beneath each fang. As he licked those sweet drops, he slid one hand down the front of her dress to cup the spot at the juncture of her thighs.

She pushed back father and a moan escaped her lips. That's when he began to drink.

Chapter Eight

Erica found the hard muscles of Max's thigh and squeezed with shaking fingers while she rubbed against his cock. His lips on her skin were like fire, his body like a wall of steel against her back.

She'd never wanted anyone so badly. It wasn't like her at all to want to surrender and it scared her. Part of her soul that she never knew existed had burst free and was clamoring for control. She wanted him to tell her what to do so she wouldn't have to wonder.

"Please ..." she whispered finally when he drew his lips away. She felt his teeth slide out of her skin and rather than relief that he was finished, she felt suddenly alone and without purpose. "You can take more ..." Had she really said that? Did she really want him to continue?

"No, I can't." His voice was raw.

She turned in his arms and leaned against him. "Isn't there more I need to learn?" Shame colored her cheeks at the request. She had to be losing her mind. Why did she want him to do this, to own her? She'd been an independent woman for all of her adult life. She'd spent more than a decade resisting the limits anyone else tried to impose on her and now all she wanted was this man, this vampire she hardly knew, to claim her and command her.

He grabbed her arms and shook her once, just hard enough to remind her that giving her will over to him was a dangerous idea.

"There's a lot you need to learn. First, you don't tell me what to take. I'll take what I want." He brought one finger up and tilted her chin so she had to meet his gaze. His voice softened. "If I take everything I want from you right now, there will be nothing left, Erica. We can't play like this, not here where there's nothing stopping me from making you mine."

Lost in his blazing eyes, she couldn't respond. Somewhere in her foggy thoughts a voice cried for him to do it. She wanted him, and she hated herself for being so weak.

He let her go and she sagged a little, her breath escaping in a shuddering sigh. "This isn't me," she said finally, wishing it were true. "I'm not usually like this."

"I know. Believe me when I tell you, I don't want to change you. I don't want to turn you into exactly what you're trying to save your sister from."

Erica glanced up sharply. "I may not know you very well, but that sounded like a lie, Mr. Hart."

A smile played at the corner of his mouth as he rolled his sleeves down and retrieved his cuff -links. "You don't have to believe me, Erica. You just have to do as I say. Rule five: Call me Max."

* * * *

'Elegant' was too mild a word to describe *Gregori's*. Like the finest human restaurants, it seemed that no expense had been spared to make the place sparkle. Chandeliers hung in the center of every room and the ornate windows held thick beveled panes of leaded glass that captured the reflections of dozens of candles. Strings of miniature lights decorated the potted trees that lined the main entry hall and each pinpoint of light gleamed off the polished parquet floor.

When Max and Erica arrived, an attendant took their coats while the concierge checked their reservations and showed them to a table that overlooked the huge central dance floor.

Erica relaxed when Max pulled out her chair for her. She sat down and he ordered her a wine spritzer. This place catered to her more delicate sensibilities, not the part of her that had been screaming for release since Max left her wanting and wondering in her apartment.

She began to fantasize that after a sumptuous meal, she might look down and see Elena swirling across the dance floor with her escort. She'd always dreamed that one day she'd see her twin happy and healthy and free of her addictions. The beauty and charm of *Gregori's* made her think it might be possible that Elena could find happiness in this world.

With a start, she admonished herself for such a foolish thought. If Elena was happy she wouldn't have called for help. Her words were burned into Erica's memory; *I need you to help me ...*

Max ordered Erica's dinner and the authority in his voice made her feel momentarily safe. He leaned forward to speak to her after the tuxedoed waiter left them. "I put out some feelers this morning. I found out there's some fresh blood in the upper echelons. Some of the people who work directly for the new king have been taking on extra feeders. That could be an important lead."

"Tell me more about the old king," Erica said under her breath. "Why did he leave?"

"He went back to Europe. It's a better place for an old vampire. Things are too liberal here for the ones that were turned before the 1900s."

"That's where you're from, isn't it?"

"London. But I haven't been there in years." He didn't dare tell her how many.

"What's the new king like?"

"He's American ... young, too. There was a bit of an upset when he took over. He does things differently. I don't understand the upsurge in new feeders. It could be they're stocking up before new rules are put in place."

"What kind of rules?"

The waiter floated into view then and Max's voice dropped. "Enough talk for now. When you're finished eating, we'll take a walk around and see if we come across anything interesting."

Erica nodded as the waiter brought her appetizer. Max was right about the food. It looked and smelled wonderful. If only her stomach would settle enough to let her enjoy it. She wasn't over the adrenaline rush Max had caused earlier. Her body still thrummed with desire for him. Food, even fabulous food, wasn't going to fulfill all her needs tonight.

While she ate, Max sipped a glass of dark wine. The liquid looked like blood but smelled sweet, like candy. She found herself wanting to ask for a taste, but afraid he'd admonish her for stepping out of line. It bothered her more that she liked the feeling. She was actually worried about pleasing him and doing the right thing. What was wrong with her? Why did she crave his approval--and worse, his demanding touch? This wasn't normal.

Max talked idly about his day while Erica studied her food. Filet mignon with a medley of baby vegetables, prepared to perfection. She wished she didn't enjoy it, wished she could push the plate away and demand they get on with their mission to find Elena. What would happen, she wondered, as she savored a bite and gazed into Max's eyes, if she did just that? Would he punish her? Would he take her home and teach her an unforgettable lesson in obedience?

She reached for her own drink and gulped. She would have put the icy glass against the heated skin of her neck, but that would be crass.

"Is there a ladies' room?" she asked finally. A few moments out of the spotlight of his heated gaze might give her a chance to compose herself.

"I'll escort you."

"To the ladies' room?"

"You're not to go anywhere alone. I'll wait outside, of course." He rose and she waited for him to pull her chair out before she stood. With his hand on her waist, they walked through the gilded mid-level of *Gregori's* to a fountained portico where a sign in gold leaf pointed to the restrooms.

"I'll be right here," Max said. "Inside, you're to talk to no one."

She nodded and let herself through the heavy oak door. Inside the quiet, perfumed staging area she regarded her reflection in the full-length mirror. In the tight black sheath, she looked perfectly calm, utterly in control. She saw no outward sign of the waves of nervous anticipation that rolled through her every time she looked at Max.

In the sink area she re-applied her lipstick and ran cold water over her wrists. After a few deep breaths she decided it was time to get back to work. As she slung her purse strap over her bare shoulder, one of the toilet stalls opened and a woman sauntered out.

She was beautiful in an exotic way, with almond shaped eyes of jade green and long black hair. She smiled at Erica showing her flat human teeth as she took her place in front of the wide mirror.

"You're new," the woman said as she leaned forward to brush her long lashes with an unnecessary touch of mascara.

Erica nodded.

"He told you not to talk to anyone, right?"

She nodded again and smiled demurely. What if she spoke to this woman? Maybe ask if she'd seen Elena? What would Max do to her?

"Don't worry. This room is soundproof. He won't know you've said anything. I'm Vera Nighe. I belong to Benton Carlisle."

"I'm ... Ricki. I ... belong to Max Hart." The emotional tumult that followed her reply left Erica dizzy. She'd promised Max she would speak to no one. Should she have told this woman she was here with him? Did it matter? Why did it give her pleasure to say she belonged to the handsome man waiting for her outside the door?

"It's nice to meet you, Ricki. I hope you enjoy yourself here."

"Thank you."

Vera smiled, finished touching up her perfect makeup and left. Erica waited a few more minutes while two halves of her psyche battled each other in her head. The logical side of her brain wanted out of this entire situation right now. She still had time to escape with her dignity intact and salvage her precarious self-image. The other, darker side of her mind was shamelessly begging for release. She pictured herself strolling out of the bathroom and baiting Max with a defiant look that would challenge him to put her in her place. She replayed the moment in her apartment, when, clutched in his arms as he siphoned her blood, she'd silently wished for him to tear her dress off and make love to her.

That part of her could not be allowed to take over. If she gave in to those abnormal desires, she'd be lost. She'd never find Elena if she became enthralled by a vampire.

The answer was simple. She had to get away now. Max would take her home if she asked him to--he'd probably be relieved by the request.

She'd almost reached the bathroom door when she heard the sound. The tinny, distant melody of voices trickled through the ductwork. That, by itself, wasn't unusual. Restrooms in public buildings often had excellent acoustics. She remembered back in grammar school when she and Elena were taught in separate classrooms, sneaking into the first floor girls' bathroom while her twin hid in the one on the second floor. They would whisper into the heating vents and share gossip and secrets.

Drawn by the memory, and the voyeuristic spirit that had awakened in her unexpectedly the night before, Erica moved toward the air conditioning duct. Covered with an ornate gold grillwork, it looked more like a wall sculpture, designed to blend effortlessly into the décor.

She listened just for a moment and what she heard made her blood run cold.

"I need you to help me. Ricki, I need you to help me."

Chapter Nine

Max crossed his arms over his chest and leaned against a marble pillar next to the indoor fountain. It had probably been sixty years since he'd waited on a woman this long. In his London years, if a female had kept him waiting longer than ten minutes, she'd have found her own way home.

He tapped his foot. Was Erica playing with him? He'd seen that galvanizing flash of mischief in her eyes and it made him want her that much more. As frightened as she was, as focused on finding her sister, there was a part of her that enjoyed the game. He'd seen it once too often to believe it was a fluke. She wanted to test him, to tease him and see how far she could go. She wanted him to lose control with her and if only she knew how close he was to doing just that--and how he would ravage her if his desire took flight unchecked--she'd probably climb out the bathroom window and catch a cab home.

Maybe that's what she did.

When a raven-haired beauty strolled out of the bathroom, a new worry assailed him. Had the two women spoken? Max vaguely recognized the woman--her name was Veronica--or Vera, something with a V. She belonged to one of Gregori Nachevik's upper echelon, one that had stayed behind to keep tabs on Jake Beaumont when the new vampire king assumed power. She was about as powerful as a human got in the vampire world. Her influence probably surpassed even that of the king's concubine, whom Max had heard was also human.

It made a strange sort of sense. A powerful male vampire would be wise to avoid a liaison with a vampiress. She'd be more apt to stake him while he slept and assume his power. A human 'mate' or even a privileged feeder was a much wiser choice to keep a man's secrets and to warm his bed--considering that humans actually had warmth.

Where was Erica?

When she came out, he'd give her exactly what she wanted. He'd upbraid her, gently but with a promise of more to come, and he'd detail how he was going to punish her for insubordination. He could tell her things that would bring that sexy blush back to her cheeks and make her tremble under his touch. He licked his lips at the thought.

Did she know how much power she had over him? He'd known her less than 24 hours and yet she was burned into his psyche deeper than any of the women who had shared his bed and fed his hunger for decades back in London.

He was one breath short of barreling into the ladies' room when she appeared. Her hazel eyes were wide and her honey-toned skin had gone deathly white.

He crossed over to her and grabbed her elbow more to hold her up than to admonish her. "Are you all right? What happened in there?"

"Elena--I heard her voice through the vents. She's trapped here."

"What? You heard her?"

"She begged me to help her. Max, she's here. We have to find her."

Max held her frightened gaze and a warning tingle went off at the back of his neck. Whatever she heard, she believed it was her sister, but the whole thing seemed so outrageous. Was it possible that Elena Talbot had been taken prisoner by a vampire mate and was actually being held against her will at *Gregori's*? It made no sense.

He tugged Erica behind the pillar where the echoing gurgle of the fountain would drown out their conversation.

"Erica, do you realize what you're saying? If Elena is here, there's no way we can get her out. I'm going to have to get back-up."

"What kind of back-up?"

"I'll call my partner and some of my colleagues. We may have to get permission from the king to search the place."

"Just do it, Max. I have to save her. I *know* she's here. I know it was her voice."

He didn't dare tell her that he found it too incredible to believe. He looked up at the ornately painted ceiling above them. There were private dining rooms upstairs, and probably a few special rooms below the main floor as well for guests with unusual tastes. A vampire might hold a feeder in one of those rooms--a feeder who had made agreements she wasn't prepared to keep.

"The only thing we can do right now is leave," he said, softening his grip on her arm.

"No! We have to--"

He clamped his hand over her mouth and pushed her farther into the corner behind the fountain. "Shh!" He hissed in her ear. "We cannot cause any kind of scene."

She struggled against him and he felt her teeth on his palm. If she broke his skin and drew blood, she'd feel it instantly. The deadly desire to drink was overwhelming when it hit. If she drew even the smallest amount of his blood into her mouth she'd be compelled to take more until the change began.

He pulled his hand away and turned her in his arms, then pushed her against the wall. "Don't do that." His breath in her ear was ragged. "Don't ever bite a vampire, do you understand?"

She nodded but didn't go still. She pushed back against him and a small sound escaped her lips. In response he held her tighter. "Erica, Erica ..." He wanted to hold her and comfort her, but at the same time, if they'd been in private, he wouldn't have been able to control himself. He had to get her out of here and get away from her before he did something *she'd* regret.

"We're leaving. Don't make another sound."

Slowly he turned her to face him. The defiant fire flickered in her eyes only for a moment, then dull fear replaced it. Max straightened and swallowed hard. There was someone behind him. A vampire.

* * * *

Erica held her breath as a shadow fell across the alcove. She saw a man, broad shouldered and barrel-chested, in a dark three-piece suit. She didn't dare raise her eyes to his.

She sank back against the wall and tried to quell her shivering as Max turned around.

"Everything all right, Maxwell?"

"Mr. Carlisle. Everything is fine." He held his hand out and Erica slipped her fingers into his. He brought her into the light and into the scrutiny of the vampire who owned Vera Nighe.

"Who is this sweet morsel? Maxwell, you've been holding out on your friends at the club, haven't you?"

"Her name is Ricki. She's very new."

"She looks it. No offense, but the lady is shivering. What have you done to her, Max?" Carlisle laughed and held his hand out to Erica. She glanced at Max who gave her leave to step forward and allow the other man to kiss her hand.

As Carlisle brushed his cold lips over her skin, he breathed in her scent and held it as one savors the smoke from a fine cigar. Erica cringed and fought off a shudder of disgust. Under other circumstances she might have found Benton Carlisle handsome and perhaps charming, but the evil light in his eyes left her terribly cold.

Vera hovered behind him. She wore a sympathetic smile and briefly Erica wondered if she might find an ally in this mysterious woman. If only she could find a way for them to be alone together again.

"I was about to take Ricki home. She's had quite enough for one night."

"Surely you have time to join us in the Round Room for dessert."

Max glanced at Erica and his look told her it was an invitation he didn't dare refuse. In a strange way, she was glad. The longer they stayed inside *Gregori's* the better her chance of locating Elena.

"We'll see you there."

Carlisle nodded and gestured for Vera to follow him toward the curving staircase that led past the fountain to the club's upper floor. With a quick glance over her shoulder, his lovely companion sashayed after him.

Max hesitated just a moment and his hands tightened on Erica's waist. "This isn't good. Benton Carlisle shouldn't have any interest in me."

"What's going to happen now?"

Max sucked in a breath and leveled a stone-cold gaze at Erica that made her heart rise into her throat. "You've been disobedient tonight. And I'm going to have to punish you for that. I'd say if you want to get out of here in one piece, you're going to have to *keep it up.*"

* * * *

The Round Room was a universe apart from the rarified atmosphere of *Gregori's* first floor dining rooms. Here, the walls were painted black, and like *After Dark*, a pulsating beat rattled Erica's bones when she stepped over the threshold.

Inside, a complex lighting system created dizzying effects on the walls and the floor. Swirling spirals of color, stark white strobe lights and prismatic arcs illuminated the patrons who were oddly transformed from the elegant personas they wore downstairs.

Everywhere Erica looked, there were vampires feeding. Rather than tables and chairs, the room held couches, divans and banks of oversized pillows. Much like *Club Dead's* grotto, the scenes taking place ran the gamut from a couple locked in a lover's embrace to orgies involving several humans and vampires trussed in tight leather, chains and spiked collars.

She pressed herself back against Max, and she felt his hesitation. In here, he might not be able to protect her from the others if they wanted her. That thought terrified her. Giving herself over to Max was one thing, but to a group of ravenous vampires--she could never do that.

"We won't be here long, I promise," he said close to her ear. He nudged her forward a step just as Vera Nighe appeared. The lovely woman Erica had met in the ladies' room looked different in the fractured light. Her skin looked much paler and her eyes seemed sunken. The delicate buttons on the front of her cream-colored dress were open, exposing the deep valley between her breasts.

She smiled at them and offered her hand to Erica.

"Come with me, sweet one ... I'll get you a drink."

Erica looked back at Max. His expression was stony. "No. She stays with me."

Vera pouted and surged closer, shimmying forward to bump her hip against Max's. "Now's not the time to be selfish."

"Maybe later." Max pulled Erica away from Vera and led her toward an unoccupied couch. He drew her down to sit next to him then gently eased her body across his. Cradled in his arms she felt another conflicting surge of emotions. Had they been alone, she would have felt cherished, and desirable, but here, on display in front of so many others, she felt exposed. She stiffened when Max lowered his head to her neck.

"Please don't," she said when she felt the tips of his fangs against her skin. "Not here."

"I have to--"

Erica struggled against him and he held her tighter. The feel of his hands commanding her to mold against him would have been irresistible if she wasn't suddenly so afraid. "No ..."

"Maxwell. I'm glad you decided to join us."

Erica looked up as Benton Carlisle's shadow fell over them once again. Also transformed, he'd become a frightening caricature of his former self. His elegant suit jacket and crisp white shirt were gone, replaced by a leather vest and pants. In one hand he held a coiled whip and in the other a leash that connected him to a woman who wore nothing at all.

"Mr. Carlisle." Max's voice was low and steely. Erica tensed as he pushed her gently off his lap.

"Max ... why don't you come with me for a moment? There's some business I'd like to discuss with you."

"Business? Now?"

"It's rather important. It involves security here at the club, and I know your department often looks into private affairs if there's a special request."

Erica stared up Carlisle, entranced. It shocked and amazed her to see this man, who only a short time ago looked like the consummate corporate executive, now dressed in leather and leading a naked woman around on a leash. The absurdity of hearing him discuss business with Max made Erica's stomach turn.

She cast a sympathetic glance at the woman, who responded by bearing bloody fangs in a vicious snarl. The vampiress, apparently bored by the proceedings, tugged on the chain that dipped from her slender throat to Carlisle's fist.

Her reward for impatience was a tap with the handle of Carlisle's whip. She pouted, but with her red-tipped fangs protruding the expression looked dangerous rather than demure.

Erica looked away.

"We'll only be a moment, Maxwell. I promise not to keep you from your lovely lady very long."

Erica's heart twisted when Max rose. He gave her a grave look that would have melted her heart, if he'd held it longer than a second. As she watched, his expression morphed dangerously and his fangs grew.

"You stay right here. Don't move, no matter what."

She nodded. She had no intention of moving an inch. As long as everyone else in the room kept their distance, she'd be fine ... for a few seconds at least.

Max moved off with Carlisle and Erica wrapped her arms around her herself. She folded herself up on the soft couch and forced herself to scan the room for a sign of Elena. With so many people writhing in the darkness, she couldn't focus on any specific features. Her gaze fell inadvertently on the sparkling chains, the spiked collars and the undulating flesh all around her. She shivered as the image of the naked vampiress tethered to Benton Carlisle played through her mind.

"Good! You're alone!" Vera's voice broke through Erica's reverie and she looked over to find the other woman kneeling before her. In Vera's hands rested a wine glass full of what appeared to be the same dark liquid Max had sipped during dinner. "I brought you a drink."

Erica eyed the glass. The sumptuously sweet smell reached her and her mouth watered for a taste, but Max hadn't given her leave to accept a drink.

"I'd better not."

Vera pouted and swirled the liquid enticingly in the glass. "It tastes like candy. It will help you relax. I know this place can be overwhelming the first time." Vera smiled at her and swayed to the insistent beat. "Once you get used to it, you'll love it here. You can be completely free." She held the glass up for Erica to sniff the sensuously sweet aroma again. The bouquet was so strong Erica could almost taste it. She wanted to so badly.

Erica looked up from the depths of the wine and gestured toward another vampiress who wore a dress that looked like chain mail. The female's narrow hips were girded with a heavy leather belt to which her arms were tethered with cuffs. Two men who appeared human led her across the room to a collection of pillows. When they pushed her to her knees, Erica looked away.

"She doesn't look very free to me."

Vera laughed. "She's a vampire, darling. She's in complete control of that scenario. In time you'll learn. *You* have all the power." The woman made a sound like a purr and settled herself on the floor at Erica's feet. "Max needs you much more than you need him."

Erica took another look around the room. In the distance she thought she saw Max and Carlisle but she wasn't certain. She leaned closer to Vera and tried to whisper over the pounding music. "Have there been a lot of new feeders around lately?"

Vera nodded. "Take a sip and I'll tell you more." She tapped the rim of the glass and held it up to Erica. As Vera looked up, the heavy curtain of her dark hair fell back to expose fresh bite marks just under her left ear. "It'll give you strength."

"Strength for what?"

Vera grinned. "Whatever Max has planned for you." Mischief sparkled in her eyes. "It's fortified with herbs like those energy drinks they serve at the human bars now."

Erica looked at the wine again. She wondered why Max hadn't offered her any during dinner. "Maybe when Max comes back."

Vera sighed and took a deep sip of the wine herself. With a shrug, she set the glass down on the floor and rose. She held out her hands to Erica. "Do you want to dance with me?"

"Dance? With you?" Was beautiful Vera coming on to her?

"Just for fun, come on!" Vera pulled Erica to her feet and tugged her to an open section of the floor where several couples swayed to the music. A moment later, as a comfortable haze descended over Erica's vision, she found herself swirling around in time to the beat. Vera's hands on her hips, guided her in an undulating rhythm that made her forget Max and Elena ... and everything else.

Chapter Ten

Max kept his eyes on Erica from across the room while Benton Carlisle asked him mundane questions about security. He didn't need to wonder if this forced separation from Erica was planned.

When he saw Vera try to give her a glass of wine, he bared his fangs. “I’ll report your concerns to my superiors, Mr. Carlisle,” he said as evenly as possible. “It’s nothing we can’t handle.”

“Of course, of course,” Carlisle grinned back and tugged on the chain of his captive vampiress. She growled. “Would you like to join in some of our private activities tonight? Your new feeder looks especially interesting.”

“She’s not ready.”

“She looks ready to me.” Carlisle inclined his head to the dance floor where Vera was dancing in sensuous circles around Erica. When the other woman leaned over and kissed Erica on the lips, Max growled, too. “I’ve got to go. I’ll get back to you in a few days.”

Carlisle nodded absently. “I’m sure you will, Maxwell, I’m sure you will.” He laughed and pulled his captive female to him as Max walked away.

Walking across the dance floor took forever, and by the time Max reached Erica, she swayed in a dreamy haze while Vera ground their bodies together. She smelled of vampire wine.

She giggled when he grabbed her wrist and dragged her toward him. “You were supposed to stay on the couch.”

“I wanted to dance!” She delivered her protest through a feathery laugh. Wrapping her arms around his neck, she pushed her hips against him. Vera tried to sidle between their bodies but Max shoved her aside.

“She’s finished,” Max told Carlisle’s woman. “Hands off.”

“So selfish. Couldn’t we share?” Vera tried again to come between them and Max pushed her aside once again. This time he pulled Erica away, toward the Round Room’s grand entrance. She stumbled after him with a mild protest.

“Do we have to go? I was actually having fun.”

“Yes, we do. There’s nothing more we can accomplish here tonight.”

Erica giggled again. “Okay.”

When they reached the door he had to physically push her through it. Out in the corridor, he had to hold her up. This wasn’t normal. He hadn’t seen her drink the wine. She’d had nothing except her meal and the drink he’d ordered for her with dinner.

Max draped Erica’s arm over his shoulder and hoisted her onto his hip. “Come on. Time to go home.”

“I don’t want to.”

“I’m sure you don’t. But you need to sleep this off.”

She looked up at him and with adoration in her eyes. It stung him. If she'd looked at him that way when she was sober, he'd probably have fallen in love with her on the spot. "Are you going to punish me, Max? I was so bad."

"We'll talk about that later. Right now, let's concentrate on keeping you on your feet."

* * * *

The trip back to Erica's apartment was a struggle. Though she dozed during the car ride, she woke as giggly and unsteady as before and he had to carry her to the front door. He searched her purse for the keys while she leaned on the doorjamb and fixed a seductive gaze on him. When he opened the door and pushed her inside, she lurched toward the couch and fell across the fluffy cushions, kicking her shoes off as she did.

"Oh, it feels good to get those off!" She laughed again as Max closed the door and shrugged off his jacket. He crossed the room and looked down at her, sprawled on the sofa, the hem of her dress cresting on her thighs just above the band of her stockings. The sliver of pale skin exposed above her garter beckoned him. Had he been a lesser man--a lesser vampire--he'd have been unable to resist a taste.

"What am I supposed to do with you?" he asked as she rolled on her side to make room for him on the couch. "I can't leave you like this and by the time you sober up it'll be daylight."

"Sober up? I'm not drunk, Max. I only had that spritzer with dinner and ... hmmm ... What else *did* I have?"

"It's not how much you drank, it's what you drank. Someone drugged you tonight."

Erica's response was a sensuous sigh that rasped against Max's heightened senses. She rolled onto her stomach and gave him a seductive grin over her bare shoulder.

"I don't believe you."

He sighed. This wasn't how he'd pictured the evening ending.

"Come on." He grabbed her wrist and dragged her to her feet. She fell against his chest and slithered one hand inside the front of his shirt.

"Take this off, Max. Let me touch you."

"Maybe later. Right now you need to go to bed." He held her up and guided her gently toward the bedroom, but halfway there she dug her toes into the carpet and stopped.

"Let's do it right here, Max, on the floor. Make love to me right here."

With her warm and pliant in his arms, how could he resist? He wanted her, in fact he'd wanted nothing else since the moment he saw her at *After Dark*. Why couldn't he just give in and do as she asked?

"You don't know what you're asking, love. If you did, you wouldn't have to say it twice."

"I need you, Max. I need to feel something. Pleasure, pain, I don't care. Just make me feel something."

Max growled. The loneliness in her voice tore through him, touching memories he'd worked hard to suppress. How could he tell her he knew how she felt? He'd spent so many years not sure if he was living because nothing touched him since the night he'd been turned, lured by what he thought was a hot-blooded woman, into a cold-water flat on the East End. No warm-blooded being came near him for decades after that unless he willed them to so he could feed from them. All he'd wanted for so long was to be touched, to be wanted like Erica wanted him now.

He allowed himself to caress her neck and shoulders, then slid one hand to the zipper of her dress. He tugged it down inch by inch to the small of her back exposing an expanse of perfect skin. When he ran his fingertips down the elegant ridge of her spine, her skin pebbled and she shivered deliciously.

He parted the V of black satin and let the dress fall over her hips and into a puddle on the floor. The sound she made as she leaned against him caused his aching cock to pulse with need. This is wrong, he told himself. If he indulged his fantasy too much longer, he'd lose control completely.

Before she made another sound, he scooped her up in his arms and carried her down the hall to the bedroom. The darkness made no difference to his enhanced eyesight. He saw as clearly as if the lights were on. The bed was larger than he'd have imagined for a woman who lived alone. Covered with a plumb-colored spread just a shade darker than the carpet, and heaped with satiny throw pillows, it invited much more than comfortable sleeping.

He drew aside the covers and placed her on the bed where she stretched sensuously. Her breasts jutted as she arched--begging him to touch the tight pink nipples and ivory mounds. She mumbled incoherently to him and reached out to draw him down on her, but he resisted.

He took her wrists in one hand and held them over her head. She writhed with pleasure at his demand, reveling in the power he held over her. Her reaction was almost too much for him. He could have her like this, dominate her and feel no guilt because she obviously enjoyed it.

If not for the drug he'd have mounted her and shown her everything she wanted to learn.

Instead he took a deep breath and commanded her to remain still. She obeyed, and her eyes fluttered closed. He touched her face but she remained that way, finally asleep.

He sighed and reached down to unfasten the garters that held her stockings in place. One at a time he rolled the black silk down her legs, exposing the honeyed skin beneath. Behind her left knee he found a beauty mark that begged him to taste it. He would have, but the aroma of her skin, her arousal even in sleep, drove him mad. He had to finish his task and leave her before he gave in to his desires.

Now, wearing only a black thong, she sighed and stretched in her sleep. He removed the skimpy scrap of cloth, lowering it over her thighs slowly and reveling in her final secrets revealed.

He'd won. He'd undressed her, touched her and drank in her perfection with his eyes. Satisfied with his own resolve, he dragged the blankets over her, tucked her in and walked away.

Tomorrow, when she regained control of her senses, he'd tell her all about it in excruciating detail and thus begin her punishment.

* * * *

Erica floated in a sea of sensations. Ribbons of colored sound carried her high up to a cool mountain peak and down to a warm ocean of golden sand. She felt wonderful, but uncertain as well. She remembered tasting the color red, candy sweet and tempting on Vera's sumptuous lips. She'd never been kissed by a woman before, never would have imagined that it could excite her.

Erica abandoned the troubling thought and concentrated on her dreamscape. The horizon stretched forever toward a blue sky filled with buttery clouds.

Elena looked down on her from those clouds and for an instant Erica tasted death. She cried out and reached for her sister. As she did, Elena's face shattered and fell to earth, making a sound like hail on glass.

She woke to that sound.

Oh God. What had she done?

She turned to look at the window and the movement caused her head to throb. Sunlight peeked in around the drawn shade but the thrumming sound continued. So where was it in coming from?

The shower. She clutched the blankets to her body and shivered when she realized she was naked beneath them. Her dress lay neatly over the bedroom chair, her shoes and stockings sat on the floor beneath it along with her garter and black thong underwear. Her careful chignon hung around her shoulders and her mouth and eyes felt gritty.

Whoever was in the shower was whistling.

She cringed.

Then it came back to her in a flood of disturbing memories. The odd hangover cleared and her stomach, which moments before had been threatening to rebel, now rumbled for food.

She remembered only vague details from the night before and though her recollection was fuzzy, it didn't include undressing herself. Max Hart had some explaining to do.

She threw off the blankets and hurried across the room to retrieve her bathrobe from its place behind the door. She looked in the mirror and smoothed her hair, then checked quickly for new bite marks before she closed her robe. Other than the spot on her neck that he'd drank from the night before, her skin remained flawless. Lucky for him, she thought.

"Max!" Standing before the bathroom door, she yelled once as loudly as possible, which only made the throbbing pain in her head resume with a vengeance. When Max didn't answer, she pounded on the door. "Get out here, now!"

She waited a beat and stepped back when the bathroom door flew open. He wore only a towel, draped around his neck.

Their eyes locked for a moment, and Erica managed to hold her comments in check while he slid the towel off his shoulders and wrapped it around his waist.

"I see you're up." He greeted her with a raised eyebrow.

"You too." She smirked and for a moment, the self-conscious look on his face made her forget her anger. Only for a moment. "What the hell did you do to me last night?"

His eyes darkened and he tilted his head. "Not half as much as I wanted to."

Erica swallowed. She felt flushed and she was suddenly aware of the fact that she wore nothing beneath her thin cotton robe.

"What was in my drink last night?" she demanded stepping back as he left the bathroom. He headed for the living room and she followed him, clutching her robe around her.

"Some vampires use a combination of herbs to relax their feeders. Normally it isn't that potent but you must have gotten an extra large dose. You're lucky I got back to you when I did."

"You shouldn't have left me alone."

"I didn't have a choice. Benton Carlisle is a powerful vampire. I had to go with him. And while I was gone you were supposed to be following the other rules."

"Well, I tried."

"Not very hard by the looks of it."

Erica crossed her arms over her breasts and watched him while he rooted around her living room gathering his clothes. A blanket from her linen closet lay over the couch attesting to where he'd spent the night.

"You wandered off and left me alone at a vampire orgy, where I got drugged and groped by another woman and--"

"And kissed. Don't forget kissed." He leveled a sardonic gaze at her.

Erica gaped. That memory came back, too. It hadn't been a dream. Vera had been all over her. "And *I'm* to blame?"

"You were supposed to be obedient."

"You told me to be *disobedient.* Didn't you? Or did I misinterpret one of your many mixed signals?"

"What mixed signals?" He spread his arms wide leaving his towel unattended and hanging precariously.

"Oh let's see--*every* one. I don't know what to make of you, Max. Before we left here, you were acting like you wanted to ..."

"Like I wanted to what?"

Erica flushed hot. She couldn't say the words. "Then you apparently brought me home, undressed me, and dumped me in bed ... alone."

* * * *

Max dropped his gathered clothes and leaned back, crossing his arms over his chest in a pose similar to Erica's. Acutely aware of the fact that she'd already seen what was under his towel, he wasn't sure he liked the direction the conversation was taking. Of course, with the sun up, he was trapped. Their argument would have to work its way to some type of conclusion and if they both didn't get dressed very soon ...

"What would you have preferred? That I took you in the state you were in? Don't think I didn't want to. Don't think it was easy for me to peel that dress off you ... to slide your stockings down over your legs, inch off your underwear and leave you there, in bed unconscious and completely vulnerable." Max paused and watched her reaction to his words. A faint tremor racked her and her breathing grew shallow. He knew she was contemplating how easy it would have been for him to do whatever he wanted with her.

"I'm a vampire, Erica. We come into the world ready to take what we want. It requires a lot of effort for us to act human sometimes. We're governed by certain desires, needs we can't ignore. Believe me when I say, it was all I could do to walk away from you last night because if I hadn't ..."

"What?" Her voice was raw. He saw the hard tips of her nipples through the thin fabric of her robe and he remembered how badly he'd wanted to taste them last night. He remembered holding her close to him while he undressed her. The memory of her stretched on the bed, reaching for him made him hard all over again.

He could have taken her so easily then. But he didn't want her that way. He wanted her with him--awake and aware and begging him to do things to her she'd only dreamed about letting a man do. He wanted to see her eyes go dark with desire and her lips part as she sighed his name.

"If I hadn't ... I'd still be inside you right now."

Chapter Eleven

Erica trembled at Max's revelation. She dropped her arms and stared as her anger drained away. Something inside her began to heat and suddenly she was aware of every sensation. The cool fabric of her robe rubbed against her breasts and an ache began to build between her legs. Max's stare felt like a lead weight, holding her in place and stealing her breath. Her knees felt weak.

Max took a step toward her and she instinctively bared her neck to him. The memory of his arms around her, trapping her to his side while he drank from her, made her shudder with desire she shouldn't have felt.

When he put his fingers on the pulse point of her neck, just above the marks he'd made, her muscles coiled and she arched against his touch.

"Do you know how much danger you put yourself in last night?" he said as he took another step. Now he was right next to her. She felt the heat of his skin and didn't question it. He smelled like steam and male power and the almond soap she loved. His fingers closed on her neck, caressing her skin beneath the collar of her robe. "You attracted someone's attention. Someone devious enough to drug you."

"Who?"

"Maybe Vera. I don't know. She may have been trying to lure you away from me. You saw Carlisle with his vampire bitch. He might have drawn me away so Vera could lead you off somewhere where I couldn't find you. Carlisle wants you. I could smell it on him."

"But I'm yours ..." She breathed the words without thinking. All coherent thought left her as Max dipped his head close to her neck. His teeth scraped her shoulder and she squeezed her eyes shut to block out the fear of losing control.

"Yes. You're mine. Or at least you were supposed to be mine last night." His fingers slid into the folds of her robe and parted it. Erica sighed as he drew a line of fire between her breasts. "When I got you home, you asked me to make love to you. Do you remember that?"

She shook her head. "I remember you standing over me."

"I did, for a long time, wondering what to do with you. I wanted to shake you. You've gotten yourself in too deep already and I wanted to scare you away from this world. I thought about tearing your dress, drinking from the spot right here--" Max thrust his hand between her thighs and Erica gasped. Her body throbbed with need for him and the feel of his fingers on her sensitive flesh was her undoing. She moaned.

"If I'd bitten you there and left you, you'd be wondering now what I did to you. I could have made you think anything I wanted. I could have left you with the memory of my cock inside you, but I didn't because I didn't want you to just *remember* it. I wanted you to *feel* it."

Max brought his fingers to the nest of curls between her legs and delved inside. Erica cried out and spread her legs. He caught her around the waist and pushed her backward against the wall.

She dropped her head to one side, offering herself to him again. When he bent his head to her neck and sucked her skin into his mouth, she gasped. She shuddered against him when his teeth pierced her skin. Instinctively, she spread her legs father to allow him access anywhere he wanted to go. Their hands met between them and battled to pull the towel from around his waist.

With the last barrier between them gone, he hoisted her up and positioned his hard thighs between hers. His free hand pushed her robe from her shoulders, baring her breasts to him. He caressed her as he drank and his erection grew until the hard length teased her to distraction.

She wrapped her legs around him and he held her another few inches higher, positioning her above him. He lowered her as he thrust upward and she bit her lip at the sweet sensation as he took possession of her body.

* * * *

Max drank deeply as he entered her, then released his hold on her neck. It wasn't about feeding anymore. He took just enough blood to fuel his desire to the breaking point. Now, with her essence inside him, he was ready to show her exactly what his world was like.

He wrapped his arms around her and carried her to the bedroom. They didn't make it to the bed. He placed her on the floor and knelt over her, delving deeper while she moved against him.

"Open your eyes," he commanded. "I need to see it."

She obeyed and he kissed her, plunging his tongue deep. She still tasted like the wine and now, mixed in her scent was musk and primal fear, lust and anger. He craved it all, every emotion, every sensation. He took it all in and let it wash over her, using his ability to shape her perception so that she felt his desperate need mixed with her own. He made her feel his heart pounding under her hands as he took her, made her feel his skin grow slick with sweat as he worked her body to the breaking point.

When her inner muscles began to pulse, he slowed his thrusts. With long-practiced skill he allowed a calming sensation to wash over her, cooling her desire just enough to bring her back from the edge. Then he started again.

* * * *

Erica felt her climax nearing. She reached for it, meeting Max thrust for thrust. She locked her legs around his back and dragged her nails over his skin, drawing him deeper until she thought she would break. At the very moment the wave crested, a cool breeze seemed to stir between them and it pulled her away from the edge of the precipice.

She lay panting beneath him for a moment, lost in his blue gaze, aware of nothing but the delicious pressure of his erection inside her. He drew out slowly and she whimpered for him. He thrust in again and bent to take one aching nipple in his mouth. He sucked the hard tip and rolled it against his tongue, causing a sensation that arrowed straight to her womb.

"Don't stop!" She begged him over and over and time and time again he brought her right to the edge, then soothed the ache just before the wave broke over her.

The pleasure became pain and the desire became a frantic battle for release. "Now! Now!" She pleaded for it but he ignored her demands and continued the exquisite torture, bringing her right to the edge once more.

"Last night," he said between thrusts, "you asked if I was going to punish you for disobedience. The answer is yes."

She threw her head back and laughed, but the laugh became a sob when she nearly peaked again. "Not like this," she gasped.

"What would you have me do? Hold you down? Tie you up? Spank you?"

Anything would be preferable to denying her release. She wanted it, needed it. Erica had never begged a man for anything, but she begged Max to let her come.

"Promise me one thing, and I'll give you what you want."

"Anything!" She agreed without thought. All she wanted was the shuddering explosion that would free her from his thrall. She bucked against him and he stilled her with his body, holding her motionless as he kissed her into silence.

"Promise me you'll let me handle the case from now on. *My way.* I won't take you to any more bars where you could be drugged, or touched by another man ... or woman again. Promise me you'll keep yourself safe and let me find your sister for you."

Erica let out a cry of frustration. She was so close, so desperate and so completely at his mercy, she would have done anything he asked, obeyed any command he gave her. But this ...

She nodded. "I promise."

He kissed her again and she cried as the ache ebbed once more. When he began to thrust into her again, she held her breath, waiting for the moment he'd take it all away, but this time he brought her to the edge and over. The orgasm she'd been dying for tore through her and she gasped as it rocked her body into utter oblivion.

She cried out as he came, the tremors of his body matching hers. She felt him explode inside her, a burst of liquid heat that had to be an illusion, a delicious, sensuous illusion.

When the shock waves ceased, her body trembled and she shivered in his embrace. After a moment, Max rose above her. He kissed her once more and then lifted her in his arms and carried her to the bed. The soft blankets felt like clouds beneath her aching limbs. She shuddered at the sensation as he drew the sheet across her body. Her nerve endings trembled as he caressed her. Every touch was like an electric shock. After a time, her inner muscles calmed and she sank into a blissful sleep as he climbed into bed next to her and wrapped himself around her.

"Erica," he whispered as he kissed her hair and settled her head onto his chest. "What am I going to do with you?"

"Anything you want," she mumbled as she clung to him. "Anything you want."

Chapter Twelve

Erica wrapped her arms around her bent knees and stared down at Max's sleeping form. At first she'd panicked to find him lying next to her, unmoving and cold. She thought he was dead.

Of course, she was right.

She reached out and smoothed his dark hair and he stirred, but his skin didn't warm to her touch and his chest didn't rise and fall.

She sat back and contemplated how she'd come to this.

She'd never experienced anything like what Max had done to her that morning. At twenty-nine, she was no virgin, though her previous lovers numbered in single digits. She'd always chosen her men carefully, with an eye toward their reliable nature, rather than expertise in bed. Up until now she'd never had a man last so long or exert so much control over every nuance of the act. She'd never had a man control her orgasm before--and hold her captive with it as he had. She'd have promised him anything ... hell, she'd have given him her body if he hadn't already been inside her.

She shivered at the memory. He'd been so alive while they were making love ... or was it just sex? If Max only wanted what her body could provide him, why had he forced her to make that promise to him? Why did he want her to stay safely out of the investigation? Was it truly because he cared about her, maybe even loved her? Or was it because he knew that his world was too much for her?

What scared her most was how strong she felt now. Surrendering to him, to her innermost desires, made her feel invincible. A small part of her wanted more even now. She wanted to wake him up and tell him yes, hold me down. Tie me up. Bite me.

Who was she? How had she become this creature who sat staring at the body of her vampire lover wishing he'd awake and punish her for her aberrant thoughts?

She shook herself out of the psychological quagmire and climbed out of bed. She hesitated a moment, her attention captured by her own reflection in the mirror. When she looked at the bed, she saw only a blur of color where Max lay. When she turned she saw him in full detail, lying on his stomach, clutching a pillow under his head.

In the mirror, nothing. She couldn't focus on his image. Did that mean he wasn't real? She glanced at the clock. It was close to noon. If she opened the window shade and sunlight struck the bed, what would happen?

She shook off that disturbing thought and strolled into the living room to straighten up. It was only when she found her robe and his towel next to the couch, which she realized for the first time in her life, she'd walked through her apartment naked.

She laughed softly. The old Erica never would have done that. Where had the old Erica gone?

She jumped when the phone rang, suddenly self-conscious. It could have just as easily been the doorbell. She pounced on the receiver before the second ring and wondered why it mattered to her if the noise disturbed Max.

"Hello?" She tried to sound normal.

"Ricki?"

Erica clutched the wall between the living room and the kitchen as the good humor drained out of her body like molten lead. The shock of hearing Elena's voice doubled her over.

"Lainey! Where are you? What happened?" The memory of her sister's voice crying through the vent at *Gregori's* rushed back into her mind. How had she forgotten that until now? "Where are you, Lainey, tell me now and I'll come and get you."

"I don't have a lot of time, Ricki. Only a few minutes. I need you to come to a place called *The Underside*, tonight. . .come alone."

"I'll come right now. Lainey, are you all right? What's happening to you? Did they hurt you?"

"It's Benton Carlisle. He's keeping me here. I need you, Ricki. You're the only one who can help me."

"Of course." Erica's hands shook so violently she almost dropped the phone. "I'll be there, Lainey--I'll come right now."

"No. Not now. Tonight. I won't be able to get free until tonight. Come after midnight and come alone. They know about Max and if they see him here, they'll hurt me. I have a plan to get away, Ricki, but I need your help."

Erica nodded. "Okay, okay. Lainey ... it'll be all right. I'll get you out and we'll find a safe place for you, I promise, this time will be different. Lainey? Lainey?" The only response was a dial tone.

Erica sank to the floor and stared at the cordless in her hand. At least Elena was alive. She sounded fine in fact, strong ... not drunk or stoned. That was good.

After a few deep breaths, Erica rose and returned the phone to its cradle. She glanced down the hall at the bedroom and listened. There was no sound. No snoring as she might have expected with a man in her bed, no gentle rhythmic breathing either. She had to remind herself, Maxwell Hart was dead to the world. Literally.

She sighed. She'd made him a promise--albeit under duress. She wondered what he'd do to her if he found out she was about to break it.

* * * *

"I'll be out of your way by 6:00," Max told Erica as he watched her washing dishes. Sitting at her small kitchen table with his notebook and a cup of coffee that she insisted on making for him, he felt as close to human as he had in over a century.

Watching her denim clad rear end wiggle as she scrubbed a frying pan certainly added to the illusion. He had a raging hard on but absolutely no hint of hunger. He wanted to make love to her, but as a man, not as a vampire who tempered his need for blood with sexual demands so that both hunter and prey could derive pleasure from the union.

He just wanted to touch her, play with her hair, taste her skin and feel her come around him without any power play. No games. No blood.

He hadn't wanted that in a long time and in truth, it worried him. He couldn't enjoy his normal male desire without wondering why it had returned after all these years of heightened vampire urges. After decades of hearing the rush of blood under a woman's skin when he touched her, of tasting her emotions on his lips, he reveled in the normalcy of this moment. He reveled in watching her wash the dishes and wondered what she was thinking.

"What are you planning to do tonight?" she asked him as she completed her task. She stacked dishes neatly in the drain-board and turned to him, the damp dishtowel tossed over her shoulder.

With her golden hair hanging down to her shoulders and not a hint of makeup, she looked beautiful. She looked sunny and warm and alive. It made the dark empty spot where his heart used to beat ache to look at her. He wanted that feeling wrapped around him, in fact he craved it now more than blood. He'd felt alive when he made love to her. He felt human.

"I'm ... uh ... going to talk to some of my contacts. There's always someone at *Gregori's* and they can snoop around. I'm also going to arrange for someone to follow Benton Carlisle and Vera Nighe."

"Why?"

"He's involved in something. I really think Vera drugged you and that has me worried. I don't want you to go anywhere tonight. Once it gets dark, stay inside and keep all the shades drawn. Don't answer the door unless it's me."

She smiled shyly at him and reached for his hand. "Will you be coming back tonight? When you're done working?"

"Would you like me to? I'll be very late. I don't want to wake you."

"Sure you do," she purred and his body stirred in response. "But I have to go to work tomorrow. And I've got to get to the bank before that so I can transfer the money to pay Elena's rent."

"I wish you didn't have to do that."

Her expression faltered. "I don't want her to lose her apartment. She'll pay me back."

That wasn't true. Max saw it in her eyes. She wasn't expecting anything in return for her efforts to help her sister--probably because she'd learned long ago not to.

"Give me her address and I'll go there tonight and get something of hers I can use to track her with."

"But the landlord--"

Max laughed. "I won't be asking the landlord's permission. I won't disturb anything. I just need a piece of her clothing. A scarf would be perfect, or a blouse with a collar. Maybe something with her favorite perfume on it."

"All right. She lived ... *lives* at 420 Fortune Drive, Building A, apartment 5."

Though he didn't need to, Max wrote it down. He'd learn a lot more from looking around Elena Talbot's apartment than just what she smelled like, and he was glad for the chance to do it without Erica along. He had a feeling he would find things there that even her sister didn't know about. His desire to protect Erica was starting to overwhelm him. He'd never felt like this before and it left him off balance and edgy.

He looked at the kitchen clock. He still had an hour until sunset.

"Come with me," he said as he rose from his chair. He took Erica's hand in his and tugged her toward the bedroom. "I want to show you something."

She raised one perfect eyebrow. "Is it something I've seen before?" Her half smile ignited him and he growled as he dragged her into his arms.

"You've seen it before, but not up close." He punctuated his words by cupping her rear and pulling her tight against him. The look in her eyes told him she understood exactly how much he wanted her.

She reached for the buttons of her blouse but he grabbed her hands and held them. "No. Everything stays on until I tell you to take it off."

She sighed happily and her breathing grew shallow. "Do we have time...?"

"We have as long as it takes. I'm not leaving here until I'm done with you."

The sound she made drove him over the edge and he scooped her up and carried her into the bedroom.

It was well after six when he left.

Chapter Thirteen

Erica felt Max around her and inside her. She tasted him and she ached for him long after he left her apartment.

Because the memories of their lovemaking were so fresh, guilt gnawed at her as she stood before her closet looking for an outfit that would help get her into *The Underside.*

She hadn't mentioned anything about Elena's phone call knowing he'd insist on being involved. Erica had no illusions that her task would be easy, but she wouldn't do anything to jeopardize her sister's life. Her trips to *After Dark* and *Club Dead* had taught her more about the vampire world and what they expected of her feeders. She could do this.

A little on-line research told her *The Underside* was more of a

Goth club, which she might have found amusing under other circumstances. What could be more Goth than vampires after all?

That thought brought her back to Max. The line between human and vampire was blurred in him. As blurred as his image had been each time she'd looked in the mirror. She hadn't asked him about it, but as they made love again that afternoon, she'd stolen glances across the room and marveled at the fact that his reflection was no more than a waxy smudge. She wondered if it was simply her own perception, clouded by the delirium of sexual fulfillment or if there was some truth at least to that bit of vampire lore.

Beyond that, she felt him and remembered him as human. Everything in the way he touched her today was different than last night. Though he'd looked at her with the same dark longing in his eyes, that dangerous look that turned her insides to liquid, he'd been gentle and slow with her. He'd kissed her senseless and caressed her body until her nerves caught fire, but he hadn't delayed her pleasure like last night. He hadn't forced her to promise him things, or tortured her with words that made her want what she couldn't have.

He'd loved her thoroughly and left her wondering once again what she'd gotten herself into.

With a ragged sigh, she thumbed through the clothes in her closet until she found a long straight skirt and a black tank top. She appraised the outfit in the mirror and tossed the top aside. A leather bustier would work better but she didn't have one.

She wished she'd insisted on going with Max to Elena's apartment. There, she'd have found a suitable outfit.

Maybe in the back of the closet with the stuff she didn't wear anymore? She dug deep, tossing things aside as she went until she came upon the item she remembered. It had been Elena's but Erica had borrowed it years ago. She laughed at the memory. A Halloween party at work was rare, but one year her manager had decided to get everyone in the spirit. Erica had dressed in an eclectic mix of beachwear and black rags, a long black wig, a broom and a bottle of suntan lotion and called herself the "Sand-Witch." The getup won a prize and garnered her a few months of teasing from her co-workers. She thought of them now and wondered if any of them would believe how she'd spent her weekend so far. She wasn't sure she believed it herself.

She found the black top she'd worn as part of the costume and pulled it out of the closet. The sleeves were laced up the sides and the front sported rips and tears held together with silver safety pins and jump rings. It would have to do.

She mussed her hair, slathered on her darkest lipstick and ringed her eyes with black liner. The look reminded her of the girl who hadn't gotten into *After Dark*. If she adopted the same attitude, they'd probably welcome her at *The Underside*.

She left her apartment at ten and drove herself across town to the address listed on the Web site. This time she didn't care who saw her.

* * * *

"Carlisle's not there tonight?" Max adjusted the volume on his cell phone headset as he turned into the parking lot of Elena Talbot's building. His partner's voice reached him over the patchy connection. With deliberate patience, Lucas Vitale repeated what he'd just said.

"I don't see him anywhere. I know he spends most evenings here, but maybe he got tired of the place."

Max worked with Lucas regularly and the other vampire investigator was the closest thing Max had to a friend. He tried to keep the frustration out of his voice when he answered.

"I don't like that Erica is alone. I've got to finish this now, but maybe you can swing by her apartment, just to see if she's all right."

"You want me to go in, or just lurk around?" Lucas' deep voice held amusement. He was a bit of a rebel and he liked his job, perhaps too much.

"Lurk. It's what you're best at. Call me if you see anything suspicious."

"All right. I've got to take Kyra home first."

Halfway out of his car, Max paused. "Kyra is with you?"

"Of course. I needed to bring a feeder with me. You know she can handle anything."

Max shook his head. He should have expected that. Kyra knew them all and she fed them all. It was her job. And her pleasure from what Max understood. A few days ago, he might have felt a pang of jealousy, but now, just annoyance that she couldn't get home by herself. "Do me a favor and don't waste any time at Kyra's, all right? I want to know that Erica is safe."

Lucas' voice took on a curious tone. "Why so worried about a feeder?"

"She's not a feeder. She's just ..." Just what? he asked himself as he rounded Building A and headed for the fire stairs at the back that would lead him to Apartment 5.

"Just what? Just a human? Just a good lay?"

"Shut up, Luke."

"Ooh. Did I strike a live nerve there? I didn't know you had any left."

"Just do what I ask, Lucas ... and keep Kyra out of it. I don't want her to know about Erica."

"Why not? Do you think she'll be jealous that her favorite biter has a new toy?"

Max hung up. Lucas was a prick sometimes, but he'd never let Max down yet. He jammed the cell phone into his pocket and cased the building. Getting in wouldn't be a problem. The fire stairs at the back of the building gave access to all the bedroom windows. Elena Talbot's was bare, no curtains, not even a shade. He wondered as he began to climb, if the landlord had already cleaned the place out.

Max pried the screen off the window and set it on the stairs, then hoisted the old sash, glad that he wouldn't have to break the window to get in. Once inside he lowered the sash again and moved out of the line of sight.

Two steps in, it hit him. The scent he'd been looking for. It permeated the place. A smoky mixture of musky perfume, heather and clove. He didn't need to take anything that belonged to Elena to remember it and he didn't need to give the scent to anyone else.

What he needed was to figure out how to tell Erica that he knew exactly what had happened to her sister.

* * * *

Déjà vu struck Erica as she took her place in line outside of *The Underside*. The back entrance was another unpainted steel fire door manned by a bouncer who could have been the twin brother to Frank from *After Dark*. This one looked less friendly, though. He scowled at the women and men lined up outside and rather than gesturing the unacceptable candidates out of line, he waited until they approached him and literally shoved them aside.

He seemed to get off on it. The smirk on his doughy face grew wider each time he refused someone entry.

Erica's fear and annoyance peaked as she neared her turn. If he threw her aside, how would she get in? She thought about calling Max and telling him about Elena's phone call but she knew he'd make her leave. Worse than considering that he'd leave her out of the rescue mission, was the thought of admitting she lied to him. She lied in the throes of passion and made a promise to him that she didn't intend to keep. What did that make her? Certainly not worthy of the adoration he'd shown her this afternoon. Certainly not worthy of his trust.

She shook the doubts aside and moved up to close the gap that had opened between her and the person ahead of her in line. She still had time to walk away and call Max for help. What if he needed time to formulate a plan? She couldn't let Elena down by not being here.

Erica jerked her head up when the bouncer called, "Next! You in black!" He laughed at his own joke. Everyone in line wore black and each outfit was darker than the last.

Erica stood out because she was the only blonde in sight and that worried her. Inside, she wouldn't be able to melt into the crowd, and she wouldn't be able to avoid a body search tonight.

Just like *After Dark*, the man checked her for needle marks, asked if she smoked or snorted and he also squeezed her ass. She forced a smile as she shoved her inside and pretended it didn't make her want to rip his head off.

The gauntlet tonight was worse than at *After Dark*, but at least the music was better. Four men lined the back room and each one of them searched every-one who came through, male and female alike. Erica noted that quite a few men had been admitted and none of them seemed to be bothered by the intimate body search. Of course they had fewer places to hide contraband than women did.

Erica bit her lip and held her breath as each of the four security guards took his turn. The first one lifted her skirt and patted down her legs from crotch to ankle. He actually ran his fingers inside the leg of her panties and leered at her before he motioned her to move on. The second one looked down the front of her blouse but nothing she had made an impression on him. He motioned her on to the third who also lifted her skirt. This one sniffed her hair and she shuddered. That was almost as bad as having the first guard's fingers in her underwear.

The fourth one patted her hips and her breasts. He pushed her collar open and stamped a fluorescent butterfly on her chest, then let her pass into the club. She figured the brand meant no one would chase her down later and insist she hadn't been properly felt up ... searched. She had proof that she'd passed the security inspection.

The Underside had an odd vibe to it, and a strange smell. It took Erica a few minutes to place the sharp, smoky scent. Cloves.

Small plates of incense burned everywhere making the air heavy with the spicy aroma.

Drinks flowed freely and here she didn't have to order at the bar. A waitress pressed a glass of sweet wine into her hand moments after she arrived. She resisted the urge to take a sip. It smelled so good, but she didn't dare take any chances.

She made a quick circuit of the place to get her bearings and then found an empty corner table where she would be able to watch everything. As soon as she saw Elena, she'd make her move.

Her nerves thrummed with anticipation. She'd find Elena tonight and this half-life would end. No more rescues after this. No more sleepless nights.

No more Maxwell Hart.

A flash of white caught her attention and she zeroed in on a figure across the room that stood out even more than she did.

A tall woman with long black hair and a flowing white dress floated across the room like a runway model. Vera Nighe. Her almond eyes lit on Erica and she smiled.

"What are you doing here, little one? Where's Max?" Vera asked when she arrived at Erica's table. She looked angelic and full of life, unlike last night at *Gregori's* when she'd appeared sunken and tired.

"I came alone tonight." Erica wanted to lie but she thought of Elena's plea to leave Max out of it.

The other woman looked around, scanning the room with her curious gaze. "Wonderful. Then you can have a drink with me."

Erica smiled and pushed her glass toward Vera as the tall woman sat down. "Here, it's all yours."

"Come on, Max isn't around. One sip won't hurt."

"I wonder what would have happened if I'd drank the wine last night. Apparently just a whiff was enough to affect me. I barely remember anything that happened."

Vera's smile became a pretty pout. "Then you forgot all the fun we had dancing together?"

Erica shrugged.

"What a shame. We'll have to make some more memories tonight, since you're on your own."

"Where's Mr. Carlisle?" Erica asked. She wanted to sound conversational but a hint of suspicion crept into her voice. If Carlisle was responsible for hurting Elena, she wanted to make him pay.

"He'll join us soon, pretty one. Very soon."

Vera sidled closer to Erica and put her arm around her shoulders. Erica pulled away but the woman resisted and dipped her face toward Erica's for a light kiss.

Erica pushed her away. "Vera, I'm flattered, but I belong to Max and he doesn't like anyone else touching me, even other women."

"He's not here. He doesn't have to know."

"He *will* know. He'll find out and last night he was very angry with me about what you did ... when you kissed me."

"I thought you said you didn't remember it."

"I didn't, but he reminded me. I'd rather not be punished again, if you don't mind."

Vera pouted again. "He's bad. We're not hurting anyone. Just a little harmless flirting. It doesn't mean anything."

"I know."

"Just one? Benton likes to see me with other women. It would make him happy and I could have him smooth it over if Max found out."

"I'd rather not."

"Just one ..." Vera dove in again and Erica tried to dodge but the woman was all hands. She took Erica's face in her fingers and kissed her on the lips again. She tasted like candy and cloves and something else ...

When she broke the kiss, Erica stared at her. "What did you do to--" The world went black before she finished her sentence.

Chapter Fourteen

Max sat brooding in the dark apartment. The same scent that permeated Elena Talbot's apartment surrounded him, along with memories of the things that had happened here.

It made him feel ill. He didn't like the feeling. It had been years since something truly turned his stomach. Between disgust at himself and anger at whatever game Elena Talbot was playing with her sister, the feeling overwhelmed him.

When his cell phone rang, he growled into the receiver. "What?"

"Problem, Max." Lucas sounded edgy. That wasn't like him.

Max sat forward in the chair. "Where are you?"

"I'm at Erica's building. She's not here."

Max sighed. She'd lied to him. Why didn't it surprise him? "Are you sure?"

"Not to be cliché, but the lights are on and nobody's home. Her car isn't here."

Max rose and headed for the door. His confrontation would have to wait.

* * * *

Erica blinked slowly until the scene before her came into focus. Her fingers were wrapped around the steering wheel of her car, which still sat in the parking lot of *The Underside*. She had no recollection of leaving the club and it took her a moment to recall if she'd even gone inside. She gasped when she saw the time. Her watch read 4:30 a.m. She'd been out all night--and didn't remember a thing after Vera kissed her.

She began to shake. A cold inner tremor became a violent shiver. What had they done to her? Where was Elena? She flung the car door open and stumbled out onto the black top. The world tilted dizzily and she clutched the roof of the car for support.

The rest of the parking lot was empty.

Without considering the consequences, she ran to the back door of *The Underside* and started banging. The cold metal hurt her hand, but she kept at it. "Let me in! Is anyone there? I have to get in!"

Nothing. She stumbled down the stairs and ran to the front of the building. Windowless. The front door was solid wood with a fierce gargoyle faced carved on it. Erica yanked on the latch, pounded on the gargoyle's face and screamed until her throat hurt. No one answered.

No Elena. Nothing.

Still shivering, she wrapped her arms around herself and sobbed as she walked back to the car. Max was right. This was not her world. She couldn't function here. Whatever Elena was involved in, Erica couldn't help her. Now she'd have to go back and confess to Max and beg for him to help her.

He'd hate her for breaking her promise.

He'd never trust her again.

* * * *

Max found Lucas in the parking lot of Erica's building. Dressed in dark jeans and a black leather jacket, his blond hair hidden under his black motorcycle helmet, he was little more than a shadow.

"You look like a second story man," Max said.

Lucas grinned, showing fangs. "I used to be one. I was damn good at it, too." He nodded toward Erica's bedroom window. "Nothing."

Max cursed. He should have known she'd go looking for her sister without him. "I'm going inside to look around, maybe I can figure out where she went. Can you spend some more time tracking Benton Carlisle? See if he shows up at his office today. And if you hear from Kyra, let me know."

Lucas shrugged. "Sure. Look, if you want backup tonight..."

Max shook his head. "I don't need it, yet. I'll call if I get into trouble."

"Suit yourself." Lucas turned to leave but glanced over his shoulder. "You look worried Max. I don't think I've ever seen you look worried."

"I am, Luke. And you know what? It's one of the few things I don't miss about being human.

Lucas laughed as he climbed onto his bike. "That's the biggest difference between you and me, Max. I don't miss anything at all."

Max watched the taillight of Lucas' bike recede, then let himself into Erica's apartment.

Her bedroom light was on and black clothes covered the bed. Max picked through them then checked the papers on the corner computer desk hoping to find something that would lead him in the right direction.

As an afterthought he nudged the computer mouse and watched the screen light up. He opened up her Internet browser and checked her address menu for recent activity. The last Web site she'd visited was a Goth message board frequented by feeders.

He should have known. He should have expected she would lie to him. He was only a vampire to her after all. Promises made to him didn't matter.

But promises *from* him, did. Whether she ever believed it or not, he cared and he was going to do what he told her he'd do whether she trusted him or not.

* * * *

Erica's fingers shook so hard she had to hold the key in both hands in order to unlock the door. Once inside her apartment, she tossed the keys aside. She had to clean off the butterfly stamp on her chest, and the wash the smoky scent of *The Underside* out of her hair before Max came back.

If he came back.

She put one trembling hand to her neck on the spot where he'd last bitten her. Her fingers came back with a smudge of dark blood. She stared at the stain for a moment, teetering on the brink of passing out cold. Someone had fed from her. . .and she had no memory of it.

That knowledge only increased her trembling. She sank against the nearest wall, gulping air and trying to regain her composure. When a hand closed over her shoulder, she screamed.

Max dragged Erica into his arms and quieted her, hushing her as she sobbed against him. He lowered her to the floor and pulled her across his lap, smoothing her hair.

"I've been waiting for hours," he murmured as her trembling finally stopped. "Why, Erica? Why couldn't you trust me?"

She looked up at him through the haze of tears that clouded her vision. "She called me, Max. She called again and asked for help. I had to go."

"And you didn't find her, did you?" His voice went hard. She swallowed and shook her head. "There's a reason for that, Erica. She's playing a game with you."

Erica sat up and stared at Max. His mouth was set in a thin line and his eyes shadowed.

"What do you mean?"

"When did she call you?"

"This morning." She hated to confess it, but with him staring at her, looking betrayed, she couldn't lie to him. "While you were asleep."

He nodded and his hands dropped from her shoulders. He sat back against the wall and stared at her.

"You smell like blood."

She looked away. A moment later he pulled the collar of her shirt roughly aside and traced a rough line from the opalescent butterfly stamp to the bloody bite marks. His expression turned to steel.

"Who did this? Carlisle?"

She didn't answer, didn't look at him. She cried out when he shook her. "Who was it?"

"I don't know! I don't know. I met Vera ..."

Max dropped his arms again and rolled to his feet. He paced behind her while Erica curled into a ball and leaned against the wall.

"You let her drug you again? What were you thinking? Did you think that would get you taken to Elena?"

"I didn't drink anything. Vera kissed me ..." Erica swiped at the tears that spilled down her cheeks. After the memory of Vera's warm lips on hers, there was nothing but a terrifying void.

Max was silent for a moment. When he finally spoke, his words made her shiver.

"Take off your clothes."

She stared at him but he wouldn't meet her gaze. When she hesitated, he dragged her to her feet and tore at the thin lace that held her shirt together.

Frightened and aroused by his actions, she didn't resist when he pulled the waistband of her skirt open and slid the garment roughly down her legs. He tore her underwear away, threw aside the tight black bra she wore then ran his hands down her body.

She warmed to him, despite his anger. She wanted him, if only to ease the ache in her heart. She needed him to comfort her, but instead he was searching her, exploring her body inch by inch.

"What are you doing?" His touch made her breathless, but the look in his eyes froze her.

"Looking for bite marks. You're lucky to be alive. For all you know a group of vampires could have fed on you. They could have killed you, Erica! Or turned you." She didn't need him to tell her that. The thought had been running through her mind all during the torturous drive home.

She held herself rigid while he ran his hand up each of her legs, between her thighs, across her lower back, up under her breasts and her hair. His intense scrutiny made her skin tingle and her body ache for him.

"It looks like that's the only mark," he said finally. He stepped back from her, leaving her cold. "If they only drugged you, the memories of what happened might come back."

"If they *only* drugged me?" She turned, seeking his embrace, but instead he wrapped her in a blanket from the couch, the one he'd used the night before.

"We can use hypnotic suggestions to control humans and sometimes even other vampires. If someone put hypnotic suggestions in your mind, you won't remember anything unless they tell you to."

"I might have seen Elena and not even know it."

Max put one finger under her chin and forced her to look in his eyes. "There are worse things you might have done, Erica. I'm not going to protect you from this. You should have listened to me. You should have trusted me!"

She pulled the blanket around her against the awful cold. "I'm sorry, Max. I wanted to. But she's my sister. She told me they'd hurt her if you came with me. What could I do?"

"She's using you, Erica. Whatever sick purpose she has, she's *not* in trouble. She's not waiting for you to rescue her. She's waiting for you to fall into her trap."

Chapter Fifteen

If Max had still been human, the hurt in Erica's eyes would have broken his heart. At that moment, he considered himself fortunate to be dead. It lessened the pain he felt for her.

Part of him wanted to walk away. He couldn't bear the thought that she'd been touched by Carlisle--or anyone else--that another vampire had held her and drank from her to nourish themselves. She was *his*. She had to be his alone.

And part of him wanted to avenge everything she'd been through and make it all right again. He wondered if she felt his hands tremble as he searched her body for marks they might have left on her. The only evidence of what had happened to her was the bloody bruise on her neck and the butterfly stamped above her breast.

"Get dressed." The order left a bitter taste. He wanted to take her to bed and sooth away with the hurt with his hands and his mouth. But it would never be over until he told her the truth, until he kept his promise and found out exactly what her sister wanted from her.

"Max, please don't leave me now."

"I'm not going to leave you. I'm going to take you with me."

"Where?"

"To see your sister." He held up his hand. "Don't ask any questions. Ask *her* when you see her. This ends now."

Her eyes fell and a sob escaped her. She turned away and walked into the bedroom. He stood rooted to the spot, fighting the urge to follow her. If he touched her again, he'd lose control and neither of them could afford that right now.

When she returned she looked better. She wore jeans and an

oversized blouse over a cotton T-shirt. She'd cleaned the blood off her neck and the dark makeup from her face. She looked innocent, like she had this morning. Innocent, and broken.

She walked past him and retrieved her keys from the floor where she'd dropped them. When she stood, he grabbed her arm and pulled her to him. "Tell me one thing, Erica. I need to know."

"What?" Her voice was thick and he saw tears well in her eyes as she looked up at him.

"Tell me you're not part of the game."

"I don't know what you mean, Max. What game? Where's Elena?"

"I'm not sure where she is, but I know where she'll end up."

"What do you mean? Where are we going?"

"To her apartment."

* * * *

Erica watched Max as he drove. She didn't say anything when he bypassed Fortune Drive and eased onto the empty highway. Wherever he was taking her, it wasn't to Elena's.

He didn't look at her. He didn't say a word until they reached a bungalow development in South Windsor. There, he parked the car, got out and waited by the back fender for her to join him.

"I don't understand, Max. How did you find her? She was supposed to be at *The Underside* last night."

"No, she wasn't. *You* were supposed to be. Don't you see? You were set up. I don't know why. Your sister has been playing you."

"No." Erica shook her head. She refused to accept that. Elena wouldn't do that. She used Erica, took advantage but only because she didn't know any other way. Her sister would never hurt her deliberately. "Elena needs help. Maybe someone is forcing her to--"

"Come on. Let me show you."

He took her hand and led her across the parking lot to one of the rundown bungalows in the development. The small house had a rusty awning over the front door. Empty flowerpots sat in a metal stand next to the concrete slab that served as a porch. The name scratched into the wrought iron mailbox was Blake, K.

Erica didn't comment when Max produced a key from under the tattered welcome mat and opened the door. "Whose place is this, Max?"

He gave her a sour look. "Maybe you can't smell it as well as I can, but come on ... can't you tell?"

He pulled her over the threshold. Inside, clothes lay on every surface in the small living room. Cartons of oriental take out languished on a round table in the corner, and on the mantle of the faux fireplace stood a picture that drew Erica's attention immediately.

She crossed the room and picked up the battered silver frame. Her own face stared out at her.

"She's living here?" She croaked the words out as she struggled to set the picture upright in its frame.

"Has been for a while. She calls herself Kyra and she's a feeder. A popular one." His voice sounded raw. She saw the truth immediately when she looked at him.

"*Your* feeder?"

He nodded but didn't meet her gaze. "Mine and a lot of others. She prefers not to be exclusive."

Erica's jaw clenched and she turned back to the picture on the mantle. It was all she could do not to smash it. "When did you...?"

"Friday night. After I left you."

"She'd been missing for two days by then." But Erica hadn't seen her sister in person for months before that.

"She was with a friend of mine tonight. Another investigator. He took her with him to *Gregori's*."

"Where is she now?"

"He said he dropped her off here. I was here earlier and by the looks of the place, she never came inside."

"So now she really *is* missing?" Panic welled in Erica again. To come this close and still not find Elena was torture.

"Not for long. She'll turn up. She has regulars."

Erica closed her eyes and sighed. "And you're one of them?"

"I was."

"Does feeding include ... other things?"

Max whispered the answer. "Sometimes."

"Take me home, Max. I don't need to see any more."

* * * *

Once again, sunrise threatened as Max drove himself home. He'd reluctantly left Erica at the door of her apartment and he hated himself for having too much pride to beg her to let him stay. He needed her. He hadn't figured out why yet, but he did. He needed to know that somehow she would forgive him eventually for the things he'd done with Kyra--Elena.

It rocked him that they were the same person. Erica's twin looked nothing like her. Acted, tasted, smelled nothing like her. The woman he'd come to know as Kyra Blake was like the negative image of Erica, dark where her sister was sunny, hard and jaded where Erica was soft and too naïve for her own good.

He made it home just as the sun broke over the horizon and he sank wearily into the dark leather couch. The case wasn't closed yet. He still had to figure out what Benton Carlisle had to do with it, and he had no intention of letting Kyra off the hook. He planned to find her and make her answer every question he had. Even if Erica had no further desire to talk to her sister, he couldn't leave it alone. He had to have the answers for her, even if she didn't want them.

He dialed Lucas on his cell phone as he unbuttoned his shirt.

"Yeh?"

"Did I wake you?" Max asked.

"It's the crack of dawn, for chrissake. Of course you woke me. What's up? Besides you."

"I need to tell you something about Kyra."

* * * *

Erica didn't go to the bank that morning, and she didn't go to work either.

When the sun rose and the first rays blazed through her bedroom window, she sat contemplating a bed she could no longer sleep in and wondering why it hurt so bad to know that Max had been with Elena.

She hated herself for being jealous over a vampire. Of course it was natural to feel a little proprietary. She'd given him things she'd never given another man. She'd experienced sensations with him that a human man could never hope to recreate. Who wouldn't want that to go on? But she'd learned her lesson. The part of her that had come out and enjoyed free reign this weekend was gone, banished now to the dark recesses of her mind where it belonged.

She called her office and told her manager she had the flu. She needed more than a day to recover, more than a day to figure out how to reclaim everything of herself that she'd lost and to mourn what she'd given freely.

At first she'd told herself there was nothing Elena could say to her, nothing she wanted to know. Whatever plan her sister had for her, whatever reason was behind Elena's making her think she was in trouble and drawing her into the vampire world, didn't matter to Erica. At first.

Curiosity burned in her though and she hated herself for it. Max could have told her a confrontation with Elena would do no good.

He probably would have told her not to go, but she decided she had to.

She dressed slowly, careful in her movements. Her body ached and it scared her to think why. Whatever had happened to her between midnight and 4:30 a.m. had left her feeling bruised and tired. There were circles under her eyes and it took most of her strength just to force down a cup of coffee and a piece of dry toast before she left home.

Surprisingly, she had no trouble recreating the route Max had taken to Kyra's. Despite the state she'd been in, she remembered every turn. When she pulled up, she turned off the car and sat for a long time staring at the bungalow that belonged to her sister.

None of it made sense. If Elena had a secret identity as a vampire feeder, why keep two apartments? Well, Erica shrugged, she wasn't exactly *keeping* them both. Two months behind on the rent didn't constitute keeping a place. But still, the apartment on Fortune Avenue was full of furniture and clothing that belonged to Elena. Why would her sister leave it all?

A frightening thought took over. What if Elena didn't know who she was? What if Carlisle, or whatever vampire was involved with her, was actually using the mind control Max spoke of to convince Elena she was someone else? That had to be it. Elena wasn't setting Erica up or trying to lure her into the dark underworld of the vampires. She was trying to escape the false persona that had been imposed on her by the creatures that fed from her.

With that thought in mind, Erica felt stronger. It wasn't Elena's fault. Erica could still save her.

She got out of the car and raced across the parking lot. She retrieved the key from where Max had left it under the mat and unlocked the door. If she had to wait all day for Elena to return she would. She'd do whatever she had to do to reach her sister.

The place looked a little different than it had a few hours before. A woman's raincoat lay across the back of the threadbare couch and a pair of high-heeled pumps lay in the corner behind the front door.

Erica's heart thudded. Was Elena here? Had she finally come home?

She called out tentatively as she moved through the apartment. The smoky smell of cloves grew more intense as she neared the bedroom.

Erica knocked on the closed door and waited. No answer. She

hadn't expected any. Elena slept like the dead.

That thought galvanized her and she turned the knob and flung the door open.

A body lay tangled in the flowered sheets of the queen-sized bed. A cap of short dark hair nestled on the pillows.

"Elena?" Erica approached the bed and drew in her breath. Her sister's face was pale, bloodless. Her lips were blue. "No. No ... Elena!"

Chapter Sixteen

"My contact told me that Benton Carlisle made a brief appearance at *The Underside* last night. He was with Vera Nighe and they had a feeder with them," Lucas said.

Max grimaced. He stifled the urge to throw the phone. "Carlisle is behind all this. I don't know why. He could have any feeder he wants. Why bother with Erica or Elena?"

"You said it yourself, Max. He can have anyone. He arranged to get what he wanted."

"If he's drugging unwilling feeders, he's got to be stopped. We have to let Beaumont know."

Lucas sighed and there was skepticism in his voice. "Carlisle is like a fortress. Letting Beaumont know might not produce any results."

"It's against our rules, Luke. If we don't live by rules then we're no better than monsters." Max rose and paced. Through a small, tempered window in his bedroom he saw the morning sky and it made him ache for Erica. He'd called her twice already, but there was no answer. She'd probably gone to work, in an attempt to get back to her life. Maybe she needed to be somewhere he couldn't follow.

"I'm not disagreeing with you, Max. But Carlisle is old school, like Gregori. That civilized veneer they wear is very thin. Vampires like him still believe they're superior to humans. They feel they deserve whatever they can take."

"He's not going to take Erica."

"From what you told me, I'd say he already has."

Max bared his fangs and made an inhuman sound. He couldn't live with that. He wanted Erica back, wanted to taste her again, to feel her.

Lucas spoke again after a long silence. "Max? Are you still there?"

"I'm here. But I shouldn't be. I should be with Erica. Luke, can you do me a favor? Luke?"

After another long silence, Lucas returned, his voice low. "Max, I've got my police scanner on." Part of Lucas' assignment as an investigator was to monitor human police activity and make sure that crimes that were reported didn't have anything to do with vampires.

"So?"

"There's been a 911 call from Kyra's development. A woman reported that her sister's been murdered."

* * * *

Strangers surrounded Erica as she sat on the sofa waiting for the ambulance attendants to wheel Elena's body outside. Friends and neighbors of the woman Elena had become had gathered to lend support to the sister they'd never known she had.

"Ma'am? I have a few more questions to ask you about your sister." A South Windsor police detective loomed before her. Erica saw only a blue blur and the gleaming brass of a badge quickly flashed in front of her eyes.

"What do you need to know?"

"Did she have any enemies? Anyone you know of who might have wanted to hurt her? What about a boyfriend? Current or ex?"

Erica blinked, tried to focus on his face framed by thinning gray hair. "I don't know. She ... knew a lot of men, but I don't think she had a boyfriend."

"If you think of anyone who might have had a reason to be upset with her, you need to give me a call, all right?" The detective pushed a business card into her hand. Erica stared at it, unable to discern the name or the numbers printed on the card. She thought of Max and nodded absently.

A moment later the detective moved off, mumbling into his radio. Before Erica could process his questions further, a woman from next door put a steaming mug of herbal tea in Erica's hands and watched with watery blue eyes while she sipped it.

"I can't believe you're Kyra's twin sister," she said in a soothing, motherly voice as she settled herself next to Erica on the sofa. "You don't look anything alike."

"They're obviously fraternal," a man said. He sat on a kitchen chair that he'd brought into the living room. Erica didn't know his name.

"That's your picture on the mantle, isn't it?" the woman asked. Erica nodded and frowned into the tea. Someone said it was chamomile but it didn't taste right. She didn't care if it was drugged. In fact she hoped it was.

"How long did you know ... Kyra?" she asked. It bothered her to think that these strangers knew more about her sister than she did. It broke her heart to think she'd never know the truth.

"She's been here a few months. Always said hello," the man said. Erica raised her eyes just enough to catch a glimpse of him. He looked about fifty. His face was puffy and ruddy and he wore a stained T-shirt, but despite his gruff appearance, he seemed kind. He smiled ruefully at her. "She leant me money last month when my disability check was late. I hadn't paid her back yet, but I'll get the money to you ... I promise."

Erica shook her head. "You don't have to." Elena leant someone money? If she hadn't been dead inside she might have laughed.

"Ma'am ... we need you to sign this." One of the ambulance attendants came forward with a form on a clipboard and handed it to Erica.

She stared at the blurry page for a few seconds. "What is it?"

"It's the release. As your sister's next-of-kin you need to give permission for an autopsy."

The mug wobbled in Erica's hand and the nameless woman steadied it, easing it from her grasp. "I'll hold this, sweetheart. You take the pen."

Erica scribbled something that might have been her name and handed the clipboard back. The attendant gave her a sympathetic look and thanked her, then he and his partner took up the ends of the wheeled stretcher. The last Erica saw of her sister was the black bag that encased her as the attendants removed her body from the bungalow.

"Is there someone we can call for you?" the woman asked. She put the mug back in Erica's hand and patted her arm. "What about your parents?"

"They're dead." The words came out with surprising ease. Erica had always had trouble admitting it when people asked. It wasn't so much the grief, which had dulled over the decade since they'd been gone, but the reminder that she was alone, except for Elena. Her twin had never been much of a family. Now even she was gone.

"May they rest in peace," the man said. "What a terrible thing to have to tell them. In a way, they're lucky."

"They are," Erica agreed. They didn't have to see what had become of their daughters.

"I don't drive, otherwise I'd take you back home. Do you live near here?" the woman asked. "We can call you a cab."

"It's all right. I'm going to stay here a while and just ... I'll call someone later if I'm not up to driving myself home." It bothered Erica that she couldn't remember the woman's name, and that she didn't care enough to ask again.

"Are you sure? In this state, it's probably better if you weren't alone."

"She won't be alone. I'm here."

Erica looked up and the tea splashed on her leg when she saw Max. He swept into the room and tossed aside the dark cape he'd held over his head. Another man, blond and brash looking, followed him inside and did the same thing.

Erica dropped the mug and flew into Max's arms.

"Max! She's dead ... she's dead ..."

"Shh. It's going to be okay. Elena isn't dead," Max said after the other man escorted the neighbors to the door.

"What!?" Erica sat up and pushed away from Max. "I saw her, Max. They ravaged her. She was bleeding, all over ... they--"

"They turned her."

* * * *

The look of defeat on Erica's face lasted only a moment, but it was long enough to cut Max to the bone. In that one fatal second he saw it in her eyes, the utter disgust with his kind. Her sister was a monster now--or would be when she woke.

Erica had found her sister, and lost her in the same moment.

She sank to the couch, her eyes blank. "Are you sure?"

"Lucas checked it out. After you called 911, the call came up on his scanner. He made a few calls. You reported the bite marks, that tipped him off and he had our ambulance come for her."

She blinked and stared at him. "What do you mean, *your* ambulance?"

"She can't be taken to a hospital. They'll put the body in the morgue and she'll wake up in a metal drawer. We lose a lot of newly turned that way."

"Lose them?"

"They go ... insane."

Erica swallowed hard and clutched at him. Her fingers dug into his shoulders. "What's going to happen to her? What are you going to do with her?"

"They're taking her somewhere safe where she can wake up in her own time. Lucas will arrange to be with her. They were close."

"They were?"

"They were friends. She may hate him now. That'll be hard for him to adjust to."

"Why? Why would she hate him?"

"Erica ..." Max pulled her close and rubbed her back as she settled against him. "Female vampires are different. Elena may not be like you remember her."

"Max, I don't know *how* I remember her. I don't know who Elena is any-more." Tears ran down her cheeks and he brushed them away. "They changed her. They made her into Kyra--whoever that is. She's a feeder, who helps her neighbors and ... sleeps with vampires. That's not who Elena was."

"You think someone used mind control on her?" Max considered the possibility. If Benton Carlisle had been controlling Kyra, it didn't make sense that she would have been the fiercely independent woman he knew. Carlisle liked his feeders subservient. Kyra/Elena wouldn't fit the bill.

"It's the only thing that makes sense, Max. That's why Elena kept calling me. She remembered who she was--maybe just a little. She wanted to get free but they kept making her forget. That's why she wasn't at *The Underside*. She wasn't using me ... I know she wasn't."

Max wanted to believe her. He didn't want to think that Kyra was involved in some despicable plot to destroy Erica just for Benton Carlisle's entertainment. "I hope you're right. If that's the case, the mind control will be erased when she wakes up. She'll be Elena again ..." Or a new, hungrier version of Elena.

"I need to be with her, Max. When she wakes up."

"No. You don't." He shook his head. "That's not something you want to see."

"She needs me, Max. You can't keep me from her."

"It may not be safe for you to be anywhere near Elena right now. If Benton Carlisle is involved, you should stay away, because I think, after what happened to you last night, he may be after you."

"Why me? What could he want with me?"

"I don't know. But I intend to find out. Whatever he wants from you, Erica, he's not going to get it."

Chapter Seventeen

Erica paced back and forth in Kyra's living room while Max made phone calls. She'd grown tired of listening to his conversations and started straightening the place up to pass the time.

The other vampire, whom Max called Lucas, had come and gone and when he left, Erica followed him to the door and looked for rain. The sky was a beautiful clear blue and there wasn't a cloud anywhere.

When Max finished his last call, she met him in the kitchen.

"Where's the rain?"

He raised his eyebrows.

"When the neighbors left before, I thought I heard someone say it was raining. Am I going crazy?"

"No," he laughed. "It's a trick we use when we have to move around in the daylight. We use the capes and we give people around us the impression of a sudden downpour so they see someone huddled under an umbrella, or a newspaper. Whatever people do so they don't get wet."

"I guess you prefer days when it really is raining." She managed a faint smile.

He nodded. "It's not the daylight so much as direct sun. It burns--but not like in the movies. We won't burst into flame. We just start to blister. It would take hours to actually reduce a vampire to ash."

Erica held up her hand. "I don't really want to know." She sat wearily in a kitchen chair and leaned back as Max began rubbing her back. "Will she remember me? Will she feel pain?"

"Yes and yes. The change is difficult. It can be violent. If she wasn't expecting it ..."

"You don't think she *wanted* to be turned, do you?"

"Kyra never mentioned it. Some feeders, it's all they talk about. Their ultimate goal is to become one of us."

"But Kyra wasn't like that?" The name felt strange in her mouth, like she was talking about a stranger. Technically she was.

"She never mentioned wanting to be turned. At least not to me."

"How often did you feed from her?" Erica hated herself for

asking. Like a self-inflicted wound, the sudden pain of it shocked her. Her eyes stung.

"Don't do this, Erica." Max sounded tired. She looked up at him and saw something in his eyes that touched her heart. She'd wounded him, too.

"I want to know."

"We feed every two to three days by necessity. More if we have a regular feeder. I visited Kyra ... maybe three times a week."

"And you slept with her all those times?"

Max gave Erica a dark look. If she insisted on opening up wounds, he could be coaxed into adding salt to them. He saw it in her eyes. She wanted to hurt. She wanted him to inflict pain.

"Most of the time."

"Did you love her?"

"No."

"Does Lucas love her?"

Max laughed, but the sound was cold. "Lucas doesn't love."

"Why not?"

"Do you want to talk about Lucas or Kyra? What do you want to know, Erica? Do you want to know if I enjoyed it? Yes, I did. Do you want to know if Elena enjoyed it? She said she did. She was always ready, so I guess she liked it. Did I feed from her the night I met you? Yes. Why? Because I wanted you so badly that if you'd let me, I'd have drained you. I'd have turned you just to make you mine and keep you with me forever, because I never met anyone who made me feel the way you did. Did I have sex with Elena that night? No, because I couldn't imagine wanting anyone but you under me." Max rose and grabbed her shoulders. He shook her gently until she looked up at him. Hot tears spilled down her cheeks.

"Max ... tell me what to do. I don't know what to do about you." She sank into his arms and he held her. At first the contact was merely for comfort. He wanted to sooth her and calm her trembling but unbidden his body began to respond to her. Pressed against him, her heart beating against his chest, she felt like part of him. She was the part he'd been missing for so long.

He rocked her in his arms for a while longer, then tilted her chin up and kissed her. "Let me love you," he whispered against her ear. "Let me make you feel something besides pain."

She nodded and tilted her head farther back. He put his fingers against the fluttering pulse at the base of her throat, reveling in the rhythm of her body. He matched his phantom heartbeat to hers and, breath by breath, in unison, they moved together.

He led her to the living room. With all the shades drawn, it was night inside even though the sun was just about to set.

"Stand still," he told her. "Don't move." She obeyed and he began unbuttoning her blouse. She wore nothing underneath, which pleased him. He opened the shirt and let his hands roam. She sighed as he cupped her breasts and kissed them.

Next he opened her jeans. The snap and the zipper were quick, but the slide down her thighs was slow and sensuous. She obediently stepped out of the soft denim and kicked off her shoes. He pushed the open shirt from her shoulders and let it fall, then explored beneath the waistband of her panties. His fingers found her wet center and delved inside. She gasped at the gentle intrusion and closed her eyes.

"Take them off."

She didn't hesitate. He guided her to the couch and stretched her out beneath him. He remained dressed for a time, lazily stroking her, kissing her and tasting her until her breathing became shallow. A gentle movement of his hips against her produced a low moan. He swallowed the sound with a deep kiss and guided her hands so that she could begin to undress him.

He took her slowly, watching her eyes dilate as their bodies joined. She sighed through parted lips each time he moved within her. This time he used his abilities to hold her reaction steady, to keep the ache from building so high that she'd beg for release. He thrust slowly, gliding in and out so that she could focus only on the sensation of friction within her. When she arched against him, he wrapped his arms around her and held her until she settled back again, content to feel nothing but the increasing pressure of his strokes.

"Let me ..." she moaned. "Let me."

"No. I want to hold you like this forever. I don't want it to end."

She smiled through the haze of sensation. "We can't stay like this forever, but we can do it all again ... and again. Let me come and then we'll start over."

He kissed her and let her feel his tongue against hers. "You have to make another promise if you're to get what you want."

Her eyes widened. "Don't ask me for promises I can't keep."

"Then make a promise you will keep." He punctuated his question with a movement that brought her to the edge. She shuddered and clung to him, ready to dive. "Be with me, Erica. Stay with me. Don't make it end."

She looked up at him, her cheeks flushed with sexual heat, her lips parted. He moved again, a gentle thrust that brought him deep inside her. He felt the first pulse of her orgasm. “Love me.”

“I do!” She gasped the words out and rocked against him as she came. The rhythm of her body brought on his own release and he gave her the sensation of liquid heat spilling inside her. She moaned. “I love you, Max. I need you.”

He slammed into her, roused by her words. Even if she only meant it for the moment, for now it was enough. He clutched her to him and held her tightly as she shuddered against him. He breathed her name over and over until she slept, wrapped in his arms, sated.

* * * *

He left her in Kyra’s apartment, asleep on the couch. Before he rose and disengaged his body from hers, he’d whispered to her to wait for him and not to think about her sister.

He hated using mind control. Some vampires relied on it to get away with everything, even murder. The ability kept those around him from becoming suspicious about his true nature, but it made him feel dishonest to use it. A side effect of the change, it relied more on pheromones than mental powers, but either way, it was a form of manipulation. Necessary now and then perhaps, but dirty as far as Max was concerned.

With someone as stubborn as Erica, what choice did he have? The last thing he needed was for her to go looking for Elena and find something she still wasn’t ready to accept.

He wanted to find a way to make it easy for her.

Lucas didn’t answer his cell, but that didn’t mean much. Max knew where to find him.

Gregori Nachevik’s old estate had changed hands relatively easily when the balance of power in the vampire world shifted abruptly last December. When Gregori chose Jake Beaumont as his successor the entire vampire infrastructure in North America rattled. Rumor had it, there was a faction brewing that planned to remove the new king from power and a faction that remained dedicated to Gregori’s choice. It didn’t matter to Max either way, as long as he had an ally in power when he needed it. He planned to make sure Jake Beaumont was that ally.

The gothic mansion had a modern flair, bright lights, and cleaner lines than before. The spiked wrought iron rails that had adorned the parapets and widow’s walks when Gregori ruled now lined a perennial garden and gave purchase to flowering vines.

Fresh blood in the vampire world meant lots of changes but not all of them were good.

A distinguished older man in a dark suit met Max at the front door. He bowed as Max climbed the front steps.

"Mr. Hart. Mr. Vitale told us to expect you this evening."

"Is Mr. Beaumont here? I'd like to speak to him as well, if I may."

"Not this evening, sir. Come inside. You can leave him a message." The butler stood aside to allow Max to step into the huge foyer. Max stood in the center of the room for a second, looking up at the enormous chandelier dangling overhead. The place seemed so different since his last visit, larger somehow and just a shade more inviting.

"I'll see Mr. Vitale," he said. "And I'd like to leave a message for Mr. Beaumont."

"Very good, sir. This way."

The man gestured to the dark paneled wall and a hidden door slid open at his approach. A narrow, dark corridor stretched beyond. Max eyed the butler skeptically. The lower levels of the mansion had always been reserved for the darker aspects of Gregori's world. He had to wonder how they were now being used.

The man bowed. "Mr. Vitale is in the room at the end of the corridor."

"Thank you."

Max entered the hallway and crossed cautiously to the far door. He knocked.

"Yeah?"

Max opened the door and peered inside. Candlelight illuminated the small room beyond. A round bed draped in red satin dominated the room. As Max entered, Lucas rolled to the edge of the bed. He gave a sardonic look as he pulled the blood red sheet around him.

A sleek, dark head bobbed up from the nest of pillows at the top of the bed. Kyra grinned at Max as she arched languidly to a sitting position, licking her newly acquired fangs.

"I'm ready for more," she purred. "How about you, Max? Come let me show you the new me."

Max's gaze bounced from Kyra to Lucas and back as his partner began collecting discarded clothes from the floor.

"I guess I don't have to ask if Kyra woke up all right," he said. Thoughts of Erica plagued him. While she worried and mourned for her sister, Lucas was welcoming Kyra into the vampire fold with a good fuck.

"I'm great!" Kyra slithered from the bed and padded naked across the room. She sidled against him and draped her arms around his neck. He avoided her gaze, too similar to Erica's, and disengaged her slender fingers from his collar.

"So this was planned. Benton Carlisle turned you by request."

She nodded, gave him a quirky grin that showed her fangs. "He had permission, too. He did it to save me from myself. Poor messed up Elena--drowning in booze and strung out on drugs. He offered me a new life."

"I've never seen you drunk or stoned." Max crossed his arms over his chest, kept his gaze leveled at a spot on the wall above the bed while Lucas yanked on his jeans and shirt. Kyra accepted the discarded sheet and draped it artfully over her thin frame.

"Of course not. I had to get clean first. Now, I can stay clean. I don't need all that stuff anymore."

"Didn't it occur to you that if you could kick your habits as a human, you didn't need to be turned?"

Kyra laughed. "No. Do you know how many times I tried? How many times I swore to Ricki that I'd give it up, I'd let her sign me into some rehab where some half-assed counselor would tell me my problems stemmed from the fact that I didn't get a pony for my seventh birthday? And that I need to 'own' my addictions in order to conquer them? Just the thought of spending twelve weeks in a 'share circle' sent me running for a fix, or a drink. I don't need that anymore. All I need is a ripe feeder." She turned a sultry grin toward Lucas. "Can you get me another one, Luke? I'm hungry again already."

"What about Erica? Why did you drag her into this?"

Kyra's laugh was ice cold. She shrugged her pale shoulders and reached for the door but he blocked her path. When she looked up at him, he saw vampire in her eyes.

"Erica will do anything for me. If you know her, you've seen that already." Kyra leaned toward Max again and she breathed in the warm essence of Erica that lingered on his skin. "Mmm. You *do* know her, don't you? She'll do whatever she has to in order to see that I get what she thinks I need."

Max grabbed her wrist and twisted. Kyra snarled, fangs extended. Lucas came up behind her, trapping her shoulders with his massive hands. "What do you mean, she'll do anything she has to do?"

"Whatever Benton Carlisle expects of her. He owns her now. In exchange for turning me, I gave him Erica."

Chapter Eighteen

Erica floated to consciousness with the eerie awareness of a presence above her.

"Max?" His name left her lips on a contented sigh. She stretched and reached toward the blurry figure standing near the couch.

"He's not here, little one. He left you alone ... unprotected."

Erica struggled to fit a name to the cooing, feminine voice. "Vera?"

"Yes, it's me. I've come to take you home."

"Home?" Erica blinked, but her blurry vision cleared only marginally. She felt heavy and warm, weighted into the soft cushions of her sister's couch by an invisible force.

Vera hovered above her, her lovely features distended and indistinct.

"What's happening to me?" Erica's question came out breathless. She was too tired to force the words out.

"You're just resting now, my sweet. When you wake up again, you'll feel better, stronger. You'll be ready to begin your new life."

Somewhere in her foggy brain, a warning bell sounded. Panic slithered through her ribcage and clutched at her lungs. Where was Max? Why had he left her?

"Please ... don't turn me," she said as her leaden eyelids drifted closed. She felt Vera's cool fingers on her forehead, brushing strands of hair from her face. A moment later all sensation left her body and she drifted into blackness.

* * * *

"We're going to need more backup," Lucas said as Max turned off the highway and headed into the rich section of town. Here, the mansions sat well back on manicured lawns and iron gates blocked the entrances to rolling driveways. Benton Carlisle's estate loomed into view before Max answered.

"If we go in with a posse, who knows what Carlisle will do to Erica. We've got our insurance policy. That's enough for now." Max jerked his thumb toward the back seat where Kyra lay unconscious, he wrists bound behind her with strips of crimson bed sheet.

She'd put up quite a struggle when Max had suggested she come with them to retrieve her sister. Knocking her out hadn't been easy and Lucas had vibrant scratches across his chest and jaw to prove it.

"Do you think Carlisle cares enough about Kyra to bargain for her?"

Max glanced at Lucas as he turned the car off the main street to circle around to the back of Carlisle's property.

"I don't think he gives a crap about Kyra. But I think he'll care about getting a chance to keep all this secret from Beaumont. An even trade--his secret for Erica's life."

"Guys like Carlisle don't like compromise." There was a dangerous glint in Lucas' eyes and Max remembered why this man was his closest friend.

"But we're going to make him like it."

* * * *

Erica awoke gasping. She clutched at her neck searching for new bite marks but found none. She struggled to sit up and take in her surroundings. The dark paneled walls seemed to close in on her and the cloying smell of cinnamon and clove drifted from the dozen or so red candles that adorned the dark wood tables and shelves that decorated the room.

She lay on a narrow bed, swathed in white sheets. Leather-covered handcuffs hung from the high brass bedposts and across the room other chains and cuffs dangled from pegs on the walls.

This was Benton Carlisle's home and it was just as she'd suspected. Nevertheless the décor in the tiny room sent chills through her.

She rose from the bed, grateful to find her clothing intact, and tried the door.

Of course it was locked. Why would she have suspected otherwise?

Panic tickled the back of her throat. She swallowed the strange sensation and tried to take deep, calming breaths.

She was practically hyperventilating when the door finally opened.

Benton Carlisle stood in the doorway. He wore a modest, dark suit and a power tie. He leaned against the door jam in a casual stance and adjusted the diamond cufflink in his right sleeve.

"How are you feeling?" He sounded as if he were speaking to a coworker rather than a captive.

"Scared shitless," Erica replied. Why lie? False bravado would get her nowhere.

Carlisle laughed, flashing fang for an instant. "My dear, I love your honesty. Of course you're scared. But you have no reason to be. I have no intention of mistreating you. I promise."

"Can I get that in writing?" Erica inched her way backward toward the bed as she spoke, her eyes on Carlisle. His wide shoulders filled the doorway, leaving no room to slip past him.

A glowing candle full of molten wax flickered inches from her fingertips. She could hurt him, distract him and run. Something inside her turned cold with the realization that she probably wouldn't leave the building alive, but it didn't matter. As long as she didn't submit to him, didn't allow him to win. Death would be a reward at this point.

"I could most certainly put all my promises in writing. If that would ease your fears. I would be more than happy to solidify an arrangement with you and I guarantee it's one you'll be satisfied with."

"I doubt it."

"Would you care to talk to Vera? She's quite pleased with the relationship we share. She enjoys a wonderful life, and you can, too."

"Do I have a choice? Waking up here after passing out at my sister's house sort of gives me the idea that I don't get a say in the matter."

"If you're willing to negotiate terms with me, my dear, you'll be surprised how many choices you have." Carlisle sobered and his dark eyes bored into hers.

"What's to negotiate? Why am I here after all? You want to own me. You can't."

Carlisle took one step forward into the room and Erica backed up. Her fingers rested on the edge of the bedside table behind her, glided toward a fat red pillar of dripping wax.

"Let's talk about what I want. And what you want. You want your beloved sister to be happy, don't you?" The tone of his voice changed then, and Erica's flesh tingled uncomfortably.

"You turned Elena. She couldn't have wanted that."

"Of course she did. Begged for it, in fact. I wouldn't have obliged her under normal circumstances. She was a junkie. Not worthy of being a feeder and certainly not worthy of being a vampire. I had her thrown out of *After Dark* one night--about six months ago. Vera felt sorry for her so we gave her bus fare and followed her to make sure she actually got on the bus. She didn't--you came to get her."

"I remember. That night was the first time she talked seriously about joining AA. She almost convinced me that she wanted to sober up for good." Almost, Erica thought. *Was I already too jaded to believe her?*

"She did want to. She wanted to be part of this world. I told her she had to straighten herself out or no vampire would want her."

"What does this have to do with me?"

"I saw you that night. You wore a gray herringbone suit and a white blouse. You had your hair up and your collar unbuttoned showing off that beautiful neck. I've been watching you since then." Carlisle's smile made Erica queasy. She heard the candle crackle behind her and tried not to react.

"When Kyra came back to us, sober and eager to please, I asked her about you and she told me who you were. She said you were the good twin. The responsible sister with a firm grip on reality and normal life, a boring job and a knack for being there when she needed you. I told her how she could kick her addictions permanently and take away all the pain, the meaningless desire to hurt herself and punish you for being better than her."

"I'm not better than her--"

Carlisle held up one finger as if scolding an errant student. "Yes you are! And Kyra knew that her whole life. You were the pretty one. She always hated that you didn't look exactly alike. She wanted the blonde hair, the healthy glow. She was always the thin, pale one. You were smarter, more popular, stronger. She loved you so much--and she hated you. She hated herself for wishing she was better than you."

"Stop it! Stop it!" Erica fought the urge to cover her ears and drown out his words. "How do you know so much about my sister? How do you know things I don't?"

"I know because she wasn't afraid to tell me. I offered her something you couldn't. An end to her problems."

"That's all I ever did! I tried for years to get her help, to give her a reason to want to get better. And then you came along and offered to make her into a vampire and you took it all away over night." A bout of shivering wracked Erica's body. She inched closer to the candle flame.

"Yes. We took away your purpose. I'm sorry for that. Elena was your project for half your life. Fixing her was your ... career, for lack of a better term."

"My curse."

"Yes! Exactly. That's over now. The curse is lifted. Elena is gone and all her problems are gone, too. She's become something else. Something invincible and immortal. In a way, you made that possible."

Erica rolled her eyes. Her sarcastic laugh made Carlisle smile. "How's that? By letting her sell me to you? By becoming your playmate?"

"How bad would that be? The humans who live in the vampire world fare well. You'd have everything. You could move freely in Kyra's world and maybe even get to know the person she's become."

"She's become a slave trader. I have no desire to know her."

"What *do* you desire? Name it."

"Nothing you have to offer."

Carlisle shook his head at her vehement response. His right foot slid forward and panic lanced through Erica's chest again. Her throat closed as her fingers found the soft, warm cylinder of wax.

Carlisle grinned, bearing his fangs and in that instant Erica hurled the candle at his face.

Chapter Nineteen

Benton Carlisle's scream echoed through the hallway beyond the candlelit room. Full of rage more than pain, it sliced through Erica's fear. Galvanized, she ran by him as he doubled over and tried to claw the hardening wax off his face. She bolted into the hallway and up a flight of dark stairs.

She heard him snarling and pounding after her as she flung herself through another hallway on the next level. She ran, checking door after door until one flew open at her touch.

She screamed and backed up as a thin body lurched toward her. Elena stumbled through the door, her eyes wild, her lips parted to show bone white fangs.

It took a moment for Erica to realize her sister's arms were bound behind her back and that the shadowy form behind her was Max.

"Carlisle's coming! We have to--" Elena's screech cut her off.

Erica whirled around, practically falling into Max's arms as Carlisle exploded into the hallway. He reached around Erica and grabbed Elena by the arm, yanking her across the hall. They crashed together into the far wall and while Elena struggled against him, Carlisle wrapped one hand around her slender throat.

* * * *

It had been decades since Max had felt anything like the emotion that coursed through him when Erica fell into his arms. The relief combined with something else he thought he would never need or want to experience again. A possessiveness laced with fear consumed him. She was his--safe in his arms again. He wouldn't lose her, wouldn't leave her ever again.

Behind him, Lucas struggled with a captive Vera Nighe. Carlisle's concubine cried and cursed when Max produced a wooden stake and brandished it at her master.

"It doesn't have to be this way, Carlisle," Max said, his eyes on Kyra. Carlisle's thick fingers dug into Kyra's flesh and blood welled between them.

Coppery sparks danced in her eyes and she hissed through her clenched teeth. "Ricki, please don't let him kill me ..."

"Do you want to watch your sister die, Erica? Call off your dogs and I'll let her live."

"Get behind me!" Max tried to push Erica behind him, and Lucas reached forward to grab her but she twisted out of his grasp.

"Don't take another step," Carlisle warned. "I'll rip her throat out." He squeezed harder and Kyra sobbed.

"Ricki!"

"That's no way to kill a vampire," Erica said. She broke from Max's embrace and tore the stake from his hand in one fluid motion. She shoved the razor sharp point at Carlisle and he backed up--just a breath, but enough to show his fear. His back touched the wall behind him.

"She said you'd do anything for her." He taunted Erica, but his eyes shifted back and forth, measuring, plotting. Behind Max, Lucas dropped Vera. She fell and lay sobbing at his feet.

"Don't let her kill him, please!"

Max ignored Vera. He might stop Erica from killing Kyra, but not Carlisle. She lunged forward again and the other vampire twisted out of her way. Kyra screamed, a thin, tortured sound. Blood ran down her chest and spread in a crimson stain on the tank top she wore.

Any wound Carlisle inflicted would heal, another gift of the change, but that didn't stop her from feeling the pain, raw and deep and so much more intense now with her heightened vampire senses.

The look in her eyes told Max this was something Kyra hadn't bargained for and for the briefest instant, he pitied her.

"I'll tear her head off--that will kill her." Carlisle's threats came in ragged gasps. "You had a chance. You could have had everything, could have saved Elena like you always wanted to."

"She's beyond saving now." Erica's voice was steel, a cold blade meant for her sister, but Max felt it, too. Her message was clear. No redemption for a vampire.

Carlisle growled and tore at Kyra's pale flesh. Her scream died on bloody lips as she sank to the floor clutching her throat. Max dove for Carlisle. With Elena out of the way, Erica was his next target. But before he could pull her to safety, Erica surged forward and rammed the tip of the stake into Carlisle's chest.

* * * *

She'd expected more resistance. The ease with which the stake plunged through Benton Carlisle's chest and into his lifeless heart surprised her. The shock and horror in his eyes did not. He hadn't expected it from her.

She held the stake in trembling hands, keeping it embedded in his ribcage as his large body sank to the floor next to Elena. He was dust before his head hit the floor--nothing more than a mottled brown skull and a pile of brittle bone fragments.

Vera screamed.

Erica dropped the stake and turned slowly. Framed in the open doorway, Lucas caught Vera and held her back. She sobbed and cursed, clawing at him to get to Erica, but Max blocked her path.

When Erica swayed, he caught her and she sagged against him, wishing she could feel his heartbeat beneath her palms.

"It's all right, it's all right," he whispered against her forehead. He spread his hands against her back and she felt the welcome illusion of warmth.

A whimper from Vera drew their attention, and Lucas dragged her back away from the scene of her lover's death. When Erica glanced back, Carlisle's feeder hung limp in Lucas' arms.

"She'll sleep for a while," Lucas said as he lowered Vera to the floor. "When she wakes up, she won't remember what happened here."

Erica broke reluctantly from Max's arms and dropped to her

knees in front of her sister. Elena's eyes were huge--like those of a wounded animal. They'd taken on a rusty hue, like old blood. She snarled when Erica reached for her and scrabbled backward.

"Help her!" Erica reached for Max. She glanced back at him, searching his eyes. "What can we do for her?"

He took Erica's shoulders in his hands and guided her away from Elena. "She'll recover. Dead flesh doesn't exactly heal, but it regenerates," he said. "She's feeling the pain now, nothing else. She doesn't know you."

"Her throat--"

"She'll be all right."

Lucas shouldered into the hallway and knelt beside Elena. She hissed at him and the sound became a pitiful sob. Erica shuddered when Elena's bloody hands dropped limply from her wound. Her head fell back as Lucas lifted her in his arms. "I'll take care of her," he said. "You two, go home."

"I can't leave her."

Max hushed Erica's protest and crushed her to him again. She clung, squeezing her eyes shut to block out the macabre image of Carlisle's dusty bones mixed with Elena's blood.

"What happens now?" she asked as Max guided her through the door. She spared a glance at Vera, crumpled on the floor, blissfully unconscious.

"Nothing. Lucas and I will take care of it." His laugh was hollow, forced. His brittle smile made her heart ache. She'd killed one of his kind ... without thought or remorse. Did he see it as self-defense or murder? Did he think she could do the same to him just as easily?

"I don't want to go home," she said.

"Where do you want me to take you?"

She met his gaze, and hoped he understood that she didn't see him as a monster. "Your place."

* * * *

More than a century had passed since the last time Max's heart had pounded in anticipation, or stuttered in fear. Despite the intervening years, though, he hadn't forgotten the sensation.

Memories of past pain plagued him now as he led Erica up the stairs to his apartment. Through their silent car ride across town, he'd tried to figure out why she didn't want to go home. He decided finally, it had to be because she didn't want him in her home, in her life anymore. She could leave him here, walk away from the horrific world he inhabited and be done with him, done with her sister once and for all.

When he unlocked the door and showed her inside, she hesitated then took his hand and drew him in with her. The look in her eyes confused him, a sultry tease mixed with sadness. Did she want him, or want to be rid of him? She stepped into his embrace and he buried his face in her neck, not for blood, but to feed the empty hollow in his chest. She felt warm and pliant in his arms and the sensation chased away the ache that thoughts of losing her forever had produced.

She drew him forward into the apartment, still wrapped in his arms, and he toed the door shut behind them.

"I'm sorry for the things I said to Carlisle--not for him, but for you." The words came out in a rush when she finally pulled back to meet his gaze.

"You don't have to apologize." His faint smile faded as he searched her earnest gaze. He molded her hips with his hands and drew her toward him. "Did he hurt you?"

She raised a finger to his lips and her touch was like fire. "He didn't do anything to me. He would have ..."

Max shook his head to clear away the dark thoughts. If Carlisle wasn't dead--he might have vowed to hunt him down and drive a stake into his chest just because he'd touched Erica--just because he'd wanted her.

She ducked her head and looked up at him from under lowered lashes. "I need you, Max. Make love to me."

He felt something then, something akin to life. She needed him. Never as much as he needed her, but the degree didn't matter. It wasn't over for them. Maybe it had only just begun.

With a dark look, he led her to his bedroom.

* * * *

Erica sank down onto the hunter green sheets of Max's bed and watched him as he moved across the room. The sparse décor faded from view and she saw only his eyes, smoldering, delving into her. The pressure of his gaze made her ache.

"Don't move," he said when she arched invitingly. She straightened and lay still but the simple command caused a pulsing in the sensitive flesh between her thighs. She bit her bottom lip against the need to slither out of her clothes for him.

As she watched him unbutton his shirt and shrug out of it, she wondered if he was using his mind control on her. The events of the day faded rapidly from her consciousness. The hurt, the fear all drained away leaving her feeling light, but far from empty.

Her gaze dropped to his hands as they unfastened his belt and the button of his pants.

A moment later he stood naked beside the bed. His eyes went dark like the midnight sky.

"Max ..." She forced herself not to reach for him, but her hands ached from the need to touch the smooth muscles of his arms and the dark hair that arrowed down his chest.

"Who do you want?" he asked, holding her motionless with his gaze. "Who do you want inside you? A man or a vampire?"

She held her breath for a moment and wished she could answer without words, but he had to hear it. He had to know she loved him, regardless of what he was.

"I want you," she said. "I don't belong to a vampire. I belong to Max Hart."

* * * *

The words didn't mean as much as the look in her eyes. Her husky whisper drove Max over the edge. He'd never wanted anyone, anything more than he wanted Erica to love him. He'd never felt the blood lust as strongly as he felt his need for her.

Driven by her words, he undressed her, exposing her soft skin inch by inch until she lay naked beneath him. Feather–light touches of his fingertips had left her near the edge already. He saw the anticipation in her eyes, and in her pebbled flesh, her tight nipples and the taut muscles of her belly.

He spread her legs with one hand, feeling the wet heat of her. The vampire in him wanted to play with his prize, to tease her until she begged for it hot and hard. The vampire wanted to taste her blood and drink in the luscious crimson drops of her desire until there was nothing left.

The man wanted to caress her until she came against his fingertips, to kiss her blind and sink into her slowly until he felt her pulse beat around him.

The man won out. He didn't drink from her, though she asked him to. He didn't ravage her, though she'd have been willing. He loved her until she shuddered in his arms and he let her feel him come inside her and fill her with his need.

Then he let her sleep.

When she awoke, she gave him her throat. She fed him with her body and her soul and he knew that a vampire didn't own her. She owned him.

The End

ETERNITY

Marie Morin

Dedication:

This one's for my fan, Shirley S, with apologies up front for any and all errors you may find here. I've never been to Great Britain except through books and my imagination, but I've done my best to be as accurate as possible and to portray the land of my forefathers with the affection and affinity I feel for it.

Chapter One

Joy filled Emily Hendrick's heart to overflowing. She had realized her dream. It had taken every penny of her inheritance and her savings. She had had to sell everything of any value she owned, and she was now in hock up to her eyeballs, but she was the proud new owner of a real Scottish castle.

Her joy sustained her throughout the terrifying flight from Georgia to NY and from there to England. Not that either leg of the trip was particularly eventful, but it was enough, in Emily's opinion, to strap her ass to a missile and trust that 'manmade' would hold together long enough to get where she was going, even if not for the added threat of lunatics roaming the world with nothing but death and destruction on their minds.

Her exultation not only sustained her through customs and the headache of renting a car--when her English wasn't exactly English--and piling her few belongings into it, her excitement grew as she drove out of Heathrow Airport and headed north.

It was disorienting to find herself on the 'wrong' side of the road whenever she managed to drag her mind, and her gaze, from the pictures lying beside her on the seat, but then she would remember, before she could cause a multiple car pile up, that she was *supposed* to be on the wrong side of the road.

"Left, left, left!" she muttered, trying to calm her wildly palpitating heart.

Her excitement diminished just a tad when she finally arrived at the village nearest her castle and discovered the land agent had already gone home for the evening. Curbing her impatience with an effort, Emily found lodging for the night and settled to wait one more night before she could see her beautiful baby.

She was pacing the cobblestones in front of Gregory MacGregor's office when he arrived the following morning. He was an older man, gray hair streaking his red beard and the hair that grew on his head like a monk's tonsure. "Mr. MacGregor?"

He turned from his door and looked her over again. "Aye."

Emily smiled with relief, surging forward. "I'm Emily Hendricks."

He frowned, as if trying to figure out why the name sounded familiar, then finally grinned. "The Yank?"

"Oh, I'm not a Yankee," Emily corrected him. "I'm from Georgia."

He looked disconcerted. "Russia?"

Emily gaped at him blankly. "No. In the United States. I'm the one that bought Castle MacKissack?"

He chuckled, nodding. "Oh, to be sure! Ms. Hendricks. I was expectin' ye yesterday." He unlocked his door and pushed it open. "Tha accent threw me fer just a bit. You're not a Yank, then?"

Deciding she really didn't want to try to explain, Emily ignored the question, following him into his office. "Actually, I did arrive yesterday, but you were already gone for the day. I had to spend the night at the ... uh ... inn." She watched him as he moved about the cramped office. "I'm really anxious to get out to the castle."

"Ye'll be wantin' ta take care of the paperwork before tha'?"

"Oh. Sure. I thought everything was already taken care of?"

He moved to a filing cabinet, flipped through a couple of folders and finally pulled one out and returned to his desk. "Just a couple more."

Emily glanced over the papers cursorily and signed her name at the bottom of each.

"Well, now, we've got everything in order now, I believe," he said, sounding somewhat relieved. "I'll just lock up an' take ye out fer a tour."

Emily frowned, but finally merely shrugged and went out to wait in the car. The pictures that she'd been sent of her castle were once more on the seat beside her and she picked them up, studying them lovingly while she waited.

The whining toot of a foreign horn jogged her out of her absorption and she looked up to see that Mr. MacGregor had pulled his car along side the one she was driving. He said something to her, but she didn't catch it. Smiling and nodding anyway, she started her car and turned it to follow him.

The accents were giving her more problems than she'd anticipated. In some ways it was rather like the U.S.--concentrate. Every few miles you encountered a slightly, or vastly, different accent. In the states, the accents usually didn't vary that much until you crossed a state line. It made it worse that they didn't seem to be having any easier time understanding her than the other way around. She had heard British accents that were really similar to her own, but that didn't seem to be the case in this particular area.

She shook it off. She'd get used to it after a while and, hopefully, they'd get used to her accent, too.

She was so busy admiring the countryside she almost rear ended Mr. MacGregor's car when he swerved and made an abrupt turn between two crumbling gates. She glanced at the gates curiously, but she was still rattled from the near miss and didn't get much of a look at them.

Almost as soon as they were through the gate, the narrow road began to curve and climb. The hair pin curves made it impossible to look anywhere except at the road and Emily kept a wary eye on the bumper of Mr. MacGregor's car. When he swerved off the road abruptly and parked the car Emily thought he'd run off the road. He got out after a moment, however, motioning to her, and she pulled off as well, glancing at the ruin casting its shadow over the patch of grass where they'd parked.

She supposed he'd decided to show her some of the sights along the road, but she really wasn't interested in sight-seeing at the moment. Sighing, she got out of the car.

He grinned at her, spreading his arms expansively. "An' here we are."

"Where?"

"The Castle MacKissack, lass."

Emily turned in a circle, looking out over the fields and finally faced the stone ruin. It looked vaguely familiar and a strange little knot formed in the pit of her stomach.

Narrowing her eyes against the sunlight that was spilling around the crumbling heap of stones and, in some places, through, she studied the wide ditch that curved around the front. A rusty set of bedsprings lay half in and half out of the muck at the bottom of the ditch. There was an abandoned appliance, as well, that looked like it might have been a stove, or possibly a washing machine. Wheels, tires, and an assortment of unidentifiable objects littered the ditch.

A narrow--very narrow--bridge spanned the ditch. It might have been wide enough for a car but looked barely wider than a walkway.

Feeling a wave of nausea wash over her, Emily opened the car door, leaned inside and grabbed the small stack of pictures from the seat. When she'd emerged once more, she shuffled through them and stared down at the western facade and 'main entrance.'

It bore an uncanny resemblance to the ruin she was staring at--except for the fact that there was water in the moat, instead of cast off belongings.

"Ahh, but she's a sight, ain't she?" Mr. MacGregor said, beaming at her.

Emily merely stared at him. "This isn't ... this isn't ... You're not saying...." She couldn't seem to get the words out of her mouth.

He nodded happily. "Speechless, are ye? It tis a sight! O' course this is just a minor holding of the clan MacKissack. Didn't see much action a'tall, but 'tis as fine a specimen of the mid ta late medieval period as there is standin' today."

"So ... where's my castle? Is it close to here?"

He turned and looked her over as if she was crazy. "Aye. Yer standin' in it's shadow, lass."

Emily shook her head. "No." She stabbed a finger at the picture she held in one trembling hand. "This is *my* castle."

Frowning, he took the photo from her and looked it over. "Aye, that's the photos I sent ye."

Emily gaped at him, feeling a twinge of outrage beginning to work its way up through her shock and dismay. "But ... But .... When were these photos taken?"

He frowned, scratching his head thoughtfully. "Well ... I couldn't say. I'm thinkin' probably after the first great war, ta be sure."

"What war? The Norman Conquest?"

He chuckled at her joke. "Nay. It was na' here then. Me grandfather had a man up from London ta take the pictures."

"Your Grandfather!" Emily gasped disbelievingly.

"Aye. They're not as recent as I would've liked, but there didn't seem much sense in paying a photographer ta come so far when I found them."

Emily couldn't seem to do anything but gape at him, her mouth working like a fish that had suddenly found itself yanked from the stream.

"Come on then. I'll show ye around. I know yer anxious ta see it."

The tour didn't help Emily's feelings much. According to the brochure she'd gotten, the castle had been 'modernized.' The Scottish idea of modern didn't coincide with her own. In the center of each of the ten cavernous rooms the small castle boasted, a cord had been dropped from the ceiling. A bare socket and bulb dangled at the end. Theoretically, these were turned off and on by the string hanging down from the receptacle, but the string was rotted and broke when Mr. MacGregor tugged on them.

Shrugging, he dragged a flashlight from his pocket, flipped it on and flashed it around the room. "The generator's not on anyway."

"Generator?" Emily asked faintly.

"Aye. The power company run lines out this way, but the storm took them out a few years ago and they've not been ta put them up again."

"How many years ago?"

He scratched his head, frowning. "That would've been sometime along '75, I'm thinking."

"Nineteen seventy five? Or seventeen seventy five?"

He chuckled. "It's na' been so long ago as tha'. I'm sure there'll be no problem gettin' them up an' goin' again now tha' ye'll be fixin' the place up."

Seeing her glum expression, he urged her toward the hallway and pushed a door open about halfway down. "In door plumbing."

Emily didn't go in. She peered at the ancient bathroom from the hall.

"O'course it'll not be workin' without the generator ta pump the water," he added after a few moments.

The remainder of the tour passed like a nightmare. Emily felt as if she was struggling to run through a thick, gray fog, being chased by something unidentifiable.

When they'd left the castle and returned to the cars, Mr. MacGregor studied her curiously for several moments.

"There's no phone, I suppose," Emily managed to say around the knot of misery in her throat.

"Nay. Went down with the power lines," he said almost cheerfully.

She looked at him, fighting the urge to wrap her fingers around his throat and squeeze until his eyeballs popped from their sockets.

"I'm thinkin' a cell phone might work, but then again, maybe not."

"It doesn't matter since I don't have one," Emily said through gritted teeth.

He nodded, scratched his head.

"Well, I'll be off then."

Emily merely stared at him, thinking that it was a very good thing she didn't have a gun. Otherwise, she'd have been tempted to shoot him and toss his body into the ditch/moat with the rest of the garbage that cluttered it. "I don't suppose you know somebody that could fix the generator?"

He grinned. "Me nephew, Angus, is a fair hand at mechanics."

Emily turned to stare at her white elephant. "And maybe you could give the power company and phone company a call and put in an order for me?"

"Sure. I'd be happy ta. If ye like, I'll ask around about some workmen ta give ye a hand."

"That would be so helpful," Emily said, gritting her teeth at him in a parody of a smile.

His brows rose, but finally he nodded, tipped his hat at her and climbed back in his car.

She watched him until his car disappeared, wishing there was a cliff between Castle MacKissack and town that he could drive off of.

Gloom settled over her once he'd disappeared. Resisting the urge to simply flop down on the ground and squall, Emily got back into her car and began to study the brochure and pictures.

There it was, the print small, but readable. 'Photos taken around 1940.'

She supposed she'd noticed the caption, but she didn't really remember it, maybe because she had assumed that the castle would be taken care of, maintained as it had been in the photos? Or, maybe, because she'd been living in a dream world ever since she'd first set eyes on the advertisement?

Sighing, she studied her castle for a while.

Finally, realizing that she was going to have to stay in the thing, at least until she could find out if there was anyway she could get out of the deal and get her money back, she climbed out of the car and began lugging her belongings inside.

She was wandering through the echoing halls trying to do a mental inventory of everything that needed to be done when Angus MacGregor showed up. Relieved, she sent him to have a look at the generator and give her an estimate on what it would take to get it going.

She was at the top of the castle, staring into the distance, when he found her again. His suggestion was that she simply scrap it and buy a new one, but he finally agreed to see if he could jury-rig it for her and get it going.

She would've far preferred simply abandoning the place and staying at the inn, but she couldn't really afford to. Stiffening her spine, she picked her way carefully back down the narrow, twisting stair that led to the tower and found the 'master's apartment.'

She'd bought the place lock, stock and barrel. The furnishings that came with it were from the 1700's, which had delighted her when she'd read it. In actuality, the pieces weren't in terribly good condition, but she supposed they could be cleaned up and restored.

So much for the idea of setting up a tourist bed and breakfast to help her pay for the place.

Shrugging off her morbid thoughts, she moved to the windows. They'd been painted closed, but fortunately the paint was cracked and peeling. She managed to get one of the windows open about two inches and another almost halfway up before it stuck.

She was lucky there was any glass windows in the place. The glass looked like it dated back to the 1700's, too. The panes let in daylight, but they were blurry, making it impossible to get much of a view.

What she mostly needed, she finally decided, was cleaning supplies. The place was coated in dust and cobwebs. The fabrics around the room were mostly rotted, but she'd brought some household linens. If the mattress on the bed wasn't rotted, too, she might be able to sleep if she could just clean the place up a bit.

The mattress, she discovered when she'd stripped the bed, was actually almost modern. It couldn't be more than fifty or sixty years old. There were a few holes in it and she suspected mice had made them, but after testing the bed experimentally she decided it would hold her weight without collapsing.

The bulb over her head winked a couple of times and finally brightened.

Emily stared at it, feeling her first upsurge of hopefulness since she'd arrived.

It went out again.

Sighing, she went back to cleaning.

A voice echoed hollowly down the hallway like the wail of someone long dead and Emily jumped.

"Miz Hendricks?"

Relieved when she realized it was Angus MacGregor, Emily put a hand to her pounding heart. "Up here!"

She met him in the hallway near the main stairs. He was grinning triumphantly. "I got it goin'."

"You did? But the light went out again."

He frowned, following her as she led him back to the room. After staring at it for several moments, he looked around and finally dragged a chair across the floor. Standing on it, he tested the bulb, twisting it first one way and then the other. He almost fell off the chair when it came on.

"It was just loose. It looks like it's about as old as me uncle though, so you'll be wantin' ta get some more."

He climbed down again. "If ye'll follow me ta the dungeon, I'll show ye how ta turn the generator off and on."

"Dungeon?" Emily echoed faintly.

"Aye. I guess you'd be callin' it a cellar now, but that's wha' it was built for, ta keep prisoners back in the old days."

Dismissing that, Emily focused on the real issue. "Can't I just leave the generator running?"

"It only holds enough fuel fer a few hours. I meant ta tell ye, ye'll want ta be gettin' a supply ta hold ye awhile."

"It figures," Emily muttered, following him down the stairs and into the 'modern kitchen.'

Picking up a flashlight, he opened a door at the far side.

"There aren't any lights down there?"

He shrugged. "None that I seen."

"This just keeps getting better and better," Emily muttered, following him down the steep stairs.

It felt like entering a cave. Beyond the narrow beam of the flashlight, there was nothing but darkness so profound it almost seemed solid. To her relief, she discovered the generator was near the foot of the stairs.

Squatting beside the generator, MacGregor pointed to a couple of valves and switches. After taking her through the process a couple of times and watching to make sure she had the hang of it, he stood up once more, fanning the beam of the flashlight around. "You'd think they would've ... ahh. There's a light, right enough. Let's see if it still works."

Before she could agree or protest, he left her standing beside the generator and disappeared into the gloom, apparently searching for something to climb up on. Emily shivered, frozen to the spot, her gaze glued to the moving beam of light. Finally, she heard the scrape of wood on stone.

After a few moments, she heard the rattle of a chain against glass and then a weak light spilled forth, chasing some of darkness back a few feet. Blinking to get her eyes to adjust, Emily looked around nervously and froze.

"That's not ... That isn't ... Is that a casket?" Emily gasped in horror.

MacGregor uttered a yelp and fell off the rickety chair he was standing on.

Chapter Two

Nigel MacKissack drifted upward slowly toward consciousness, wondering what had disturbed his rest. There seemed to be a great deal of activity outside his coffin, things being slammed about and cursing and he frowned, feeling anger slowly penetrate his grogginess.

O'Neal knew better than to disturb him. What the devil was he about?

The noise finally ceased and he considered drifting off once more, but a hunger pang hit him about that time. Sighing, he realized he wasn't going to get back to sleep unless he did something to assuage it. Feeling around for the latch, he pushed up on the lid, discovering in the process that it was all he could do to lift it.

He was winded by the time he'd managed to shove it open. Resting for a few moments, trying to fight the alarm growing inside of him to discover he was so weak, Nigel finally managed to climb out. He had to brace himself once he'd done so.

The first thing that caught his gaze as he looked around curiously was a broken chair. He stared at it for several moments and finally looked up at the light illuminating it.

A candle hung from a length of rope attached to the ceiling.

He stared at the strange sight blankly for several moments and finally realized it wasn't a candle at all. As he moved around the casket for a better look, his kilt fell off. He looked down at the faded, dusty wad of cloth, too stunned for several moments even to think why it might have simply dropped off of him. Finally, he bent and picked it up, studying it curiously.

It was so old it all but disintegrated in his hands.

"Bloody hell!" Dropping the rag, he examined his shirt. It, too, fell apart the moment he touched it and he found himself standing in the chilly dungeon without a stitch of clothing on.

His stomach protested again, reminding him that he was weak with hunger.

How long had he slept? O'Neal was supposed to have awakened him no later than 1800, sooner if his health began to fail. And, in the event O'Neal hadn't been able to come himself, his son was to come.

But the clothing he'd been wearing was damned well older than fifty years. At a guess, he'd figure more than a hundred.

Hearing noises from above, he glanced up and was distracted once more by the strange light.

Moving toward it, he paused when he was beneath it, staring up at the glass ball. It wasn't a candle. It wasn't a flame at all as far as he could see. Gas? But even that had a flame and required air to burn. This thing was completely encased in glass and as far as he could see it wasn't burning, but merely glowing and far more brightly than any candle he'd ever seen.

"Some new contraption," he muttered, wondering what else had changed since he'd decided to sleep for a while.

Losing interest in the light, he closed his eyes, commanding his senses, but he discovered he was too weak to detect much of anything. It was still daylight. He knew that much. He was so hungry, he was tempted to go out anyway, but in his weakened state, the sun would probably drain him of what little energy he had. Besides, he didn't think he was strong enough to catch anything in the daylight and he didn't just need food. He needed the energy he could only find in a living thing.

Sighing with a mixture of weariness and disgust, he settled weakly on the stairs, waiting for dusk, listening to the activity above him and wondering who the hell was in his house.

* * * *

Emily couldn't get her mind off the casket. Angus had taken off like a cat shot in the behind as soon as he'd clambered up from the floor, disclaiming any knowledge of it.

It couldn't be occupied, she finally decided. It would be in the ground, or a mausoleum or something, not just sitting in the basement--the dungeon, she corrected herself.

She did her best to concentrate on cleaning the room she'd chosen as her bedroom, but just about the time she noticed that the shadows in the room were growing long, it occurred to her that she needed fuel for the generator if she didn't want to sit in the castle in the dark. She needed a lot of things, actually.

She was dirty from working, but she didn't have time to bathe and get to town and back before dark. She probably didn't have time to get back before dark if she left immediately, she thought wryly.

Finally, she merely brushed as much of the dust off her clothes as she could, went into the bathroom to wash her face and hands and, after grabbing her pocketbook, headed for the car, making a mental list of the things she absolutely, positively had to have immediately.

* * * *

Nigel's ass was cold and numb from sitting on the stone step by the time he judged that the sun must be setting. His head was also throbbing with a combination of hunger and the noise from whatever that thing was at the foot of the stairs that had been growling and coughing non-stop since he'd woken. Rising with an effort, he made his way up the stairs.

The room at the top of the stairs, which had once been the quarters for the kitchen staff, had been transformed into a kitchen. From its condition, he was fairly certain it wasn't anything that had been done very recently, and he wondered again just how long he'd overslept.

He was merely curious, however, not alarmed. He had more pressing matters to attend to at the moment.

He wasn't really surprised to discover that his room had changed, as well, but he felt anger for the first time. "Bloody hell!" he roared. "Where the bloody hell are my things?"

Striding about the room, he checked the armoire, grinding his teeth in impotent fury when he found it bare of anything but dust. It was the same when he checked the chest at the foot of the bed. Finally, he flopped down on the edge of the bed, too weak despite his anger to do much more than glare angrily at nothing in particular while he tried to figure out what to do about his situation.

The bed creaked ominously the moment he deposited his weight on it and he held his breath, wondering if it would collapse from age.

When it didn't, he allowed his anger to absorb him again. He wasn't squeamish about running about without his clothes, but it was going to be damned hard to parade about the countryside naked without arousing attention.

After a while, he grew bored of entertaining himself with what he meant to do with O'Neal once he got his hands on him and realized that he'd been staring for some moments at a mound of what looked like it might be traveling trunks. It hadn't dawned on him just at first because he was too furious to think straight, and also because the things didn't look like any portmanteaux's that he'd ever seen. He finally decided that that was what it was, though.

Someone was going somewhere.

Well, if O'Neal thought he'd get off that easily, he had another think coming!

Striding toward the bags, he lifted the largest. It was surprisingly heavy for its size and he wondered if it contained clothing at all, but decided to have a look. Dropping it on top of the trunk at the foot of the bed, he examined it and saw it had a tiny latch on it.

The latch looked like it was broken. It merely flopped around when he flicked at it with his finger, but he finally decided to see if he could get it to work anyway. Grasping it between his thumb and forefinger, he pulled at it. To his surprise, it made a strange noise and slid sideways. As it did, the contents inside, under what appeared to be considerable pressure, began to expand, pushing it even further and opening the strange case wider.

It was a curious sort of thing, but he saw that there was indeed clothing inside, and Nigel decided he'd examine the odd closure mechanism later. At the moment he couldn't think of much besides his hunger.

The clothing was as odd as the case and the closure to the case.

None of the fabrics the articles were constructed from was the least familiar to him and the clothing was only vaguely recognizable. He took the pieces out one by one and examined them.

Clearly, it was men's clothing, but the man must be a midget. He held up a pair of breeches, examining them with a frown and finally held them up to his waist. Either they were an odd length, or he'd been at least partly correct. The breeches hit his legs about halfway between his ankles and his knee ... too long for knee breeches, too short for casual wear.

Tossing them aside, he dug around in hopes of discovering a kilt. There wasn't one, but at the bottom of the case, he found what he thought must be some sort of under garments. They were made of a silky fabric and too sheer, he felt sure, to be worn as outer garments. "What the bloody hell could ye cover with so dainty a patch of fabric, I'd like ta know," he muttered, holding one bright red piece up that was strung together with strings and examining it.

Dropping the article finally, he picked up a matching red piece that looked more like some sort of harness than anything else. "Well, its fer sure tha's na' fer no man's ballocks."

Men's outer wear and a woman's under garments?

Sighing with disgust, he began trying the clothes on, discarding them one by one when he discovered he couldn't get his arm in this one, his leg in that one. Finally, he found a shirt that had no buttons at all. It didn't even have so much as a drawstring at the neck and he wondered if he could get his head through the hole. To his surprise, the thing seemed to grow larger as he tugged it on, then small again. He pulled on the fabric, wondering what sort of fabric it was made of that it could change form so easily.

Despite the miraculous properties of the fabric, it fit him almost like a second skin and it wasn't particularly comfortable. Shrugging, he dug through the clothing and unearthed the piece he remembered seeing that was the same pale pink in color and made of the same fabric.

He didn't much care for the color. He didn't much care for the way it fit, but at least his arse was covered.

He couldn't find any shoes that would fit his feet. There were probably a dozen in the second portmanteaux he opened, but he knew he'd never get his big toe in them.

Dismissing it finally, he left in search of food. He couldn't wait any longer. He had to have something. Once he'd fed, once he'd regained some of his strength, he'd come back and deal with O'Neal and find out just where the hell the man had put his personal belongings.

Chapter Three

It was already completely dark by the time Emily pulled up in front of the castle and parked. To her relief, she saw that the lights were still on, which meant that the generator was still going.

Unfortunately, the castle didn't boast any exterior lights. Leaving the car's headlights on to see, she dragged a can of fuel from the trunk of the car and headed inside.

Before she did anything else, she intended to make sure the generator wasn't going to run out of fuel and shut off.

It really gave her the creeps going down into the dungeon, knowing there was a casket in it.

It'd be a lot creepier sitting in the dark in the crumbling old castle, however.

She tried not to look at the coffin, but her gaze kept straying to it as she filled the generator's tank. When she'd finished, she set the can down and scurried back up the stairs, chill bumps creeping up her spine.

By the time she'd finished unloading the car, she realized that she absolutely was not going to be able to sleep in the castle knowing that casket was down in the dungeon unless she was sure it wasn't occupied.

Steeling herself, she grabbed up a flashlight and headed down the stairs. Her heart nearly failed her when she saw the thing.

"It's empty. If anyone was in it, it would be in the ground. It wouldn't have just been left out like that."

She didn't feel very reassured.

Finally, she edged her way toward it slowly, as if something might suddenly spring out of it.

The lid was surprisingly heavy. She had to set the flashlight down and use both hands to lift it. The hair on the back of her neck stood on end when she finally managed to lift the lid, and she jumped back.

The lid promptly slammed closed and the noise nearly scared her witless.

Dragging in a deep, sustaining breath, she struggled and finally managed to open it again, pushing it back until it was balanced on it's hinges.

Steeling herself, she picked up the flashlight and flicked it over the interior. To her relief, she saw it was empty except for some rotted pieces of cloth. She was about to set the flashlight down and close it again when the beam caught a glint of something in one corner. Curious, she trained the light on the spot. Her heart seemed to stand still in her chest.

It was a gold coin!

"Oh my god!" Emily whispered, caught between hope and disbelief, wondering if it was only a button and her mind was playing tricks on her. Moving to the end of the casket, she reached inside and picked up the round, golden object, studying it closely. It *was* a gold coin! Minted in the early 1700's! Excited now, she thrust the coin in the pocket of her jeans and examined the coffin more carefully to see if there was another coin.

She didn't see any, but she wasn't about to give up without checking it out thoroughly. Setting the flashlight down on the lumpy fabric that covered the bottom of the casket, she tugged at the material that had been tacked to the sides. It was rotted. The tacks held, but her finger hung in a tear of the fabric and it shredded. As the fabric came away, coins poured out onto the bottom of the casket.

Emily stared at the coins, too stunned even to think for several moments. Finally, a sound that was half sob, half laugh tore its way up her throat. "I'm saved," she gasped weakly. "I'm saved!"

Slowly, it flooded into her mind that the coins were gold, and ancient. They could be worth a *lot* of money. "I'm rich!" She laughed giddily, then covered her mouth. "Is it mine?" She thought it over, but she couldn't remember any 'ifs, ands, or buts.' The paperwork had said the land, the buildings and anything on or in them were hers. She began to dance around the coffin, laughing and crying. It was hers, hers, hers! She wasn't going to starve to death. She wasn't going to lose everything she'd put into it. She must have at least enough money to make the place livable, maybe even more than that. Maybe it was enough she could pay off the loan and she wouldn't have to turn it into a bed and breakfast after all?

She'd made several circuits around the casket when it occurred to her to wonder when and how the money had gotten there. She stopped, frowning, but it didn't seem likely it could have been anything recent, like a drug deal. It had been in a secret pocket in the lining of the casket and the material was rotted with age.

She didn't think it was likely that whoever had originally owned it would still be alive, or coming back to get it.

Angus had seen the casket, though. He was bound to talk about it. She couldn't count on people not being curious. She could have local kids sneaking in here while she was out, just to have a look.

She had to move the gold to a safer place. She couldn't just leave it sitting in the coffin, in broad view.

She went back to examining the casket and discovered that the coins were sewn into pockets all the way around. There was far too much to try to carry it in her jeans pockets. After studying the fabric in the coffin for several moments, she realized it was too rotted to use. Finally, she lifted up her T-shirt and formed a pouch. By the time she'd collected roughly half of the coins, the neck of her T-shirt was stretched down to her nipples.

"This isn't going to work," she muttered.

She couldn't bring herself to leave the coins even for a few minutes, however. Taking her T-shirt off, she tied a good knot in the bottom and began dropping the coins into the neck. When she had all the coins in it, she could barely lift the thing. Grunting and groaning, she finally managed to lift it out of the casket and began to struggle toward the stairs with it, wondering where she was going to hide her treasure.

She was sweating profusely by the time she made it up the stairs to the kitchen. She had to set her makeshift bag down and rest. When she'd caught her breath, she began searching the room for a likely looking hiding place. Nothing she found made her feel particularly secure, however. Finally, she decided to keep looking. She wasn't going to be able to rest until she'd found a really safe place to hide the coins where she could be sure her security wouldn't just vanish as abruptly as it had appeared.

After lugging the coins from room to room, she finally decided that even if she'd found a spot on the ground floor she wouldn't have been able to sleep for worrying that someone might break in during the night and find them. She stared at the stairs for several minutes, wondering if she could possibly make it up them with the bag full of heavy gold coins. Finally, she decided the safest thing to do would be the 'child' climb.

Placing her butt squarely on a step, she pulled the bag up to the step below her and then moved up another step. It was slow going, but at least there wasn't much risk of having the coins overbalance her and send her tumbling down the stairs.

By the time she'd worked her way to the top, she'd decided to see if she could hide the coins in the mattress, at least temporarily. There were holes in it already. She could just drop the coins in the holes after she'd counted them so that she knew how many she'd need to retrieve once she found a better spot.

She was dragging the bag by the time she reached her apartments, no longer able to lift the heavy thing at all. Groaning with effort, she pushed the door open and backed across the room until she reached the bed.

The moment she straightened, one hand on her aching back, she saw the ass print in dust on the mattress. She stared at it blankly for several moments and finally glanced around the room. Two of her bags were open, the contents strewn all over the place.

"Oh my god! I've been burgled!"

She clapped a hand over her mouth, wondering if the burglar was still in the castle. He would've heard her coming up the stairs, though. She'd been making a lot of noise.

It was a 'he.' She had no doubt of that, and a pretty damned big 'he' at that if the size of his feet was anything to go by. He'd left bare footprints in the dust on the floor.

And then there was the perfect print of a bare ass on her mattress.

She stared at it, wondering if it was some weird kind of graffiti, or maybe something the local teen gang did as a sort of gang signature.

Moving to the suitcases, she was on the point of checking them when it occurred to her that she probably ought not to touch them or move anything. She should leave them for the police to look at.

At a glance, she couldn't see that anything was missing--nothing important at any rate.

She was going to have to drive back into town to contact the police. She didn't have a phone and she hadn't seen a house between here and the village.

She didn't really want to go back to town, not again tonight.

She damned sure wasn't going to leave her gold lying around.

For that matter, she didn't think she wanted the cops in her room after she'd hidden it in her mattress.

She sat down on the edge of the bed to think it over, staring at that ass print.

Finally, she decided just to hide her gold, check the castle and make sure nobody was in it with her and then lock up. She could report the burglary in the morning ... after she'd found a really good hiding place for her gold.

She'd hefted her makeshift bag onto the bed, counted the coins and was on the point of dropping them into the holes in the mattress when she got to thinking about the posts of the bed. The foot board of the bed was only about half the height of the head board. Catching hold of the ornamental finial that toped one post, she twisted it back and forth a few times and finally managed to pull it off. She post, she discover with a surge of excitement, had been made similar to a cask. Instead of having been made from one solid piece of wood, it was made from several planks glued or nailed together and hollow in the center.

She'd have to take the bed apart to get the coins out again, but surely that was preferable to having someone plop down on the bed and hearing the jingle of coins?

It certainly seemed so to her, and she scooped the coins up and dropped them in, replacing the ornamental top carefully and using a shoe to hammer it down tightly.

When she'd finished, she grabbed a shirt from her suitcase and went down to get the rest of her cleaning supplies.

It was just as well she'd decided not to go back to town, she thought wryly, because she'd been so excited about her discovery, she'd forgotten she'd left the headlights on. Climbing into the car, she turned the key and, to her relief, managed to get it started. Leaving it running so that the battery could recharge, she carried her cleaning supplies inside.

Taking the broom, which was the only weapon looking thing she had, and a flashlight, she did a room by room search. Finally, reassured that she was alone in the castle, she bolted the front door and went upstairs to finish cleaning the room while she waited for the car to charge up its battery enough that she felt safe to turn it off.

* * * *

Nigel felt considerably better after he'd fed. He still didn't feel entirely up to snuff, but he certainly felt far better than he had.

It had disturbed him a good deal when he'd discovered that he was too weak and ill to morph. He hadn't had that problem since he'd been a mere youngster.

He didn't realize just how deeply it had shaken him until he thought about morphing for the return trip to the castle and realized he wasn't at all anxious to try it.

It wasn't that far to walk anyway.

The door was bolted when he got home.

He was on the point of pounding on it furiously when it

occurred to him that O'Neal had undoubtedly discovered that he'd awakened and was so arrogant as to think he could keep Nigel out with nothing more substantial than a door!

It took him two tries to dematerialize and flow beneath the door like smoke.

It shook him.

It also infuriated him, not the least because he discovered he hadn't managed to make the transition with his clothes. Snatching the door open, he retrieved them from the other side and struggled into them once more.

When he was dressed again, he looked around the shambles of his front hall for a victim.

He'd already opened his mouth to bellow for O'Neal when a distinctly feminine scream filtered to him from the second floor. There was such terror in the sound that his heart seemed to stand still in his chest. His blood ran cold.

Jerking all over in reaction, he ran to the stairs and bolted up them, following the series of screams to his own apartment.

When he flung open the door, a young woman whirled to look at him with terror stricken eyes. Before he could even ask her what danger lurked, she whacked him up side the head with the broom she was wielding like a sword.

He was too stunned to duck, certainly too surprised to think about dematerializing.

As she swung at him again, however, he collected himself and moved.

* * * *

Emily had never liked spiders. In point of fact, a spider was the one thing in the world, besides snakes, that could almost instantly turn her from a rational human being into a blithering maniac with only one thing on her mind--kill.

She'd thought the cobwebs were just that, abandoned, uninhabited--trash.

When the eight legged monster dropped from the web she swept down, she screamed in mindless terror, swinging her broom at it frantically as it darted in first one direction and then another.

It chased her a while. She chased it awhile, but there was one thing Emily was absolutely certain of, she was going to kill the thing if she had to take the room apart.

She'd just managed to beat it into a smear when the door to her room crashed open. Whirling at the new threat, Emily didn't so much as spare a split second to consider the wisdom of attacking the mammoth standing just inside her door with nothing but a broom. Adrenaline was still pumping wildly through her. Uttering a feral shriek, she went after him, swinging for all she was worth.

She might have missed him except for the fact that he came to an abrupt halt on the threshold as if he'd been pole-axed. She managed to hit him twice before she swung and missed.

Her momentum swung her in a wide circle and she discovered as she spun around that he'd managed to leap behind her. Screaming gibberish that didn't even make sense to her, she went after him again.

Again, he managed to slip past her. Sneaking up on her blind side, he grabbed her from behind, catching her hands.

"Now what'er ye gonna do, ye termagant!"

Emily let out a growl of pure fury, lifted one leg and stomped his instep. At the same moment, since he'd grabbed her hands, preventing her from swinging the broom, she pivoted it, whacking him in the middle of the forehead with the broom handle.

He yelped and released her, hopping on one foot and rubbing his forehead. Emily whirled on him and grabbed his "Achilles heel."

He went instantly still, his eyes widening.

"Make one move, you fucking pervert, and I'll crack your nuts like pecans."

He stared at her wide eyed, unmoving, hardly breathing. "Kindly take yer hands off me ballocks."

Emily gave them an experimental squeeze and he winced. "What the hell are you doing wearing my clothes, you pervert!"

"Yers?" he yelped, aghast. "Ye wear men's attire then, do ye?"

"Men don't usually wear pink jogging suits," Emily said dryly. Her adrenaline rush was rapidly departing and concern took its place as she realized she had the bull by his horns and didn't know what to do with him now.

His eyes narrowed. "Pink or no, things 'ave changed a bit more than I'd've thought if women are running around in men's breeches."

Emily stared at him. "Where have you been? Mars? My god, women have been wearing pants for...." She frowned, trying to think how long it had been and realized she didn't know that much about the history of clothing. "Years and years. And they're not men's breeches, damn it. They're *my* breeches ... I mean my jogging pants. What kind of nut case breaks into a woman's home only to steal her pink jogging suit?"

"Yer home? Tha's a fine one. This is *my* home, I'll have ye ta know, and has been for several hundred years at least."

He was obviously pissed off, but he didn't really seem dangerous and, frankly, Emily wasn't terribly comfortable about holding his balls.

Releasing them cautiously, she stepped back and looked him over.

It was her jogging suit all right. He was so big, though, that not only did it fit him like a second skin, but the sleeves of the top ended about halfway between his elbows and his wrists, and the pants looked like pedal pushers.

Then there was the middle.

It didn't quite meet and exposed a very nice, tight belly. There was a narrow trail of dark hair from his belly button downward.

She shook the thought off. Either he was gay, or he was one of those guys that were 'in' to wearing women's clothes. Either way, it didn't matter how good he looked, because the interest wasn't likely to be mutual.

He looked pretty damned good, though, all over. His hair was the next thing to black, and long, hanging well past his shoulders. His eyes were a beautiful, bright shade of blue, and his craggy, purely masculine features made her tummy jumpy.

She frowned. "Several hundred ... Are you trying to make me believe you're a ghost?"

He looked taken aback. "Are ye daft, lass? Do I look like a bloody ghost ta ya?"

Emily gave him a narrow eyed glare. "No, you don't. You look like a pervert."

His eyes narrowed. "Ye've called me that three times now and I'd like ta ken what ye mean by it."

She plunked her hands on her hips. "Well, you *are* wearing my clothes. You figure it out."

He studied her for several moments. "In my day a woman who'd wear breeches would be the pervert. And now I think on it, what sort of lady are ye ta be grabbing me by me ballocks? Cause I'm thinkin' yer no lady atall," he growled at her.

The comment almost surprised a chuckle out of her. She pretended to cough instead. "What I am is the owner of this property. And what you are is an intruder. Leave!" she commanded, pointing toward the door.

He leaned toward her threateningly. "*I* am the owner, and what's more I'm a hell of a lot bigger than ye, lass. I could toss ye out on yer arse without a bit o' trouble."

"Well, you're wrong there, buddy," Emily said, stepping up to him until they were practically nose to nose and stabbing him in the chest with her finger. "Because I happen to know a little something about kick boxing and if I can't kick your ass, I can damn well make you know you've been in a fight. And, if you do manage to put me out, I'll go straight to the cops and have them back here to arrest your sorry ass before you can spit!"

"Maybe I'll just eat ye instead," he growled.

That comment surprised a snorting laugh from her. "Thanks for the offer, but I'm good. My boyfriend gave me head before I left home. Right now I'm a lot more interested in getting you out of here than 'in' to me."

He straightened, studying her with a look of surprise. "Ye are daft, lass. Ye talk strange an' I've no idea what yer sayin' half the time."

Emily shrugged. "Not my problem. I want my clothes back before you leave, too."

"What've ye done with me own things, then, I'd like ta know? Ye expect me ta walk about swingin' in the breeze? Fer I've not a stitch ta my name with my clothes rotting off in tatters and everythin' else gone.

"And now I'm at it, where's O'Neal? Did he sell ye my place? Is that what yer sayin'?"

"I bought it through a land agent, MacGregor--fair and square--all paid. I think he was selling it for the taxes, but I don't know much about British law and I wasn't really clear on why it was up for sale except that nobody seemed to own it anymore."

He frowned. "But I had all tha legal work done up on it. This is tha truth, lass? My castle was put up fer sale?"

Emily felt a sinking sensation in the pit of her stomach as it occurred to her to wonder if the man was telling the truth and somehow he'd been cheated out of his place. He seemed sincere, and puzzled, and more than a little stunned by the turn of events. "Look, I'm really sorry. But I did buy the place and as far as my lawyer could see everything was in order. When did you do this legal work you're talking about? Maybe, somehow, things got screwed up and it wasn't properly recorded."

He frowned. "April, I think."

"This year? Last year?"

"Seventeen fifty three."

Emily gaped at him. Cold washed over her, making the fine hairs on the back of her neck prickle. "Oh. Well, that's been a little while," she said faintly, realizing suddenly that the man must be an escapee from a mental hospital. "I tell you what ... let me just run downstairs to find my papers and I'll let you have a look at them. How's that?"

His eyes narrowed suspiciously as she began inching toward the door. "How long ago?"

Emily gave him a blank look. "How long ago, what?"

"You said it had been a while. How long?"

Emily had managed to work her way to the door by that time. She glanced toward it out of the corner of her eye and was relieved to see it was standing ajar. "I'm ... actually, I'm really bad at math. I'm not exactly sure."

His lips tightened. "Tell me the year. I'll do the math."

"Two thousand four," Emily flung at him, leaping out the door and making for the stairs as hard as she could run.

Chapter Four

She couldn't hear him behind her, but then her heart was pounding in her ears like the drum section of a marching band. She almost tripped and rolled to the bottom but managed to catch herself just in time. She skipped the last three stairs, leaping from the fourth and landing in the hall at a run.

She'd left the car running to charge the battery. It was nothing short of a miracle that the damned thing hadn't run out of gas. She broke three nails getting the door open and dove inside. She wanted to throw it in gear and take off, but all the doors were unlocked and there was no way she was going to drive, at night, with a lunatic on the loose, with her doors unlocked. What if she came upon another one?

As she hoisted herself across the back of the front seat to slam the rear door locks down, she saw the man appear in the door. Sliding back into her seat, she put the car in gear and dug two strips of dirt and rock into the air, then burned rubber as she hit the pavement. The car swerved wildly. With an effort, she managed to straighten the vehicle on the road. When she glanced back in the rear view mirror, she didn't see a sign of him, but she couldn't convince herself that he wouldn't suddenly land on top of her car like the killer maniacs always did in the movies.

"Oh god! I was talking to him!" she muttered, feeling a shiver skate down her back. "Just standing there like a complete idiot making conversation with a lunatic!"

Maybe he wasn't a dangerous, psychopathic lunatic?

The escapee theory *would* explain why he didn't have any clothes, though. He'd probably thrown the hospital gown away.

She glanced down at the gas gauge and was dismayed at the level.

"Don't panic! There's more gas in the back," she reminded herself when she remembered she'd only taken one of the cans inside.

Something fluttered near her window and Emily gasped, turning to glance at it several times before she finally realized it was ... or it looked like ... a small bird flying right beside her car.

She ran off the edge of the road. By the time she'd straightened the car again, she'd lost sight of it.

She realized at just about that same moment that she was on the wrong side of the road--again. Jerking the wheel, she veered sharply into the lane she was supposed to be traveling in. Almost at the same instant, the little bird that had been flying by her window smacked into the front wind shield so hard it cracked the glass. Screaming, Emily slammed on the brakes instinctively.

She sat gasping for breath when the car came to a halt, fighting the urge to burst into tears.

She lost the battle. "Poor little bird!" she sobbed.

Looking around, she gauged the distance she'd put between herself and the castle and decided it was safe to get out and check on the bird she'd murdered with her rental car.

She found it lying in the road several yards in front of the car. It must have been thrown from the hood, she decided, when she slammed on the brakes.

It wasn't a bird.

It was a bat.

A shudder went through her, but, really, it was kind of cute and so helpless, the poor little thing. As she bent down for a closer look, she saw that its tiny, little chest was still moving.

Maybe she'd only stunned it?

But what should she do? If she left it where it was, somebody was liable to run over it. After a few moments, she ran back to the car, opened the glove box and popped the trunk, then grabbed a hamburger wrapper off the floor of the car. She didn't want to touch it. It was bleeding and there was no telling what sort of diseases the thing might be carrying.

It was still lying where she'd left it, barely breathing. She nudged it with the toe of her shoe, just to make sure it wasn't conscious enough to bite her, and finally opened the paper wrapper and picked it up.

It felt warm. She felt a welling of nausea and revulsion as she scurried around to the trunk and very carefully laid it inside.

She slammed the trunk lid quickly as soon as she'd let go of it, raced around the car and jumped into the driver's seat, slamming the door and locking it.

She was still crying about running over the poor little bat when she finally got to the police station.

* * * *

For several moments, Nigel stared blankly at the vacant spot where the woman had been standing before it dawned on him that she was probably running for help. The one thing he definitely did not need at the moment, when he was still so weak and disoriented, was problems with the local authorities.

He was so shocked by her assertion that it was Two Thousand and Four, however, that he'd slept for two and a half centuries, that he couldn't seem to think beyond that and the implications of it.

Finally, he shook himself and started after her.

He'd lost valuable time, though, and by the time he reached the door, she'd leapt into the strange carriage he'd seen sitting out front.

God only knew why. There weren't any horses attached to the thing. How the hell did she think she was going to get away from him like that?

The thought had barely registered in his mind when the carriage took off like a bullet shot from the barrel of a gun, kicking up clods of dirt and rocks that peppered him like cannon shrapnel.

He could do nothing but gape at the retreating carriage in stunned surprise for several moments. Finally, he regained enough presence of mind to concentrate on morphing. Unfortunately, he quickly discovered that his powers were still not quite what they had been before he'd gone into deep hibernation. He morphed, but his clothing did not. By the time he'd managed to extricate himself from the garments he'd been wearing, the tail of the carriage was already disappearing from view.

Gritting his teeth, he launched himself into the air. Whatever that strange looking carriage was, he knew he could fly faster than it could cover the ground and he had the added advantage of being able to gain on her by being airborne when she was forced to follow the road.

It was stunningly fast. Not only had it taken off like a bullet, but it continued to gain speed. As rapidly as he covered the distance, it was a struggle to gain on the carriage.

A sense of triumph filled him as he drew even with it at last and he poured forth more energy, gaining upon it slowly but surely, drawing abreast of her.

She glanced at him through the glass and he knew she realized she was done for now.

The last thing he remembered was the expression of horror on her face when her carriage overtook him and he slammed into the glass.

* * * *

Emily glared sullenly at the cops as they glanced around her room, scribbled on their pads and exchanged speaking glances.

Admittedly, she'd been in a state when she'd arrived at the police station. First she'd had the wits scared out of her by the lunatic, and then she'd run down a poor, defenseless animal. The two incidents so closely together had her nerves all to pieces, particularly when added to the disaster the castle was.

They had assured her there were no reports of any lunatics missing from any insane asylums. In fact, there wasn't even a mental hospital within a hundred miles. She knew, even when they had finally agreed to come out and check things out for her that they'd already made up their minds that she was the one that was crazy.

It hadn't helped that they'd found her pink jogging suit lying on the threshold--the pink jogging suit she'd told them the lunatic was wearing.

The first cop to reach her door had squatted down and examined it and asked if it was the item that had been 'allegedly' burgled from her home.

Everything had gone downhill from there.

After a grand total of thirty minutes, tops, they had completed their 'preliminary' investigation and cleared out. She knew they wouldn't be back.

She knew everybody in the tiny little town would be talking about the kooky American that had moved into the ruins of the Castle MacKissack.

It wasn't until they drove off that she thought about the bat again.

Chastising herself for heaping thoughtlessness on top of carelessness, she ran out to the car and climbed in. Popping the trunk, she craned around in the seat to watch it fly out, certain it would've regained consciousness by now.

She didn't see anything and after a few moments she climbed out of the car again, moved around it cautiously, and peered into the trunk.

The lunatic was lying in her trunk, buck ass naked!

"How the hell did you get in my trunk!" Emily demanded.

Holding his head, he looked around in confusion and finally began struggling to climb out. Emily was of more than half a mind to slam the hood on him, but she couldn't help but notice he seemed injured.

Her sympathy lasted until she saw the hamburger wrapper stuck to his back. "Oh god! You crushed it!"

"What?"

"The bat! The bat I hit with the car! I was trying to save the poor little thing and you've crushed it, you big jerk!"

She couldn't bear to look. The poor little thing had looked bad enough after it hit her wind shield.

"Is it dead?"

He looked at her curiously. "Is what dead?"

"The bat, damn it!"

"Not quite," he muttered, staggering a little drunkenly toward her front door.

She forgot about the bat when she saw him heading toward her door. Racing around him, she planted herself on the threshold and grasped the door frame on either side, barring his entrance. He stared at her for several moments when he reached her and finally grasped her around the waist, lifting her off the floor. Turning, he set her just outside, crossed the threshold and slammed the door in her face. Before she could grab the latch, she heard the bolt slam home.

Emily gaped at the vibrating door a good five seconds before rage set in. She began hammering on the door with her fist, kicking it when her fists started smarting from the pounding. "Let me in, you ass hole!"

"Not by the hair of my chinny, chin, chin," he growled from the other side of the door.

"Smart ass!" She rattled the door again, but she knew there was no way she was going to be able to beat it down.

Turning, she studied the car speculatively for several moments, but finally dismissed the thought. She didn't want a car sized hole where her front door had been and, besides, the whole fucking castle would probably disintegrate and all she would have was a bigger pile of stones.

She was tempted to try the windows, but it was black as Hades and she didn't particularly like stumbling around in the dark. Finally, realizing there was no hope for it, she slammed the trunk lid closed and climbed into back of the car, locking the doors and then finding what comfort she could on the back seat.

She was just starting to doze off when she heard a roar from inside the castle that made her hair stand on end. Sitting up, she listened intently. A few moments later, the lunatic, wearing her jogging pants, wrenched the front door open and stalked toward her.

Leaning down, he glared at her through the window. "Where's my bloody gold, woman?"

Emily didn't know why she was surprised that the guy was claiming her gold, too, but she was--maybe because it seemed strange that he knew about it if he hadn't put it there?

She tried to give him a look of total incomprehension, but she felt the guilt creep into her expression. After trying to stare him down for several moments, she decided retreat might be the better part of valor and climbed over the seat back into the front seat of the car. That was when she discovered that the keys weren't in the ignition. They were in her pocketbook, inside the castle.

Feeling a prickle of uneasiness creeping down her spine, she scooted to the center of the front seat, staring at the man fixedly, wondering if he was about to bust the glass out of the window and come in after her.

To her surprise, the look of rage slowly changed to one of speculation and then concentration. His image began to waver. She closed her eyes, rubbed them. When she opened her eyes again he looked as if he was slowly disappearing into nothingness--well, not nothingness, smoke.

She rubbed her eyes again and leaned toward the window to peer down at the ground. Her pink jogging pants lay on the ground. Wisps of smoke swirled above them, moving sinuously, almost purposely, along the car, as if testing the doors and windows. After a few moments, it disappeared under the car.

She sat up, peering down at the ground where the snake like coil of smoke had disappeared. It didn't reappear and after a moment, she sat back, turning to move to the other side of the car to see if it was visible from there.

She didn't have to move that far, however. Even as she turned, she saw that the smoke was drifting through the vents. As she watched, it settled in the seat beside her, thickened, became more and more substantial. Her jaw dropped lower and lower and her eyes got wider and wider.

Solid once more, he grasped her upper arms and hauled her across the seat until they were almost nose to nose.

Emily managed to suck in a breath. She licked her dry lips. "You *are* a ghost," she said weakly.

He frowned. "I'm no ghost, but I'll gi' ye a wee hint, lass," he said gruffly, curling his lips in a parody of a smile and displaying a set of very white teeth which featured two very long, very sharp fangs.

Chapter Five

Dizziness washed over Emily as she stared at that set of pearly white fangs and her brain sluggishly tried to add, fangs, plus coffin, plus sleeping for two and half centuries, plus changing into smoke and wafting through the car's ventilation system.

"Werewolf?" she hazarded weakly.

His eyes narrowed. "Vampire," he snarled.

It was the coward's way out and she knew it, but she welcomed the dizziness and the encroaching darkness, tried to concentrate on summoning it. Instead, it seemed the harder she wished for unconsciousness, the further it slipped from her reach.

She couldn't faint, but she was so weak with terror that she couldn't move either.

Apparently satisfied with her reaction, he climbed out of the car, dragged her out and hoisted her into his arms, heading back inside the castle.

Emily leaned weakly against him, trying to formulate a plan.

Her keys were in her pocketbook on the bed in the master suite. If he took her there, she would have the chance to get it, but, then where to go? The cops already thought she was a nut case. If she showed up at the police station again tonight, this time claiming the man was a vampire, they'd probably lock her up.

She considered that as he climbed the stairs with her, wondering if she would be safe from him if they locked her up.

It didn't seem likely if he could change into a puff of smoke and ooze through the tiniest cracks that a jail cell would be all that safe, besides which she'd be trapped.

What were the rules about vampires, she wondered a little frantically? She'd never really been 'in' to that particular cult, but she'd seen some vampire movies. She ought to be able to remember something useful.

'Church' popped into her mind abruptly. Vampires were evil creatures and ungodly and couldn't go inside a church.

She also remembered that they couldn't come in unless they were invited, but how would that pertain to a house that they claimed? So far as she could see the fact that the house now belonged to her hadn't even slowed him down. So, even if she managed, somehow, to get him outside, it probably wouldn't do her any good to try to bolt the door to keep him out.

When they reached her room, he strode to the bed and lay her very carefully on the lumpy surface, then stood back and studied her thoughtfully.

Emily watched him through half closed eyes, trying to catch a glimpse of her purse without moving her head. She couldn't see it and concentrated instead on trying to remember the position of it.

She finally remembered that she'd moved it from the bed and set it on the floor after she'd given the cops her identification to look at.

It was at the foot of the bed, near the leg where she'd poured all of his gold to hide it.

The bed dipped as he sat down.

He waved a hand over her face and she realized that he must not be convinced that she was under his power. She considered it frantically, but she simply could not remember that the women in the movies had done anything in particular. They'd only lain perfectly quietly, as if they couldn't move and they hadn't seemed frightened.

He leaned over her, until his mouth was near her ear. "I'm thinkin' yer fakin' it, lass."

Emily tensed fractionally, but she managed to keep her breathing slow and even.

He sat back, studied her a long moment and finally settled one hand on her breast, squeezing it.

She came off the bed as if she'd been spring loaded, smacking him squarely on one cheek. "Pervert!"

To her surprise, he chuckled. Before she could roll off the bed on the opposite side, he launched himself half atop her. Capturing her flailing arms after a pathetically brief battle for dominance, he dragged her back to the center of the bed, manacled her arms to the mattress on either side of her with his hands and used the weight of his body to pin her to the bed.

Realizing that fighting him was a useless expenditure of energy at the moment, Emily ceased abruptly, glaring up at him.

He looked amused. "Seein' as how yer in my bed with me cock tucked between yer thighs, I'm thinkin' we should introduce ourselves."

Emily's eyes widened as she realized he wasn't joking. There *was* a hard ridge tucked tightly against her pubic bone.

His dark brows rose when she merely stared at him speechlessly. "I'm Nigel of clan MacKissack, once Laird of the clan, now no more than the last of my clan."

Emily swallowed with an effort, fighting the sense of sympathy that swept over her at his words. "How do you know you're the last?"

"If I was na', ye'd na' be claimin' ownership of me castle."

She stared at him, but it was just too much to take in. Her mind was telling her to accept what she saw as real, but it was also telling her it couldn't possibly be real, that somehow he'd hypnotized her or something to make her think she'd seen something she really hadn't seen.

"Ye did na' give me yer name, lass," he said chidingly.

"Emily ... Hendricks."

He frowned. "And where d'ye hail from, Emily Hendricks?"

"Georgia."

His dark brows rose. "The colony in the Americas?"

She gaped at him. "It hasn't been a colony since seventeen...."

A look of surprise crossed his features. After a moment, he released his grip on her arms and slid off of her, leaving only his leg thrown across her hips to hold her down. Propping his head in one hand, he studied her. "It's na' under English rule no more?"

She shook her head slowly. "We gained our independence. It's part of the United States of America now."

"Is that a fact? An' how did ye manage tha' when the British Empire is the most powerful in the world?"

Emily bit her lip. "Actually, I think they just got tired of fighting us."

He grinned. "If they're all like you, I've na' a bit of trouble believin' it."

Emily felt a blush creep into her cheeks, but she didn't think it was a compliment.

His gaze moved from her face and traveled down her body in a leisurely examination. "I'm thinkin' the world's changed more than a wee bit since I've been ... sleeping."

Emily licked her lips. "You're ... you're not really a vampire, are you? I mean, you just used some kind of trick to make me think you disappeared and reappeared inside the car--like hypnosis? You don't ... drink people's blood?"

His gaze snapped to her face once more, his face hardening with anger. "I'm no bleedin' savage. Why would ye think I'd be a ... bloody cannibal?"

"But ... vampires drink people's blood, don't they?"

"Ye've known a lot of vampires, then, have ye?"

"Uh ... no. But I heard...."

"Ye heard wrong, or there's some that's no more'n savages. I've heard tell of such, but I figured it was no more than tales. I'm na' convinced it ain't."

"Then you're not going to ... bite my neck and suck me dry?"

A wicked smile curled his lips. "I'll na' make no promises o' tha', Emily Hendricks. In fact, there's na' much I'd rather do at the moment than suck every inch of ye."

Chapter Six

Heat rushed through Emily at the look in his eyes as much as his words, sucking the breath from her chest and forcing her heart to labor faster.

"I'd be more than a bit tempted to use me powers to enthrall ye, except fer the wee problem that I can't seem ta remember the half of the things I once did without even thinkin' about it," he murmured. "Then again, this could be a lot more interestin'."

"What?"

He chuckled, laying a hand lightly on her abdomen and skating it slowly upward until he was cupping one breast in the palm of his big hand. Emily looked at him sharply. He shifted closer until his lips brushed hers. "This," he murmured, melding his lips to hers for a fraction of a second before he parted the fragile barrier of her lips and swept inside, exploring the tender inner flesh with his tongue.

Emily gasped sharply at the intrusion, sucking in his taste and scent. It curled in her belly like potent liquor, rushing through her bloodstream to her head and creating a wave of weakness and dizziness. She lifted her hand, placing it on his hard shoulder. Inside her, a war waged, the desire to pull him closer, to enjoy the sensations he was creating inside of her just a few moments longer, and the more rational urge to push him away swaying back and forth, each striving for dominance.

Finally, she pushed at his shoulder lightly.

To her disappointment, he released her at once and drew back.

"We've a bit of coil here, Emily Hendricks."

"We do?"

"Aye, we do. Yer sayin' ye bought me castle and ye own it fair and square. I'm sayin' I built the castle and I've a prior claim. Ye've hid me gold from me, an' me with no notion of what it might take ta get me money from the bank, or even if the bank's still there after two and a half centuries.

"Ye can stay fer now, lass, but ye should give it some hard thought, because I've na' been with a woman in more'n a little while an' yer just ta my taste. I'm thinkin' it's na' gonna be easy ta remember I'm supposed ta be a gentleman. If ye hang around here long, yer gonna find yerself on yer back with yer legs spread."

His words washed over her like an aphrodisiac, strengthening the desire he'd already stoked inside her.

Her first reaction when he rolled off the bed and strode from the room was disappointment.

Her second, dawning anger, both with herself and with him.

She got off the bed, stalked to the door and slammed it, locking it decisively.

She heard his chuckle waft up to her from the stairwell and ground her teeth.

* * * *

Nigel's amusement faded as he picked up Emily's shirt and examined it. He hadn't liked it before he'd found out it had been made for a woman. He'd liked it even less when Emily had looked at him as if she thought he was a man milliner. Sighing in disgust, he dragged it over his head and shoved his arms into it.

It couldn't be helped. Two hundred fifty years, and god alone knew how long since O'Neal had been gone, and his sons. There should have been a wardrobe waiting for him. There wasn't and the annoying female sleeping in his bed had taken his emergency stash, as well.

He couldn't go parading about the countryside bare arsed, but he needed some answers.

Opening the door, he strode outside and picked up the breeches he'd dropped beside the car when he transformed himself. He was really going to have to remember how he'd managed to take his clothes with him before. Losing them each time he morphed was becoming tedious.

It made him uneasy. Was it just memory lapse from such a long sleep? Or something else?

He didn't like to contemplate the possibility that he might not regain all of his powers ... or even that it might take him years to re-learn everything. When he'd pulled the breeches up, he studied Emily's carriage, walking around it. It was a strange looking carriage, to be sure, and stranger still that the thing could go at all without horses to pull it, especially so fast.

It had been two and a half centuries since he'd known mortal man, though. Maybe they'd learned some of the ways of the vampire?

Emily had been truly frightened, though, when he'd morphed and drifted inside the carriage.

He glanced up at the window at that thought, frowning. He'd been angry. He'd wanted to scare her, but he hadn't been particularly pleased when he'd done it. He liked it better when her lovely eyes flashed with temper, amusement, even slyness.

He wondered if she was as unique as she seemed to him or if women had really changed so much. He might have been tempted to think her mannish, with her absurd clothing and her hair chopped off nigh as short as his, except for the minor little detail that there was nothing mannish, or boyish, about her body. That part was all woman, and her reaction to him seemed proof enough she was not 'strange.'

Irritated to find himself dwelling on her when he had things far more important to worry about, he dismissed her from his mind and set out toward town. It was annoying to have to walk, but he didn't think he could figure out how to drive Emily's carriage and he couldn't afford to attract attention by arriving naked.

On the positive side, he managed to mesmerize a hare along the way and he felt much stronger after he'd eaten again. He stopped at the first cottage he came to and looked around for water to wash up. There was no well, but he found a pitcher sitting on a table in the garden that contained water.

It was late as he strode down the streets, glancing to his left and right, searching for the name MacGregor. Few people were about, but those that were glanced at him curiously. Uncomfortable with the attention he seemed to be drawing, he moved to the shadows along the edges of the buildings.

He was near the center of town when he looked up and saw a couple of young men coming toward him. They stopped when they neared him, blocking his path. Dressed in black leather from head to foot, with long, stringy hair and rings protruding from their noses, lips, brows and ears, he thought at first that they must be in costume, perhaps returning from a ball.

The taller of the two snickered, digging his elbow into the young man beside him. "He's a pretty one, eh?"

The other young man grinned. "What's yer name, then, lass?"

Nigel's eyes narrowed. Before he thought better of it, he grasped one by the front of his shirt and the other around the throat, lifting him clear of the pavement. Slamming the one he held by the throat against the wall of the building they stood beside, he gave the youth a long, dangerous look. "I'm looking for MacGregor, the land agent."

The one he was holding by the throat only croaked and gagged, his eyes bulging.

Nigel turned to the other one and snatched him closer. "MacGregor?"

The boy's mouth worked. Wordlessly, he pointed down the road.

"Which house?"

"The white one on the corner of Hobbs and Kensington."

He allowed the boy he was holding by the neck to slide to the ground. "You boys could do with a lesson in manners," he growled. He contemplated it for several moments but finally decided against it. Releasing them, he shoved past them and continued on his way.

The cottage of MacGregor was dark. Nigel studied it for a few minutes and finally stepped through the gate and made his way around to the back door. After glancing around to assure himself there were no witnesses about, he dematerialized and slipped under the door.

He cursed under his breath when he materialized once more and found he'd left the clothing outside, but finally dismissed it, glancing around at the room he found himself in. Closing his eyes, he summoned his senses, feeling his way through the cottage until he located the mortals within.

The man had a wife. That was unfortunate.

When he reached the threshold of their bedroom, he paused, closing his eyes, concentrating. To his relief, he gathered the threads of their consciousness and will to him. No doubt, he thought wryly, it had been easier because both were asleep, but he wasn't going to look a gift horse in the mouth. Moving inside, he stopped beside the bed, staring down at the sleeping man.

Finally, he summoned the MacGregor's consciousness.

MacGregor sat up, staring at him fixedly. Slowly, fear filled his eyes.

"I'm Nigel MacKissack, of the clan MacKissack. Ye've sold me castle an' I'd like ta ken how it is ye managed tha'."

MacGregor resisted, but it seemed to be more from fear than anything else. He didn't actually appear to have much knowledge of the events that had led up to the sale of the property. It seemed to have been caught up in some sort of legal limbo for several decades while one petitioner after another laid claim to it. That left a couple of hundred years unaccounted for and Nigel assumed that the trust he'd set up had protected it far better than he'd deemed necessary at the time.

The question of why he hadn't awakened when he was supposed to wasn't something that MacGregor could tell him. Nigel suspected, though, that at least a part of it was due to the fact that mortals had withdrawn from him so completely that he had not had their life force to support him and had sunk deeper and deeper in hibernation. The only flaw he could find with the theory was that Emily's presence should not have been enough to arouse him if that had been the case.

Shaking it off as the least important part of the mystery, Nigel extracted what information he could from MacGregor before thrusting him back into deep slumber. He looked around then for a lamp or candle, but could find nothing that looked familiar. There was something on the tables on either side of the bed that he thought must be lamps, but both had the strange looking glass balls protruding from their tops. He couldn't see any way to light them.

He was stymied for several moments. Finally, he stalked around the bed to MacGregor. "Get up, man and show me how ta light tha bloody lamps."

MacGregor sat up, fumbled with the lamp for a moment and then light flooded the room.

"I've no more need of ye," Nigel muttered, placing his palm on MacGregor's forehead and pushing him down once more.

Studying the lamp, he moved the handle MacGregor had used, turning the lamp on, then off, on, then off. He still couldn't figure out how the thing was producing light, but he finally decided it wasn't really important so long as he knew how to make it work and turned his attention to selecting the makings of a wardrobe for himself.

MacGregor was a bit stouter than him, not quite so tall, but he figured the MacGregor was a sight closer to him in size than Emily and the clothes should fit well enough until he could find a tailor.

He found a kilt in the armoire. It wasn't his clan tartan, of course, but it was a kilt. He took it anyway, since beggars couldn't be choosers and a pair of breeches and a couple of shirts. Stockings required another lengthy search, but he found some and then settled to looking for shoes. They pinched like the very devil, but he was tired of having to go barefoot. He decided he would make do with them until he could find a shoemaker.

It had occurred to him after he'd gotten over the worst of his anger that he'd been so furious he hadn't even thought to look to see if Emily had discovered the other emergency stash he'd hidden in the dungeon. He'd put the bulk of it in the casket with him, of course, figuring that was the safest place since he would certainly have awoken if anyone had tried to take it while he was in the casket. He hadn't considered the possibility that someone would find it while he was out feeding.

No matter. Sooner or later he'd find out where she'd taken it and in the meanwhile--assuming she hadn't found the rest--he would have that to take care of his needs.

He discovered when he got back to the castle that she'd locked him out.

Irritating woman!

Once he was inside, he unbolted the door, retrieved his clothing and bolted the door again.

She had locked him out of his room, as well ... and stuffed clothing under the door.

Torn between amusement and annoyance, Nigel transformed

once more, drifting into the room through the keyhole. She was asleep, he saw, dead center of the bed, a pillow nearly as long as she was clasped beneath her, her heart shaped buttocks aimed enticingly in his direction.

His mouth went dry. Both his amusement and his irritation vanished.

Dimly, he remembered uttering something asinine about being a gentleman. He looked down at his cock, which had lifted its head with interest. “Ye needn’t look so hopeful, Laird MacKissack. She’ll na’ be happy ta see ya.”

After a moment, he moved around to his side of the bed climbed in.

She had all the cover, too, he noticed.

She muttered in her sleep when he pried it from her grip and covered himself, but there was a definite chill in the air, and he was of no mind to freeze his arse off only for the sake of being a gentleman.

The Laird had finally settled down in disappointment and Nigel had just composed himself for sleep when she rolled over and flung one arm and leg across him. He sucked in a sharp breath, held it for several moments and slowly released it, but there was just so much a man could take and still retain his sanity.

Chapter Seven

There was a man in her bed. Emily felt a tiny prick of alarm, and then she remembered that it was *his* bed. She was in his bed. It was odd, this feeling that she belonged to him, and in his bed, when she couldn’t remember having a significant other.

Maybe it was a one night stand? It wasn’t something she’d ever tried, but....

When he skated a large, faintly rough palm over her bare skin she realized it was Nigel--the vampire, Nigel.

Something about that disturbed her, but she wasn’t entirely certain what it was. In a few moments, she didn’t care either, because his mouth and hands felt absolutely wonderful as he caressed her sensitive flesh with them.

He pushed the long, loose nightgown/T-shirt she slept in up until it was wadded across the tops of her breasts. Her nipples puckered and stood erect as the cool air of the room caressed them, blood thudding in the distended tips as anticipation began to grow inside of her.

His hot mouth wandered along the valley between her breasts and then meandered up one slope to the crest. He teased it for some moments with his tongue, making her gasp and move restlessly beneath him. Finally, when she thought he meant only to tease her, he sucked the aching bud into his mouth. Heat coursed through her the moment his mouth closed over the sensitive tip. She moaned in pleasure and encouragement, gripping his shoulders and then stroking his arms, and shoulders, and back. With each sucking motion of his mouth, a new, harder jolt of sensation went through her, creating a corresponding tightening of muscles low in her belly and gathering moisture in her sex until she found she was panting in an effort to draw enough air into her lungs, so dizzy she felt drunk with desire.

Hunger grew inside of her apace with the sensations--burgeoning, building, making her body grow taut, and then tighter still until she felt herself nearing her peak.

Briefly, disappointment filled her when he released the nipple and began to wander down hill again to the valley, but her belly tightened in expectation, her neglected nipple throbbing a plea for attention.

He bestowed it with fervor, making her body leap upward to the wrung it had been perched upon and then begin to climb higher still. Uncomfortable with her growing need, she shifted beneath him. His engorged cock was digging into the soft flesh of her belly and she needed it lower. Satisfaction filled her as it nestled between her thighs, nudging her cleft each time she arched her hips and evoking welcome waves of pleasure.

Groaning, he broke off his attentive caress of her nipple and sat back on his knees, dragging her panties down her hips and off her legs impatiently and then settling between her thighs once more, guiding the head of his cock along her cleft until he wedged the rounded head in the mouth of her sex. She moaned, lifting up to meet his thrust. His cock slipped through her wetness, breached her passage and was caught in the taut, unyielding grip of the throat of her sex as it tightened convulsively around him.

Grinding his teeth, he withdrew slightly and bore down again, gaining a little more ground before her muscles fisted around him and halted his progress once more.

Despite the chill in the air, moisture beaded his body as he struggled to hold onto his control, as he fought his way past her clinging muscles and finally buried himself deeply inside of her.

Emily wrapped her arms tightly around him as he paused to catch his breath, held him for several moments and then began to stroke his back, rotating her hips in invitation when he seemed slow to respond to her needs. Uttering a sound between a growl and a groan, he captured her mouth beneath his and began to thrust inside of body with his cock and his tongue, caressing her mouth and her nether mouth with the same erotic rhythm. Emily's body leapt with excitement, shaking as it scaled the limits of pleasurable endurance. Without warning, she crested, her body quivering, quaking and finally exploding with release. Crying out, she closed her mouth around his tongue, sucking him as her body convulsed around his cock in delightful waves.

He shuddered, jerked as her release provoked a hard response from his body, driving him beyond control and into crisis.

The release of tension sucked her back down into oblivion once more and Emily went perfectly limp, smiling faintly as she drifted away on a warm cloud of satisfaction.

Something was tickling her nose when she woke. She twitched her nose but the tickle persisted, rousing her to an awareness that the mattress was harder and lumpier than she'd thought. It was moving, too--up and down.

Emily opened her eyes to a fleshy brownish-pink color that refused to come into focus because it was against the tip of her nose. Lifting her head slightly, she blinked the blurriness of sleep from her eyes and tried again. The color resolved itself into a broad chest with a light dusting of dark hair across the male breasts and puddling between them. Emily shoved herself upright and stared down at Nigel blankly, feeling outrage slowly filtering through her groggy brain.

Snatching a pillow up, she clocked him with it.

Slowly, he opened one eye a crack. "What time is it, then?" he muttered huskily.

Emily glared at him. "How the hell would I know? I just woke up! What are you doing in my bed?"

His gaze flickered past her to the window and slammed shut again. "It canna be more'n eight of the clock. Wake me noonish," he growled, rolling over and burying his head in *her* pillow.

Emily stared at him in disbelief.

He didn't have a stitch of clothes on! She was beginning to think the man never wore any. And what he was doing in *her* bed, naked, as if she'd *invited* him, she didn't even want to imagine, particularly since she began to have a dim recollection of a wildly erotic dream she'd had the night before.

She'd bolted the front door and the bedroom door, and what's more she'd stuffed a sheet in the crack under the bedroom door, just in case he tried the smoke trick again.

That thought prompted another one and she glanced toward the window speculatively. As she'd thought, sunlight was streaming through it since she hadn't drawn the drapes the night before.

Vampires roamed the night. Sunlight killed them.

Her eyes narrowed with suspicion as she turned to look at him again.

She'd never believed that hooey about him being a vampire anyway. He was just some kind of ... magician ... or maybe a hypnotist!

She smacked him on his bare ass with her palm "What kind of vampire are you, anyway?" she demanded.

"A tired one," he muttered into the pillow, scarcely flinching when she popped his bare buttock.

"What I'd like to know," Emily said gratingly, "is, if you really are a vampire, like you claim, why is it that the sunlight doesn't seem to be bothering you?"

"It *is* bothering me. Close tha bleedin' drapes, will you?"

"Sunlight kills vampires," Emily stated emphatically.

Nigel struggled up onto one elbow and peered at her blearily. "Are ye daft, lass? Why the bloody hell would sunlight kill me?"

"You're not a vampire, are you?"

He studied her for a long moment and finally collapsed on the pillow once more. "More of tha' vampire nonsense ye been hearin' about, eh? Well, it's too bleedin' early in the day fer arguin'. Come back later, lass, an' we'll go a round er two when I'm up ta it."

On one level, she knew he was right. She hadn't even had her coffee, and she felt like hell. Her own brain felt as if it was functioning at half speed ... or maybe less, because she remembered just then that she had *not* gone to bed naked. She occasionally slept nude, when it was particularly hot and the air conditioner couldn't keep up with the muggy heat of the deep south, but she wasn't in Georgia anymore and it wasn't hot and she knew damned well she'd had a nightie and panties on when she'd gone to bed.

"You ... you ... Asshole! Where are my damned clothes?"

He turned his head to one side and cracked an eye open. She wasn't fooled, however, there was definite wariness in that one, bright blue eye. "Did ye lose them?"

Her eyes narrowed. "I didn't dream that ... what happened last night, did I...?"

"I'm a vampire, na' a mind reader. How am I ta ken what ye dreamed, or ye didn't dream, lass?"

Emily ground her teeth. "I'm sure as hell not dreaming now and there's ... semen on my thighs."

He raised up enough to study them with interest. "Here, let me have a better look," he murmured, grabbing her legs and prying them apart.

Emily slapped his hands, but he dragged her beneath him despite her struggles, grabbing her hands and manacling them to the bed. He was shaking with laughter when he pinned her to the bed with his chest and that made her madder. "You ... you hypnotized me ... or something."

"I'm na' sure what this hypnotize thing is, but I'm fair certain I didn't. I'm thinkin' ye was sleep walkin' and molested me in my sleep when I was defenseless."

She hated to admit it, but not only was he sexy as hell with his tousled hair and his morning whiskers, he was also cute. She bit her lip, trying to keep from smiling back at him. There was no sense in encouraging the rogue. "You did the vampire thing, then, and made me *think* I was dreaming it."

Something flickered in his eyes. "If I had, ye'd na' remember a thing about it."

"I didn't have to remember! You left ... evidence!"

His dark brows rose, but his eyes were still twinkling with suppressed laughter. "I'll have ta remember ta tidy up after meself then, won't I, lass?"

"Ha! You admit it then?"

"I dinna, but I'm thinkin', seein' as how ye've got me all roused up an' awake now, I may as well partake."

Emily gaped at him, all traces of humor gone. "You think I'd *let* you?"

He sighed irritably. "Aye, I think ye will," he murmured, pinning her with a piercing gaze.

Emily blinked, feeling heavy suddenly, weak, dizzy. She struggled against it. Bit by bit, however, the lethargy gained the upper hand until she found she no longer wanted to struggle. She felt strangely peaceful as she stared up at him, totally aware, and yet devoid of emotion about the situation.

Releasing his grip on her wrists, he rolled off of her, propping his head in his hand and allowing his gaze to roam her length in a leisurely inspection that seemed to miss nothing. Emily watched his eyes darken and cloud with desire, feeling a reflection of his need growing inside of her.

He caressed her with a slow thoroughness that left no part of her untouched, building an inferno inside of her that made her feel scorched from the heat, feverish.

Spreading her thighs, he settled between them, breaching the mouth of her sex and thrusting inside of her even as he covered her lips in a searing kiss. Emily gasped as her body adjusted to his intrusion, feeling her body fisting tightly around his engorged cock. With each stroke of his flesh along her passage, quakes of delight rippled through her, growing harder, winding tightly through her until she tore her lips from his and uttered a throaty groan she could no longer contain.

He increased the tempo of his thrusts then, driving more rapidly into her until the stimulation was nearly unbearable. When the sensations reached her limit of endurance and burst, fragmenting in white hot ecstasy, it dragged an exultant cry from her that he echoed moments later as he reached his own culmination.

Shuddering with the force of it, he settled weakly against her, gasping for breath.

Awash with satisfaction, Emily lay limply beneath him, vaguely aware of a sense of completion that went beyond mere sexual release and an anxiety that nearly matched it that she should feel anything of the sort.

Placing a gusty, open mouthed kiss along her neck, Nigel rolled off of her and onto his back. Lifting the hand nearest her, he stroked her temples with his long fingers. "I'd say yer na' ta remember, lass, but yer tha' stubborn an' I ken ye will. I'm na' complainin', mind ye. I've a notion I'd na' awoke when I did if na' fer the life force ye bear, an' my affairs in such a mess as it is, but as much as I need to feed from it, I'm thinkin' is na' such a good notion ta keep ye here.

"Mortals make pur companions for vampires an' a wise vampire stays clear of a mortal when there's danger of growing attached. Fer both our sakes, ye need ta be thinkin' about goin' back ta the colonies, lass."

Chapter Eight

It was bright in the room when Emily awoke. She lay staring at the ceiling for some time, feeling lethargic, strangely satisfied and yet ill at ease, too.

Nigel was dead to the world.

Maybe that wasn't the best sort of metaphor to use in reference to a vampire?

Frowning, she sat up and eased off of the bed.

He felt around the bed when she moved, as if searching for her, but after a moment, he ceased, sleeping deeply.

Creeping around the room, Emily found a change of clothing and moved to the door. It was still locked, and the cloth she'd stuffed under the door untcuched. She studied it in puzzlement, wondering how he'd gotten in, and finally glanced toward the window. It, too, was still closed and locked.

Nigel didn't seem to follow any of the 'rules' she knew about vampires--he might or might not be a vampire--but it was for certain he wasn't just an ordinary fellow.

The door creaked when she let herself out and she glanced toward the bed, her pulse jumping. When he didn't stir, she closed the door behind her and went down the hall to the bathroom.

There was no sense in trying to lie to herself about what had happened. She had thoroughly enjoyed Nigel's lovemaking--he was a skilled and considerate lover. What made her uncomfortable was that he seemed capable of depriving her of will in a way that went beyond merely 'turning her on' to a point where she simply didn't care anymore.

She wasn't in the habit of engaging in recreational sex, or casual sex. She had needs, just like everyone else, and she didn't consider herself a Miss Goody-goody. She just didn't get anything out of sex, generally, unless there was also a bond of affection.

She found Nigel likable--for a complete nut. She also found him very attractive, but she didn't feel comfortable about falling into bed with him on such a short acquaintance and knew she wouldn't have willingly.

He'd done something--besides being a charmingly handsome rogue.

Dimly, she remembered saying something about not 'letting'

him have his way with her--and directly after that, had.

What was she to do about him?

She supposed she could go back to the police station and demand that he be removed, or arrested, but what if what he'd said was true? What if this place had been his and he hadn't agreed to the sale, thought he had it taken care of?

It wasn't her problem. She'd bought it. Everyone that was supposed to know about these things said everything was in order. Legally, it was hers.

The problem with legal was that it wasn't always right.

It also wasn't infallible. It was possible that Nigel might be able to prove a prior claim and come up with the papers to back it up that would negate her title. Then she'd be out her money and the place, because she didn't think for one moment the people she'd paid would just turn around and hand it back to her. She would almost certainly end up in court ... and then the little nest egg she'd discovered would be gone, too.

She could leave, of course, but in the U.S. possession was nine tenths of the law and if she gave up possession and moved out, it might weaken her situation even worse. Besides, she didn't really have any where to go unless she was willing to use the wind fall she'd discovered in the dungeon and she was afraid to use it until it was absolutely necessary.

By the time she'd finished her bath, she had decided to yield possession of the master suite to Nigel and take the next one down the hall. At least then he couldn't claim that she was sleeping in his bed, which nine out of ten men would consider constituted an open invitation--with Nigel obviously among them.

She couldn't quite decide why it was that she wasn't totally pissed off about the fact that he'd taken advantage of her. It occurred to her that she should have been and that her acceptance of the situation so philosophically just wasn't like her. Regardless, she couldn't summon outrage, fury--anything at all beyond a mild sort of discomfort at the sense of acceptance that gripped her and wouldn't let go.

She didn't know what she was going to do if he persisted in considering her as part of his property. She decided, though, that she would cross that bridge when she came to it.

The most important thing at the moment was to figure out how she was going to get her coins out of the bed and into a safe place now that Nigel had so inconveniently decided to lay claim to the bed.

She discovered when she got downstairs that a handful of local men had arrived looking for work. It disconcerted her, but finally she told them to have a look around the place and assess the damage while she went to the kitchen to scrounge up food to jump start her day.

The milk was tepid. Since the refrigerator was turned all the way up as far as she could see, she mentally added a refrigerator to her list of needs and tried the stove. It seemed to function reasonably well, but after charring the bread she put in the oven to heat she decided she was going to have to figure out its little idiosyncrasies before she could actually cook with it. Breaking off the burned areas, she buttered the remainder and ate it with a cup of instant coffee, pondering her situation.

She supposed she hadn't adequately considered the difficulties in renovating a structure several hundred years old, but then she'd expected the castle to be in far better shape than it actually was. She'd figured the building would need modernization, probably some repairs, but she'd thought it would be basically livable. She supposed it was, but not by most people's standards and only in the sense that it beat living on the street. The unpleasant truth was that the castle was pretty much a disaster area. If it hadn't been a historical structure, it would probably have been condemned.

She'd seen buildings that looked better that *had* been condemned.

It was going to take a *lot* of money to make this place the jewel she'd envisioned, and she wondered if there was enough gold in the world to do it. That thought reminded her of the coins she'd tucked away and she dwelt irritably on the fact that Nigel was barring her from it at the moment. It suddenly occurred to her, though, that she'd tucked that first coin she'd found into the pocket of her jeans. It wasn't likely to bring much, but at least she could have the coin assessed so she would know the value.

She'd left her jeans in the bedroom--with Nigel.

Leaving the kitchen, she went to assess the situation with the castle again, this time with an eye toward repairing it. Two of the men were wandering around the great hall, staring at the walls, the ceiling and the floor doubtfully. When she entered, they stopped and turned to look at her. She could tell just from their expressions that they figured tearing it down and starting over might be the best bet, but that wasn't an option.

After a little thought, she decided just to start with basic cleaning. The place was so filthy from so many years of accumulated dust and mold and cobwebs that it was pretty near impossible to tell what needed discarding, repairing, or just cleaning. Whatever the value of the coin, she thought she could pay the men for one day anyway.

Briefly, they haggled over a days' pay and she put them to work sorting and moving the furnishings. Any piece that looked sound was to be left where it was. Anything that needed repairing was to be brought to the great hall. Whatever looked beyond repair was to be placed in a separate pile so that she could study it herself and decide whether to attempt repairs or give up on it and consider it a total loss.

They didn't look particularly thrilled with the job, but they went to work readily enough. Shrugging inwardly, Emily figured the job itself would take care of 'weeding out' those who really wanted, or needed, the work and those who'd come because they thought they might make more money working for the American. Outside, she found three others. She put them to work cleaning; cutting the overgrown brush, collecting the stones that had fallen that would need to be reworked, and building a rubbish pile.

Satisfied that at least some progress was being made, she went back inside and stood staring up the spiral stairs for some moments. Finally, girding herself, she went up.

Nigel was sprawled in the center of the bed on his belly, a pillow over his head, but he didn't so much as twitch when she quietly entered the room. The pillow was the only thing covering his bare body. The coverlet had slid off on the floor.

Emily stared at him for several moments, captured by the sight of all that bare flesh.

As much as she would've liked to dismiss any interest in him, she found she couldn't. He was a big man, and very nicely built. He did not have the 'cut' and definition of a body builder, but his body was taut and muscular and, as she recalled, hard all over.

A shiver went through her and she dragged her gaze from him almost reluctantly and looked around the room. Her belongings were still scattered and she didn't want to linger in the room long enough to gather them all up. After a moment, she spied her discarded jeans and shirt from the day before and collected them. To her relief, the coin was still inside the jeans pocket.

Turning, she scurried from the room, feeling a sense of triumph.

The sense of jubilation lasted until she got her first good look at the rental car in the light of day. Dismay filled her.

The windshield was cracked. The lord only knew what the

rental agency was going to charge her for repairing it.

She had a week, however, before she had to face them with the damage, and she dismissed it, pulling out the road map and studying it. It wouldn't hurt to look for a coin shop in the village, but she rather thought she wanted more than one opinion on the value of the coin.

Telling the workers she was off to get supplies, she headed out, hopeful, working out a story in her head to explain her possession of the coin that she thought might be believable.

Chapter Nine

The racket could not be ignored. Nigel tried his best, but slowly the bumps and pounding and talking and whistling filtered through his cocoon of comfort, disturbing the sense of well being that had held him in blissful thrall. Irritation surfaced. The servants knew better than to make so much noise when he was sleeping. What the devil were they about?

He didn't realize that he'd been trying to identify the sounds as individuals until it occurred to him that he heard nothing familiar. Sluggishly, his mind connected with that lack of recognition and it finally dawned on him that he wasn't listening to the day to day work of his servants. Those mortals were long since gone. Whoever it was stomping about the place and making such a racket, it was no one he knew.

Yawning, he stretched and rolled over. After a little while, he managed to lift one eye lid enough to peer toward the window. It was still early. Eleven, perhaps eleven thirty.

In the days before he had taken the notion to hibernate for a time, it had been his habit to roam the night, drop into bed near dawn, and sleep till early afternoon, but he could see that until he'd trained a new staff that wasn't a habit he was going to be able to take up again.

He felt around the bed for his woman and discovered she was gone.

That roused him enough to make him sit up and look around the room.

He frowned when he saw that the room was empty save for himself, far more irritated that his concubine was missing without his leave than he was about being awakened. He'd claimed her twice--thoroughly. She should have been completely under his spell. He couldn't figure out how it was that she didn't seem to be, but he didn't like it. He didn't like it at all.

She should have been waiting for him to waken to do his bidding. He felt invigorated from the life essence he'd absorbed from her thus far, but he needed her again and she'd fled, leaving him with no way to assuage his hunger.

In the light of day, he found he was less inclined to attribute her with powers of any sort ... beyond mortal stubbornness. He felt strong now. Perhaps he hadn't yet attained his former strength, perhaps he was still a little lacking in some skills because of his prolonged sleep, but he was certain he was once again fully capable of summoning most of his powers.

And yet Emily still managed to effectively resist him.

Finally, he decided it was an enigma that would sort itself out with time. At the moment, he was more interested in discovering what was going on in his castle. Rolling from the bed, he looked around for a chamber pot.

There wasn't one. There also wasn't a washbasin or pitcher for bathing. Irritated all over again, Nigel stalked down the stairs and through the deserted kitchen. Flinging the kitchen door open, he leaned against the door frame and took a piss in the garden.

There was a strange man moving about the kitchen garden, hacking at the weeds with a sling. He stopped when Nigel opened the door, stared at him curiously a moment and then went back to his task.

"You there," Nigel called when he'd finished. "By what name are ye known?"

The man stopped again and looked him over. "Sean. Are ye the yank's husband, then?"

Nigel frowned. After a moment, he realized the man must be referring to Emily. He was on the point of denying it when it occurred to him that he didn't particularly want the locals gossiping about his woman. "I'm laird here. Fetch me up some water for bathing."

The man frowned. "Is the water na' workin' in the castle then?"

Nigel gave him an assessing look. He wasn't accustomed to having anyone counter an order with a question, but he was curious enough about the comment to let it slide. "Have a look."

"I'm na' much of a plumber, but I'll see if there's aught I can do about it."

Nigel stepped to one side as the man reached the door. After glancing around, he headed for the sink to one side of the kitchen and grasped a knob. Water spilled forth the moment he turned it.

Intrigued, Nigel strode across the kitchen and stared at the water flowing through the spout. It appeared to be coming right out of the wall. He tilted his head, listening to the movement of the water and trying to determine the direction it was coming from and realized that it was moving through the tubes that ran across the ceiling and down along the wall.

"Yer right. It ain't gettin' hot. Maybe the breaker on the water heater's tripped?"

Nigel stared at the man uncomprehendingly.

"Ye ken where the breaker box is?"

Since he didn't ken what a breaker was, or even a water heater, although that sounded rather self-explanatory, he certainly had no clue of where the box might be that held the breakers--whatever those were. He merely shrugged.

After glancing around the kitchen, the man finally turned and made his way down into the dungeon.

The thing at the bottom of the stairs was still growling and coughing and the strange flameless light still glowing, Nigel saw. He didn't see a box of any sort beyond his sarcophagus.

Sean glanced at him over his shoulder a couple of times. "It's a bit chill down here ta be walkin' about in the altogether."

Frowning, Nigel grasped the man around the throat with one hand. Lifting the man clear of the stairs, he pulled him close, peering through his bulging eyes into his thoughts. "I'm a patient, good-natured fellow else I'd na' ha' put up with yer impertinence as long as I have, my lad. Ye'll watch yer tongue when ye speak ta me or ye'll na' have it long. Do ye ken?"

When the man's eyes glazed, Nigel set him on his feet once more.

"Now ... I dinna ken breaker box, nor plumbing, nor water heater for that matter. Ye'll explain it ta me an then we'll find these things and ye'll show me how they're to be done."

Nodding, Sean held forth for a good ten minutes, but he might just as well have been speaking a foreign language for Nigel found he simply did not know enough to make sense of it. His library was gone, but it seemed doubtful it would have been of use to him if it was still intact. In the days before, he'd kept abreast of advances in science, but he hardly felt that a two hundred year old book would be of much use to him even if he still had the books. Finally, he simply cut Sean off and urged him to explain the simple workings of the things he described so that he could use them. When he had time--and money--he'd locate some books and bring himself up to date on the things that had changed since he'd last walked the Earth.

They located the breaker box and Sean flipped the breakers back and forth, plunging them into darkness at one point. Finally, he expressed it as his opinion that all the breakers were working as well as could be expected considering their antiquity and they went up the stairs once more.

When they reached the hall once more, Nigel rummaged through the bundle of clothing he'd left there and finally merely donned the kilt. From there, they proceeded up the stairs to the second floor and Sean displayed the wonders of the bathroom. Pleased, Nigel sent Sean about his business and made use of the facilities. Despite Sean's assurance that the water heater was working, the water was barely less than frigid, but since servants seemed to be a thing of the past, he made do.

There was a rectangular piece of fluffy fabric hanging over the shower curtain rod. It smelled of Emily and was still damp from her drying her own body with it. He used it to dry off and tossed it aside.

Donning the kilt once more, he headed down the stairs again and into the kitchen. There were no servants to cook and no food to speak of even to cook himself. Inside some sort of cooling chest, he discovered a block of cheese. Peeling the strange skin off of it, he closed the door of the chest again and looked around for something to go with it. He found bread, but not so much as a single bottle of wine.

Angry now, he settled his hip against one of the tables and consumed the bread and cheese, washing them down with water from the thing Sean had called a faucet.

It was a disappointing meal to say the least. He was accustomed to eating far more elegant meals, but he decided he could remedy the situation far sooner if he could lay his hands upon some of his money.

Brushing the crumbs from his hands, he made his way back to the dungeon. There were no torches, no light source at all beyond the light bulb Sean had explained that used electricity and could not be moved around. After scrounging for a bit, he broke a rickety chair and took one of its legs then pulled some of the lining from his sleeping cask to form a makeshift torch.

Discovering he had nothing to light it with, he climbed the stairs once more and collared Sean in the kitchen garden.

"I've need of flint to light me torch."

Sean scratched his head, staring at the wad of cloth at the end of Nigel's makeshift torch blankly for several moments. Finally, he dug into his pocket and withdrew a small, rectangular object.

The lighter Sean produced pleased Nigel. He pocketed it and thanked the man, striding purposefully inside once more.

Rubble, he discovered, blocked the narrow hall that led to his secret chamber and he nearly lost his patience altogether. Curbing his temper, he trudged back up the stairs once more and rounded up the men working in the castle, setting them to the task of clearing away the rubble and shoring up the hall. He watched them for a while, but grew bored and went back upstairs to assess the magnitude of his situation.

Emily had not reappeared and, as little as he liked to admit it, he wasn't at all pleased with her absence. She'd taken the carriage, he saw, but he couldn't decide whether that meant she had gone upon a long trip or would be returning shortly.

She'd left her belongings. She would return. He was certain of that.

Deciding that, perhaps, she had gone for food, he dismissed her from his mind and examined the castle from top to bottom. By the time he'd finished, he was of the opinion that it was beyond repair. Perhaps he should simply have it pulled down and rebuild?

Emily seemed strangely attached to the pile of rubble, however.

Not that he was particularly concerned about whether she was pleased, or displeased, about his decision, but he finally decided he was rather fond of the place himself and that it warranted the work needed to put it to rights. There was a wealth of memories attached to the place for him, some good, some not so good, some rather unpleasant, but overall he was inclined to look on those of a more pleasant nature and the desire to preserve something of such familiarity was strong, as well.

Everything had changed so drastically since he'd decided to hibernate. It was going to take a great deal of effort to accustom himself to the changes as it was. He didn't particularly relish the thought of also having to grow accustomed to a new residence.

Having settled that in his mind, he went outside. None of the outbuildings still stood. The stables had vanished altogether and he felt an unaccustomed pang of regret for the horses that had once lived there. He'd been particularly fond of Caesar, his bay stallion. He'd expected to wake to find Caesar's descendants awaiting to attend him as Caesar once had.

He supposed he should consider purchasing himself one of the new horseless carriages everyone seemed to use now, but he'd always preferred to ride and he didn't particularly feel up to trying to master a carriage that looked so strange and moved so fast. Eventually, he knew he would have to, but he saw no reason to rush things. He had all the time in the world.

Chapter Ten

Emily found herself humming as she headed back to the Castle MacKissack. It had been a long and very tiring day but enthusiasm buoyed her flagging energy.

She'd taken the coin to a dozen different shops in almost as many towns. No two had appraised the coin at the same value, but after she'd made the rounds she had a far better idea of the worth of her discovery. She just wished she'd had the chance to check on the internet before she'd had to sell the first one. Unfortunately, she didn't have a land line ... yet. She hoped to have one before she had to sell more of the coins, but she was still very happy with what she'd done, even knowing she'd probably sold the coin for a lot less that it's actual value.

The car was full to bursting with the things she'd bought. She had deliveries scheduled for supplies and building materials ... and she still had enough money left to pay the workers!

Her good humor vanished as she pulled into the parking spot she'd claimed and turned the car off. The place looked very little different than it had when she'd left hours ago! What had the men been doing all this time?

Trying to tamp her rising ire, Emily climbed from the car and headed across the narrow bridge and into the keep. She could see the men were working, but they were still pretty much working in the same spot as they'd been working when she left.

"You haven't made much progress," she said as she reached them.

The men exchanged a glance. "Yer man had us down in the dungeon clearing a bit of rubble."

"My...." Nigel. Emily's lips tightened. She turned away, heading for the main entrance, intent on giving Nigel a piece of her mind for 'posing' as her man and having the nerve to pull her workers off the job she'd given them to do something for him instead.

"He left with Sean a bit ago," one of the workers volunteered.

Emily halted in her tracks, turning back to the man. "Sean?"

"Connors. The bloke that give us a ride up here."

"Oh." Emily frowned, remembering the old truck that had been parked beside her car earlier when she'd left. Disconcerted to discover she had no outlet for her temper, she stood indecisively for several moments and finally stalked back to the car to begin unloading it. When she came back outside, the men had gathered around her car to unload it. Mollified, she directed them where to put the supplies and went inside to see if she could discover what Nigel had been up to.

* * * *

The operation of the carriage seemed a bit more complicated than Nigel had expected it to be and seemed to require a surprising amount of coordination, as well. There were three pedals on the floor. Sean had depressed the one in the middle when he'd turned the key. Nigel had wondered what the key was for--for the placement of the lock seemed odd to say the least. The moment Sean turned the key, however, the carriage began to bounce and growl like the contraption in the basement that he'd been told was a generator to produce electricity.

When he'd pumped another pedal for several moments, Sean grabbed a stick protruding from the floor of the carriage, wrestled it a moment and lifted up on one pedal, depressing another at the same time. The carriage jerked and, to Nigel's surprise, surged backwards. When Sean turned the wheel in front of him, the carriage changed directions.

It was at this point that Sean stomped down on the third pedal, jolting the carriage to a halt. He then went through the entire ritual again, except that this time when he raised one foot and lowered the other, the carriage shot forward jerkily.

It did not make for a comfortable ride. The carriage was not well slung at all and jolted every bone in his body as they bounced along the roadway. He wasn't exactly thrilled with the speed either. As much as he'd always enjoyed racing horses and carriages, those had never attained such speeds and he wasn't at all certain Sean had the skills to handle a carriage moving so fast. After a time, however, when Sean proved that he did indeed have control of the speeding carriage, some of the tension left Nigel and he concentrated on watching and learning. By the time they arrived at the shop where Sean had said he should be able to sell his jewels, he decided he was ready to give it a try himself once they were out in the countryside again and there weren't nearly so many obstacles to avoid.

The shopkeeper seemed inclined to rob him. Nigel was in no mood to haggle over the price and simply mesmerized the man. Once he'd made the man tell him the true value of the necklace, he was perfectly willing to settle for a sum that would allow the man a modest profit. Pocketing his money, he went out again.

Sean, he discovered, left much to be desired as a servant. He remained seated in the carriage, staring at Nigel through the window instead of rushing around to open the door. Irritated, Nigel glanced around. He saw then that everyone seemed to be opening their own doors and finally decided that he would have to accustom himself to the new customs.

"I've need of a tailor and a shoemaker," he announced when he'd climbed into the carriage once more.

Sean frowned. "I canna think of one of either hereabouts. There's a shoe repair shop, but I don't think they make shoes."

Nigel stared at the man in disbelief, but his senses told him Sean was still under his control and therefore could not be lying to him. "Ye've clothes an' shoes. An' everyone else from what I can see. How is it tha' ye've these things when there's no tailors nor shoemakers about?"

"The shops sell both, ready made ta fit."

"They canna ken my measure. How's this?"

Again, Sean frowned in confusion. "Ye just find the closest fit."

Nigel wasn't happy with that, but it seemed he had no choice and he directed Sean to take him to a shop. He was even less happy with the clothing and shoes he was able to purchase, but he supposed they fit as well as the garments he'd taken from MacGregor.

Deciding there had to be skilled tailors still in the world and shoemakers, for that matter, who could produce garments and footwear specifically to his measurements, he purchased only enough for his immediate needs and returned to the carriage Sean referred to as a truck.

Once they'd left the congestion of the town behind, he had Sean pull over and stop the carriage.

"Ye'll need ta teach me how to drive the carriage."

Shrugging, Sean got out and moved to the passenger side of the carriage. Nigel switched places and, once he'd settled in the seat, studied the workings for several moments, remembering the things that Sean had done to start the thing.

The moment he turned the key, the carriage growled, lurched forward and died.

"Ye have ta push the clutch all the way in."

"Clutch?"

"Tha' pedal in the middle."

Nodding, Nigel pushed the pedal as far down as it would go and tried again. This time the carriage hopped forward for several feet before it again died.

"Ye have ta ease out on the clutch and ease down on the gas pedal at the same time. Too much petrol and the engine floods out. Too little an' it chokes."

Nigel was feeling rather more like choking Sean at this point than the carriage. He was tempted to simply give up on it, but he had need of transportation. Grinding his teeth, he tried again and again. Finally, just as he was considering climbing out of the carriage and taking a limb to it, he managed to get the carriage going.

"Now, when ye hear the engine start ta whine a bit, shift ta the next gear."

It made a horrible grinding noise as he tried to comply.

"The clutch. Push it, then let out again and push down on the gas."

He discovered it was a lot harder to keep the carriage on the road and shift gears than it had appeared when Sean had done it. While he was focused on shifting the stick into the correct place, the carriage veered off the side of the road. Righting it, fighting the edge of panic that seemed determined to grip him, he focused on keeping the speeding carriage centered on the roadway.

"You're supposed ta stay ta the left. Otherwise, ye'll hit the next car ye meet."

The carriage was traveling at such speed by now, Nigel didn't even dare take his eyes from the roadway long enough to glare at his 'teacher.' Instead, he gripped the steering wheel in white knuckled fists and concentrated on keeping the thing where it was supposed to be on the pavement.

"Shift to third now."

They met an oncoming carriage as Nigel wandered across the road while attempting third. The blare of its horn alerted Nigel to imminent disaster and he looked up, shouting. "Whoa! Whoa!"

"The brake man! It's na' gonna help ta yell whoa at the bleedin' thing!"

Nigel stomped down on the brake, jerking the wheel at the same time. They missed the oncoming carriage, but ended up in the ditch on the side of the road.

Shaken, Nigel decided he'd had enough practice with the new carriage for one day.

Chapter Eleven

A week of backbreaking, mind numbing cleaning passed before Emily finally worked her way through the lower floor of the castle and turned her attention to the rooms on the upper floor once more. It was just as well, Emily thought wryly, that she hadn't grown up in a cushy sort of life. She was exhausted and she was used to working hard. If she hadn't been, she would've either had to give up or she'd have dropped from exhaustion long since.

Even with modern cleaning tools and supplies, and the aid of a couple of women from the town nearby, it was hard work. She couldn't imagine what it must have been like to have to clean the place in the old days when all the water had to be drawn from a well and lugged into the castle with buckets.

Beyond a cursory cleaning of the room she'd taken up residence in, she hadn't even scratched the surface of her 'apartment,' which included a large bedroom and a small sitting room.

As tired as she was from having worked all day in the lower regions, Emily decided to at least sweep the dust and cobwebs from the two rooms before settling for the night. That way, she could tackle scrubbing down the walls, floor and ceiling first thing in the morning instead of wearing herself out sweeping first. It would also give the room longer to dry out.

She discovered quickly enough that there was far more dust than she'd expected. Within only a few minutes she was choking on the clouds she'd stirred up. There weren't any screens on the windows, but then she hadn't noticed that there was a real problem with insects--not mosquitoes at any rate.

Moving to the windows, she opened both as wide as she could and went back to her task. She'd been listening absently to an odd fluttering sound and a squeaking noise for several moments before it occurred to her that it wasn't creaking wood, or hinges, or, in fact, anything of a non-threatening nature. The hair on her arms and neck stood up as she stopped abruptly and looked around.

She smiled when she saw the small animal fluttering about the ceiling. "Silly thing! You flew in the window. You can go out the same way."

He appeared to have forgotten how he'd gotten in, however, flying round and round the upper part of the room, almost clipping the light dangling from the cord in the center, dipping low, then darting upward again.

The moment he lit, she discovered it wasn't, as she'd thought, a small bird. It was a bat.

She screamed when it turned to look at her and bared its teeth, hissing. After looking wildly around for a weapon, she grabbed the broom up and swung at it, screaming again when it took flight and began to circle the room again.

"Shoo! Out!"

Instead of heading toward the window, it dove toward her.

"Nigel!" she screamed at the top of her lungs, swinging the broom wildly as the thing zipped around her. "Nigel! There's a bat in my room!"

When it dove at her again, she ducked, running in circles in a blind panic. She stopped when she discovered she'd run toward the windows instead of the door. Before she could decide whether to make a run for the door or not, the thing dove for her again.

Catching the broom up in her hands in a batter's stance, she waited until it whizzed past her and swung for all she was worth. She caught it with the straw end of the broom, swatting it in the general direction of the window. To her relief, she managed to bat it out one of the open windows. Dropping the broom, she raced to the window and quickly closed it, then ran to the other windows and closed them, as well.

Below, she heard the resounding thud of the heavy oak door that fronted the castle as it was slammed open and then closed again. Next, she heard the heavy, smacking sound of bare feet as Nigel stalked across the great hall and started up the stairs.

Grabbing up the broom, Emily went to meet him.

"Nigel! There was a bat in my room. I think it was rabid! It hissed at me!" she gasped the moment she saw him, fighting the urge to burst into tears now that the fright was behind her.

It was several moments before she realized he was looking distinctly displeased. Without a word, he snatched the broom from her hands and broke it over his knee, tossing the two pieces over his shoulder.

Emily gaped at him. "You broke my broom!"

"Aye!" he snarled.

Anger surged through her. She plunked her hands on her hips. "I need my broom! What did you break it for? What if that thing gets in the house again? I'm telling you, I'm almost a hundred percent certain that thing's rabid! It looked straight at me and bared its teeth at me and hissed. And then, it attacked me!"

He glared back at her. "He was na' rabid and *I* am a hundred percent certain he'll na' be stupid enough ta try flyin' in yer window again, woman!" he growled. With that, he stalked down the hall to his room and slammed the door behind him.

Emily stared at the reverberating door for several moments and finally turned to look at her broken broom. After several moments, she gathered it up and trudged back to her own room.

"Ass," she muttered as she passed his door. "I had to fight the damned thing off by myself. You'd think he could at least give me a reassuring hug or something! But what does he do? Snarl at me and break my damned broom. Men! They're always such sullen beasts and completely useless in a crisis!"

* * * *

Emily saw the horse and rider out of the corner of her eye as she passed the gates leading up to Castle MacKissack. Slamming on the brakes, she screamed as the rider, laughing like a madman, urged his horse into a leap that just cleared the hood of the car as the horse and rider soared majestically over the drive and car, landing on the other side and racing away at a gallop.

Her heart was still hammering unpleasantly in her chest as she watched the two disappear over a rise, Nigel MacKissack's black hair and tartan flying behind him like flags in the wind.

"Lunatic!" she yelled shakily, frightened into anger.

Finally, gathering herself, she depressed the gas pedal and proceeded to the castle. He was waiting for her when she arrived, walking the horse now, patting it's neck appreciatively.

Still more than a little shaky, Emily glared at him as she emerged from the car. "You scared the *hell* out of me!"

Nigel lifted his dark brows at her. "Ye were in no danger. I would na' have allowed harm ta come ta ye."

Emily ground her teeth. "I wasn't worried about me!" she

snapped, realizing belatedly that she could certainly have been injured if she had hit him and the horse, but then she could scarcely get any angrier than she was already.

He shrugged and finally grinned. "I was na' in any danger either. Samson here's a wee bit fresh. I've a notion he thought ta ditch his rider when he saw the car, but he came ta hand well enough. He's nae Caesar, but he'll do."

Emily shook her head. "The horse ran away with you?" She frowned. "Where did you get him, anyway? And what do you want with a horse?"

He prodded the horse with his knees, guiding it up to her, and reached down. Emily sidled away.

"Come. I'll give ye a ride on him."

"No, thanks. I don't like horses. I especially don't like wild things like that beast you're riding."

He frowned, fixing her with a hard look that seemed to go right through her. Emily felt her resolution wavering. Looping the reins around the pommel, he leaned down, grasped her beneath her arms and hauled her onto the saddle before him.

Despite the strange lethargy that had come over her, Emily felt fear. She clutched at him, wrapping her arms tightly around him and burying her face against his chest. He pushed her slightly away and tipped her chin up. "I'll na' allow you ta come ta harm, lass."

Strangely enough, the words reassured her. A calm seemed to settle over her and she leaned against him more trustingly as he grasped the reins and wheeled the horse about.

"I really need to unload the car," Emily protested a little weakly. "And pay the workers."

"I'll handle the workers."

Emily frowned, vaguely disturbed by that comment, but the reason eluded her. Instead, she found herself caught up in the exhilaration of racing across the open field on the back of the horse with the wind ruffling her hair and singing in her ears, the heat and strength of Nigel's body pressed tightly against her. If she closed her eyes, she could imagine herself as a medieval lady, being borne away on the steed of her knight into the happily ever after of a fairy tale princess.

After a time, Nigel reined the horse to a slower gait, then to a brisk trot and finally to a walk. Dismounting beneath the shade of a tree, he left the spent horse to graze and carried her to the grassy knoll beneath the spreading limbs. Without a word, he lay her upon the ground and covered her body with his own, making love to her with a slow thoroughness that built the passion within her to a fever pitch before he gave her the release she craved.

The sun was setting when they made their way back to the castle. Reining the horse to a stop before the wide entrance door, Nigel caught her cheek in his hand and tilted her head back for a lingering kiss. "I hunger for ye, lass. I canna seem ta get enough of ye," he murmured.

The words sent a shaft of heated pleasure through Emily. To her disappointment, however, he released her and helped her down from the horse.

"Wait for me in our room."

Emily watched him as he turned the horse and disappeared into the gathering gloom, feeling the warm glow slowly dissipate and anger and resentment begin to simmer in its place. She felt almost like a sleepwalker coming awake in a place far removed from where she'd lain her head to sleep.

Shivering, she glanced around. The workers had gone home. Vaguely, she recalled that Nigel had said that he would 'handle' the workers. Her irritation grew.

They were her workers. She'd hired them. How dare he appropriate them!

How dare he pat her on the head and tell her to go await him in the bed for his pleasure!

Grinding her teeth, she stalked to the car and began to unload it. Darkness caught her before she'd finished and, reluctantly, she gave up on unloading until she had daylight to see.

She'd been too angry about his highhanded manner to think much beyond that, but as she'd worn off her anger lugging her supplies inside it occurred to her to wonder where he'd gotten the horse, and how he'd paid for it.

Glancing upward, she felt her heart plummet to her toes. She'd been counting on that money to get her out of the fix she was in financially. Abandoning her supplies in the hall, she raced up the stairs, arriving in the master suite breathless. Pulling the finial from the post where she'd hidden her stash, she peered down at it. From what she could see, the gold looked untouched.

It comforted her somewhat, but she was still uneasy, wishing now that she'd moved the gold when she'd taken up residence in the other room. She'd had plenty of opportunities to do so, but the castle was overrun with workmen and she hadn't liked the idea of taking the gold from such an ideal hiding place and risking having it stolen from a less desirable one.

That horse had to have cost a pretty penny, though, and now that she thought on it, Nigel had been wearing new clothes, as well. He'd gotten money from somewhere.

Or he'd used his vampire powers and stolen the goods.

Dismissing it for the moment, she went to her own room and collected one of her suitcases. When she returned, she dropped it on the floor beside the bed and began fishing coins out. When she'd gotten all she could, she zipped the suitcase up and dragged it down the hall to her own suite.

Nigel still hadn't returned, but he'd promised to do so.

Creeping back down the stairs, she went into the kitchen and fixed herself a quick meal, then dashed up the stairs again and barricaded herself into her own suite, trying not to think about what the vampire, Nigel MacKissack, was doing while she consumed her own supper.

When she'd finished eating, she worked on setting the room to rights until weariness began to weigh upon her and the urge to seek her rest. She'd heard nothing to indicate that Nigel had returned. After a brief debate, she finally decided to risk a shower since she was certain she wasn't going to be able to sleep without one.

The bathroom was dark and creepy, like the rest of the castle. There was nothing about it to encourage her to linger and she was uneasy anyway that Nigel would return and catch her unawares. That being the case, she confined her efforts to a simple soap down and rinse, then scurried back to her room and bolted the door.

After she'd dressed for bed, she spent another fifteen or twenty minutes sealing every crevice he might use to enter her room and finally turned off the light and climbed wearily into her bed.

She roused some time later as she felt two strong arms scoop her from the bed. Drowsily, she looked up with little surprise to discover Nigel had come to collect her. She murmured a protest, which he ignored, striding down the hall with her, settling her in his bed and making love to her until she was delirious with passion.

She woke the following morning feeling deliciously sated, but also firmly resolved to do something about the situation she'd found herself in. There had to be some way to keep Nigel's fingers out of the cookie jar, and she meant to find it!

Chapter Twelve

The workers were standing around outside when she went downstairs the following morning. Giving them the task of unloading the car, she went to grab a quick breakfast. They'd finished by the time she returned and, since she hadn't had the chance to do so earlier, she went over what they'd done the week before.

It didn't seem to her that they'd accomplished as much as they should have considering the length of time they'd spent on it. When she questioned them about it, they explained that her 'man' had set them to other tasks while she was away from the castle. She didn't correct their assumption that he was her man, though it irritated her, both the fact that they assumed he was head of the household and his arbitrary countermanding of her orders.

Dismissing it for the moment, she interviewed them to see if any of them had any particular areas of expertise. To her surprise and relief, she discovered that Mr. MacGregor had sent her men skilled in those things she most particularly needed. Setting them the task of working up a list of what they needed to replace the antiquated wiring and plumbing and figuring mortar and stone to fix the castle itself, she went to examine the furniture they'd moved.

The craftsmanship of the furniture spoke for itself. Despite the age of the pieces, despite the fact that nothing had been cared for as it should have been, the majority of the pieces looked as if they could be repaired. Collecting the books she'd bought on antique restoration, she found herself a comfortable spot and settled down to reading and compiling a list. By the time the workmen returned with their own lists, she felt like she had what she needed to get started and, after comparing their list with the materials she'd already bought, she set them to work and went off to order more supplies.

After Emily had ordered the supplies the workmen needed, it occurred to her that she might find some answers to her other questions in books and she stopped by the local book shop. They had a number of novels about vampires, but only one book of mythology and the occult. She wasn't certain whether the novels would be of any use to her or not, but she decided to buy them, as well.

She was feeling rather pleased with herself when she reached the castle once more, until she saw Nigel astride his horse, gesturing to the workmen, who were nodding and gesturing in turn. Grinding her teeth, Emily climbed out of the car and went over to see what they were doing.

"Are we working on a new project?" she asked with exquisite politeness.

"Aye. The barn and stables for my horses," Nigel responded absently.

"Horses? You have more than one?" Emily gasped, surprised out of her outrage that he'd commandeered her workmen again.

"Na' yet," Nigel said, dismounting and tossing the reins to one of the men as if he was a stable hand. "I mean ta acquire a dozen or so."

"Horses?"

"Aye."

Emily blinked up at him. "What for?"

He gave her a look, as if *she* was the one who was crazy! "Ta ride, lass," he said off handedly and looped his arm through hers, guiding her toward the castle. "And for the carriages."

"Carriages?" Emily said faintly. "What are you going to do with a carriage?"

"I'll need transportation now and again."

"Uh ... people don't drive around in carriages anymore."

He lifted his brows. "An' what's that you dash about in, then?"

"The car? It's not a carriage. It has an engine."

He was silent for several moments, obviously displeased about something. "I suppose I'll hae ta learn ta drive one, but I'm na' anxious. I had Sean show me the other day when he took me into town, but my lack of skill scared him nigh as badly as tha carriage scared me."

Emily bit her lip to contain a smile. It was on the tip of her tongue to offer to teach him, but she hardly thought it was a good idea to fraternize with him when her goal was to oust him from her property. Resolutely, she disentangled herself from his grasp as they reached the main entrance to the castle and then put a little distance between them. "I didn't want to say anything in front of the men, but I hired them to repair the castle. I don't appreciate you dragging them off to do something else after I've told them what I want them to work on."

His brows rose. A flicker of amusement crept into his eyes.

Crossing his arms over his chest, he leaned against the door frame. "I thought we'd settled the matter of who was master here."

Emily's eyes narrowed. She plunked her hands on her hips. "We haven't settled anything! Don't think for one moment that you've won just because you've been using that voodoo bullshit on me, because you haven't! This is my castle and those are my workmen! And I hired them to repair the castle, *not* to start building something else!"

"Then we're in agreement."

Emily gaped at him. "We are?"

"Aye. The castle's in sore need of repairs an' tha's a fact. I'll tell them ta leave off on the stable awhile an' repair the castle first."

"You'll tell...." Emily compressed her lips in impotent fury. Whirling, she stalked back to the car and started unloading the supplies she'd bought.

She didn't realize he'd followed her until he bellowed for the men. They came trotting up at once, grabbed her parcels and started carrying them inside. Favoring Nigel with an irritated glare, she grabbed her books and headed inside.

Chapter Thirteen

The garlic positively reeked. Inside of ten minutes, Emily had a blinding headache from the fumes and her eyes were watering. The book had been very specific, though. Garlic warded off vampires. Tonight, she intended to sleep in her own bed, undisturbed and free from the anxiety that Nigel would simply come for her when it pleased him.

Maybe she shouldn't have cut the cloves? It didn't seem to her, though, that they really smelled strongly enough to ward off anything before they were cut. Besides, she hadn't gotten nearly enough. Once she'd cut them in half, she was not only able to make a garlic chain to go around her neck, but she had enough left over to mince and place in bowls near the door and windows.

She sat up to wait for him.

It was well into the wee hours of the morning before she saw the drift of smoke into the room and Nigel abruptly appeared at the foot of her bed.

He was holding his nose. “What the bloody hell is tha’ smell?”

Emily blinked the tears from her eyes and pasted a smug smile on her lips. “Garlic!” she announced triumphantly.

“I ken that, but where’s the bleedin’ stench coming from?”

Emily lifted the garlic lei she’d formed for herself and waved it at him tauntingly. “Garlic wards off vampires.”

“I’d think it would ward off anyone. What the bloody hell are ye doin’ wearin’ it?”

“I told you. It wards off vampires. I’m warding off a vampire,” Emily said with determined patience.

He glared at her a moment over his pinched nostrils and finally strode to the windows opening them one by one and tossing the bowls of garlic out. Dragging in an untainted breath of air, he returned for the bowl she’d left by the door and tossed that out, as well.

“The garlic doesn’t affect you,” Emily said, daunted.

“Like hell it doesn’t! I’ve na’ smelled anythin’ less appealin’ in many a day!” Nigel growled, planting his fists on his hips. “If you weren’t in the mood for lovin’ why dinna you say so?”

Emily gave him an indignant look. “As *if* you’d listen to any damned protest! You just use that voodoo shit on me and do whatever you please!”

“I don’t do voodoo shite. I dinna even ken what it is!”

“Mumbo jumbo, then!”

“Tha’ neither! You’re na’ gonna sit there an’ tell me ye dinna enjoy it as much as I do!”

Jerk! He just *had* to throw that up to her! “That’s beside the point! I didn’t tell you you could just move in with me! I don’t recall offering to be your fuck buddy! I didn’t tell you just to help yourself any time you wanted to fuck!”

He reddened. “Ye’ve the mouth of a sailor on ye, lass! Nay, worse! I’ve a mind ta turn ye over my knee! Yer my concubine. I claimed ye. It’s na’ fuckin’. It’s makin’ love an’ I’ll thank ye ta keep a civil tongue in yer head!”

Emily gaped at him in disbelief. “*You* claimed me? And just like that, I’m yours?”

He frowned. “Tha’s generally the way of it. I’m a vampire.”

“Which is supposed to tell me exactly what?” Emily snatched her book up and shook it at him. “I looked up all the rules about vampires and I can’t see that you follow any of them! I’ve nailed up crucifixes and strewn garlic all over the place and you just waltz right in here like I invited you! Sunlight doesn’t bother you!

You don't suck blood. What kind of vampire are you anyway?"

"A real one," he growled. "I told ye na' ta pay any mind ta tha' nonsense! I'm na' undead, na' an unnatural. I was *born* a vampire, lass. It's no different than bein' born ... with red hair or a different color of skin. I may be as much a freak of nature as an albino, but I'm just as much a part of nature as ye are."

Emily blinked at him, stunned. "But ... people don't live that long. You said you'd been around for centuries."

He gaped at her. "Ye mean ta tell me ye'd have an easier time believin' I was a walkin' dead man than tha' I happen ta live a good deal longer than a mortal?"

Put that way, she supposed he had a point, but his comments had prompted a worry that hadn't occurred to her before. "Go back to the other thing. You said you were *born* a vampire?"

"Aye. Why?"

"As in pregnant?"

He gave her an uneasy look.

"Are you saying I could get pregnant?" Emily demanded.

He paled slightly. "Nay."

Emily's lips tightened. "Why don't I believe you, I wonder?"

His eyes narrowed. "Mayhap because ye've na' believed a word I've said so far?" he growled. Turning, he stalked toward the door.

Emily pulled the garlic lei off and threw it at his head. "If you've gotten me pregnant, you ass, I'll ... nail a stake through your heart myself!"

He vanished. The garlic smacked into her door and then hit the floor.

Emily felt vaguely nauseated, but she wasn't certain if it was because of the garlic or the sudden realization that she'd been playing without protection. Not that it had been *her* idea any of the time!

All right. Granted it was the best sex she'd ever experienced in her life and if it hadn't been for the circumstances she would've been more than willing to take him for a lover, but there *were* circumstances that made that a very bad idea. Besides, she would've gotten protection if she'd had the option of choosing.

She was a little relieved when she realized that she was probably in the middle of the least fertile period of her cycle, but not completely easy.

After a few moments, she climbed from the bed, gathered a change of clothing and headed for the shower. If the garlic wasn't going to ward him off, no way in hell was she going to try to sleep reeking of that smell.

Anyway, she'd made it clear enough that she didn't welcome his attention. Very likely he wouldn't bother her again with or without the garlic.

She'd just stuck her head under the shower spray when Nigel appeared in the shower behind her, wrapping his arms around her and pulling her back against his broad chest.

"I knew you'd come around, lass," he murmured huskily, nibbling along the side of her neck as he skated his palms over her breasts, cupping them, massaging them. Emily jumped all when he grabbed her. Weakness surged behind the startlement, and directly behind that, warmth as his fingers plucked gently at her nipples, making them stand erect and sending pulses of burgeoning desire through her.

"Nigel!" she gasped in a strangled voice.

"Aye, luv?" he murmured, running one hand down her stomach and cupping her mound.

She gasped as his fingers parted her flesh, delved into her cleft, rubbing the tiny nub of her clit and sending shafts of pleasure stabbing through her. Her mind melted into chaos. "What are you ...? You left."

"I'm never far from ye, luv. Ye're my concubine. I feel all that ye feel, ken what ye ken."

The play of his finger made it difficult to gather her thoughts into any semblance of order. "Ken? Know, you mean? You're not saying you can read my mind?"

"Aye."

"You can't!"

"Aye, I can ... Oft times."

That comment created a thread of uneasiness, but before it could fully form into a specific dread, he'd stroked her ability to think right out of her. When he nudged her away from him and turned her to face him, pushing her back against the shower wall, she didn't even think to protest. She lifted her arms and looped them around his neck, stretching upward to plaster her body against his hard form.

Heat surged through her as he hooked a hand beneath one thigh, lifting it and fitting his body into hers. She gasped, arching her hips to meet him, luxuriating in the feel of his turgid flesh as it melded with her own, stretching her, filling her.

Grasping a handful of her hair, he tipped her head back, sucking kisses along her throat and finally covering her mouth with his as he thrust into her, deeply, his strokes aggressive, possessive. A fresh, hard wave of desire swept through her as his taste filled her mouth, as he stroked his tongue along hers.

Feeling the advent of her climax, she tightened her arms around his neck, sucked his tongue. He made a growling sound deep in his throat. A hard shudder went through him. Abruptly, even as her crisis caught her, and she began to moan as bliss shot through her, he began to thrust harder and faster, desperation in his movements as his body hovered near it's own culmination. He groaned into her mouth as it caught him, kissing her hungrily.

Weak in the aftermath, Emily clung to him, shivering, wondering as her mind slowly kicked into gear again what had come over her to yield to him ... again, without a whimper of protest.

Finally, he released her, allowing her to slide slowly down his length until her feet touched the shower floor once more. Her body felt about as substantial as gelatin. With an effort, she locked her knees and pushed against him, demanding release. Almost reluctantly, he stepped away from her.

Refusing to make eye contact with him, she moved beneath the shower spray, rinsing herself and finally stepped from the shower. "I thought I'd made it clear I'm not here for your convenience!"

"No?" he growled, anger threading his own voice. "I find it ver' convenient myself. An' most enjoyable, as well."

"You hypnotized me ... again," she muttered accusingly as she snatched her towel up and began to rub herself briskly.

"Mesmerized."

"Whatever!"

"I did na'."

Her head snapped up. "You did."

He shrugged. "I did na' have ta, but if it makes ye feel better ta think so...."

Emily's eyes narrowed on his back as he put his head beneath the shower. Without even stopping to consider the possible consequences, she stepped over to the toilet and depressed the handle. The moment she did, he let out a roar as the water cascading over him instantly turned uncomfortably hot. Her eyes widened guiltily as he jumped away from the shower spray and snatched the curtain back to look at her. Without a word, she whirled and darted toward the door. Snatching it open, she ran toward her room as fast as she could. She didn't make it. She was less than halfway there when Nigel suddenly appeared before her. Before she could skid to a halt, he caught her, snatching her off her feet and tossing her over his shoulder.

"It was an accident!" she lied.

He smacked her bare buttock with the palm of his hand. "I'm na' likely ta believe tha' with the look ye gave me!"

"Damn it, Nigel! Put me down!" she screamed at him as he strode down the hall with her and into his suite of rooms.

He did. He dropped her in the middle of his bed so hard she rebounded almost a foot. One of the boards supporting the springs slid off the bed rail and the mattress collapsed beneath her as she landed again. The tilt of the mattress helped her as she rolled away from him. She almost managed to make it off the bed before he dove after her, collapsing the other side of the bed.

Chapter Fourteen

They tussled, but there was no contest and the wrestling match was brief. Emily glared up at Nigel, huffing for breath as he pinned her down with the weight of his body, his hands clamped firmly around her wrists.

"Ye want ta tell me what tha' was all about?" he asked mildly.

Emily pursed her lips. "You know very well what it was about!"

"Nay. I do na'."

Emily gave him a look. "You're not serious!"

He lifted his dark brows, but finally frowned. "Ya took issue with tha' comment about convenience?" he guessed.

"It was such a totally chauvinistic comment!"

"I can't say I'm familiar with the word."

"Well, you're certainly well versed in the attitude," Emily said tartly. "You're such a ... such a...." Words failed her.

"Man?"

Emily gave him a look. "Yes!"

His lips twitched. "Tha's a relief, at any rate."

Emily pursed her lips. "That wasn't a compliment!"

"I dinna take it as one, but I'd na' be happy if ye thought otherwise, I can tell ye."

Emily rolled her eyes. "Look! The only reason I'm still here is because I bought this place. I've got everything tied up in it and I'm not about to leave. I don't know how you got the idea that I'm your woman, but I'm not!"

"I never like ta argue with a woman, particularly since it's usually a waste of breath, but ye are my woman. I ken ye don't understand the way of the vampire, but I've marked ye as my own, lass, and there's no gettin' around tha'. I've never apologized for takin' what I need an' I'm na' about to start now." He lowered his head, breathing deeply of the scent of her skin. "Your life force is a powerful one, an' I've need ta feed of it ta regain my strength. I canna do otherwise, for I've no notion when I might run into an old enemy an' have need of my powers. If ye want apartments of your own, I'll na' deny ye, but I'd prefer it if ye stayed here."

He nuzzled the tip of one breast with his nose until it stood erect and then sucked it into his mouth. The moment his heated mouth closed over the turgid flesh, her belly clenched. Heat spread outward, filling her with desire she struggled to ignore.

It was a losing battle. She felt herself weakening almost at once. By the time he released her nipple and moved to its twin, she'd ceased to struggle against him and began to writhe and twist from mindless need instead. He settled himself on his arms, slightly above her, watching her face as he entered her. Emily gasped with pleasure as she felt him possess her, felt the stroke of his hard length along her clinging passage.

He moved slowly, stroking the length of her nether throat almost caressingly with his hard flesh. The pleasure escalated inside of her at a far more rapid pace. Within moments, she was hovering near culmination.

It seemed he held her there with deliberation, pausing each time she began to feel the first flutters of fulfillment.

The pleasure burgeoned, rose to a near unbearable level, until she was gasping for breath, moaning almost incessantly, writhing as if fevered. And still he withheld release from her torment.

Finally, she clutched at his shoulders, gasping his name.

"Aye, luv?"

"Please."

A shudder traveled through him. Lowering himself until he lay fully against her, he scooped his hands beneath her hips, lifting them and tilting them up to him, driving deeply inside of her. The air left her lungs on a groan of ecstasy. Tremors began inside of her at the rough pace he set, quivers of sensation that erupted within moments into an electrifying, mind shattering explosion of near painful rapture.

Oblivion swept in around her in its wake, bathing her in a warm glow of satisfaction as he found his own surcease. She was scarcely even aware of her surroundings when he gathered her close, pillowed his head on her breasts and joined her in slumber.

She awoke, stiff, sore, uncomfortable. Lifting her head with an effort, she saw that the bed was a shambles, tilted crazily. Dimly, she recalled that the boards supporting the mattresses had slid off when Nigel had tossed her into his bed like a rag doll. One heavy arm and leg were thrown across her.

There was no way to extricate herself without waking him. Irritated, she shoved weakly at the weights pinning her to the bed. With a grunt of displeasure, he rolled away from her, sprawling on his belly on the other side of the bed.

Sitting up, she glared down at him blearily. After a few moments, she looked around in confusion, located her towel and crawled off the bed.

The shower revived her enough to allow memory to flood back, but they gave her little comfort or pleasure.

He hadn't even tried to deny the accusation that she was a convenience to him--nothing more than a handy body that he could somehow 'feed' upon to draw whatever it was vampires needed.

She'd known that.

Why then did it hurt to have it laid out in the open--bare, unembroidered, the plain, unpleasant truth?

He was an annoyance to her, an impediment to her claim of ownership, nothing more. She was still more than half inclined to believe he was some sort of lunatic than the vampire he claimed to be.

It wasn't like she cared anything about him, was it?

But then, why did she feel like crying?

Swallowing against the knot of misery in her throat, she stepped from the shower, dried herself and went down the hall to her room to dress.

Downstairs, she was greeted not only by the workmen, but a workman from the power company. The realization that she was soon to have a steady, more reliable power supply than the ancient generator was enough to perk her spirits up and when, later that afternoon, the phone man arrived she was able to push her depression firmly into a back corner of her mind.

Mid afternoon, Nigel came down, consulted with Sean briefly and then, after glancing at her for several moments speculatively, climbed into the passenger seat of Sean's truck without a word and left. Sean returned some time later alone.

Emily had to fight the urge to ask Sean where Nigel had gone. Despite her burning curiosity, however, she knew very well that the workmen all thought that Nigel was her significant other and she couldn't bring herself to display her ignorance of his whereabouts.

She supposed it was contrary of her to feel slighted. She didn't appreciate Nigel's highhanded assumption that she was his only because he'd claimed her and she'd been at pains to convince him that she didn't feel that way at all. She really didn't have a leg to stand on insofar as demands of any sort, but she couldn't help but feel completely unimportant to Nigel, despite his claims to the contrary, when he so obviously didn't consider her important enough to even tell her where he was going or when he would be back.

She supposed he must have decided to check into the legality of her claim, but even that didn't arouse enough anger to chase her feelings of ill usage away.

Firmly dismissing it from her mind, she held her depression at bay throughout much of the day by occupying herself with watching the progress of the workmen and working on one of her refinishing projects. It returned tenfold, however, when she retired to her apartment that evening.

Undoubtedly Nigel had decided to take the bed apart to fix it.

The gold coins she'd discovered in the dungeon had been stacked very carefully on her dressing table.

Chapter Fifteen

Emily stared blankly at the gleaming pile of gold, too stunned to think for many moments, too surprised to fend off the emotions that washed through her.

Gladness and relief should have been uppermost. Neither emotion was. Instead, a faint nausea washed over her and the depression she'd been firmly holding at bay all day flooded through her with a vengeance.

"He found my gold when he was putting the bed back together and brought it to me," she said aloud, feeling it on her tongue, questing for the relief she knew she should feel.

It evaded her. Instead, the uncomfortable sense of having been paid for services rendered crept into her mind.

Gritting her teeth, she stalked over to the table and stared down at the coins. "They're mine," she said more loudly. "He merely acknowledged it by returning them to the rightful owner when he found them."

They blurred before her eyes. Her chin wobbled. Sniffing, she crossed the room and climbed into the center of the bed, thinking. After a few moments, she realized that she was carefully avoiding any thoughts at all about Nigel. She decided it was best to continue that way. She had better things to do, and far more important things to do, than to weep into her pillow like a lovelorn teenager.

Nigel was gone and he'd left the gold.

He might, or might not, be coming back. It was possible he'd left the gold as his way of saying he was giving up his claim to her castle.

That depressed her so much she had to struggle against the tears again. When she'd fought the urge to a standstill, she tried to consider it on the good side.

It *was* a good thing. It meant she wasn't going to have to find a lawyer to help her slug it out in court. It meant she wouldn't have to worry about spending her windfall on lawyers and court when she really needed it to set the place to rights.

It meant she didn't have to worry about Nigel's unwanted attentions anymore.

She did cry then until she finally fell asleep.

She woke the following morning feeling as if she'd been beat down. Somewhere in the rounds of feeling sorry for herself, however, she'd found her backbone and decided what to do.

It wasn't safe to keep the coins in the castle. She was liable to get robbed, or worse. Fortunately, she'd fallen asleep a good bit earlier than usual the night before and, consequently, woke earlier, as well. By the time the workmen arrived, she'd managed to stow the gold in the trunk of the car.

"You're off ta London too, then, Missus?"

Emily turned and stared at Sean in surprise, trying to think how she could respond to the remark without displaying the fact that this was the first inkling she'd had that that was where Nigel had gone. A poker face wasn't something nature had seen fit to give her, however, and it took her too long to respond in any case. Sean reddened. "I was just thinkin' if ye were off ta London ta stay with Mr. MacKissack tha' you might na' be needin' us for a few days."

Emily felt faint color rise in her own cheeks. "No. Unless you need a few days off?"

"I'd as soon work. Can't pay the creditors sittin' around the flat."

Emily forced a smile. "Too true. I expect to be back later this evening, though. I might spend the night in the city, but, at the latest, I'll be back tomorrow and I'd rather y'all kept at it now that things are finally starting to come together."

She hadn't actually planned to drive all the way down to London, but once Sean had put it into her mind she decided that would be the best. Besides, an international city would give her more avenues for sale of the coins.

It was scary driving in London. She'd thought she'd grown accustomed to driving on the opposite side of the road, but she'd been driving for years in the U.S. and it was hard to grow accustomed to everything being exactly backwards. Besides, it was a strange city and driving in any large city that was unfamiliar was unnerving.

It had taken longer to make the trip than she'd expected and she was exhausted by the time she arrived.

The banks were all closed.

Since there was nothing else for it, Emily located a hotel for the night. The bellhop looked at her strangely when he hefted her bags, but she pointedly ignored the curious look he sent her way, leading the way to her room.

She couldn't help but wonder if Nigel had indeed come to London and, if so, where he was staying, but she curbed the desire to search for him, spending a quiet evening in her room. The following morning, Emily rose early and had her bags brought down again, drove to the bank she'd chosen and rented a safety deposit box big enough to hold her coins. She felt better once she had them stored, at least in the sense that the fear of being robbed subsided. Keeping one of the coins, she left the bank and spent the next several hours checking with the shops for a likely buyer.

It was nearly noon by the time she managed to locate the last shop on her list and she was beginning to feel pressed for time. She supposed that was why she collided with the man in the shop.

He grabbed her as she rebounded.

"Excuse me! I'm so sorry! I was in a hurry and not watching where I was going," Emily apologized, throwing a glance upward at the man whose hands lingered on her shoulders and then freezing in surprise.

"That's quite all right."

The accent was British and yet surprisingly similar to the southern accent she was familiar with. As pleasant as that was, however, it wasn't his accent that arrested her attention.

He was tall, nearly as tall as Nigel or perhaps even a little taller. It was difficult to tell, for his build was slighter. His face was handsome in a purely male sort of way, all harsh planes and angles.

His eyes, a shade of palest blue, sent a shiver skating down her spine and it was that that seemed to freeze her to the spot.

It was several moments before she realized that he was smiling.

.... And he hadn't released her.

To her surprise, he leaned toward her, sniffing deeply, as if inhaling the aroma of a flower.

Something glittered in his eyes, a look almost of satisfaction. "Your perfume is almost as enticing as your lovely face and accent."

Emily felt a blush rising, not the least because the only perfume she was wearing was from the bar of soap she'd showered with. "Thank you. I'm sorry I almost ran you over."

Almost reluctantly, he removed his hands at last, to Emily's vast relief. "I'm afraid I can't agree. Simon ... Umphreys."

Emily blinked. It took her a moment to realize he'd introduced himself. She glanced around a little uneasily, wondering where the shopkeeper was. "Emily Hendrick," she said finally, extending her hand.

"Touring?"

"What?"

He lifted his brows. "Are you just visiting?"

"Oh. Actually, I moved. I bought a place ... uh ... north of here."

"How may I be of service today?"

"Excuse me?" Emily asked blankly.

He lifted his brows and stepped away from her at last, gesturing broadly around the shop.

"Oh. You're the ... uh ... proprietor?"

He smiled faintly, almost seeming to shrug. "When one collects antiquities it becomes a necessity after a bit to buy a larger house or to set up shop."

Emily chuckled dutifully, but the story seemed a little farfetched to her. He just didn't seem the type to have a pack rat tendency. She had no trouble picturing him as a collector, but something just didn't seem to right quite right about the man as a shopkeeper. Inwardly, she shrugged. "Actually, I was looking to sell, not buy. I have a small collection of old coins."

He stood looking down at her for several moments. "May I see it?"

"Oh. Yes." Feeling strangely unnerved by the man's gaze, Emily dug around in her pocketbook and finally produced the coin. Taking it from her hand, he moved behind the counter, looked around for several moments and finally produced a magnifying glass to study the coin. Ill at ease for no reason she could put her finger on, Emily wandered around the shop, trying to pretend an interest in the items in his store she didn't feel.

"What's this?" she asked finally, after staring at an odd looking leather and metal harness thingy for several minutes.

Simon glanced up, lifting his head to see what she was studying. He grinned. "A chastity belt."

Emily reddened all the way to her toes. "You're kidding, right?"

"I beg your pardon?"

"Joke?"

He grinned. "Seriously. It comes with a bit of history."

"I'll bet it does," Emily muttered.

He chuckled at that, but Emily's own sense of humor had vanished as she stared at the thing. An idea was forming in her mind.

An absolutely outrageously insane idea.

"How much is it?"

"Excuse me?"

"The chastity belt."

He studied her a long moment and finally gave her a price that sounded remarkably cheep, all things considered. To her relief, he didn't ask why she was interested in it. "Do you have the key?"

"It's attached to the belt."

"I'll take it," Emily said decisively.

He looked at her curiously for several moments, but finally laid the coin down and moved around the counter. When he'd wrapped it up and took her money, he went back to his examination of the coin.

"It's in good condition," he commented after a while.

Emily said nothing. The coin was in mint condition--didn't look as if it had ever been in circulation at all. It was possible some of the coins had taken a little abuse in the leg of Nigel's bed, but she certainly hadn't noticed anything wrong with the coin. Most likely, she thought, he was trying to drive the price down.

"You have a collection you say? Of these? Or various coins?"

"Those."

He nodded, set the coin on the counter and began leafing through books.

Emily glanced at him surreptitiously from time to time. She began to have the feeling that he wasn't carefully searching out the value of the coin so much as he was stalling for time. She didn't know why she thought so. He didn't appear nervous. He didn't even appear to be all that excited about the coin.

"Quite valuable. A bit above my touch, actually. Have you considered selling them at auction?"

Emily looked at him doubtfully. "Actually, no. The outcome is really pretty unpredictable, isn't it?"

He shrugged. "It can be. I suppose it depends upon the auction house, and then, of course, your starting bid. You might well end up with far more than you could get selling them in a shop. Auctions draw collectors."

Emily had moved back to the counter when he started talking. Smiling, she held out her hand for the coin. "I'll give it some thought. I'm in no real rush."

He studied her intently for several moments when he placed the coin in her palm. "Have lunch with me?"

Surprise rendered Emily speechless for several moments. "I ... uh ... actually, I have to get back ... but thank you for the offer."

His smile broadened. "You can't simply dash off, Emily Hendrick. How will I get to know you?"

Emily blushed, feeling suddenly torn. He was an attractive man, and his interest was flattering, particularly after the way Nigel had treated her so off-handedly.

She didn't know why she felt so uneasy about accepting.

"There's a restaurant just around the corner with outdoor dining."

Relief flooded Emily. If they would be dining outside, there could surely be no harm in going with him. "I guess I don't need to leave right away."

Chapter Sixteen

Simon Umphreys was charming. By the time they'd finished their luncheon, Emily was wondering why she'd felt uneasy about him at all.

".... I expect that's probably about the most miserably boring story you've ever heard, but that's how I came to own the little shop around the corner."

Emily blinked, feeling as if she'd just woken from a daze. Color rose in her cheeks when she realized she couldn't remember hearing the half of the 'boring' story he'd apparently been telling her. Had she been staring, she wondered? Gaping at him like an awed adolescent?

She frowned, thinking it over, but she didn't know why she would have. He was handsome, and his accent fascinated her almost as much as the deep resonance of his voice, but she hadn't been aware of being simply 'fascinated.' She felt almost as if she'd just woken. With an effort, she smiled politely. "I didn't think it was boring at all."

"So ... what brings you to the UK ... besides the sale of those coins?"

She didn't want to tell him about the castle. She didn't know why she didn't, but something held her back. Instead, she shrugged. "I suppose I just felt like I wanted a change of scenery."

His brows rose questioningly. "You didn't have to travel halfway around the world to find that, surely? The U.S. is a pretty big place, if I recall my geography."

It took an effort to smile that time. "It is. I considered moving to a different state, but when I went to the Realtor, I happened to see this brochure of ... a place here and I just fell in love with it."

His gaze was assessing. "It wasn't because of one of those excessively jealous and obsessive husbands one hears about, was it?"

The comment irritated Emily. She wasn't certain if she'd taken it the wrong way or not, but it sounded like an insult. "The U.S. hasn't cornered the market on nut cases. From what I can see everyone else still has their share ... but, no," she responded tartly, and glanced at her watch. "I should be going."

Irritation flickered in his eyes briefly. "Not without giving me some way to get in touch with you again, I hope."

Emily sent a vague smile in his direction and focused on gathering her things.

"You will give some thought to the auction? If you'd like, I could make some inquiries for you ... find the best sort of place to deal with."

Emily glanced at him indecisively, but the truth was, she really needed to turn the coins into cash and settle it in an account. "That's really nice, but I wouldn't want to impose on your good nature."

"Not at all! I'd be happy to. The truth is, I think I know of someone, but I do need to check before I go any further with this. I could ring you up when I know something for certain."

"Uh ... I don't have a phone yet."

"I'll drop you a post card, then."

She couldn't help it. She blushed to the roots of her hair. "Actually, I don't remember my new address."

He chuckled. "That's putting me in my place."

"No! I really don't! You could email me," she added tentatively.

He frowned. "I thought you said you didn't have a phone?"

"I don't--yet. But I should have one in a few days. Anyway, I can check my email at any phone."

He took out two business cards while Emily scratched around in her purse for something to write on. "Use my card. And take the other with you. It has all of my contact information on it."

Emily had mixed feelings about the entire encounter. She was strangely drawn toward the man, and yet, at the same time, he made her feel very uneasy. She couldn't quite decide why that was. Try though she might--and she did--going over and over in her mind the conversation they'd had, his expressions, his gestures--she couldn't think of anything he'd said, or anything about his manner that had set off warning bells.

It was irrefutable that something had. She finally decided, though, that she was either suffering from paranoia or guilt.

She had no reason to feel guilty, of course.

She didn't have a relationship with Nigel.

They were lovers, plain and simple, and she'd never even agreed to that much. Moreover, he'd certainly made it clear that, regardless of his nicey nasty attitude about calling a spade a spade, it was just sex. They hadn't shared anything else, not really. He considered his business his own, and didn't appear to have any interest in hers, either, so long as she was handy when he needed to 'feed' off her life force.

She glanced at the package on the seat beside her and grinned. Boy was he in for a surprise!

* * * *

Nigel wasn't home. Emily didn't know whether the discovery irritated her or depressed her more. She'd convinced herself that he would've returned by the time she got back and he'd been really upset that she'd gone off without telling him.

Instead, it looked as if she was going to be sitting in the damned castle like a dutiful slave, awaiting his return!

She was mollified once she'd made her rounds to see what had been done in her absence. She had lights! She had a phone! Even her new range and refrigerator had been delivered and installed.

She had no one to call, of course. She toyed with the idea of calling Simon and giving him the phone number but discarded it after a little thought. She just wasn't comfortable with the idea of him knowing where she was when she knew so little about him. Supposedly, he'd given her a good deal of background on himself while they had dined, but she couldn't recall much of anything that he'd said. Even if she had, that didn't mean a thing. Anyone could lie.

Finally, after a solitary meal, she dragged her notebook computer out and connected it to the phone line. Her mailbox was full--not much of a surprise. She hadn't checked it in weeks. After deleting the junk mail, she discovered a couple of dozen messages from friends ... and three from Simon.

A little thrill that was part excitement, part uneasiness went through her when she saw the emails with his name on them.

For all that, the messages weren't actually anything to get too worked up about. After responding to the last one, which asked if she'd had a good trip back, she began reading and responding to those from friends back home.

A new message from Simon popped up while she was still online. Emily had a feeling she should simply ignore it, but found she couldn't. Finally, she yielded to the urge to chat with him and they moved to a chat room.

The anonymity of it made her feel safe, soothed her sense of uneasiness and she found herself flirting back when the tone of his messages changed from purely business to a flirtation.

Chapter Seventeen

Emily woke three nights later to find Nigel standing beside her bed, staring down at her. There was that in his expression that seemed to reach deeply inside of her, a need that went beyond sexual. Instinctively, Emily lifted her arms to him, welcoming him.

Relief flickered across his features. Without a word, he disrobed, climbed into bed with her and took her into his arms, kissing her with the hunger of a starving man.

Stroking his hard back and shoulders, caressing his silky hair, she kissed him back with a fervor that matched or surpassed his, realizing only with his touch how much she'd missed it, missed him.

After a few moments, he dragged his mouth from hers and focused upon her body, skating his hands over one shoulder and down her arm to her thigh and then moving his hand upward once more as he lavished hungry kisses along her throat, over her breasts and belly as if impatient to touch and taste every inch of her at once.

Her own need raged out of control and she moaned and twisted against him, pulling at him, urging him to claim her fully.

"What's this?" Nigel asked abruptly, breaking through the haze of her passion drugged senses.

"What?" Emily asked vaguely.

He tugged at it. "This."

As suddenly as if she'd been thoroughly doused with cold water, Emily remembered the damned chastity belt.

"Uh," she said, stalling for time.

Nigel climbed from the bed and turned the light on, glaring at the offending thing. "It has the look of a chastity belt."

"Does it?" Emily said, still feeling more than a little disoriented from being jerked from the edge of release into a cold, unpleasant reality. "Uh. Well, it is."

Nigel plunked his hands on his hips. "Take it off."

Emily gazed up at him resentfully, torn now between the desire he'd aroused in her and the urge that had prompted her to put it on in the first place, the grim determination to deny him, and to deny the passion he aroused in her so easily.

"I can't. It's locked. I need the key."

He gave her a look.

"It's on the molding over the door," she said with some

dudgeon.

Having retrieved it, he placed a knee on the mattress and leaned down to fit the key in the lock. After twisting it back and forth for several moments, he removed the key again. "It's the wrong key," he said accusingly.

Emily felt her jaw drop. "It can't be the wrong key! It's the *only* key!"

He studied her suspiciously for several moments. "It does na' work," he said flatly.

"Give it to me!" Emily snapped, snatching the key from his hand and shoving it into the lock herself. "Shit! It must be rusted ... but I *oiled* the damned thing!"

"It's na' rusted. It's the wrong bleedin' key. What the bloody hell are ye wearin' it for anyway?"

Emily gave him a look, torn between indignation that he could even ask, frustrated passion, and a deep anxiety that she wasn't going to get the thing off now that she'd gotten in on. "Could we just discuss this *after* we get this fucking thing off of me?"

"Just what do ye suggest, seein' as how ye dinna think ta check the key before ye put it on?"

"Oh! So now it's my fault that the man that sold it to me gave me the wrong frigging key?"

"No. If's yer fault fer puttin' it on ta start with!" he growled. "An' it's yer fault ye dinna think ta check the key before ye put it on."

Emily glared at him for several moments and finally slid out of the bed. "That's not helping me get the thing off," she said stiffly, stalking to the door and flinging the door open.

He followed her down the hall, down the stairs and into the kitchen, watching her as she dug around in the cabinet drawers for something to pick the lock. When that didn't work, she began sorting through the kitchen knives, looking for one with a serrated blade.

"Why did ya put it on ta start with, lass?"

Emily glanced at him. "If you gave it a little thought, I'll bet you could figure it out," she said tartly.

"Ta keep me out of the honey pot?" he hazarded.

Despite her irritation, she felt the urge to smile at that. With an effort, she quelled it. He took her silence as a yes.

"Ye welcomed me," he said tentatively. "I dinna dream that?"

Emily sighed. "I was half asleep, damn it!" She mulled over it while she struggled to fit the knife she'd chosen between her skin and the narrowest piece of leather. "It's complicated."

Gently, he took the knife from her hand, set it on the countertop and knelt in front of her. After studying the belt frowningly for several moments, he leaned forward and blew into the keyhole. Emily heard a metallic click and the lock opened. She stared at it blankly a moment. "How did you do that?" she demanded in stunned amazement.

"I'm a vampire, lass. I've learned a thing or two in the past several hundred years."

Standing, he grasped her shoulders, studied her for several moments and finally leaned down, kissing her lightly on the forehead. When he leaned away from her again, he simply vanished.

* * * *

Nothing, Emily reflected glumly could more surely dampen your enthusiasm for life in general than to discover just about the time you managed to run a man off that you really didn't want to run him off.

The chastity belt seemed to have done the trick all right, but she couldn't seem to garner any sense of triumph at her success. When Nigel had first vanished from the kitchen, she'd been disbelieving, then angry.

It wasn't like she'd *intended* to get him all roused up and then leave him hanging.

If she had, she certainly wouldn't have allowed him to arouse her and leave her hanging.

She didn't know if he was in his room or not, but she glared at the closed door as she stalked past it to her own room and slammed the door.

She'd been avoiding him for several days before she realized he hardly seemed aware of her efforts. In fact, he was hardly at the castle at all unless he was asleep, and it was really starting to bug the hell out of her, wondering what he was up to.

She was afraid she knew, but she didn't want to think about it.

When she couldn't stand it anymore and finally realized that he wasn't going to spare her by coming around, she gathered her courage and offered an olive branch.

"I've got to return the rental car. I've already extended on it twice. I figured I'd look for a car while I was in town. If you'd like, I could give you driving lessons."

Nigel, who was ensconced in his partially restored study, looked up absently from the book he was reading. "I'm sorry. I dinna catch that?"

He'd been so deeply engrossed in what he was reading, she realized, he hadn't heard anything she'd said. Somehow, she couldn't seem to get up the nerve to try again. "Nothing. Never mind."

It was probably just as well, she told herself as she packed an overnight bag and headed for the car. She'd told Simon she would meet him to discuss the sale of the coins.

Chapter Eighteen

It was tempting to buy a new car, but except for the inheritance from her parents, money had never been easy to come by and Emily found she just wasn't comfortable with the idea of buying a new car even though she felt that she could probably afford it without demolishing the money she expected to get from the coins.

Then again, they weren't sold yet, and she couldn't afford to count her chickens before they hatched.

Settling finally on a late model in excellent condition, she headed for the hotel where she'd stayed the time before and checked in.

Simon, she discovered, had left a message for her at the desk.

A vague sense of uneasiness moved through her. She couldn't recall that she'd told him where she had stayed before, or that she intended to stay in the same hotel.

She supposed she must have. Otherwise, how would he have known?

She decided she was just being silly.

A sense of guilt had swamped her. Rationally, she knew she had no reason to feel guilty. In the first place, she had no romantic interest, or sexual interest, in Simon. She was here purely for business reasons.

In the second, she couldn't be guilty of cheating even if she had felt either, because she wasn't involved with Nigel, not even tentatively anymore.

She still felt as if she was doing something wrong. She couldn't shake the feeling and she realized it was because, in spite of everything, she was tied to Nigel.

She loved him.

How could she have been so pigheaded as to have lied to herself about it so long? And why did she have to realize it now, when it was probably too late to do anything about it?

She sat in the room for a time, staring at the wall and trying to decide whether to check out and return home immediately, or call Simon as she'd agreed and go through with the sale of the coins.

She didn't know what to do.

If she accepted that everything that Nigel had told her was true, and in her heart she did, then she also had to accept that the castle and everything in it was rightfully his, regardless of what was legal. So the coins weren't hers to sell.

Except that he'd given them to her.

The question was, why?

He'd never said and she'd been too upset about it to ask. Truthfully, she'd done her best just to put that particular incident out of her mind.

She couldn't sell the coins, she finally decided. She would give them back to Nigel and demand to know why he'd given them to her. She had to know.

She couldn't just return to the castle and say nothing, however. She'd agreed to meet with Simon about the sale, and it wouldn't be right to just stand him up when he'd gone to all the trouble to try to make the arrangements for her.

Moving to the bed, she fished Simon's card from her pocketbook and dialed his number. He picked up on the fourth ring.

"Simon?"

"Hello, Emily. Did you just get in?"

She was oh so tempted to lie to him and tell him she wasn't in town at all. "A little bit ago. Listen ... I'm really sorry, but I can't sell the coins. I know you went to a lot of trouble arranging things and I'll be happy to pay your finder's fee, but ... I can't sell them."

He was silent for several moments. "Problems?"

Emily gnawed her lip. "It's kind of complicated."

"Why don't we discuss it over dinner? You haven't eaten yet?"

She thought that was a really, really bad idea. "No! I mean, I haven't, but I'm really tired from the drive."

"If you're not comfortable with discussing the business, we won't, but I'd like to see you anyway."

Which was exactly the problem. She had the feeling that he wanted to pursue a personal relationship and she couldn't do that.

On the other hand, she'd been flirting with him online. She'd encouraged him. As tempting as it was to take the coward's way out and dump him on the phone where she wouldn't actually have to look him in the eyes, it wasn't right.

"Where?"

"Would you like me to pick you up? Or would you prefer to meet me someplace?"

It didn't take long to decide that. She far preferred the latter option since she couldn't think of anything more uncomfortable that having to ride back to her hotel with him after she'd dumped him. "I'll meet you."

They arranged a time and then he gave her directions from the hotel since she wasn't familiar with London. Her stomach tightened with nerves the minute she hung up and she was tempted to call him back and cancel.

"Chicken!"

She wanted to call Nigel, but she fought the urge. What could she say?

When she checked the time, she discovered she was going to be late meeting Simon anyway unless she rushed. After a quick shower, she dressed and left the hotel, the driving instructions in her hand.

She began to suspect she'd walked into a trap long before she pulled up in front of the huge house in the purely residential area. Simon hadn't given her directions to a restaurant! He'd told her how to get to his house!

Emily knew she should just drive off, return to the hotel and call Simon on the phone. If she parked and went up to the door, he was going to assume she was open to his seduction.

Upon reflection, dumping him over the phone seemed like the better part of valor.

As she stared up at the mansion, however, she found herself pulling the car into the drive and turning off the ignition.

Simon was standing beside the car when she got out. Catching her hand, he lifted it to his lips in an old world salute. "I've been expecting you."

Emily stared at him in consternation, wondering how she'd come to park the car and get out when she'd just made up her mind not to. "I don't--why am I here?"

He slipped an arm around her shoulders, walking her toward the front door. "We need privacy for what I have in mind."

Alarm skimmed a chilling finger down Emily's spine, but

somehow she discovered she couldn't seem to pull away from him or even to object as he led her inside and locked the door firmly behind him.

"What's happening?"

He smiled. "Nothing just yet. We'll have to wait until Nigel arrives."

Emily frowned, but discovered her thoughts were more and more disjointed. "He's coming here?"

"I expect so," Simon responded pensively. "I have his woman."

Chapter Nineteen

Emily found herself in a bed, unclothed. She couldn't seem to move. Struggling, she finally managed to move her head enough to check her wrists, but, to her consternation, she discovered she wasn't bound in any way that she could see.

Simon's face swam before her gaze.

"I can't move," she whispered plaintively.

He lifted his brows. "You didn't expect to be able to, did you?"

The comment confused her. "Did you drug me?"

He chuckled at that. "I've no need of such things."

"You're a vampire."

"Very good, but then I thought you were a clever little thing the moment I met you. How did you manage to get Nigel's gold?"

As difficult as it was to put her thoughts into order, Emily had managed to figure out that Simon was out to get Nigel and thought he could use her to do it. "Who's Nigel?"

He smiled thinly. "Good try." He leaned toward her. "But I smelled him on you the moment you walked through my door. I knew he'd claimed you as his woman." Settling on the edge of the mattress, he traced a finger along her body from her throat to her mound. "Lovely. I always admired Nigel's taste in women. Perhaps I'll keep you when I'm done with Nigel. Would you like that?"

"No."

He grinned, displaying his fangs for the first time and Emily felt another quiver of fear course through her. "I've always enjoyed a challenge. Meek women can be so boring."

"He won't come."

"I think he will."

"Why are you doing this?"

"Funny you should ask," Simon said, rising and pacing across the room. "Revenge ... over a woman. Does that wound you?"

It did, but she wasn't about to admit it. "Mortal or vampire?"

He tilted his head, studying her. "Like you, she was partly both."

Shock went through Emily. "I'm mortal."

"But the blood of vampires runs through you, as well. A tiny dollop, but it's there. I expect he sensed it, but perhaps not. Perhaps he doesn't realize why he found you so irresistible, but one is always drawn to those of one's own kind."

"That's insane. I'd know if I was a vampire!"

He chuckled. "How, pray tell?"

Emily stared at him in confusion. "I'd know."

He shook his head. "Those of the blue blood, like myself and Nigel--we know, because we know our roots. You would not know unless you'd been told, anymore than you would know if you had an ancestor who was of any other race. You don't just 'know.'"

"Then how do you know?"

"Because you have the 'way.' Mortals do not."

Emily frowned in confusion. "The way?"

"You can resist the *mesmer*. No mere mortal can. If you were purely mortal, you wouldn't be asking so many questions. You'd be lying there like a good little lamb, awaiting your fate."

The comment sent a surge of hope through Emily. She remembered that Nigel had found her 'resistance' confusing. He'd thought it was because he was weakened from his long sleep, but maybe Simon was right. And, if he was right, maybe she could free herself?

"You can't. You don't have the strength."

"Can't what?" Emily asked cautiously.

He smiled thinly. "You don't guard your thoughts at all well."

"You might just as well let me go. Nigel won't come. I'm not his woman."

He tilted his head, studying her. Finally, he crossed the room and settled beside her on the bed once more, stroking her face. Instantly, Emily felt as if she was falling asleep, felt the same sense of drifting downward and losing awareness of her surroundings.

She found herself in her own bed, looking up at Nigel. He was staring down at her, his expression guarded, but filled with need.

A sense of welcome flowed through her, warming her. Her body quickened with desire and she lifted her arms to him.

Dimly, she realized that she was dreaming of their last time together. Distress filled her when she remembered how terribly wrong everything had gone from there.

"I didn't mean it, Nigel. Please. Don't be angry with me. I love you."

To her relief, he seemed to accept her apology, climbing into the bed with her and gathering her in his arms, kissing her as if he needed her more than anything else, even the air he breathed.

Desire, full blown, exploded inside of her as he kissed her, filled her with his heat, with his essence.

Abruptly, the kiss changed completely and she realized it wasn't Nigel who was kissing her. She struggled, trying to push him away, but she found that it was useless. She couldn't fight him.

"Nigel," she whispered in despair as she felt herself slipping into Simon's thrall.

She woke to full awareness almost as abruptly as she'd fallen asleep and blinked up at Simon in stunned surprise. A satisfied smile curled his lips.

"I believe he will come ... now."

Horror and confusion filled Emily. "What did you do?"

He chuckled. "I? Nothing but summon your memories--those you share with Nigel."

"It was a memory? Not a dream?"

"A memory you share with Nigel," he emphasized.

"You made him see that!" she said accusingly. "You made me call him!"

He shrugged. "That was the point. Don't get me wrong, I find you vastly appealing, but I'm more interested at the moment in my revenge. Later, perhaps...."

"Never!" Emily snapped. "I can't image how you could be so conceited as to think I would even consider leaving Nigel for you, but you're wrong!"

He shrugged. "His last concubine did."

"Well, she was a damned fool!"

Anger flickered over his features for the first time. "If Evangeline were still here, perhaps she could explain the appeal, but since Nigel took eternity from her, she cannot speak for herself. She died. Long years ago."

"I did not take it," Nigel growled, appearing abruptly just inside the door of the room.

With a snarled hiss, Simon whirled, changing even as he turned into a wisp of smoke. He reappeared directly in front of Nigel, grasping him by the throat and tossing him across the room as if he were no more than a child. Emily screamed as she saw his body fly through the air and collide with the far wall so hard it shook the house.

Without even glancing in her direction, he leapt to his feet and launched himself toward Simon. They collided mid air, struggled, and broke apart.

Emily squeezed her eyes closed, unable to move, unable to watch. She couldn't close her ears to the sounds of their battle, however, and she finally realized it was more frightening only to hear and not see the battle raging around her.

Within moments, the two had trashed the room and broken almost every stick of furniture. The bed where she was held in thrall was like the eye of a hurricane, the only area of calm in a sea of struggle.

They were surprisingly evenly matched, considering that Nigel was a bigger man physically. Unfortunately, Simon seemed to have an edge in magic.

Slowly, as the battle waged on, Simon's grip upon her began to dissolve and she realized that he was weakening, though he showed little sign of it. With a tremendous effort, she threw off the last of his hold and sat up, grabbing the coverlet up and covering herself.

"Stop!" she shouted. "Please stop! She's dead. Evangeline is dead! You can't get her back, no matter what you do to each other!"

Her shout distracted both men. It was all the distraction Nigel needed to gain the upper hand. He captured Simon by the throat, pinning him to wall. Gasping for breath, he grasped Simon's hand and placed it upon his forehead. "See, damn you! I tried to spare you!" he growled.

A distant look came into Simon's cold blue eyes as his hand settled on Nigel. After a moment, however, his expression became one of confusion and finally pain. Abruptly, he vanished in a puff of smoke.

Shuddering, Nigel turned, leaning against the wall while he fought to catch his breath.

Emily was almost afraid of the look on his face. "What happened?"

"I gave him the truth," Nigel said harshly.

Chapter Twenty

Nigel didn't look as if he was in the mood to talk and Emily discovered she had a great reluctance to question him.

She might not like the answers any better than Simon had.

She dressed in silence, hardly even daring to look at Nigel. Daylight was breaking as they left Simon's house and headed back to the hotel to collect her belongings. It confused Emily. She hadn't been aware of any time passing. How could she have missed the entire night?

Simon had enthralled her.

She wondered what else he'd done.

He'd said he had shown Nigel memories Had the part where Simon had been making love to her been a memory, too? How could it be when she didn't remember any of that happening--except in the dream?

The silence became unbearable after a while and Emily searched her mind for something that might be safe to talk about.

"Did you take care of your business in town?" she asked after glancing at him several times.

"Did you?"

Blood flooded her cheeks. Anger warred with remorse inside of her, however. Nigel knew very well that Simon was capable of mesmerizing her and that it didn't necessarily follow that she'd gone to him willingly.

She supposed she had, but not in the sense that Nigel apparently believed.

"Why did ye go ta him?"

Emily searched her mind for an explanation. "I didn't--exactly."

He gave her a look that made her blood run cold. "He dinna take ye from Castle MacKissack."

Emily pursed her lips angrily. "Have it your way," she said tightly.

She could hear him grinding his teeth. "Can this thing go no faster?" he demanded.

The urge to burst into tears washed through Emily. He couldn't *wait* to get away from her! She sniffed the tears back with an effort. "If it's not fast enough to suit you, damn it, then do one of your damned disappearing acts!"

To her consternation, he did.

She was glad.

She didn't want to talk to him anyway!

She was the one that should be mad if anybody was!

Both of them had used her. And they'd been fighting over another woman, right in front her!

How dare that bastard act like she'd been cheating on him when he'd come to Simon's house to fight with him over that damned Evangeline!

By the time she'd reached the castle, Emily had managed to work herself into a royal rage. It wasn't easy to stalk inside lugging the suitcase full of coins, but she did her best.

Nigel was pacing the great hall when she entered.

She pitched the suitcase at him. Unfortunately, it was far too heavy to really throw it. The suitcase hit the floor at her feet and burst open, spilling gold coins in every direction. After glaring at him, Emily stalked across the great hall and up the stairs.

Nigel appeared in her room while she was stomping back and forth, furiously packing her bags.

Folding his arms over his chest, he leaned back against the door. "Where're ye off ta this time?" he growled.

"Home!" she snarled at him.

"Ye are home!"

Despite her best efforts, Emily's chin wobbled. "No, I'm not! Georgia's home and that's where I'm going!"

"Why?" Nigel asked quietly.

"Because!" Emily wailed, giving up the effort to keep a reign on her emotions.

Pushing away from the door, Nigel crossed the room and caught her shoulders. "That's no reason atall, lass."

"Because ... I hate you!" Emily flung at him furiously, trying to push him away.

"Do ye?"

"No!" she wailed.

He chuckled, to her surprise, wrapping his arms around her and pulling her tightly against him. "I'm glad ta hear it, Emily Hendrick, because I love ye so much sometimes I feel like I can't breathe."

The words washed over her, sucking the air from her lungs. "You do?" she gasped in surprise.

"Aye, luv, I do."

Emily burst into tears, burying her face against his chest. "I thought you loved Evangeline."

"There was a time, long ago, when I thought I did, too. When she left me fer Simon, I was furious. It took me awhile ta realize tha' was all there was ta it. I was angry because she'd left me. If I'd really loved her, I'd have been hurt. When she left Simon and asked me ta take her back, I knew then tha' she'd wounded nothin' but my pride, na' my heart."

Sniffing back her tears, Emily pulled away to look up at him. "Really?"

"Aye, 'tis the truth."

She frowned. "Why were you fighting Simon, then?"

He gave her a look. "He had ye, lass. Ye dinna think I'd've gone fer anythin' else?"

She wasn't completely convinced, but he was saying all the right things and she desperately wanted it to be true. Sighing, she leaned against him. "I've missed you so much. I'm so sorry for ... everything. I just wanted ... I don't know what I wanted."

Nigel gave her an affectionate squeeze. "I'm na' like the men today. I can learn the things I've missed, but I'll never be like the men ye've become used ta, Emily. I was born long ago, an' lived in times unlike these, an' I'm a vampire besides. I ken ye felt tha' I gave ye no say in the matter ... Well, an' ye were right. I dinna. I'm tha' used ta takin' what I want, an' I told ye tha'. I dinna think I've got it in me ta change my ways, luv."

Emily shook her head. "I love you, Nigel. I fell in love with you just as you are. I don't want you to change."

"No?" he asked, pulling away slightly to look at her.

"Well ... maybe a couple of little, tiny adjustments," Emily said, smiling up at him as she looped her arms around his neck and lifted her head to nuzzle his neck.

He uttered a sound that was half growl, half chuckle. His arms tightened around her. In the next moment, he leaned down and scooped her up, carrying her to the bed and falling upon it with her.

Emily gasped as they landed, expecting to hear splintering wood, but Nigel's lips drove all other thoughts from her mind as he explored every inch of flesh that was exposed to his touch. When he'd thoroughly explored open territory, he tugged her clothes off and reacquainted himself with everything beneath.

Emily felt her libido shoot skyward from the first touch of his lips. Her playful amusement vanished, replaced by desperate need. Her need fueled his and they began to struggle to rid themselves of the remainder of their clothing until both lay completely bare, every inch of their flesh touching, melding with one another as they kissed and stroked each other until their passions reached fever pitch.

And when at last their bodies joined, Emily realized why it was that his touch had turned her blood to liquid fire from the very first time they'd made love and every time since. They were made for one another.

Afterwards, as their bliss slowly mellowed to a pleasant warmth, she lay her cheek along his chest, caressing him as she listened to his heart slow its pounding rhythm.

"Why did you give me the gold?" she asked after a time.

"It was yers."

Emily frowned, lifting her head to look at him. "But it wasn't. This castle and everything in is yours and you knew that."

"Aye, everythin', includin' ye. Yer my woman. All that I have is yers."

A sense of peace settled over Emily. She relaxed against him, relieved.

She was almost asleep when she thought of something else. "What did you mean when you said I couldn't get pregnant?"

Nigel stiffened. "It's the price of a long life, luv. It's a rare thing fer a vampire ta breed a child an' na' somethin' I can give ye."

"Oh," Emily said.

"Yer na' angry?"

"No."

His arms tightened around her. "I'd feared ye would be when ye found I could na' give ye a child."

"To tell you the truth, I really never thought about wanting one. I guess that's because I never loved anyone before. It's different now."

His hand stilled. "Is it?"

"Mmm."

"Yer sayin' yer all right with it then?"

"Mmmhmm. Because I am."

"Am?"

"Pregnant."

Nigel sat up abruptly. "Yer what?"

Emily started laughing.

Nigel glared at her. "Ye've a warped sense of humor, Emily Hendrick!"

"I wasn't laughing because it was a joke. I was laughing at the expression on your face."

He stared at her a long moment and finally frowned. "Are ye with child, lass, or na'?"

"With."

"Yer certain of tha'?"

"Positive."

"It canna be mine," he said in a strangled voice.

Emily sat up and smacked him across the ribcage. "Who else would it belong to!" she demanded indignantly. "I haven't been screwing anybody else, damn it!"

"Makin' luv," he corrected her. "Yer sure, then?"

"I said I was, didn't I?" she snapped.

A smile curled his lips. "An' it's mine."

She glared at him.

"Dinna look at me like that, lass. It's just tha' I'm havin' a hard time acceptin'. I was na' accusin' ye of anythin'."

Slightly mollified, Emily settled back once more.

"Do ye think it's a boy or a girl?" he asked after a time.

"One or the other."

"I'm serious."

"So am I."

He fell silent and after a while Emily began to drift away again. "Did you take care of that business you had in town?"

"Uhn," he grunted absently.

"Is that a yes?"

"Aye."

"Satisfactorily?"

"Aye. I had ta mesmerize the bleedin' nodcock in charge of my account at the bank, but it's come along nicely over the years."

"Bank account? How nicely?" Emily asked curiously.

"I can't recall the word the man used. I half suspected he'd made it up, fer I've never heard the number before, but it looks ta be in order."

Emily sat up again. "If you've had a bank account this long, it must be up in the millions!" she gasped.

"Nay. That wasn't the word."

"Billions?" Emily gasped disbelievingly.

"Aye. That was it. I'm thinkin' that'll tide us over nicely fer a few years."

Epilogue

Emily jumped as she felt Nigel's touch, then smiled as he slipped his arms around her waist, caressing the slight mound of her belly. "I still have trouble believin' we're ta have child," he said quietly.

"You've felt him kick," she reminded him. "He's definitely there ... and growing."

"Is it a male child, then?"

"Do you really want to know? I got the results of the sonogram."

"Nay. I want it ta be a surprise."

She lifted a hand to his cheek. "I'm so glad you gave me a child."

"It's ye who've given ta me, Emily ... somethin' I never even thought ta hope for. I love you."

"I love you, too."

"I've somethin' I want to give ye."

"What?"

"Eternity."

Emily felt her heart skip several beats. It wasn't something she'd ever considered before, but she knew beyond a shadow of a doubt that she wanted to spend forever with Nigel. Dragging in a shuddering breath, she tilted her head, offering her neck.

She felt the heated brush of his breath as he dropped his lips to her throat, placing a kiss on the pulse of her jugular. Expecting to feel the sting of a bite, surprise filled her as he lifted his head once more and placed something cold and metallic around her throat.

Looking down, she saw the glitter of blue fire. "What is it?" she gasped.

"A blue diamond."

Emily felt a flicker of uneasiness. "Aren't they supposed to be unlucky?"

He smiled faintly, leaning down to kiss her neck once more. "Na' for those of the vampire clan, luv."

Emily swallowed. "But, I'm not."

"Sure an' you are, lass, else you'd na' so easily resist *mesmer*."

Emily digested that in silence. "It's a symbol then? Of having vampire blood?"

"In a sense. But more than that. So long as you wear it, time will hold no sway over you."

Emily wasn't certain whether she believed that or not. She studied the beautiful stone for several moments and finally lifted it in the palm of her hand. "Does it have a name?"

"Aye. Eternity."

The End

Printed in the United States
48304LVS00002BA/124-411